COLLIDE

COLLIDE

BAL KHABRA

BERKLEY ROMANCE
NEW YORK

BERKLEY ROMANCE
Published by Berkley
An imprint of Penguin Random House LLC
penguinrandomhouse.com

Library of Congress Cataloging-in-Publication Data

Names: Khabra, Bal, author.
Title: Collide / Bal Khabra.
Description: First Berkley Romance Edition. |
New York: Berkley Romance, 2024.
Identifiers: LCCN 2023056238 (print) | LCCN 2023056239 (ebook) |
ISBN 9780593818268 (trade paperback) | ISBN 9780593818275 (ebook)
Subjects: LCGFT: Romance fiction. | Novels.
Classification: LCC PR9199.4.K4727 C65 2024 (print) |
LCC PR9199.4.K4727 (ebook) | DDC 813/.6—dc23/eng/20231208
LC record available at https://lccn.loc.gov/2023056238
LC ebook record available at https://lccn.loc.gov/2023056239

Collide was originally self-published, in different form, in 2023.

First Berkley Romance Edition: May 2024

Printed in the United States of America
1st Printing

Book design by George Towne

PLAYLIST

SUNFLOWER | Post Malone ft. Swae Lee

PRETTY BOY | The Neighbourhood

SELF CARE | Mac Miller

DADDY ISSUES | The Neighbourhood

LAVENDER HAZE | Taylor Swift

COME THROUGH AND CHILL | Miguel ft. J. Cole, Salaam Remi

BOYFRIEND | Ariana Grande ft. Social House

TENNESSEE WHISKEY | Saltwater Saddles

IF YOU LET ME | Sinéad Harnett ft. GRADES

WILD HORSE | Darci

I WANNA BE YOURS | Arctic Monkeys

TOO FAR CLOSE | Chase Shakur

I WANT IT ALL | COIN

GILDED LILY | Cults

CHANGE | Arin Ray ft. Kehlani

BODY LANGUAGE | Big Sean ft. Ty Dolla $ign, Jhené Aiko

SUNSETZ | Cigarettes After Sex

YELLOW | Coldplay

SHE'S MINE PT. 1 | J. Cole

SNOOZE | SZA

To the girls who love hockey,
especially when it's written in ink.

ONE

SUMMER

SHE'S HOLDING A gun to my head.

Well, figuratively at least.

The gun in question: hockey. The woman holding it: Dr. Laura Langston, Ph.D.

"Hockey?" I repeat. "You want *me* to do my grad school application on hockey?"

Langston has been my grad school advisor for the past year, but I've been working under her wing since I started at Dalton University.

She's everything I want to be, and I've obsessed over every academic paper she's written. She's kind of my celebrity crush in the nerdiest way possible. With her Ph.D. in sports psychology, countless papers published, and experience with Olympians and athletes around the world, she's inspirational.

Until you get to know her.

When they said *Don't meet your heroes*, they were talking about Laura Langston. She's the human equivalent of an angry swarm of wasps. There are plenty of professors who treat their students like total garbage and think their fancy piece of paper means they can be tyrants, but Langston is a different species. Her brilliance is undeniable, but she is patronizing, dismissive, and purposely difficult when she knows you need her help.

So, why the hell did I choose her as my advisor? Because her success rate in getting students into Dalton's prestigious master's program is too enticing to ignore. It's the number one program in North America and students vetted by her are guaranteed acceptance. Not to mention she chooses who will be eligible for co-op—a competitive program that allows one student from our cohort to work with Team USA. It's been my dream from the age of eight, so I'll suffer through her monstrous dictatorship if it means I'll soon have my own master's degree in sports psychology.

"You need to start using your resources to your advantage, Summer." She surveys me above the rims of her glasses. "I know you hate hockey, but this is your last chance to submit a solid application."

The word *hate* slips past her lips as if my aversion to the sport is completely fabricated. Considering she's one of the few people who know why I stay far away from the icy rink and the similarly icy men skating on it, I barely keep my composure. Sticking me right in the center of that blue circle with an empirical research study that determines the fate of my future is pure evil. An evil only Dr. Langston and her molten heart can manage.

"But why hockey? I'll choose football. Basketball. Even curling. I don't care." Does Dalton even have a curling team?

"Exactly. You don't care. I need you to do something you care about. Something you feel strongly about. Hence hockey."

I hate that she's right. Sweeping aside her overall ominous nature, she is a smart woman. I mean she didn't get her Ph.D. for nothing, but being her student is a double-edged sword.

"But—"

She lifts a hand. "I won't approve anything else. Do this or lose your spot. The choice is yours." It's like the universe sent me my very own *Fuck You* in the form of my professor. Years of working my ass off in undergrad only to be told hockey is my saving grace. What a joke. Clenching my fists, I swallow the urge to scream. "That isn't much of a choice, Dr. Langston."

"If you can't do this, then I overestimated your potential, Summer." Her voice grows sharp. "I have four students who would kill to have your spot, but I took you under my wing. Don't make me regret this."

She didn't exactly choose to take me under her wing. I had a 4.2 GPA and killer reference letters. Not to mention the extremely difficult advisor's exam she implemented last year to pick out the best students. I got food poisoning from the campus cafeteria that week, but I still dragged myself to the exam. I beat every student, and I'll be damned if they take my spot now.

"I understand what you're saying, but as you know, I'm not very fond of hockey. For good reason, might I add, and I doubt my research will be an accurate representation, considering that."

"Either you get over your apprehension or lose what you've worked for."

Apprehension?

Ignoring the pointed jab feels like trying to ignore a bullet lodged in my sternum. "There's no reason why I can't choose basketball. Coach Walker would happily let me collaborate with one of his players."

"Coach Kilner has already agreed to allow one of my students to work with his players. Get me your completed proposal by the end of the week or forfeit your spot, Ms. Preston." Her dismissal is clear when she twists away from me in her chair.

If I could commit one crime and get away with it, I have a feeling it would include Dr. Langston.

"Okay. Thank you," I mutter. She's typing aggressively on her computer, probably making another student's life a living hell. I imagine she goes home and crosses off the names of students she has successfully tormented. My name and the doll she sticks pins into are at the top of that list today.

I've successfully avoided everything to do with hockey for the past three years, only for it to be my front and center for the next few months. I'm beyond screwed, and I have to suck up my distaste for the sport of my Canadian ancestors.

I use all my willpower to not slam her door on the way out.

"You look pissed." The voice comes from the hallway leading to the advisor's lounge. Donny stands against the wall, dressed in cashmere and his brown eyes focused on me.

I've made a few mistakes since I got to college. Donny Rai is one of them.

An exhausting two-year relationship later, we have no choice but to see each other every day because we're both getting the same degree and applying to the same post-grad program. It doesn't feel like a competition between us, but I know Donny wants that co-op spot just as bad as I do.

He falls into step with me. "An ultimatum?"

"Exactly." I look over at him. "How did you know?"

"She gave one to Shannon Lee an hour ago. Shannon's thinking of dropping out now."

My eyes widen. Shannon is one of the smartest students on campus. Her work in clinical psychology was sent for review, making her the youngest student considered for publication.

"That's ridiculous." I shake my head, knowing how screwed I am. "You're so lucky you submitted your application early. The rest of us are stuck completing this new requirement."

He shrugs. "It's only a conditional acceptance."

"Right, like you would ever let your 4.0 drop."

"4.3," he corrects.

Donny is at the top of the dean's list every year; he's in every club and committee imaginable. He is the poster child for the Ivy League, so it's no surprise he managed to carve his way into this competitive program. I like to think I'm academically gifted too, but I might as well wear a dunce cap in comparison.

"I have a meeting right now. But I'll help with your application; we both know you'll need it."

The insult stings, but Donny just smiles and peels away to head to his meeting with the Dalton Royal Press. Yeah, he works on the school paper, too.

When I finally stomp into my dorm, I fall flat on the living room couch. "If I gave you a shovel, would you hit me over the head with it?" I ask Amara.

"Depends. Am I getting paid?" I groan into the throw pillow, but she pulls it away. "What did she do now?"

Amara Evans and I have been roommates since freshman year. Luckily for me, being best friends with a tech genius means getting perks from the university for her contributions. The most important one was securing Iona House. The only student living complex with two-bedroom and two-bathroom units. It's still cramped, but anything is better than the communal bathrooms where athlete's foot lurks in every corner. "She's making me do my application on hockey," I tell her.

Amara drops the pillow. "You're kidding. I thought she knew about everything."

"She does! This is what I get for sharing my secrets with her."

"Can't you find another advisor? She can't be the only one who gets students accepted to the program."

"No one has her success rate. It's like she's rigging acceptances or something. But maybe she's right. I should put aside my *apprehension*."

Amara gasps. "She did not say that!"

"Oh, but she did." I sigh, rolling to a sitting position. "How come you're back so early?"

"Sitting in that lecture hall with a bunch of sweaty dudes isn't how I want to spend my first day back."

Majoring in computer science means ninety percent of Amara's class is dudes. Which isn't something Amara's used to, coming from a family of five sisters. She's smack in the middle and says she's never known a moment of peace. Stuck between the impossible position of being the older and younger sister, and simultaneously having to deal with teenage hormones and adolescent tantrums. As someone with twin sisters who were born when I was already a handful of years older, I can't relate.

"Are you going to the party tonight?" she asks.

Being surrounded by hundreds of drunk frat dudes sounds like a nightmare. "I have way too much to do."

Her exasperated look tells me I'm in for a lecture. "Last semester you said you'd loosen up and enjoy your senior year. You said you would go out more, Summer. If I have to drag you along, I will." I did say that. To be fair, it was after I cried over a particularly difficult assignment and Donny's perfect score sent me over the edge. That's when I vowed that I'd let loose, because only focusing on school wasn't making my grades better.

I shoot her a sheepish look. "But I have to start that proposal, and I have readings to do."

She huffs out a breath. "Fine. I'll go with Cassie, but you have to promise to take a few breaks."

"Promise. I'll even go for a run later."

Amara's head hangs in disapproval. "Not the type of break I was talking about, but I'll take anything if it gets you out of here."

TWO

AIDEN

SHE'S WATCHING ME sleep.

Drawing away from the last remnants of my dream means I'm hyper-aware of my current surroundings. Either she's enjoying the view, which I wouldn't blame her for, or she's planning on ripping off my skin and wearing it later.

The latter seems more likely, because I fell asleep on her last night.

The welcome party at our house had gotten a little out of control. By a little, I mean *extremely* out of control. When Dalton University's left-winger and one of my best friends, Dylan Donovan, is in charge of a party, it's meant to turn into a rager. Mostly because I decided not to be the one policing it. We had just come back from break, so it was the only time I'd let myself drink before the season starts up again, and I'm not sure how much I'll regret that decision until I've seen the aftermath.

Opening my eyes means having to deal with the aftermath.

When Aleena, a smoking hot redhead, picked me out of the crowd to do body shots last night, it was only right that we found ourselves in my room, naked and all over each other. Though that didn't last long, because sleep debt is real, and I am its latest victim.

I train every day and take a full course load, and when I'm not doing that, I'm keeping the guys out of trouble. So, as I laid her on my bed and kissed my way down her stomach, I fully knocked out. It would have been embarrassing if I was conscious, but the sleep was so great I had no complaints.

"Morning." I stretch my arms out and under my head, opening my eyes to see exactly what I expected.

Red hair pools on my chest and full pouty lips are trapped between white teeth. "Good sleep?" she asks. "I hope you're not feeling too lazy this morning."

Anyone else would have been emasculated by the comment, but I couldn't be. Not when practically every girl on campus knows that *lazy* and *Aiden Crawford* have never been used in a sentence together. This was a one-off, and judging from her darkening blue eyes, she knew I'd make it up to her.

I chuckle. "Great sleep, actually."

"Well, if you're awake now"—she runs a red fingernail down my chest—"we can start the day off right."

What kind of host would I be to turn down that offer? When her hand trails lower, I flip her over and make up for last night.

By the time Aleena finishes up in the shower, I'm already downstairs making breakfast. Turns out women are big fans of steam showers, and I am the proud owner of the only one in the house. Rightfully so, because my grandparents had bought the house when I got accepted to Dalton. But that didn't stop Kian Ishida, the team's right-winger and our roommate, from fighting me tooth and nail for it. The captain card never failed to win a disagreement, but now he's across the hall with his loud music and constant pounding on my bedroom door.

I offer Aleena breakfast, but she only shakes her head in response before walking out the front door. I smile to myself. There is nothing better than a one-night stand who doesn't try to be your girlfriend after.

Eli watches the exchange with raised brows. "That's a first."

"What is?"

"It's past ten. You've never had a girl stay that long. Did you finally find the one?" His eyes widen with a grin that I'd like to punch off his face.

"I fell asleep last night before we got to do anything. It was only right."

"How chivalrous," he says dryly. "You've been exhausted lately. Think you need to cut back?"

Now it's my turn to laugh. Elias Westbrook, Eli as everyone knows him, and I have known each other since we were in diapers. His worry doesn't irritate me like everyone else's because I know he says it with great caution, and I must really be cutting it close with practice and school if he's saying something. "I'm fine. I've made it work for this long; what's a few more months?"

He doesn't seem to like that answer, though he only nods and plates his eggs.

"Sick party, guys." An early-morning straggler walks out of the house wearing just boxers, the rest of his clothes dangling from his arm. The pin on his jacket tells me he's one of Dylan's fraternity brothers.

Dylan is the only one out of us who is part of a frat. Kappa Sigma Zeta treats him like royalty, and although he lives with us, he could easily have the master suite in the Greek Row house. But according to him, having to be in the same house as the "ass-kissing freshmen" is the last thing he wants.

I eat a spoonful of oatmeal. "Where are the rest of the guys?"

Eli scrolls through his phone and shows me the screen. It's a picture of Kian passed out on the grass at the front entrance of our campus. Behind him, the monument of Sir Davis Dalton is trashed. I squeeze my eyes shut, hoping there is a simple explanation for this. Maybe a really good Photoshop job. "Who took that?"

"Benny Tang."

I pause mid-bite. "Yale's goalie? What was he doing here?" Having Yale come here after we slaughtered them in a game before winter break would be the worst possible scenario. The last thing I remember before heading upstairs was telling Dylan to shut it down soon. Clearly, he didn't listen.

"Might wanna ask Dylan. I wasn't here."

Of course he wasn't. If Eli, the only other responsible one, hadn't been at the party, that means the two overgrown children, Dylan and Kian, were in charge.

This all started when they lost a bet last semester that has us throwing the majority of the parties on campus. The parties we don't throw, we have to provide the booze. When I found out, I had both of them benched for two games straight.

Despite everything, I'm hoping this is a nightmare and I'm still in bed with Aleena. "And do I wanna know where Dylan is?" I ask cautiously.

When Eli picks up his phone again, I groan.

He chuckles. "I'm kidding, dude. He's passed out in the living room."

"IT WAS ME."

Every eye in the room zeroes in on me, and I regret ever learning how to speak. The pounding in my head persists because Coach wanted to torture us with practice before we gathered in the media room for a mandatory meeting. The bright white of the rink had sent my headache doubling in pain. I don't drink often, and my body never lets me forget when I do, so today was no exception. Everything was intensified, including Kian's loud voice, which spewed paranoia about why Coach called a meeting. The kid woke up with grass stains on his body and still wondered what was happening.

When Coach Kilner entered, he was fuming, his pale skin glowing red. He even knocked the hats off the heads of the juniors, who immediately cowered to the back row, and I began regretting my decision to sit up front. Kian and Dylan were way in the back too, hiding behind our goalies.

"A fucking party that trashed campus?" Coach yelled, and suddenly everything made sense. "Is this a fucking joke to all of you? Never in my twenty-five years of coaching have I had to deal with this kind of blatant disregard for the school code of conduct."

That part wasn't all true. I know for a fact that Brady Winston, the captain from the year before mine, threw a house party that landed a yearlong ban on Greek Row. The dean's car went missing, the swim team's pool was trashed, and all extracurriculars were canceled. So I'm pretty sure trashing the campus and vandalizing the monument of Sir Davis Dalton isn't the worst thing to happen to the school.

"When I became a coach after years in the league," Coach started as Devon muttered, "Here we go," beside me, "never did I think I would be giving my senior players a lecture on throwing parties."

"Coach, the party—"

"Shut it, Donovan," Kilner scolded. "We are in the fucking qualifiers that will get us to the Frozen Four and you are messing around with other colleges. At this stage?"

"Yale came here. Shouldn't they be getting the brunt of this?" asked Tyler Sampson, our alternate captain, and one of the smartest guys on the team. He's headed to law school instead of following in his hockey superstar father's footsteps.

"They are not my problem, you idiots are! I should have every single one of you suspended," he says, rage pouring out of his sweat-covered forehead.

"But then we wouldn't be able to play the Frozen Four." Kian's chiming in didn't help the rest of that speech, and now he's stuck with laundry duty for a month. It was originally a week, but Kian kept protesting, and everyone knows if Coach gives you a punishment, you shut your trap and take it.

After that, no one interrupted, except when I opened my big mouth to incriminate myself.

"What do you mean?" Coach asks, staring daggers at me now. I've seen that sharp glare too many times, and it should scare me enough to sit my ass back down, but I don't.

"I'm the one who threw the party."

Eli curses behind me, but he doesn't say anything else because he knows when I make a decision, there's nothing anyone can say to talk me out of it.

Coach runs a hand over his mouth, muttering something under his breath. Most likely about how much of a dumbass I am, and I'd have to agree. "This is how you wanna play it, Crawford? You sure it wasn't a collective mistake?"

He's giving me an out. More out of desperation than anything, because when the school gets wind of this, I will be punished. My only hope in putting myself on the line is that they'll check my academic standing and my hockey career before shelling out anything too severe. My fate will be better than anyone else's on this team.

"It was all me. I let Yale attend." Kilner nods, and I can't help but notice the minuscule flash of respect that flickers through his features before it's replaced by the usual anger. "I'll report to the dean. If someone has a different story than your captain, speak now."

The atmosphere in the room shifts, and I know the team wants to have my back, but the expression on my face must convey what I hope, because they reluctantly sit back in silence.

"Then why the hell are you still here!" he shouts, forcing us to shuffle out of the media room. Coach pulls me back. "My office after you've showered."

The locker room is eerily quiet for the first time ever, and when I step out of the shower, I'm greeted with Kian's sullen face. "Cap, you didn't have to do that," he says, looking guilty.

I run a towel over my hair. "I did. I fucked up last night; I shouldn't have let my guard down."

Eli sits beside me. "If that's your takeaway, you're looking at this all wrong. This is everyone's fault, mine too."

The locker room murmurs in agreement.

"I know you guys want to have my back, but it's on me to be a good example, and last night I wasn't. This isn't a united front kind of thing. The dean's involved, which means he'll see to it that everyone gets punished. We can't have that going into the season. If it's just me, the consequences can't be too bad," I say confidently.

My confidence withers when I enter Coach Kilner's office. It's never an exciting event to be here, but today it's especially grim. He's at his desk, tapping the mouse with a heavy hand. When he finally decides to give me his attention, he gestures for me to sit. He continues torturing the mouse until he chucks it at the wall.

It clatters to the floor in two pieces.

I swallow.

Kilner leans back in his chair, squeezing his stress ball tight enough to burst. "Where were you the last Friday before the end of semester?"

The question throws me off. I just confessed to a pretty heavy account of reckless abandon, and he's worried about last semester? I barely remember what I had for dinner last night, let alone what I was doing two weeks ago.

Except the memory hits, clearing the haze of my lingering hangover. "After practice ended, I headed to the house," I say.

"The boys?"

"Same thing."

"Party?"

Fuck. Why does he look so pissed? The only thing I remember from that party was a pretty blonde. It had started to get a bit out of hand, but I trusted the guys to handle it. It's the only reason I let myself relax last night. However, I've never lied to Coach, and I won't start now.

"Yeah, a party."

"So, you're telling me a party—mind you, one that you boys have multiple times a week—is the reason you missed the charity fundraiser?"

Oh, crap. The charity game.

In an attempt to pacify Kilner, I signed everyone up to coach the kids before their charity game. Spending two days a week with unfiltered children takes its toll, and it didn't help that it was finals season. So, when I stopped showing up, so did everyone else.

"Those kids were waiting on that ice, and you didn't show. What about the weekend before that? Same thing?"

I nod. Dalton parties never eased. If you can't find one, you're looking in the wrong place.

He lets out a derisive laugh. "You missed the mental health drive that the psychology department put on specifically for athletes. The hockey team didn't show, and neither did football or basketball."

To be fair, I don't pay attention to campus events. "How is that my fault?"

"Because instead of knowing where you had to be, there was a party all you idiots were at! If my players don't honor their commitments, do you know what I do, Aiden?"

"Bench them," I mutter.

He's fuming now. "Good, you're paying attention. And do you know why I called you in here?"

"Because I threw last night's party," I answer, "and I'm the captain."

"So you know you're the captain? I thought maybe you're too hungover to remember!" he shouts.

I wince. "I'm sorry, Coach. Next time—"

"There will be no next time. I don't care if you're my star player or Wayne fucking Gretzky, you will be a team player first." He releases a deep, agitated breath. "You should be leading your team, not partaking in their stupid games. Those boys respect you, Aiden. If you're at a party thinking with the wrong head, so are they. Smarten up, or I will have no choice but to put you on probation."

My face contorts with confusion. "What? There's no chance I get academic probation."

"We're not talking about your classes here. The party is being investigated."

Ah, fuck. Remember when I said I wouldn't know if I regretted drinking until I saw the aftermath? I regret it now. Probation is bad, like tearing your ACL bad. If the news gets to the league, they'll send agents out here to assess me as an eligible player. I had just signed with Toronto, because draft didn't mean shit until you put pen to paper. Making a mistake now would be fatal.

"I can't be on probation."

Coach nods. "You're in luck, because before the dean went on sabbatical, he informed the committee that anyone involved in the trash fiasco is to be dealt with. Since you have taken on that very stupid responsibility, your name is first on the list."

I am going to kill my fucking teammates. "What does that mean?"

"That they gave me the option of probation or community service."

An air of relief fills me. "That's great. I'll do community service. I will single-handedly scrub every inch of Sir Davis Dalton."

Coach gives me an unsettled look. "As great of a mental image as that is, it's not that simple," he informs me. "A lot goes into eligible community service hours, and since we don't have a precedent, it's going play-by-play."

I snort. "Like a prison sentence where I get out on good behavior?"

"You're in no place to be a smart-ass," he reprimands. "I would have been forced to put you on probation if it wasn't for her."

"Who?"

THREE

SUMMER

DESPERATION REEKS. OR maybe it's the hockey team's locker room after practice. Running showers and loud voices drift through the halls as I try to find Coach Kilner's office. Staying away from the rink like it has a contagious disease is proving to be a disadvantage when the long hall of blue doors resembles a maze.

When a phone rings behind me, my eyes meet a shirtless guy in a low-hanging towel. "Summer?"

Crap. "Hey, Kian." I awkwardly wave.

Kian Ishida was in every psychology class I took in junior year. We became friends when we got partnered at an extra credit seminar about brain dysfunction. I was happy to have someone who cared about sports psychology as much as I did, until I found out he's a hockey player. Much to my dismay, the six-foot-two right-winger has been playing for Dalton since freshman year. After I learned that, our friendship fizzled because even the depth of the ocean couldn't take me as far as I wanted to be from hockey. Just hearing someone talk about it made my insides churn at a slow, agonizing rotation.

He steps toward me. "I texted you about my schedule. Do you have Chung for Advanced Stats?"

I saw his text, and we do have two of the same classes this semester. I was hoping I could find a seat in the back of the lecture hall to avoid him. "I do, and Philosophy with Kristian."

"Sick, I'll see you in class, then." My plastic smile doesn't match his bright one. "What are you doing here? I didn't take you for a hockey fan."

"I'm not. I'm here to see Coach Kilner. Do you know where his office is?"

His gaze moves down the hall in confusion before he suppresses a smile.

"What's so funny?" I ask warily.

"Nothing." He clears his throat. "He's the last door on the right. See you in class, Sunny." He's gone before I can analyze his expression or the weird nickname.

Finding Coach Kilner's door, I knock on the translucent glass panel, and a gruff voice says, "Come in."

The door creaks ominously like it's telling me to run before I get caught in a mess. I'm met with a smiling Coach Kilner and someone sitting before him. Shower-damp hair and the Dalton logo sit on the back of his shirt.

I pause, thinking I'm intruding, but Coach waves me in. "Have a seat, Ms. Preston." The guy doesn't acknowledge me when I sit beside him, and I don't bother to, either. "Laura contacted me about your assignment. I understand you would like to do your project on hockey."

I would rather do it on the gum on the bottom of his shoe, but I can't exactly say that. "Right. It's research on college athletes and burnout for my grad school application," I say.

"Great. Then meet Aiden Crawford, the captain of our hockey team."

My eyes widen in alarm. The captain? They're making me do my research with the *captain*? "Oh. Uh, that's cool, but I can work with a third or fourth line. I don't want to disrupt the team."

"You won't be disrupting anything. Besides, Aiden needs it," he says, a tight string of tension suffocating his words. They clearly had a heated conversation before I entered. That would explain why the captain is simmering beside me. "*Right*, Aiden?"

This time I turn to him. Wavy brown hair and flawless skin meet my eyes. His side profile could be mistaken for one of the models off Amara's firefighter calendars. Despite all that, he still looks like a prick.

"Coach, this is a waste of my time." His deep voice is filled with poorly contained irritation. "This can't be my only option."

Surprise, surprise. My prediction of the hockey captain has been proven to be accurate. "My grad school paper is not a waste of time," I say.

"Maybe not for you," he retorts, without even looking at me. The guy can't even bother to insult me to my face. This is my worst-case scenario, and now I have to deal with him on top of it?

"Look, I don't need to sit here and listen to you be an asshole." I fail to suppress the anger that boils to the surface.

That's when he turns, deep green eyes narrow when they meet mine, but Coach Kilner interrupts the charged look.

"All right, that's enough. Aiden, you don't get to argue about this."

"I'm not doing this, Coach. I'll do fundraisers and teach the kids, but not this."

He's acting like I'm not even here. His little tantrum is inciting the anger that Langston had kindled earlier. Aggravation shoots up my spine. "Don't think I'm so eager to do this with a hockey player, either, Clifford."

"Crawford," he corrects.

Coach sighs. "I'm not here to babysit either of you. I've given you the assignment. The rest you can figure out like adults."

"But Coach—"

"You know the consequences, Aiden." He shoots him a stern look and Aiden's jaw tightens. "And Ms. Preston, you're free to discuss a switch with your professor. But even you know you won't get a better candidate than the captain."

When he walks out, Aiden curses under his breath. He runs a frustrated hand through his hair before turning to me. "Look, I'm sorry, but I can't help you with this. You can find someone else."

He doesn't sound the least bit apologetic. "Clearly. You're not exactly the belle of the ball."

The way his head rears gives me a spark of satisfaction. "I'm the captain of the team. I'm quite literally the belle of the ball."

"You're also the asshole of the ball, and those two don't mix well."

He glowers. "Glad that's established, because we won't be working together. I'm not your research experiment."

"Good! I don't want you to be," I say, pushing my chair back. "Damn hockey players." I slam the door behind me. I couldn't have gotten out of there quicker if there was a fire. Judging from the way his eyes flamed, there might as well have been.

Cold January air doesn't cool my skin as I storm over to the psychology building. Halfway there, I'm wrapped in a bear hug.

"Sampson," I wheeze.

Sampson loosens his hold. "Ah, so you remember me?"

"Shut up, I saw you before break," I say, pushing him away.

Tyler Sampson is the only hockey player I can stomach without breaking out in hives. We grew up together because our dads are best friends and we've stuck by each other's side at every grueling family event.

He watches me. "Why do you look so pissed at that building?"

"I'm not pissed at the building. I'm pissed at the devil inside it." I take a deep breath, glancing at him. "You're going to laugh."

He gives me a look to continue.

"You know that research paper I have to submit with my grad school application so I'm considered for co-op?"

He nods.

"Langston assigned hockey as my sport."

Tyler knows about my turbulent relationship with my dad, so his surprised reaction is expected. "And you're going in there to tell her off? Are you sure?"

I lift my chin confidently. "I'm standing up for myself."

"Summer, just think for one second. She gave you your assignment and you're going to go in there and tell her no? The woman who rejected a student's thesis because he double pasted a reference?" He gives me a pointed look. "You think *she* is going to be okay with you refusing something she assigned?"

I remember that story circulating, but I don't know the full truth. Langston is strict; she isn't unreasonable. Though she did threaten to give away my spot.

My stomach takes a dip. "I don't feel so good."

I'm close to tears when Sampson takes hold of my arms. "You'll be fine, it's only a few months. But if you really can't do it, at least present her with an alternate proposal."

"You mean, like a different sport? She already said no."

"Give it another try."

FOUR

AIDEN

GOSSIP TRAVELS TO the hockey house faster than I can skate a lap around the rink.

Kilner's lecture put me in a shitty mood yesterday, so I spent the day in my room and away from my inquisitive roommates. Living with three seniors and two juniors makes keeping secrets impossible. The juniors, Sebastian Hayes and Cole Carter, are our very own gossip columnists. But today as I get back from the gym, Kian stands by the door, hands on his hips like a nagging mother.

My English literature class starts in twenty minutes, and I don't have time for whatever Kian Ishida heard through the grapevine.

I ignore him, jogging upstairs to gather my things. When I come back down and head to the front door, he stops me. "Is there something you want to tell me, Aiden?"

"Depends on what you know."

His gaze narrows. "You were in Kilner's office for a while yesterday. I saw Summer Preston going in there too."

Irritation bites at me. I'd rather not think about her, even if I feel a little bad for being rude. It isn't her fault that I took the blame, but it doesn't seem like she is eager to work with me either. She wanted a duster, for Christ's sake.

"Nothing you need to worry about."

His eyes narrow. "Except there is, because we're all in this too. Whatever it is, we'll help."

It's obvious Kian feels guilty, and he won't stop until he rectifies it. If he finds out I pissed off the girl who could save my ass, he'll have an opinion.

"I'm late to class." I close the door behind me before he has a chance to argue.

When I get to Carver Hall, I shove my phone into my pocket and focus on the lecture rather than how much shit is going wrong. It doesn't last, though, because I get an email from Coach Kilner that heightens my stress ten-fold.

It's short, sent from his phone, and says, **Come see me**.

I am so fucked.

Trying to focus in class after that is already a challenge, but when my phone buzzes in my pocket repeatedly, it's impossible.

BUNNY PATROL

Eli Westbrook: Kilner is pissed.

Sebastian Hayes: On a scale of Kian's streaking to Cole's tire-slashing incident where does he land?

Eli Westbrook: Tire slashing.

Cole Carter: Uh. I'm gna miss next practice. My stomach hurts.

Sebastian Hayes: K. I'll tell Kilner u have a tummy ache.

Dylan Donovan: Thought we all knew about Kilner's perpetual stick up his ass?

Kian Ishida: Shhh. I swear the man can somehow read these.

Kian Ishida: Coach if you're reading this, I love you <3

Dylan Donovan: How'd you know he's pissed?

Eli Westbrook: Heard he broke a junior's hockey stick.

Kian Ishida: So? He's broken like 6 of mine.

Eli Westbrook: Over his own head.

Kian Ishida: Oh yeah, he's totally pissed.

Dylan Donovan: Wtf happened?

Eli Westbrook: @Aiden care to explain?

Kian Ishida: Cap? What did he do?

Did I mention I'm fucked?

Coach's threat to put me on probation didn't scare me enough to go ahead with that damn brain experiment, so now he's ruining everyone's lives. I send the screenshot of the email to the group chat.

Aiden Crawford: He's going to rip me a new one.

Dylan Donovan: Want us there for emotional support?

Kian Ishida: Fuck that. Coach will just see my face and get more pissed. Good luck, buddy.

Two hours later, I find myself at the rink as Coach steps off the ice with the kids.

"Help me with the equipment, would ya?" From his face, a person would assume he's our usual grumpy coach, but to the trained eye he's fuming. Absolutely livid. I know he's imagining biting my head off.

"Aiden, you promised you would come to our game. Where were you?" The tiny voice of Matthew LaHue reaches my ears as I'm collecting cones.

"Sorry, Matty, I got busy with school." That is the most PG-rated version I can give him. I feel like shit when he walks off with a sad nod.

I follow Coach into his office for the second time this week.

"Sit down," he orders, his tone rougher than usual. "Are you proud of yourself for the disappointment you caused in those kids?"

"No, sir."

"They look up to you, Aiden. What does it say about the team when the captain doesn't care enough to show up for the people in his community?"

"Coach, if this is about that girl's project—"

"It's not only about that. I've been watching you recently, and the patterns you're creating are not healthy. You're playing at the top of your game, but don't you think I see how exhausted you are? You're stretching yourself thin, kid."

First Eli, now Coach. I guess I'm not hiding it well. "Does it really matter, as long as I'm playing well?"

Coach exhales an irritated breath. "Hockey can't be your entire life. You have to think about the future."

"The future? Coach, you've said that I play so well because I'm only focused on the present."

"For now, but it can't always be like that. Once you go to the NHL, it's one bad game and it's all over. I don't want you to burn out."

I laugh. There is no way I'm getting a lecture on burnout right now. My stats are great, and the team is doing well because of the extra effort we all put in. "Is that what you think is happening? I feel fine."

"Are you sure? Because you've been missing commitments and losing sight of your players. You are not the captain I chose in junior year."

His words cut deep, but I don't let him see it. "I'm managing."

"I don't need you to manage, I need you to sustain. I've been coaching for twenty-five years, Crawford. Patterns are all I see.

"You are one of my best players. I'm not going to let this happen to you. You need to learn balance. Partying should not be a main priority, especially not in your senior year."

"It was only a few parties. I've been letting loose for once. Shouldn't that help prevent my supposed burnout?"

Coach shakes his head. "That's the wrong way to go about it. Find a balance, Aiden."

"So you want me to balance my classes, hockey, coaching, and a research project on top of everything else? Isn't that counterintuitive?"

"Maybe. But only if you're making room for the wrong things. Let's not forget that you willingly took on this punishment. I'd rather not give one to you, but these are the consequences. Deal with it, or I will."

THE LAST TIME I bought a girl flowers was, well, never.

I'm not an expert in botanics, but this situation calls for some serious damage control. Coach is seconds away from putting me on probation, so I have no choice but to *deal with it*.

In the flower shop, I'm immediately overwhelmed by the sheer volume of plants. A guy beside me holds a big wreath that could go nicely on a dorm door. Christmas passed a month ago, but don't girls like this stuff?

"Hey, I'm trying to say sorry to someone. You think those flowers would be good?"

He looks confused and the sadness on his face is evident. He must have really fucked up. He only shrugs and walks to the cashier. Not wanting to waste time browsing the aisles, I pick the same one.

Kian's blowing up the group chat for no reason again when the cashier rings me up.

BUNNY PATROL

Kian Ishida: Just saw two girls come out of Dylan's room.

Eli Westbrook: Dirty motherfucker

Aiden Crawford: That's what you were doing last night? We were supposed to go to the gym, D.

Sebastian Hayes: At least he got his cardio in.

Eli Westbrook: Double the cardio, apparently

Kian Ishida: I'm home Tuesdays. I'd prefer not to run into anyone
    on my way to the kitchen.

Dylan Donovan: Don't be ungrateful, Ishida. They're probably the
    only naked girls you've seen all year.

"My condolences," the cashier says, making me look up from my
phone. "Cash or credit?"

With my flowers in hand and spirits high, I pull into Iona House.
Rejection doesn't accompany anything I do, so each step to her dorm
is met with easy confidence. Luckily Kian knew where she lived, so
I didn't need to ask Coach and get my ears chewed.

When I knock, muffled voices can be heard through the door.

"I swear to God, if you invited some asshole over—" The words
die on Summer's lips the moment she sees me. "I guess I got the asshole part right," she mutters.

I smile. "Can we talk?"

She rolls her eyes. "I'm busy. I don't have time for whatever this
is." She gestures to the flowers, then slams the door in my face.

What the fuck?

I stare at the brown door in disbelief.

I knock again. No answer.

"You won't even let me explain?" I knock harder with each passing minute.

My pounding halts when the door swings open to a very irritated
blonde. "I have the worst hangover, can you shut up!" She drops her
hand from her temple and looks up at me. *"Aiden?"*

"Hey, Cassie."

Cassidy Carter is the twin sister of Cole, a junior defender on our
team. Cole lives with us, holed away in the basement. She occasionally shows up at the house to yell at him for hitting on her friends. I
had no idea she lives in Iona House, or that she's friends with Summer Preston.

"What are you doing here?" she asks.

"Getting your roommate to forgive me."

She voices a dramatic gasp and turns to Summer. "*This* is the guy who ruined your project?"

I can't hear what Summer says, but I'm pretty sure it includes the words *jock* and *douchebag*.

"Cassie, can I come in?"

"I don't know, Aiden. You didn't exactly leave the best impression," she whispers.

"I know, and I want to change that. Which can only happen if you let me in. Please?" This smile failed me once tonight, but I try anyway. When Cassie opens the door wider, I smell victory.

Summer's sitting on the couch with her laptop when her eyes come up to mine. She shoots a glare at an apologetic Cassie. Instead of helping alleviate the tension that clips the air around us, Cassie turns and runs out the door.

"Roommate?" I ask.

Summer doesn't answer. She also doesn't look at me. My confidence is withering by the second. "Can I at least apologize?"

Silence.

"Come on, Sunshine."

Her head snaps up so suddenly, I take a step back.

Wrong thing to say.

"Don't call me that." Blazing brown eyes pierce mine, and it's kind of terrifying. She pushes her laptop off her legs and comes to stand a few feet away from me. "I know you're the captain, and you think people should bow at your feet when you ask for something, but you won't get that from me. I don't care if you feel bad now or if you've decided to retire that asshole behavior and turn a new leaf. You made your decision, and I made mine." She opens the front door. "You're free to go. Don't waste your breath on me."

I watch her in a trance. There's so much fire in every word she spits at me, it's like watching a captivating performance. Momentarily, I'm distracted by the thin T-shirt she's wearing that reaches her thighs, and I'm busy reading the text on it when she snaps her fingers to bring my attention back to her face. Impatience riddles her features, but I don't move. I need her, and if I have to deal with her uptight behavior, so be it.

"I was rude."

She arches her brow.

"Fine, I was an asshole, and you deserve an apology. I'm sorry for the way I acted in Kilner's office; he sprang it on me with no discussion. It's nothing against you or your research."

Summer stands by the open door with a stony expression. In a move that may get my balls crushed, I walk right up to her and push the door closed. Her eyes mark the movement, but I don't see her knee come up, so I continue.

"Will you give me a chance?" I ask. "Let me prove to you that I'm not the asshole you think I am."

Her gaze drifts to the flowers in my hand. I extend them to her, but she doesn't move to take them. "You got me a mourning wreath?"

A what? I look down at the flowers again and blink at her. But the sound of a creaking door makes both of us turn.

The girl stares wide-eyed. "Need some privacy?"

How many roommates does she have?

Summer snorts, then pushes me away to walk back to the couch. "No."

Her roommate eyes me. "I've seen you before. Where?"

"Not sure, but I'm Aiden." I extend my hand and her eyes widen before she takes it.

"Oh shit!" She beams. "You're notorious in these dorms, Captain."

"For good reason, I hope."

"I'd say so." She smiles, then turns to Summer, mouthing something that I don't see.

Summer ignores it. "You're free to go." She dismisses me like I'm an annoying child.

I try again. "One chance."

"No."

What is it going to take? I've never had to fight this hard to keep a girl's attention. Majority of the time, I don't have to try at all.

"What did you do?" her friend asks.

"Amara," Summer warns, and I watch them have a silent conversation. Amara purses her lips before eyeing me up and down, and then she opens the door with a sympathetic look.

When I don't move, there's a small smile on her lips. "She said no, pretty boy."

"Come on, Amara. Don't you think I deserve one chance to fix my fuck-up?"

She twirls a braid around her finger, eyes settling on the flowers in my hand. "Whose funeral did you go to?"

I give her a strange look. "What?"

"You're holding a mourning wreath. Like the ones at funerals," she explains.

Now that I really look at it, I realize I've seen the wreath before. That explains all the looks and condolences I received on my way here. I try to recover. "I'm showing just how sorry I am."

She chuckles, her expression contemplative. "You'll need that when she's done with you." The ominous threat should have me walking out, but when she closes the door, triumph lifts my lips. "Good luck. I'm not getting in the middle of this," she declares, walking back to her room.

Well, there goes my plan.

I turn to the fuming girl who's typing intentionally loudly on her laptop. Funeral flowers in hand, I approach her like a man would a lion. With a slow lift of her eyes, she watches me take her laptop and place it on the coffee table.

"Let me help you with the assignment."

"I don't need your help. I could easily walk over to the basketball team and get their captain."

There's no doubt about that. He would be all over her if she wanted him. My damage control is failing. "Anything you want, I'll do. Do you want rinkside seats, or I can set you up with one of the guys? What about Eli? All the girls love Eli."

Unimpressed, she folds her arms. "You think the equivalent of having you in my research is sitting rinkside and a date with one of your teammates?"

I shrug innocently.

"I've never been to a Dalton hockey game, and I'm not planning on going."

My head rears back in surprise, because everyone at Dalton loves hockey. Especially women. Half of our stands are filled with sororities. "Not a fan?"

"You haven't done anything to make me one."

"Probably because you haven't seen me play . . . or without a shirt on." The joke doesn't give me the desired effect. Instead, her glare sharpens. "Fine, is there something else I can do?"

"You're wasting your time. I'm sure you can talk Kilner out of whatever he's holding against you."

"I'm not doing it for him," I say honestly. This is about creating a balance and standing up for my team regardless of the shit they do. "At least think about it?"

She lifts her chin. "Fine. I'll think about it."

Not wanting to give her any reason to rescind her offer, I head to the door. "You won't regret it."

"I haven't said yes yet."

I smile. "You will."

FIVE

SUMMER

AT TWELVE I took up swimming solely to piss off my dad, but by some miracle, I fell in love with it.

My mom would take me to competitions, and my dad would try to entice me with a new pair of ice skates. It never worked, but I stared at those skates for hours after. Lately, when that sour taste in my mouth becomes heightened, the cold water takes me far away from the thoughts.

Mehar Chopra, one of the athletes on the Dalton diving team, let me borrow a key to the facility to use after hours. If you aren't an NCAA athlete, you aren't allowed to use it, but luckily for me, I helped her pass her statistics final last year, and we've been friends ever since.

Finishing my last lap with burning arms and cramping calves, I pull out of the water before the afternoon rush. After changing out of my wet bathing suit, I check my phone.

Dad—Two Missed Calls.

A call from him always sends me into this spiral where I wonder if I'm a shitty daughter who's holding a dumb grudge, or if my silence is valid. His first call came early this morning, and I ignored it until now. Until I see the text from him that reads, **Give your dad a call, Sunshine.**

I don't realize I'm holding my breath until I'm lightheaded. Speaking to him would ruin a perfectly good day, so I ignore the text too. I finish drying my hair, and my phone rings so incessantly, I already know who it is. There's only one person who doesn't understand what a missed call notification is for.

"Sometimes I think I'm mistaken that I have a daughter in college, because I'm sure my kid would at least call me."

"We talked yesterday, Mom." Divya Preston has the propensity to exaggerate. I fight the urge to fake a disconnect as I head over to the cafeteria for lunch.

"That's too long," she says stubbornly. "Your father said you haven't returned his calls. He hasn't heard your voice in months."

My mother has the propensity to make my ears bleed, too. "He can listen to my voicemail."

"Your radio silence is not appreciated, beta."

I let out a heavy sigh. "You can't blame me for not wanting to talk to him." I've been away from home since I was eighteen, with the occasional travel back for the holidays. However, I stopped going home then too, because seeing my dad pretend we were a happy family left a bitter taste in my mouth.

"I don't, but he's making an effort to have a relationship with you. Your sisters have seen that change in him. You can at least try." It took him ten years to want to *try*. "He loves you, Summer."

Her words curdle like milk in my stomach. My father can't even say the word *love*, let alone feel it in any capacity, at least not for me. He loves my mother in every meaning of the word. I grew up with their love suffocating the room while I yearned for a morsel. Except I realized that it didn't belong to me. Not to the baby they had at eighteen who almost derailed my father's hockey career. Definitely not the oldest daughter who has too much to say and isn't afraid to want better for her sisters.

"I'm sure," I mutter as I pay for my food.

"How about dinner? We can swing by Bridgeport. I'll make your favorite sweets."

She knows my weakness for her gulab jamun. "It's my last semester; I can't just take a break in the middle of it."

"Fine, then during spring break."

"Sure," I say in acquiescence. "I'll call you later, Mom."

"Talk to your father!"

By the time I make it to class, there's only one empty seat at the top. The walk across campus, and now to the top of the sweltering lecture hall, has me huffing and puffing. It's the four hours of sleep and the empty tea box that has my mood a lot hotter than usual. I'm barely hanging on as we get to our break with two hours still to go. The pencil in my hand is moments from snapping when someone pulls out the chair beside me.

"Hey, Summer," Kian Ishida chirps, sitting way too close.

I glance at him. "Hi."

"You're gloomy for someone with that name."

"Haven't heard that one before." I turn away, but Kian's gaze continues to warm my face.

"Can we talk?"

I look up at his sincere expression and tone down my irritation. "Sure."

"So, I heard about your assignment. If Aiden doesn't help with your project, he'll be on probation, and considering you study sports, you should know how much it would suck for the captain to be gone."

I raise a brow. That guy seriously won't quit. First the dorm, now sending his friends to me? "What are you, his lackey?"

"Teammate, best friend. Either or." He smiles, not even slightly offended. "Seriously, I know he's an idiot, but if you could reconsider."

"You just called him an idiot. Why would I want him on my project?"

"'Cause he's your only shot to get into the program." How the hell does he know that? My plan to create an alternate proposal failed. I knew it when Shannon Lee came fuming out of Langston's office after trying to get her to take back the ultimatum. I tossed my alternate proposal in the trash and got the hell out of there. "How do I know that? I have my ways, Sunshine."

"Don't call me that."

"Sorry," he apologizes. "Look, you're supersmart and you can totally figure out something else, but we need this. The team is ready to help in any way."

I perk up. "The whole team?"

"Yes, as long as you let Aiden in. He's a good guy and you'll find that out soon enough."

"Are we talking about the same guy? Because the one I met insulted my career and told me he wasn't my research experiment."

He winces. "It sounds a lot worse when you explain it like that, but his intentions are pure."

"You can save that for his best man speech."

"He's a genuine guy," he argues.

"And let me guess. He saves cats from burning buildings in his spare time?"

His lips twitch. "Look, he might be intense at first, but he's the nicest dude you'll ever know. Coach is pissed at him for the parties, but those weren't his fault. Since he's been captain, he makes sure we stay within our limits. The only reason he loosened up is because the guys were having a hard time at home, and he didn't want them to lose a place where they could forget about all that."

He must see my softening gaze, because he continues. "He would kill me for telling anyone this, but he's the same guy who got a job freshman year to pay my fees when my dad died. I would've lost my spot here when I left for Japan, but he told me I got financial aid."

The murmur of the class stops, and our heads turn to Professor Chung, who resumes the lecture.

"Think about it?"

My eyes move to Kian again, and I find myself nodding. My focus is shot, so I spend the rest of the lecture finishing my proposal. Just ten minutes after the lecture, I'm pulling into the hockey house driveway.

As I climb the steps, Eli Westbrook walks out the front door. The only reason I know his name, despite my stance to not know any college athletes, is because at one of the parties last year he made sure everyone got home safe. That included him personally driving home at least thirty students. One of them was a very drunk Amara, who swears she fell in love with him that night.

"Hey, is Aiden here?" I ask.

Eli's head tilts with curiosity when he sees me. "He should be. Come in." He unlocks the door. "Upstairs, first door on the left."

The house is unexpectedly tidy considering they host frequent parties. The faint smell of sweat and alcohol is still fresh in the air, but I suppose that's soaked into the walls.

When I knock, I step back but hear nothing. Impatience riddles me, so I knock harder. Then again, briefly halting with hesitation, before easing the door forward.

Aiden's room is bathed in shadows from the glow of a flickering candle. Who would have thought the captain studied by candlelight?

"I've been waiting for you all day," a sultry voice purrs. I freeze, my gasp catching in my throat.

Naked. So, so naked.

A girl lies on Aiden's bed, whipped cream covering the apex of her thighs and nipples, a bowl of strawberries sitting on the nightstand. When I make a garbled noise, her eyes find mine and she screams, sending me scrambling backward to hit a dresser.

"Oh my God! I'm so sorry!" I rush out. Just as I'm going to bolt down the stairs, I bump into someone. A very hard, warm-chested someone.

I stumble back to see Aiden staring at me, concern marring his striking features. He looks irritatingly perfect with his sharp bone structure and full lips. "You good?" he asks.

My eyes are still wide, and I have to physically remember to blink them. "Fine," I squeak.

He looks to his bedroom door. "Were you in my room?"

"Thursday," I state, ignoring his question. "Our first session. We'll meet at the rink."

His entire face lights up. "I'm in?" He takes a step forward like he's about to hug me but stops when I take one back. He clears his throat. "What changed your mind?"

Kian's little speech had a lot to do with it, and when I look at Aiden, I know Kian wasn't lying. There's something about his eyes that makes me believe it.

"Your desperation," I say instead.

"Pity? I'll take it." He beams.

I purse my lips to keep from smiling. "Don't get too comfortable; you're on thin ice."

His expression grows tight like he's annoyed at the comment. But when his bedroom door creaks, our attention shifts to the girl, melting whipped cream not doing a great job of staying in place.

Aiden rubs the back of his neck with a sheepish look. The tips of his ears go a little pink, and I'm fascinated that Aiden Crawford feels even slightly embarrassed. The girl's really pretty and completely naked. You'd think he would be parading around the fact that he's constantly getting laid.

Before he can give me an explanation I don't want, I bolt down the stairs.

THURSDAY ROLLS AROUND, only for me to regret each step I take toward the cold rink. On the secluded ice, I hear the swish of a puck hitting the net.

Aiden is so focused he doesn't notice me by the ice waving at him.

The raw talent is visible in the way he moves like he's not breaking a sweat. The contour of muscles in his back ripple under his tight shirt.

"Aiden!" I call, but he doesn't turn.

So I try again, louder this time. Still no response.

I had allotted one hour for our meeting and a second over will mean barely catching up on the sleep I've lost this week. Groaning, I do the one thing I didn't think I ever would again. I trudge over to the spare equipment room and grab a pair of beat-up skates. They're too tight, and my ankle feels all wrong. The simple act of tying the laces makes my chest swirl. I desperately push away the memory of putting skates on for ten years of my life to skate with my dad.

I glide onto the ice with a rusty form, as Aiden speeds through drills.

"Hey," I call when I get closer, though he only sends another puck flying. Fed up, I tap his shoulder to get his attention. "Crawford!"

When he spins, I'm standing way too close, because his elbow hits my shoulder, throwing me off-balance. I scream and fall to the ice, my back taking most of the brunt, and my head being spared from hitting the ice. The thought of my skull cracking causes a shiver to roll up my spine. There was a video circulating last year of a Dalton figure skater cracking her skull on the ice at the Olympics. Since then, even stepping foot on Dalton rinks without a helmet meant getting your head chewed off by staff.

"Shit. Are you okay?" Aiden asks, pulling out an earbud. "I didn't hear you."

"Fine," I mutter, still lying flat on the ice.

His concern dampens when he hears my tone. "If you don't know how to skate, they keep cones for the kids right over there."

"Very funny. I can skate just fine." I wipe ice from my thighs. "I could probably beat you in a race."

He's looking down at me with amusement. "Beat me? You're literally still on the ground from falling."

He offers his hand, but I scramble up on my own. When I regain my balance, I stare into his eyes. "Scared?"

"For you? Yeah."

I shoot him a blank look.

"You're serious?" he asks, his tone disbelieving.

I nod.

"What's the bet?"

"That I win." An overstatement that I regret as soon as I voice it. I'm confident, not stupid, but right now his smug face is challenge enough. Even if I may not be able to walk tomorrow.

"I only play for stakes."

Seriously, is he some kind of gambler? "Fine. If I win . . ." I think for a bit, then smile. "You have to agree to anything I suggest during our sessions without complaint."

His jaw hardens, and I smile, knowing I have him. "And when I win, you'll tell Coach I was so great, your research is complete early."

My jaw drops. There is way too much work to do. Too many questionnaires and assessments to complete. There is no way I could produce accurate results on my own. "But that's not possible."

"Scared?" He throws my word back at me.

I grind my teeth to stop myself from making an insolent comment. I almost deny him, but his cocky smirk makes me clench my fists and remember exactly why I don't like hockey players. "Fine. I'm going to win anyway."

His low chuckle ghosts over my skin. "And they say I'm cocky."

"*Confident*," I correct.

That makes him smile wider, and I ignore it to skate to the boards. "Straight shot to the other end?"

"Yeah," he says, but he still doesn't put his back against the boards.

"Ready—"

"Helmet."

"Huh?"

"Put on a helmet or we're not doing this."

"You're not wearing one," I accuse. "Is your massive head made of steel?"

"I can manage not cracking my skull open. You, on the other hand, I'm not so sure."

I scoff. "Well, too bad, because I don't have one."

I should really put one on. After attending that brain dysfunction seminar last semester, I know better than to compromise my brain health.

Aiden turns to grab something from behind the net. "Here."

I stare at the helmet in his hand. It's not a cage; instead, it's a visor they wear for some practices. "How is my head going to fit in your helmet?"

"Better than slamming your bare head on the ice."

Reluctantly, I take it from him and pause before allowing it to touch my hair. "Just so you know, you're ruining my hair-wash schedule." He gives me a blank look as if my hair health is of the least importance to him. The helmet hangs loosely, providing very little protection, and on the verge of tipping off.

"Tighten it," he says, pointing to the buckle.

"I did." I forcefully tug on the strap.

He lets out a breath and skates to stand just a few inches from me. He's so close that I can smell his clean scent as he towers over me. How he manages not to smell disgusting is beyond me. If the locker room is any indication of how bad hockey players can stink, he's an anomaly.

I'm staring right at him when he straightens the helmet. His eyes are almost hypnotizing, and I can hear the chant in my head to look away. The green looks hazel around the edges, with specks of gold scattered throughout. When he brushes my hair out of my face, I snap out of it.

"If you pull on the left strap, it gets tighter," he explains, tugging on it. "Should fit right under your chin." He secures it as much as he can. "Good?"

I nod.

He skates backward. "On three."

We push off the board after the countdown and shoot across the ice. He's fast. Insanely fast. I start to wonder why I thought I could win against a D1 athlete. Especially since the last time I skated was years ago. My legs burn from only a few strides. My eyes aren't doing a great job of focusing on the finish line. Instead, I watch him move like lightning, and that's when I trip on a divot in the ice.

The squeak that leaves me must reach his ears, because I hear the scraping blades before I hit the ground. Again.

I'm reminded that head protection is very necessary, especially when my helmet cushions the blow when I fall. Other than my very fragile pride, I think I'm fine when Aiden kneels beside me.

"Fuck, that seemed bad. Are you hurt?" His cold hand slides to the back of my neck to lift me up. "What day is it?" he suddenly asks.

There's no way I hit my head hard enough to need a concussion check. I'm mostly worried about how soaked my new leggings are. "I don't have a concussion."

"Humor me." Traces of concern bleed through his calm voice.

"Thursday."

As he's asking the questions, I realize that he technically hasn't won yet. And neither have I lost. Biting down the smile that begins to bloom at the thought, I let him lift me off the ground.

"Where are you right now?" he continues when I stand.

"Staring at your big-ass head," I say before I turn and bolt, using every muscle in my body to my advantage.

Aiden calls after me before his skates scrape the ice. Fast. My body burns, but I'm so close I can taste the damn boards. I don't look back, afraid that even one look will cost me.

SIX

AIDEN

I LOST.

I'm the fastest hockey player in the NCAA and I lost to a five-foot-six sports psychology student who hates hockey.

"Holy shit! I won!" Summer skates circles around me.

"You seem surprised for someone who was so confident," I grumble.

"'Cause you're a college athlete. You literally do this every day and I beat you!" She does a wobbly twirl, beaming brightly. Her wet leggings snatch my attention, the discolored area highlighting her ass. I pry my gaze away before she notices me staring. "Please tell me they have cameras here. I need the footage."

"For what?"

"Future purposes."

Blackmail. "That would also mean it recorded you cheating," I say.

She lets out an animated gasp. "Cheating? I've never cheated in my life." She stops in front of me and a sudden waft of something sweet hits me. "You decided to stop, and you were one second behind me. It was a fair race."

"Depends. If you define *fair* as heavily skewed in one's favor," I say, and she stares back unamused. "Fine. You win. I'll do your sessions without complaint." Honestly, even if I won, I would have done anything she wanted. It was a miracle she let me on the project to begin with.

"Don't act like you're doing me a favor. I might have used distraction, but admit it, it was fair in the end."

I sigh. "It was fair."

Content, she skates toward the exit, and we head to Coach's office. He's letting us use it as long as we don't touch anything. Once I fill out the preliminary self-assessment, she reads over it. "You're an English minor?"

I nod. I took the responsible path and chose economics as my major but decided to do a minor I would actually enjoy, hence English.

"So, you like reading?"

"Yes."

"Like real books?"

I give her a blank look. "You mean those blocks of paper? Oh no, I've never held one, let alone read one of those."

She ignores my sarcastic remark and skims the paper. "You left this blank. What's your five-year plan?"

"Don't have one."

Alarm strikes her face. "Three-year?"

"Nope."

"What about hockey? Don't you have a dream team you want to go to?"

"I'm already signed to them."

The Toronto Thunder signed me to a three-year entry-level contract a few months back, which means I'll be playing with them later this spring. Eli also signed with them a month after me, so we're headed there together.

"What about personal goals?"

I have no idea what she wants from me. I've lived and breathed hockey since I was four; there is nothing else I ever needed to focus on. I haven't dated anyone in college because between playing, studying, and being a full-time dad to the guys, there isn't any extra time.

"Maybe it'll help if I give you an example," she suggests. "I have five-, ten-, and twenty-year plans."

Holy shit, she's insane.

She eyes my reaction. "Don't look at me like I'm crazy. I just know exactly what I want."

"Life is unpredictable. You can't plan it." I know that much from experience.

"I can. When I was younger, I was in love with psychology. Everything about it, to the point where I had a thorough life plan at the age of eight. At seventeen, I would graduate high school and move here with a full ride to Dalton. Complete the accelerated degree program and get into grad school."

I blink. "You figured that out at eight years old?"

"Yes."

Jesus. The only thing on my mind at eight was how long my mom would let me play hockey before dinner. "What if you don't get in?"

She stares at me as if I threatened her. "I will. I have one shot, and I won't let anything or *anyone* mess it up."

I try to cut the tension. "But you're basically done with all that. What's your plan now?"

"After my master's and Ph.D., I want to work with Olympic athletes as a sports psychologist. Then I'll probably marry an accountant and have two kids, a boy and a girl."

"An accountant? You're into bald dudes who would rather choke on their coffee than sit in their cubicle?" I'm not even going to touch the fact that she had the kids all figured out. She probably knows what zodiac sign they will be, too.

"They're good with math. People who excel in STEM fields are generally better equipped to last in partnerships."

"So, you want to marry a robot."

"I want to marry a stable man."

"A stable man who probably can't make you come." The words fly out of my mouth before I can think better of them. To my relief, she ignores them, but not before rolling her eyes.

"Anyway, that's my example. Your turn."

"I don't have one. I'll go to the NHL, play as hard as I can, and hopefully win a Cup one day."

"What comes after that? Do you want to have a family?"

"That's not on my mind right now." When you live and breathe hockey, there isn't much else to care about. Everything I have is spent on making sure I don't let anyone down—my teammates, coaches, or family.

"So, your only goals are hockey and"—she pretends to check her notes—"hockey?"

"Exactly. That's why I don't go a day without practice."

Surprise morphs her features. "You practice on days you don't have practice?"

I lean back in my chair, nodding. "I gotta make sure I'm keeping up. I'm heading to the NHL in a few months."

Her expression is incredulous. It takes her several seconds to form a sentence. "You think working out seven days a week is good for you? When do you rest?"

"I get plenty of rest after practice and I usually get eight hours of sleep."

"That is not healthy, Aiden."

Her concern isn't something I need. I've heard it enough from everyone else around me. "It's been working fine for me."

"But—"

"Are we done here? I have to be up early for more volunteering," I say, with false excitement.

A twinge of guilt hits me when her expression falls, and I have the urge to fill the tense silence. Summer gathers her stuff and exits the office so quickly I barely have time to think. When I follow her out, she murmurs a quick bye when the heavy doors lock behind us and takes off in the opposite direction. The cold air hits my face as I slip on my jacket and eye her impractical attire. Her half-dry leggings and thin sweater were not meant for January in Connecticut.

"Where's your car?" I call after her.

"I walked. My dorm is right there." She points to the direction of the building closer to campus.

"I'll give you a ride."

"I'm good," she says, trying to tame her long brown hair that flows in the direction of the wind.

"Let me give you a ride."

She stares at me.

I stare back.

When it seems like she would rather stay out here and freeze under the windchill, I let my gaze soften. "Please?" I almost don't recognize my voice, but this girl is damn stubborn, and I don't want her walking alone so late.

She concedes and follows me to my truck. "Is that like the standard jock-mobile?"

With the click of a button, the black F-450 lights flash. "I see you're a fan of hockey stereotypes."

"More like empirical evidence. All you need now is a country playlist to seal the deal."

I open her door and try to help her up with a hand on her waist, but she swats it away to climb in herself. Sliding into my seat, I let the heat blast through the vents and turn on the seat warmer for her wet thighs. When my Bluetooth connects, the first song plays, and much to my pleasure, it's a country song.

She laughs suddenly, forcing me to look at her to fully grasp the sound. I thought a laugh from Summer Preston was the last thing I'd ever get to hear. I'd made attempts at jokes with her all night and nada, not even a smile. But now that I know what it sounds like, I want to make it happen again.

She looks around my truck with a frown. "It smells good in here."

"Are you usually in smelly cars?"

"No, I just mean your gear is probably back there."

I shake my head. "It's in the truck bed. Can't have my back seat smelling bad."

She snorts. Not quite a laugh, but close enough.

"Did you date a hockey player or something?" I find myself asking as I pull onto the road.

She stares out the window. "Or something."

Ex-boyfriend it is. Clearly, her aversion to the sport is due to a bad experience. It can't solely be because she dislikes me.

The rest of our car ride is silent until I pull up to her dorm. She's out and speeding to the entrance before I get the chance to walk her in. I'm watching her head inside when my phone buzzes in the center console, and I answer immediately. Missing a call from Edith Crawford is not a position anyone wants to be in. "Hi, Grandma."

"Did you get my package? I had Eric send it through the post," she says.

"Yes, all the guys loved them. I'll send you pictures."

She knit sweaters for the team and wouldn't listen to anyone, not even her arthritic hands when she spent the last few months knitting. She said it gave her something other than their diner business to focus on.

It's been a while since I visited home in Providence, but my grandparents understand that my schedule is so packed I barely have time to come up for air. Asking them to come down for games doesn't feel right, especially since it's hard for them to schedule around managing their diner.

The last time I had any family in the stands, I was thirteen and both my parents had come. I remember that feeling like it was yesterday. I was full of joy, and it was one of the best games I ever played. So good I got recruited to the major junior team as a bantam player. That was also the last game my parents ever attended, and though the stands are filled with screaming fans wearing my jersey, it has never felt the same. I have a feeling it never will.

"Okay, I just wanted to check in. Will you be coming home for break?"

Spring break felt so far away I hadn't thought about it. The only thing on my mind is making sure we make it to conference tournaments without anyone getting ejected, suspended, or put on probation. Which is harder than it seems when the guys are hell-bent on doing stupid shit.

"Yeah, I am."

"It would be nice if you brought a guest one of these days."

My grandma isn't slick with her questions, so I know what she wants to hear. She has pestered me about a girlfriend for the past two years, saying she's getting old, and I should use my looks for something other than *monkeying* around.

"Just me. But I'll let you know if anything changes."

"You know, we would like to be coherent enough to talk to a girl you bring home."

They love playing the old age card, though they are the most energetic seventy-year-olds I know. They would be in the mountains hiking if it weren't for my grandpa's knee replacement.

"I'm sure you two will be as spry as ever when that day comes." Not anytime soon, because a girlfriend hasn't been on my mind ever, and bringing one home isn't something I'm willing to subject myself to. Casual hookups are the only thing I can sustain throughout the season, but now that seems impossible too.

"How are things with hockey?"

"Good. I'm coaching a class of mini mites tomorrow." I omit that it isn't of my own volition.

"You know, your dad used to volunteer for those when you were younger. Helped keep an eye on you too."

I laugh. "Probably the reason I don't get into nearly enough fights now."

"Let's keep it that way; I don't need you losing any teeth," she says sternly. "Well, I'll let you go. Call me with some exciting news next time. You are boring an old woman."

"I have plenty of exciting stories, Grandma."

She hums. "None that you need to be telling me, I suppose. God knows what you college kids are doing these days."

"Not me. I'm an angel."

"I'm sure you are. Good night, bean."

"Night, Grandma."

SEVEN

SUMMER

IT'S FOOLPROOF.

Those are the words I said to my therapist before she gave me a long list of reasons why my self-proclaimed foolproof formula is extremely detrimental.

One of the prerequisites for grad school was to attend a counseling session with an on-campus therapist last semester. I was all for it until we got down to the nitty-gritty and unearthed my abandonment issues. Who said therapy isn't fun?

Sophia, my assigned counselor, had a lot to say about how I treated relationships. Apparently, my plan to abandon people before they abandoned me isn't healthy. Go figure. She said my only friends since freshman year have been Amara and Cassie, as well as Sampson, who doesn't count since I've known him forever, because I don't create attachments to people in fear I won't be good enough for them to stick around. Thanks, Dad.

Heavy stuff, but we worked through most of it. I say *most* because I still haven't talked to my dad. Sophia suggested that calling him would give me closure without having expectations. That was our last session, because after I completed my credits, there really wasn't any motivation to go back.

A splash from someone diving into the pool sends water to hit the glass of the waiting area. Sitting in the DU Aquatic Center, I watch the doors for Aiden, who's meeting me here for today's session.

My phone buzzes with a text from my sisters. It's a picture of the Dalton hockey team at last night's game.

THE PRESTONS

Serena: You go to school with these guys?

Serena: Because holy hotties.

Shreya: I knew your 'stay away from hockey dudes' spiel was so you could keep 'em for yourself.

Shreya: Do any of them have brothers?

Summer: You two are fifteen. Keep it in your pants.

Summer: How did you even get that picture?

Serena: We went to the game with our school. UofT got their asses kicked by your boys.

Summer: Is Dad with you?

Serena: You don't know? Dad's in Boston. He's their Interim Coach.

My heart sinks into my stomach. My dad is here. Well, a few hours away, but he's *here*. Has he come closer to work on our relationship? Or is he doing it for his career again? It makes sense that my sisters snuck off to a game that I'm sure they weren't supposed to be at. However, the love for hockey runs deep in Preston blood, so I can't fault them for it.

"How did you manage this?" Aiden's voice pulls me out of my thoughts.

The afternoon light surrounds him like he's some kind of deity, and I don't know how he looks so put together after traveling for hours after his game. I offered to reschedule, but he insisted we don't waste time. Safe to say we're both eager to get this project over with.

"You're not the only one with connections, Crawford."

The Aquatic Center is empty on very rare afternoons. It took me weeks of memorizing schedules to figure out the best time to sneak in. Today, the divers are gone for competitions, so the pool is pretty much empty.

We head into the respective changing rooms, and I regret my choice of bikini when I see myself in the mirror. I probably should have donned something more conservative. Though this is the only bikini I could find both pieces of. The rest are missing a bottom or strings.

Aiden's waiting for me by a bench when I step out, and his gaze glides up my legs to fix on my face. He's in red swim trunks and nothing else, obviously, but I'm stunned. Trying to bring my eyes to his face is challenging because the guy is *shredded*.

"You know, if you wanted to see me shirtless all you had to do was ask, Sunshine. You didn't need to plan a whole swim lesson."

"Don't call me that." His voice slices through my thoughts. "Besides, there are enough shirtless pictures of you circulating Dalton's gossip page. You're not exactly a hidden gem."

"Keeping up to date, eh?" He chuckles, gaze not moving a millimeter away from my face. "So, what is this supposed to do?"

"It's an alternative. Branching out into multiple sports is beneficial for student-athletes. It also eases the rigorous workout routine you put on your body." If he won't heed my word on rest, I'll give him minimal workouts to sate his hunger for working out seven days a week.

"The last time I swam in a pool, I was fifteen."

"There's no lifeguard. If you drown, I'm not saving you."

He feigns offense. "I'm your research; you can't let me die."

"A few casualties along the way won't hurt my application." He throws me a dark look that pulls a smile from me. "Last one in the pool has to pay for the other's dinner," I say before taking off. Just as I'm about to hop off the edge and dive into the pool, Aiden's arm hooks around my waist, and we spin into the water, his back hitting it first. I'm engulfed in chlorine-treated water, and him. When we break through the surface, I'm still trapped against his hard body.

"I don't lose, Preston," he whispers against the shell of my ear.

An involuntary shiver ghosts my skin before I disentangle myself from his arms and swim away. It's a wonder how my skin still burns when I'm submerged in cold water. "I guess that U of T win is getting to your head."

He swims around me. "And every win before that."

Wiping that cocky grin off his face has become my sole purpose for the next thirty minutes. We start with slow laps until he speeds through every marker I set. I have an inkling he lied about not being a big swimmer.

When my phone rings by my towel, I pull out of the pool to reach it. If a lifeguard saw me, they'd chuck the thing in the water. Dalton has a strict no cell phones by the pool policy, after one rang during a competition and one of the swimmers actually stopped to check their notification. They hammered us with announcements about phone addictions and how our brains are rotting.

I quickly answer the phone. "Hello?"

"I hope you're not avoiding me, Sunshine."

His voice drops a lead weight in my stomach. "I've been busy, Dad."

"Too busy for your family?"

My chest heaves as my grip on my phone tightens. "Guess I learned from the best."

He's silent for a minute, but he ignores the pointed jab. "I'm in Boston for a few months. I'd like to see you."

A hot tide of resentment coasts up my spine. Aiden swims closer with questioning eyes. He must notice how rapidly I'm blinking. "Can't. I'm not free," I say, hanging up just as Aiden approaches.

I drop my phone on the towel when he stops by my legs. I'd be stupid to think he doesn't see that my eyes are red, and not from the chlorine. Before he can speak, I sink into the water and start swimming. The burning sensation in my lungs helps me subdue my thoughts. My dad was busy for twenty years, and now he's trying to pry open the door I nailed shut long ago. It isn't fair.

A large hand encircles my arm and stops my rapid movements. Aiden pulls me in so we're only a few inches apart. Concern is etched on his features. "What's wrong?"

I shake my head. "Nothing."

"Summer."

"I said it's nothing," I snap, yanking my arm away. When I reach the edge of the pool, he follows, stopping me from leaving with a grip on my ankle. Damn, he's persistent.

Aiden pulls out of the water, wet droplets gliding off the smooth planes of his body like we're shooting a *Sports Illustrated* ad. Meanwhile, my eyes are bloodshot and my hair messily sticks to my face.

From the windows that surround the pool, the orange rays warm our skin as we sit on the edge, legs dangling in the water, shoulder to shoulder. My awkward outburst and the smell of chlorine curl around us like twine. My breaths come out harsh as I focus on the water droplets falling from my nose to my wet thigh. Aiden sits in silence, but his presence is massive.

"Sorry." It slips out so suddenly I almost try to catch it in my hands and shove it back down my throat. The vulnerability in the one word is so raw it terrifies me that he would want to dissect the meaning of it. I grip the edge of the pool on either side of me and stare at the water, unwilling to make eye contact. Then his large hand covers mine, forcing me to release the tight hold I have on the pool wall.

"Don't apologize for your feelings. Especially not to me," he says, meeting my eyes. The sunlight makes his green ones shine like emeralds, and his wet hair glistens. He doesn't say or ask me anything else. But he relieves the tightness in my chest with a gentle squeeze to my hand, and I let him.

"WOW." DONNY DROPS my paper and leans back in his chair. It isn't a positive *wow*, that much is clear from his caustic tone. "Your methodology is bland."

My shoulders slump. I emailed Langston my draft, and she made notes on every sentence. The feedback would be helpful if there were actual words and not a bunch of question marks. When I reluctantly texted Donny for help, he came by the student lounge.

"Bland how?"

"It's boring. You need more tests."

"I'm doing biweekly assessments and ending with an ACSI-28 test. That's more than the criteria asks for." The self-assessments are questions Aiden had to answer, and the athlete coping skills inventory will be led by Dr. Toor, our campus sports psychologist. It's basic methodology, but it easily showcases everything I know, and that's what admissions are looking for.

"Just trying to give you my expertise."

Frustration tunnels through my skin. "I'll see what I can do."

"It's not totally miserable. Just remember you're applying to one of the most competitive programs on the East Coast."

Rocks of stress jostle in my stomach. "Thanks," I mutter when he collects his things, taking his stressful presence with him. When I let out a breath, the chair is pulled out again, and I startle.

"Hey, Summer."

Blond hair and brown eyes greet me. If the letterman jacket isn't enough, just the outline of his body would tell me he plays football. Connor Atwood is the quarterback of our football team and Sampson's friend, so I've known him since freshman year. Other than that, we've never talked.

"Hi, Connor."

He exhales a breath of relief. "I totally expected you to forget my name." His smile is sweet when he runs a nervous hand through his hair. "You don't mind if I sit here, do you? Unless you're waiting for someone."

I'm not sure if that's his way of asking if I have a boyfriend. But athlete or not, I need a distraction.

After the weird pool moment between Aiden and me, things got awkward, on my end at least. When I insisted on paying for his dinner after losing the bet, he stopped me. His pitiful look irritated me enough that I shoved a bill in his hand and walked off. I'm hoping delaying our next meeting will help with the lingering unease.

Bringing my attention back to Connor, I shake my head. "Nope. Just me."

EIGHT

AIDEN

GETTING SLAMMED INTO the boards by six-year-olds is how I've been starting my mornings. The contrast between my life only a few weeks ago and now is an upsetting revelation.

"How's the girl? Piss her off yet?"

Coach's voice drifts out of his office when I pass by after the lessons. He sits at his desk, glasses lowered to the bridge of his nose as he works on his computer. I'm unsure if my teammates have big mouths or if Summer complained about me. Did she tell him about the funeral flowers?

After our swimming session, things settled into an uncomfortable lull. Not initiated by me. I'm not sure what she was embarrassed about. Everyone has off days, and that phone call just happened to cause one of hers. I'd be lying if I said I'm not curious about who called her, though. Could it be that hockey player ex she hates? Do I know him? If so, I'll happily set him straight so he never calls her again. Her bloodshot eyes and sniffling had sent a prickling feeling to skewer my chest, and I didn't like it. At all.

"She didn't drown me. I think that's a good sign."

Coach makes a noise in his throat. "Keep it that way. The last thing I need is Dean Hutchins breathing down my neck."

I take a cautious step into his office. "Have you tried talking to him about reducing my community service hours?"

He finally meets my eyes, and the wrinkles on his forehead deepen. "Of course. I asked him at our sleepover after we giggled about our crushes."

I'll take that as a no. Coach turns back to the computer screen, dismissing me.

The walk out of the arena and the drive home are the only calm I've felt all week. The breeze cools my heated skin, and the evening sky sets a peaceful backdrop. But that feeling is eradicated as soon as I step foot in the house.

My roommates huddle by the kitchen counter. Dylan sees me first and presses a finger to his lips. I spot the green blob on the counter, a phone trapped inside it.

Cole flies past me and gasps in horror. "Fucking asswipes!" He drives his fist forward to smash his phone out of the Jell-O square, but Kian intercepts his punch.

"This took hours, you're not ruining it. Enjoy the beauty of science."

"Fuck your science, Ishida." Cole digs out his slimy phone, leaving a mess everywhere. Messing with Cole is everyone's favorite pastime, probably because he and Sebastian are the only juniors in the house.

"Good to know this is what you all are doing with your free time." I grab a drink from the fridge.

"Not free time. These are crucial hours before tonight," Kian says through a mouthful of Jell-O.

"What's happening tonight?" I ask, wholly disinterested.

"The toga party? The one our favorite sorority hosts every year? God, where have you been?"

He means *his* favorite sorority. They treat him like a celebrity because he's overly generous at their annual car wash. Safe to say they have a mutually beneficial relationship.

"You guys have fun."

Kian gawks at me. "You have to be joking. It's Beta Phi. Those girls are like your personal cheerleaders."

"Can't. I'm meeting up with Summer later."

He washes his Jell-O-stained hands in the sink. "Reschedule. It's time you stop holding the burden of guilt over the Yale thing. It was our fault too."

It isn't about guilt. The entire thing just highlighted what I've been trying to avoid as captain: that I can't handle balancing different aspects of my life. It was hockey and school growing up, and thanks to my parents, that had been balanced for me. In high school, it was grief, which I miserably failed at, and now it's my personal life. Over the years, there has only been one constant in my life—hockey. It's what got me through my teenage years and led me to the top-performing Division 1 team in the NCAA. Ruining my chances to play would be a huge failure.

"Summer is not going to let me reschedule because of a party."

Kian pulls out his phone. "I'll text her. She likes me better anyway."

"You have her number?" Thoughts of them hooking up cross my mind, but I can't even imagine it. Even if it may explain why she hates hockey players. However, if that were the case, I'd expect the hookup to have been a douchier guy on the team, rather than our very own golden retriever.

"Since junior year. We're friends."

Of course they are. I head upstairs for a shower, and by the time I'm out, he's sent me a screenshot of her response.

Okay. I'll reschedule.

I guess she really does like him better than me.

When I'm halfway down the steps, I pause, seeing Kian wear-

ing a toga. He's got the golden leaf crown and a brooch tying it together.

"You know dressing up isn't mandatory, right?"

He rushes past me. "Just giving the girls what they want. Dylan
got you one too." He points to the toga draped on the banister.

Reluctantly, I head into the bathroom to strip out of my jeans and
into the white garment. It's best not to argue when Dylan has a vision
for costumes. For Halloween, I was Snow White and they were my
dwarfs. That one played out surprisingly well.

We arrive at Beta Phi to a sea of white. I greet a few people playing beer pong in the living room. Kian wanders off as soon as we step
over the threshold, and Dylan is pouring Patrón into every passerby's
mouth before he starts chugging another bottle. The frat guys cheer
him on, chanting "Double D!" and I manage to barrel past them. Eli
is nowhere to be found as usual, and the juniors are probably smoking
outside where I can't see them.

After a few rounds of beer pong, and watching Dylan manage to
sober up, then get even more drunk, Kian bumps into me with a
gasp. "Shit," he slurs. "You're going to hate me for this, but I think
you should hide."

When he tries to shove me out of the kitchen, I stop him. "What
are you talking about?"

He swallows, eyes darting around frantically. "Remember how I
did that nice thing for you by asking Summer to reschedule?"

I nod slowly.

"Well, it wasn't so much of me asking as it was telling her you
were violently ill." Seeing my expression, he blanches. "I said it was
food poisoning! Nothing too serious. Technically, you could have
recovered."

"You lied to her?"

"A little white lie that couldn't possibly hurt anyone. But for good
measure, just hide in the bathroom or something."

"I'm not hiding in the fucking bathroom."

He lets out an exasperated breath. "Come on! Do it for me. She's kind of scary when . . ." His words trail off, and he pales.

Suddenly, an angry brunette stands before me, and I can't help but stare at her tiny outfit. It's a white scrap of a dress that has me swallowing. But when her grip on the red Solo cup tightens, I'm reminded of my current predicament. "I guess you're not too violently ill for a sorority party, huh?"

"It's not what you think," I say.

Her gaze bounces between my eyes, as if assessing the truth before she lets out a disappointed breath. Summer turns, and Kian lets out a curse before scrambling to go after her. When he pushes past me in a hurry, he trips and empties the sticky liquid from his Solo cup all over my bare torso.

THIS BATHROOM SMELLS like candy.

It's so small I have to cram into the space and nearly knock down the toiletries on the counter. But one good thing about getting a drink spilled on you in a sorority is that the bathrooms have everything you need to clean up.

As I'm wiping my abdomen, the doorknob rattles.

"Someone's in here," I mutter, but the rattling doesn't stop. "It's occupied," I say louder. Still, whoever it is doesn't stop. Finally, I yank open the door to tell them to fuck off, but a girl trips into the bathroom and right into me.

"OMG!" Her hands slide up my wet abdomen to my pecs. Then she squeezes.

Fucking sororities.

"It's really you! Totally thought that bitch Bianca was lying, but it's seriously you!"

"Yeah." I pry her hands off me. "Come back later. I'm using this bathroom."

She pulls out of my loose grip and grabs my waist. "Oh, trust me, we can put this bathroom to good use." She kicks the door closed. "Guess what color my panties are?"

I almost choke on my saliva. That's one way to get my attention. Though unfortunately for her, I am focused on a different girl tonight. The sliver of hurt that swam through Summer's eyes when she saw me hit me harder than I expected.

"Look, you seem like a nice enough girl, but—"

"Wrong answer," she interrupts. Her hands travel to the hem of her white dress as she lifts it all the way up. "Correct answer is . . ."

She's not wearing any.

I pinch the bridge of my nose to alleviate the tension in my head. I don't know if I'll regret this later, but I really need to get out of here. "I don't even know your name," I say.

"You always ask the name of every girl you hook up with?"

Well, no, but it seemed like the right thing to say. "I don't know you."

"I know you." That's all she says, but I don't budge. "Ugh! Fine. My name is Crystal. What kind of guy asks a girl's name when she's getting naked?"

No guy. Ever.

When she comes close, I smell alcohol, and it's a relief knowing she's not this insane when she's sober. Just as I try to politely remove her from my body and place her outside the bathroom, someone knocks.

"We're busy!" Crystal calls. With her distracted, I manage to squeeze away.

"Sorry, not tonight."

I don't hear the rest of her curse when I close the door and head downstairs. I'm fixing my beer-stained toga when I spot Summer in the hallway.

As I weave through the crowd, I notice she's talking to someone. He steps closer to tuck a strand of her hair behind her ear. She smiles at him, but it's small. So small, I know she's annoyed by the touch.

As I move closer, I hear him mumble something about a drink before he takes her empty Solo cup. "I didn't get your name," he says.

"Summer. Like the season."

The guy smiles that douche-y white teeth smile. "Your eyes are radiant like the sun, Summer."

I hold back my laugh. Is he going to recite a whole goddamn novel about her eyes? This guy is seriously embarrassing. To my surprise, she actually giggles, and a blush paints her cheeks before he ducks into the kitchen.

"Summer, like the season?" I muse. "As opposed to what? Summer, like the . . . name?"

She gives me a sideways glance. "Stalking isn't a good look for you."

"Not stalking. Just came over to see how you were doing, but I guess Summer, like the season, is doing great."

She doesn't find it funny at all. I, on the other hand, can barely contain my laughter.

"You know, I give updates to Kilner about your performance every week. Maybe playing in the final isn't in the cards for you," she says deceptively sweetly.

I shouldn't be laughing. Not when she's annoyed with me, and definitely not when she has my probation in her hands.

Reeling in my laughter, I take a step closer, and she stays confidently rooted in place. "What can I do to pass?"

"For starters, don't lie to get out of a session."

I wince. "I'm sorry. I didn't know he made up an excuse. When Kian said you agreed to reschedule, I decided to come. I would never lie to you, I promise."

Her head tilts with contemplation. "I'll take that with a grain of salt since your promises hold no weight for me."

"Then let me show you that they do."

The poet himself reappears with Summer's drink. "They only had beer."

I shut my eyes in annoyance. Her eyes were softening and that anger from earlier toned down a few notches. I just need a few more minutes with her.

"Thanks." I snatch the cup from him, down the drink, and shove the empty cup back into his hand. "Now go away."

I'm towering over the dude and he's fuming, looking to Summer for something. He doesn't get the answer he's looking for, because he walks off with a sad nod that makes me feel kind of bad.

"You want to make it up to me?" Summer pulls my attention back to her.

She asks the question seriously, but I can't help but take it suggestively. How could I not? She watches me in a way that has my abdomen tightening, and her bottom lip is caught between her teeth. The barely-there top of her dress would have me sporting a semi if she wasn't so mad.

Who am I kidding? I'm still hard, even as she glares at me like she'd rather see me covered in dirt.

I swallow. "Yes."

My heartbeat changes tempo when she enters my orbit. In this dim light, I can't tell what she's thinking, but I'm hoping it matches my thoughts. When her hands draw up as if she's going to drag them up my pecs and hook her arms around my neck, I feel charged with anticipation. There is no way this is happening right now. If this is her way of teaching me a lesson, it's not a very good one. I'd piss her off again just for the sheer reaction my body erupts with when she's this close.

But instead of whispering that I should make it up to her in a bedroom or a vacant bathroom, she steps back completely. "Then you better get some sleep tonight."

The smile she gives me is pure evil, and I have a feeling tomorrow's going to kick my ass.

NINE

AIDEN

THE HOUSE IS always quiet the morning after a party. Sometimes we can even hear the birds chirping and see the sunlight finding its way inside. Except today, that sunlight is Summer Preston and she's out for vengeance. And the chirping birds are the blaring of an alarm that jerks me awake. My pillow doesn't cushion the ringing coming from downstairs, and when I throw off my comforter to yank open my bedroom door, Kian's across the hall in his Shrek-themed boxers, with both hands over his ears.

"For the love of God, make it stop!" he cries.

"Are we in hell?" groans Sebastian from the bottom of the steps.

"I'm going to throw up," says Dylan, ducking back into his room.

Suddenly, the noise stops, and Summer appears with a bright smile. "Rise and shine!"

When Kian sees her, he pierces me with a glare. "Haven't you learned not to piss her off?"

"What is this about?"

Her smile is smug. "Since you missed our session yesterday, I rescheduled. We're going on a hike!"

Sebastian snorts from his place on the floor. He's still holding his head in his hands when he peeks at her. "Yeah, right, I'm pretty sure I'm still drunk."

"Kian said you all were at my disposal for this project. Unless that's changed, and you would rather your captain enjoy probation, I'm going to need you to get dressed." Grumbles erupt, but Summer turns on the godforsaken alarm again. "You have five minutes."

"IF I HAD the energy to throw him off this cliff right now, I would," mutters a hungover Dylan.

He's glaring at Kian, who chats animatedly with Summer. All the guys are paying for his generous voluntary effort. Eli got lucky because he was MIA this morning, and Cole locked himself in the basement.

Trying not to stare at Summer's ass during this five-mile hike is my own personal brand of torture. She's wearing tights that outline the perfect curve of her ass and a matching long-sleeve that leaves her midriff exposed. After last night, it's been hard for me not to think of how close she got to me.

"This is the only reason I'm not on probation," I say.

Dylan grunts. "Probation would be much preferred over this."

"Come on, guys! I thought you were D1 athletes." Summer glances over her shoulder.

"There's a reason we skate on ice, Summer. If I wanted to wear sneakers and walk in the woods, I would be a serial killer," argues Dylan.

She lets out an amused breath. "It's not my fault you drank yourself stupid last night."

For how much Dylan drinks, his hangovers are usually nonexistent. The fact that we can see the effects of it today tells me he went overboard. I, on the other hand, only had one drink.

"If I knew you wanted to drag us up a hill, I might have cut down. Besides, your problem is with Aiden. Why torture us?"

"I didn't do this to torture you."

"Tell that to my ass," he groans. His dirt-covered shorts are a result of him tripping over a tree branch. The only one who found that amusing was Kian, who took pictures when Dylan fell. "You were at the party, too. Did you drink a gallon of coffee this morning to want to do this?"

"I don't drink coffee, only tea," she retorts.

"You *like* drinking bitter hot water?" chimes Sebastian, who hasn't spoken the entire hike.

"*Chai.* With milk and sugar."

Dylan mumbles something under his breath while I try to figure out how to get Summer alone. I've been hoping I can at least talk to her today, but Kian's been on her like a leech this entire hike. There's something about her voice that makes me itch to hear it. So, as we climb down after the anticlimactic mountaintop view, the guys walk ahead, and I pull her back.

She comes easily. "I haven't talked to you all day. I'm thinking this punishment is a bit cruel," I whisper against her ear.

She shifts to look at me. "Not talking to me is punishment?"

"The worst kind."

Summer falters, and when I take a step to try to close the distance between us, she takes one back. The move surprises me, and just to see what she does, I take another, sending her even further. "You scared of me, Preston?"

She scoffs. "Yeah, right, you couldn't scare a baby if you tried."

Dry leaves crunch under my feet. "Fine," I say, lowering my voice. "Then I make you nervous."

She swallows when her eyes level with mine. "Nobody makes me nervous."

"Yeah?" I take a step closer and her foot hits a branch. She lets out a squeak when she topples, but my hand hooks around her waist. "Careful, Summer, or I might think you're nervous."

As soon as I smell her sweet scent, I hold her tighter. She's close enough that something is happening to my chest. The sensation is so unsettling that I let her balance on her feet again.

She takes several steps back. "I don't know what you think you're doing, but that won't work on me." Summer pivots, stepping on a wedged rock. I know it's a mistake as soon as she does. Her squeak cuts off when I catch her before she hits the ground.

"Ow, ow, ow." She grabs her ankle, and her pained expression tells me she sprained something.

"You twisted it," I say, lifting her into my arms.

"I'm fi—*fuck*," she curses. "You don't have to carry me." The words barely leave her mouth with how hard she clenches her teeth.

The guys are already a few feet ahead of us. "Is she okay?"

"I've got her." I'm moving fast down the slope. Fast enough that Kilner would kill me for risking an injury. When we're back on concrete, I spot the medical aid room, and Summer wraps her arms around my neck, closing her eyes in pain.

Inside, it's run-down and dirty. It's an old place, so I'm surprised they even have a room.

"Do not put me on the dirty counter," Summer warns. I pivot to grab a handful of paper towels to put under her. She's watching me as I pull out the first aid kit, then take off her shoe and sock, trying to turn her ankle to see where it hurts.

"*Fuck*," she hisses. "Are you doing that on purpose?"

I gentle my touch. "Sorry, just checking how bad it's twisted."

She tips her head back and groans. "I haven't had enough caffeine today, and you're giving me a headache."

"I thought you didn't drink coffee."

She massages her temples. "Chai. I need like two cups a day, more if I'm dealing with you."

I ignore the remark and eye her high ponytail. Feeling brave, I pull her hair tie and let her soft brown waves fall around her shoulders. When she tries to snatch the hair tie, I slide it on my wrist. "Maybe you have a headache from your hair being in a death grip."

"That's how I like it," she declares.

I raise my brows, making her roll her eyes. "I like it down."

She snorts. "Good to know. I'll throw out all my hair ties because Aiden Crawford likes it when girls wear their hair down."

Wrapping the bandage around her ankle, I glance at her. "Not girls. You."

Summer's smugness slips off her face, and the crease between her brows deepens. I know her mind is working overtime, but the comment slipped off my tongue so quickly I couldn't stop it.

"Done," I say coolly, dropping her leg. She immediately hops off, wincing when she lands on her foot. "Lay off of it for a bit."

She attempts to hop away again, but I block her path. "Not happening. This is only going to work if you let me help you."

"Fine." She lets me lift her again, soft hair dusting my arm. "Thanks."

TEN

SUMMER

FOR THE FIRST time in a long time, someone's proud of me, and I don't know how to act.

Dr. Müller hands my paper back. "This is great work, Summer. If you complete these tests and get some literature to back this up, they will beg you to join the co-op."

I sigh with relief. It's been stressful trying to get my paper structured, and knowing I've finally nailed it means I'm one step closer to achieving my goal. Dr. Langston's emails have only given me negative feedback. I dropped by to see her, but Dr. Müller, one of my favorite psychology professors, stopped me to chat.

"Would it be too much if I ran my final draft by you too?"

"Not at all, email or stop by my office. I'll be happy to help. But shouldn't you be running this by Laura? She's ultimately the one to sign off on your project, not me."

For this program, you can't submit an application unless it's given approval from your advisor. So I couldn't go behind Langston's back and toss my name in the hat if she hated it. "I know. I just want to have more than one opinion."

Müller agrees, and I ask him a few more questions, enjoying not feeling patronized, before I head out. Langston being the chair and on the admissions board doesn't give me an advantage. The only reason she can do both is because she's proved countless times that she is unbiased. I have a few more weeks until my application is due, so I'm looking at every possible angle to guarantee acceptance.

Donny made me nervous by talking about the low percentage for acceptance each year and how my life will look worse than a pileup on the I-95 if I don't get in. He's clearly great at pep talks.

My phone pings with a text from another one of my headaches.

AIDEN

Aiden: I found handcuffs in your room.
Aiden: *sent an image*

I halt in the middle of the sidewalk when I see the picture of him smiling wide, standing in my room, holding a pair of fuzzy pink handcuffs. The mischievous glint in his eyes tells me he thinks they're for something nefarious, not just last year's Halloween costume.

A passerby knocks into me, snapping me out of my daze.

Summer: Why are you in my room?
Aiden: Practice ended early. Amara let me in before she left.
Summer: Don't touch my stuff, and definitely don't look in any
    more drawers.
Aiden: Too late. You're kinkier than I thought, Preston.
Aiden: And your bed is super comfy. I'm exhausted, I think I'll
    take a nap.
Aiden: Naked.

God, he is irritating. I make a mental note to buy a lock for my drawer in case the captain of the hockey team decides to snoop, and some bleach to wash my sheets. Shoving my phone back in my pocket, I ignore the twitch of pain in my healing ankle when I sprint to my dorm.

Inside, I try to catch my breath, but it gets caught somewhere in my chest when I see Aiden in the kitchen. His blue Under Armour long-sleeve outlines the movement of his back muscles so perfectly, I hate it.

The dip in my stomach reminds me of my high school boyfriend.

I met Ryan Levy at the rink, where I skated while waiting for my dad to finish volunteering. I was in a Ryan-induced coma for those three months. However, I hated when he came to my house because he would spend his time talking to my dad. Pretty soon, I realized he wasn't dating me for me, he was dating me for my dad. Weird, but understandable, I guess, for a kid who had his sights set on the NHL.

I didn't learn my lesson, because my prom date was another hockey player. He was popular and hot, so I said yes, like any sane teenage girl. At the after-party, we found ourselves in a hotel, and I was prepared to lose my virginity that night. But the words that came out of his mouth had dried me up like a desert. "*I can't believe I'm fucking Lukas Preston's daughter.*" It was so revolting I grabbed my dress and got the hell out of there.

So, it's safe to say hockey players have been off my radar. Completely.

But as Aiden Crawford stands in my kitchen with his killer smile and shining green eyes, I feel tempted to break that oath. I drop my keys on the counter as I watch him place a pot in the drying rack. The scene is so domestic I have the urge to pinch myself.

"That was fast," he says, drying his hands with the dish towel.

My attention catches on the steaming cup on the counter. "What's that?"

"For you."

I peer into it. "You . . . made me tea?"

"You said you drink it twice a day, more if you're dealing with me, and I was already here." He shrugs, and the air of nonchalance throws me off. "Didn't know which one you liked, but I didn't open this." He lifts the green tin, and my heart stutters.

I lunge to snatch it from him and stash it back in the drawer. "Don't touch that."

He stands frozen. "You good?"

"Fine."

"*Fine?*" he asks, incredulous. "You practically mauled me."

Aiden waits for an explanation, and my shoulders tense. "My dad bought me this from a shop in Chicago when he traveled for work. It's my favorite, and this is the last one I have."

To escape the soft look in his eyes and his sympathetic nod, I bring the cup to my lips and take a sip. It's a miracle how I hold in the noise that wants to escape when the taste hits my tongue. The strong cinnamon flavor and the overuse of honey coat my tongue in a bitter formula. But for some reason, probably because he looked so sweet providing the simple act of service, I can't bring myself to say anything.

He made me tea.

Forest green eyes watch me. "Good?"

"It's . . . it's—yeah. It's good."

His eyes flicker, and the curve of his smile does something swirly to my chest before it starts to burn. Though that might be the spoonful of cinnamon I just ingested. With an itchy throat, I put the cup down. "I'm going to change. I'll be right back."

I've just slipped on a sweatshirt when a curse pulls me from my room. Aiden's standing at the counter, my cup in hand and a look of disbelief on his face. "This is disgusting." With a sour face, he places the cup in the sink. "It's a good thing I already ordered you an actual drink and some food."

"You didn't have to do that. It wasn't that bad."

"Summer, it was so bad that you were being *nice* to me. That tells me everything I need to know."

"Hey! I can be nice." His barbed look irks me. "The only reason you're here is because I was being nice by giving you a chance."

"Yeah, after I begged you."

"That's what you call begging?"

He smirks, all too intrigued. "Wanna teach me? Maybe with those handcuffs . . ."

"They are not what you think they're for."

He nods with a suppressed smile. When his phone dings, he pulls it out. "Food's here."

When we've eaten, I hand him the assessments. The sooner he gets this done, the sooner I can write my analysis.

"Are you done?" My impatience seeps into my tone.

"Almost. I wanna make sure I do it right."

"It's really not that difficult."

A short beat passes before he sighs, and his warm hand stops the anxious movements of my bouncing leg. "Summer, what's going on?"

"What do you mean?" The exasperated look I give him makes him take a long look at me.

"I *mean* you're irritable and have this faraway look like you're stressing over a million things."

"It's nothing. Can we just get this done?"

He sits back and crosses his arms. "No."

"*No?*" Did he not know how close I was to strangling someone? "This is not a good time to test me, Crawford."

I clench my jaw as his gaze drags over my face in a slow assessment. "Tell me what's wrong."

"You know you're not *my* captain, right? That whole demanding thing won't work on me."

He leans in, eating up my personal space. "Won't it?"

The challenge in his eyes is clear, but I oblige. "Langston said my intro needs work, so I'm redoing the entire thing, along with the methods section, because Donny thinks it's missing something."

"You're just as smart as Donny. Smarter. Why does his opinion matter?"

Aiden's dislike for Donny isn't something he bothers to hide. And as much as I may feel the same, I've become so accustomed to Donny's feedback that I can't imagine not having it. "Because he knows what he's doing. Besides, there are only three of us eligible for co-op—Donny, Shannon, and me. I'm his competitor, yet he's still willing to help. I have to be grateful for that."

Aiden doesn't comment on that. "Okay, let me help you, too. You still have a few weeks, and I can read over your paper."

"No offense, but what do you know about psych papers?"

"Nothing, considering I'm an econ major, but sometimes an extra pair of eyes can help."

His earnest look kindles a warmth in my stomach. "That is really nice of you."

"Don't be fooled, I've been told I'm an asshole."

"WHO'S SHE?" AIDEN asks.

He pestered me into taking a break, so I put on my favorite Turkish drama to spite him. Turns out he loves it.

"That's his ex-girlfriend. She doesn't know about the fake engagement," I explain.

"Shit, she's going to see the contract." Aiden nudges me.

The suspenseful music builds, and we wait for the big reveal. We're sitting on the edge of the couch, the sides of our legs pressed together. Then the credits roll.

Aiden groans. "Seriously?"

"That's how they get you."

He collects our containers and chuckles. "I'm starting to get your whole 'stay inside and not have a life' thing. It's kind of fun."

"I have a life, asshole. In fact, I met up with someone last week,"

I lie. Well, not entirely. Connor sat with me in the cafeteria. It's the closest thing to a date I've had all year. Pathetic, I know.

"Who?"

"Connor Atwood."

He makes a noise in his throat. "What can you possibly have in common with Atwood?"

"You know him?" Of course he did. They were both athletes, and the captains of their team.

"Yeah. The dude's at every party, and he's been with his fair share of girls. Now, apparently, one of them is you."

I backtrack. "I haven't *been* with him. We just studied together."

He cocks his head. "That's your type, huh? Football players."

"*Player*. Singular. But, no, I'm still figuring out my type."

"You keep working on that," he says. "I'm going to take off. I'll see you Thursday at the pool."

I hide the satisfied smile that breaks free. I wasn't sure if my paper was helping him, but Aiden started taking a day off and swimming for one workout. It feels like a big accomplishment.

I stand too. "Wait, I'll walk you out. I need to change."

"For what?" he asks, but I'm already in my room changing into a random pair of leggings and a sports bra. I walk out with my sneakers in hand, slipping them on by the door.

"Where are you going?"

"For a run," I say, gesturing for him to exit.

"Now?"

"I didn't have time this morning." I lock the door, then check for my pepper spray and keychain alarm as Aiden stares at me.

"You shouldn't be running alone this late."

I almost laugh, but his expression is so serious I hold it. "Thanks for the concern, but I can handle it."

He's quiet the whole way down, until I'm turning onto my usual path. "Walk me to my truck?"

"Scared?" I follow him into the parking lot.

He appears deep in thought. "Something like that."

"Don't worry, Crawford. I won't let the boogeyman get you."

At his car, Aiden tosses his bag in the back seat and locks it.

I stare at him. "What are you doing?"

He stretches his legs. "Running."

"You just had practice." He walks past me. "Aiden, I'm not running with you. You said you were exhausted."

"Did I? I feel great. I'm just running the path over there."

"That's my path!"

He throws me a grin over his shoulder. "What a coincidence."

Before I can protest again, he takes off, and reluctantly, I go after him.

ELEVEN

AIDEN

THE INCESSANT BANGING on my bedroom door rips me from my exhaustion-induced sleep.

"Cap! You're late, man."

Pulling the comforter over my head isn't enough to keep Kian's voice out. I shouldn't have gone up against him for this room. I'd be better off downstairs.

"Aiden!"

Fuck. I throw off my comforter, my muscles screaming in agony. I'm accustomed to dealing with body aches after practice. Today though, I feel the pain in my fucking jaw, that's how deep it is.

I open the door and lean against it for support. "What?"

Kian gives me a once-over. "You look like shit."

"Thanks," I grumble, going back to bed.

Kian follows. "What the hell happened?"

"Went for a run last night."

"No, you didn't. We had practice last night."

"After," I say, wincing as I lie down.

"Why would—" He watches me curl back into bed and bursts

into laughter. "You went to Summer's last night. You ran with her, didn't you?"

"It was late and she was alone." My voice is muffled by my pillow.

"Oh, man. This is too good." He barks out a laugh that somehow hurts my bones. When he pulls out his phone, mine dings from the nightstand and I know he's texting the group chat. He's still typing when he glances up. "By the way, you're going to be late to the rink."

My head snaps to the clock, and I curse, springing out of bed. Kilner would have my head if I missed today's coaching session.

Running a hand through my hair on my way inside the arena doesn't help how disheveled I look. As for the pain that shoots through me with every stride, I can't focus on it too much because I'm going to have sixteen kids slamming into me for the next hour.

"Every minute adds a lap around the rink." Kilner has the superpower of materializing where you don't want him.

My eyes squeeze shut. "I overslept."

The crease on his forehead deepens. "Don't give me an excuse. You know the consequences."

Glancing at the time, I groan. "That's five laps."

"Six now."

I should know better than to complain. My smile is plastic when I look at him. "Have I told you lately that you're my favorite coach?"

"Get on the damn ice before we make it to seven."

Holding in my groans as I tie up my skates proves to be a challenge. I slip on my instructor jacket and beckon the kids into a line on the ice. Today I appreciate how long it takes them to form a straight line, because I'm still trying to stretch out the soreness in my body.

"Okay, who's ready to show off what they've been practicing?" Tiny cheers erupt. "We'll skate and learn some stick handling before we finish off with a game."

By the time I get a few trainers on the ice, we're in full swing.

SUMMER

WHEN I WILLINGLY drove to the rink today, I didn't think I'd be sweating while seated so close to the ice. But I guess that's what happens when you're watching a burly hockey player teach six-year-olds how to play defense. The zip-up he wears hugs every dip of his muscles. I try to stop the bubbling reaction that climbs to the surface. Aiden's so secure in himself, in school, and in hockey. It's insanely attractive, and I'm not too proud to admit that.

When a kid slips and starfishes on the ice until Aiden sets her back on her skates, I can't hold back my laugh.

My cheeks heat when green eyes find me. *Get it together, Summer.*

The buzzer sounds, and the kids high-five the instructors before clattering off the rink. By the exit, Aiden talks to the parents, his gaze cutting to me every few seconds.

Finally stalking over to me, he pulls off his helmet. "What alternate universe did I fall into that you're willingly at the rink?"

"Apparently, the one where you're still impossibly annoying."

"And lovable?" he asks with a boyish grin.

I laugh despite myself. "Maybe I just wanted to see if you're actually helping these poor kids."

"Ah, so you're assessing how good I look as a DILF."

"That was you as a dad? I saw you push them to the ice."

"I was checking their stance. It's all a part of being a good teacher. Though I don't expect you to know anything about that."

"Keep talking, Crawford, and I might just tank your evaluation."

His gaze narrows. "Evaluation?"

"Coach asked me to write you one," I tell him. "It could get you out of community service."

"And you said yes? Are you sure you're feeling okay?" His face etches with fake concern.

"This is another thing I can hold over your head to make you do what I want." I flutter my lashes.

"You don't need blackmail to get me to do what you want, Summer."

The words slip off his tongue in a smooth concoction that drips into my stomach. I have no comeback, and he seems to realize he got me to shut up, because a slanted smile fixes on his lips. It's gone just as quickly when he nods toward the hallway. "So, let me guess, you're going to say I've been a difficult asshole."

Recovering rather quickly, I follow him. "Far from it."

"Is it because you've seen me shirtless?"

"You are so full of yourself."

"Someone has to be," he mutters before clearing his throat. "So, what did it?"

"You care," I say, sitting on a bench. "About hockey, about your team and your friends. You would do anything for them. You're a great captain, and probation is the last place you belong."

His eyes flicker with surprise. "With an evaluation like that, Coach might think I'm bribing you."

"Now that you mention it, I wouldn't mind a tip."

"Come here and pull it out yourself."

I scrunch my face in disgust. "You know what? I take back what I said."

Aiden stands in front of me, attacking my eyes with his bare chest. "We can't have that. What can I do to make it up to you?"

I incinerate the first thought that pops into my head and look up at him. "Nothing. I already made up my mind."

"Dinner?"

I shake my head, and the smile on his face falls before I supply, "Takeout. My place."

"Deal, but no data set. This isn't a session."

"But—"

"Just dinner," he says firmly.

"DON'T STOP." AIDEN'S deep voice vibrates against my skin, sending goose bumps to riddle the surface. With his body between my legs and my fingers digging into his muscular shoulders, he groans softly.

"If you just listened to me, you wouldn't be having this problem."

"Hmm," he murmurs in pleasure. "If this is the outcome, I'd do it again."

Upon receiving a text from Kian asking if I enjoyed torturing hockey players in my spare time, I found out that Aiden's been a walking zombie after our run. The team did conditioning and strength training yesterday, but his soreness is somehow my fault.

Now I sit on the couch with him on the floor between my legs as I massage his tense muscles. Every so often his biceps brush against my legs, and a weird sensation crawls up my spine. Trying to ignore it has become my own silent game of the night.

"Wait, so the mother-in-law likes her now?" he asks, pointing at the TV with his fork.

We stopped at an Indian place by Dalton that Aiden swore had the best butter chicken. I laughed for a good two minutes after I said I didn't trust his palate, and he looked wounded. He proved me very wrong when I tasted the food. It was almost as good as my mom's cooking, though I'd never voice that thought. Then Aiden put on *his* favorite Turkish show since he won't give me credit for putting him on to the series.

Sitting in my dorm and eating takeout feels oddly comfortable. "Yeah, 'cause she sees that she's good for her son," I explain.

The end credits roll, and my hands are tired from running over his back. "That's all you get. Any more and I'll need payment."

"What about my glutes?" he asks with a buoyant look.

"I'm not going anywhere near those," I spurn.

He chuckles. "You're so much better than Hank. His hands are like two boulders. You should become my physical therapist."

"Great idea. I'll switch majors to become your personal PT." I grab my laptop. "So, I know you said no data sets, but this—"

"Summer, can you relax for once? We can look at your work next time; it's not going anywhere." He takes my laptop and stashes it beside him. "You know how to relax, right?"

I deflate. "Donny just freaked me out about the whole application. It needs to be perfect."

"You know this stuff better than anyone. Don't let his opinion affect your work."

"I know," I say unconvincingly.

He looks like he wants to say more but instead heads to the kitchen, taking our trash with him. "Got any drinks?"

"We have some seltzer in the back and Slink if you wanna drink your weight in sugar."

He chuckles, grabbing two water bottles instead, and handing me one before falling onto the couch. "Those things are horrible. I had a few boxes after I worked with them."

"You worked with Slink?"

He nods. "It was an endorsement."

"You do . . . endorsements?"

He gives me a sideways glance. "You seriously don't follow hockey at all?"

"I don't follow athletes," I correct.

"Right," he says. "When I came to Dalton, I was offered deals I never took. But I needed the money a few semesters ago, so I promoted Slink."

"When you paid for Kian's tuition?" I blurt. Biting my tongue, I peek over at him with a sheepish look. "Kian told me about that when he was convincing me you were a good guy."

"Of course he did." He shakes his head. "Did it work?"

"Jury's still out."

He smiles. That straight-teeth smile that would melt any girl's panties. Not mine, though. Definitely not mine.

"So, you're like an influencer," I say.

He shoots me an annoyed look and gathers his things.

"You are! Do you post shirtless pics? Nude photoshoots? Puck covering the goods?"

"I'm out."

He's already heading to the door. "Was it something I said?" He doesn't answer. "I just want to know if you skated nude promoting a cereal box!"

The door slams shut, and I laugh so hard I clutch my stomach.

TWELVE

AIDEN

Summerluvin started following you.

Seeing the notification, I do what I never do; I follow her back. Social media isn't something I spend a lot of time on, but my curiosity wins when I see her profile. Oddly enough, the entire hockey team is already following her.

SUMMERLUVIN

aidencrawford: I see you've reconsidered your stance on following athletes.

summerluvin: Temporarily. But I have to say, I'm disappointed.

aidencrawford: And why's that?

summerluvin: No nude cereal box ad. Unfollowing.

aidencrawford: I'll do a private one just for you. Can't afford to upset a fan.

summerluvin: pass.

aidencrawford: You have other suggestions?

summerluvin: You, clothed, not trying to distract me from my
    research.
aidencrawford: pass.

I shove my phone back in my pocket and climb the steps to the psychology building. The reason for my irritated mood is sitting in the lounge like a prince.

Is Donny Rai seriously Summer's type? Preppy and academic? Finding out she dated Donny was a huge shock. Kian was the one to tell me, because he knows everything about everyone at Dalton. Sometimes I think he runs our school's gossip page.

"Rai."

Donny turns in his chair, and his friends eye me as if the doors to the building had jock repellent that I managed to break through.

"What's up? Need a tutor for English 101?"

I've never been the one to incite violence off the ice, but right now nothing is as appealing as the idea of my fist driving into Donny's jaw. Though, his uninspired insult misses the mark because I'm sure he's aware of every student on the dean's list, and I'm one of them.

"I'm good. You're not my usual type for tutors." I revel in the way his jaw clenches. "I want to talk about Summer."

"Do you need my permission?"

"Apparently I do, because you seem to think you can control her. She's been working hard on her paper, and I'd appreciate it if you cool your drop-ins. She's stressed, and you're not helping."

"I'm just trying to give her some of my expertise."

"She has plenty."

He laughs. "You met her like, what? Five minutes ago? I've known her for years, and she trusts my opinion. You should be glad I'm even willing to help her."

Prick. "Look, I'm telling you how she's feeling and that her project won't be any better with you breathing down her neck."

An air of tension settles between us until he steps back. "Fine. I want to see how this pans out anyway."

I falter. "What does that mean?"

He releases a sardonic breath. "Give it up, Crawford. If she lets you hit, you'll be on the curb faster than you can finish."

"Excuse me?"

"Sorry, does all the brain damage you've amassed make it hard to hear, too?" My clenched teeth feel like they'll turn to dust from the pressure. "Summer's not going to sleep with you because you act like you care. That girl has spikes around her thicker than your head. I'd tell you not to waste your time, but you're already doing that. So, I'll be watching when you inevitably fail." The air of arrogance that oozes out of every pore follows him out the door.

Later that evening, it's closing time when I skate off the ice to head to the showers. My solo practice session went longer than intended, probably because I imagined Donny's face as the puck.

Though we won our last game, it's the worst we've ever played. And when I entered the arena, Kilner made sure to castrate me for the shitty performance.

When I twist off the faucet and pull a towel around my waist, light footsteps sound against the tiled floors. As I open the door, the faint smell of peaches hits my nose before I see her.

"Summer?"

She spins, long brown hair in waves down her back. Full lips part when her gaze drifts to my low-hanging towel. Then, as if clearing her thoughts, the fire of anger lights her expression and she marches right up to me, almost walking into the stall before faltering. She crosses her arms to create some type of barrier between us, and I stifle a laugh.

"Trust me, you won't be laughing when I'm done with you."

I beam. "I hope not."

She glares. "Care to explain why Donny just became a student aide on my paper?"

That jackass. I should have known that smirk was bad news. "I didn't say anything like that to him."

"You said plenty. Don't try to pretend you didn't go all macho man and screw everything up."

"I was trying to help."

"I never asked for your help!"

"You wouldn't. You could be hanging off a damn cliff, and you still wouldn't ask for help."

"But you did it anyway? Maybe I didn't do anything about Donny because I know how he is. He's pissed about what you said, and now we're stuck with him. Why couldn't you leave it alone?"

"You were stressed," I try again.

"And how does that affect you?"

"Because I ca—"

The creak of the door cuts me off before Kilner's voice drifts through the locker room. "It's the damn plumbing in my bathroom. I need it fixed, Brent."

"Fuck." I pull a distracted Summer into the stall and close the door. My hand covers her mouth before she can make a sound. Judging by the way her eyes flare, she might bite me.

"You can't be in here," I whisper. Her brows scrunch, and her grip on my wrist tightens like she's trying to break it. "I'll remove my hand if you promise not to scream."

She reluctantly nods, and I uncover her mouth, still caging her against the wall. She's breathing hard, and I don't mean to, but my eyes fall to her rising and falling chest, which grazes my bare torso. A water droplet from my hair hits her collarbone, making her flinch when it slides down her skin, leaving a wet trail as it slips between the swell of breasts.

I'm caught in a fervent trance when a sharp pain in my abdomen forces me to jerk back.

Summer pulls away her assaulting finger, and if looks were

tangible, this one would be throwing me off a cliff. She meets my sheepish smile with an eye roll.

Being this close to her makes me hot. That isn't ideal, because I'm in a towel, and she's pressed against me so perfectly; just one wrong move, and everything is going to get even more uncomfortable. I try to force the thoughts out of my head, but that's impossible when she brings her lips between her teeth. I have to hold in a groan. I'm wrapped in a bubble of her, and I feel like I'm damn near suffocating. *What the hell is happening?*

The sink running and crumpling paper breaks my attention from her. "Crawford? You still here?" He must see my gear on the bench, because he stops in front of the stall.

I clear my throat. "Just finishing up, Coach."

"Well, hurry up. They're locking up early tonight."

"Got it."

His footsteps retreat, and Summer's head falls back on a sigh.

"And Crawford? Tell your girlfriend no shoes in the shower."

Then the door closes.

"Oh my God! That is so embarrassing." Summer's cheeks flush pink. "You're like a furnace!" She moves away and wipes the water droplets off her arm and chest before swinging open the stall door. Puzzled, I pull on my sweats to go after her.

"That's it?" I ask when she's already down the hall. "You came all the way here for that?"

"Yeah, guess so." The heavy doors bang closed behind her.

"WHEN A SKINNY fucker chirps, it is not a jab at your manhood!" Kilner grabs Dylan by the collar and shoves him with the strength of an enforcer. "Where the hell is your head at?"

In case you couldn't tell, we lost. Bad.

Disappointment clogs the locker room air. When I faced off against Brown University's centerman, I managed to get the puck in our possession, except poor communications and unfortunate timing muddied the play, and Sebastian fumbled my pass, causing a turnover. Brown's counterattack from their forward left us scrambling to catch up. Our defensive coverage crumbled like a termite-infested foundation after that, and Brown capitalized on power plays and netted two goals.

"Crawford's too busy making sure he looks pretty for his next photo shoot," says Tyler Sampson.

The energy drink ad let Kian stay in school, but it meant getting ragged on for months. Especially since Slink renewed the ads and one of the juniors saw the poster at a store in Providence.

"Fuck off, Sampson," sneers Dylan, who's only trying to get on my good side because he got ejected for unsportsmanlike conduct.

"He's just jealous you're prettier than him," whispers Kian.

I shrug him off and turn to Kilner. "We can win the quarterfinal. Today's loss was a one-off."

"One-off or not, we can't afford to lose to Yale." Sampson aims a sharp eye at me.

"That's enough." Coach steps forward. "Yale is tough, but with the right changes, we can win."

"What kind of changes?" Kian dares to ask.

"No more parties. No more drinking." Coach glares at Dylan, who slumps on the bench. "No more girls." A chorus of groans erupts from the guys, and I don't even recognize when my own leaves me. Except everyone else does, because Coach eyes me suspiciously, and Eli snorts. "Those are my orders. Your captain will enforce them. Now get the hell out of here."

I'm fine with rules and great with discipline. Having self-control comes naturally, and I thrive on delayed gratification. Except where Summer Preston is concerned. After having her pressed against me in the shower, I've had a difficult time thinking about anything else. I even googled serial killer tendencies because I'm sure smelling someone's hair is a fucking weird thing to do. But hers is different. It's soft and smells like sweet peaches.

I don't even like peaches.

It's bad, and I need my mind off her, but with Kilner's new rules, that isn't happening anytime soon.

"The *no more parties* thing really has you upset, eh?" Dylan and Kian snicker as they pass me.

I flip them off and slip into my truck. Without a distraction, I have the foolish urge to see an angry girl tonight. I just have to find her first. Which proves to be a difficult task when she doesn't answer my texts. Fortunately, Amara is in a helpful mood when I show up at Iona House and tells me Summer's at the library. It's finding which one that's the issue.

A thorough and exhausting search later, I spot long hair and a pale pink sweater in the quiet study area. The sound of the chair being pulled out drags Summer's attention to me. She assesses the rain sprinkled across the shoulders of my gray hoodie. She brings her attention back to her work.

"Don't you have a game?" she finally asks.

The reminder of the loss feels less painful when I'm with her. "It was earlier. I came here to study."

She nails me with a skeptical look. "You never study in the library."

"Needed a change of scenery." I shrug. But she's right. I prefer the chaotic nature of the house. Libraries are too quiet for me.

"So you came to the farthest library on campus?" she presses.

"Took me three tries."

"For what?"

"To find this one."

"The others didn't have what you were looking for?"

I smile. "Not even close."

She waits for more, but she isn't going to get it. I've been doing a lot of things I don't understand lately, so I've stopped trying to analyze them. "You can ask me anything you want. Show me all your data sets."

She resumes typing, brushing her hair from her face. "I can't."

"You don't have any more questions?"

"I do, but that's for Wednesday."

"Right, 'cause you can't stray from your calendar even a little."

"As someone whose head only has a puck running through it, I don't expect you to understand," she snipes.

"Trust me, I have a lot of things running through my head."

"I'm sure the influx of nudes you get on a daily basis keeps you occupied."

My attraction to her insults is mildly concerning. I'd talk to a therapist about it, but I'd rather not divulge that. I chuckle, and I can see her lips tip up before she looks away again.

"If you thought I'd shift around my schedule so you would be off the hook this week, I can't. So feel free to leave."

"I'm good right here."

She appears dubious. "Trying to get on my good side after sticking us with Donny?"

"Fingers crossed." I notice a crumpled paper under her textbook. "What's this?"

She tries to snatch back the flyer. "Nothing."

I hold it away from her reach. "*Mental health initiative for athletes*?" I glance at her. "You set up an event?"

"Kind of." She shifts uncomfortably. "It was supposed to be once a semester, but the last one did terribly, so I'm scrapping it."

"When was the last one?"

"December. Only the extra credit students were there. No athletes showed. Except for Tyler."

That's the one Coach was pissed at me for missing. It was Summer's event. "You should do it."

She laughs. "And get humiliated again? No thanks."

"I'll come, and I'll tell everyone I know about it." I'd be ignorant to not recognize the influence I have on campus. There's a certain reputation that comes with being captain.

She gathers her hair and tucks it to one side. "No way. I don't need you advertising my event and people thinking we're something we're not."

My head tilts. "We can't just be friends? I don't have to be fucking you to go to your event."

She scowls. "We're not either of those things."

"Don't change the subject. Are you doing it or not?"

She looks away. "No. It's a lot of work."

"Since when do you shy away from work? You took me on."

"You annoyed me into taking you on." She reaches for the paper again.

I don't give it back. "You should do it. It'll look really good for your application." She bites her lip, mulling it over. "Come on, you know you want to."

I almost think she'll refuse again, but she sighs. "Fine. I'll check with the department, but I can advertise it on my own. Thanks for the offer."

Satisfied, I lean back in my chair. "Look at us, agreeing on something without bickering."

"We did bicker."

"That wasn't bickering."

"Yes, it was."

"No—"

"We're doing it right now!" She lets out an irritated breath, but I don't miss the amused chuckle that accompanies it. Once again, she gathers her hair and moves it behind her shoulders. Instinctively, I remove the hair tie that's been sitting on my wrist for way longer than it should have and hold it out.

"Here."

She stares at my hand until recognition crosses her features. "That's mine."

"Good observation. Take it."

"You kept my hair tie?"

Now that I think about it, it is kind of creepy. Who in their right mind holds a girl's hair tie for weeks without having plans to use or return it? The look on her face tells me she might be thinking the same thing. "You said you like your hair up."

"So you just, what, kept it on your wrist this whole time?"

"Turn around, Summer," I order, evading the question.

Although she still looks unsure, she turns her back to me. Her peach scent clouds my senses as I gather her soft hair and twist the hair tie around, not too tight, so she doesn't get a headache.

When I'm done, she touches it. "Not bad. You practice on a lot of girls?"

I smirk. "Just you. But I am naturally good with my hands."

"Are you incapable of having a normal conversation?"

"No, but I do like seeing you blush."

"I do not blush," she argues, blushing.

We study for two more hours. Well, she studies, and I pretend to. It's way too hard to focus in the quiet of the library. When she finally closes her laptop, I want to rejoice, but she simply packs it into her bag and walks off. I catch up to her outside.

"What are you doing now?" I sound like a clingy toddler, but I can't help myself.

She throws me an unreadable glance. "Going to my dorm."

"Need company?"

She laughs, then seems to realize I'm not joking. "I have a quiz to submit, and I need to confirm with Dr. Toor about the test you're doing on Wednesday."

"We just spent two hours studying. Don't you want to relax?"

"*I* spent two hours studying. You stared into space." She walks faster, as if she can't wait to get away from me.

"Okay, but shouldn't you take a break?"

"If I wanted a break, I would have taken a gap year."

I laugh, but her expression tells me that's not a joke. "It's only eight. We should do something."

"I am doing something. I'm going to my dorm." She sighs when

I don't quit walking beside her. "Look, you obviously still feel guilty about the Donny thing, but I'm over it. You did something impulsive, and now we have to live with the consequences. It's whatever."

"Let me at least make it up to you. I'll take you out for dinner. You have to eat, right?"

"Goodnight, Aiden," she sings, leaving me in the quad.

THIRTEEN

SUMMER

IS THIS HOW normal people feel? Because being stress-free is peaceful and terrifying all at once. Currently, everything is on track, and there's an empty stress-shaped hole in my stomach. It feels too good to be true, like I'm forgetting about a fifty-page essay that's due tomorrow.

I'm packing my bag when I see Amara's sparkly dress and heels to match. "Are you ready?" she asks.

"Ready?" My brain runs into overdrive. "For what?"

She groans. "Do not tell me you are skipping plans to study. Unless you're aiming for the hot tutor look, in which case, I'm totally digging this."

I recall that Amara and Cassie had talked me into going to a concert tonight. "Shit, I forgot about the show."

"I will fight you if I have to. You are not going to the library tonight." I have a feeling that's not an empty threat.

"I'm going over to Aiden's, but I can cancel."

She perks up with a grin that shouldn't be that mischievous for what I've told her. "Cool, have fun, then."

I pause mid-text. "You're not mad?"

She chuckles. "It's Aiden fucking Crawford. Why would I be mad? You know who would be mad, though? Like half the student body."

She's right, but if they knew our time together is spent filling out assessments and analyzing data, they would opt out. "What are you talking about?"

"The texts. The frequent visits. Not talking to any other guys. You're *so* into him." There's a teasing note to her voice as if we're in the sixth grade and I just admitted I have a crush.

"For someone so smart, you've completely misread this situation."

She raises a brow. "You're telling me you haven't even kissed him?"

"No, I haven't."

Her forehead creases with concern. "Are you feeling okay? Poor judgment? Poor *eyesight*?"

"He's the subject of my paper. That's it." I haven't ever thought about kissing him. Okay, *ever* might be a stretch, because his lips were right there when he pressed me against the locker room shower, and they were pink and plump and—*never mind*.

"Mm-hmm, is that why you study him all night long?" She emphasizes her words by running her hands down her body.

"I'm not doing this with you. Have fun at the show."

"I will. You have fun *studying*." Her snicker follows me out the door like an annoying fly. On my way to Aiden's house, I try not to focus on her words, which is easy when Aiden lets me in, and Kian and Dylan are arguing in the kitchen.

"It was 2017, you dimwit."

"Are you kidding? Detroit was '17. It's '16, ask anyone." Kian turns to Aiden. "Cap, who won the Winter Classic in 2016?"

"Montreal," I murmur, removing my coat. Three pairs of eyes land on me before I realize my mistake. *Crap.* "I think?"

After an uncomfortably long minute, Kian looks up from his phone. "No, you're right, Sunny."

The spotlight only gets brighter with each passing minute. That was the year my dad played the Winter Classic, and fourteen-year-old me stood with my mom to cheer him on. Aiden's eyes are calculating, almost like he's trying to figure out a riddle.

Instead of saying anything, he takes my coat and hangs it on the rack. "We'll be upstairs."

I walk up the steps, and when I reach for the door, I falter. Stepping back, I bump into Aiden. He looks from me to the door. "What if you have a sushi girl waiting for you this time?"

He rolls his eyes. "You're a brat, you know that?"

I'm grinning at his unamused expression. "It's a valid concern."

He opens it and pushes me inside with a hand on my back. "Not a fan of sushi on women, unfortunately."

"Only whipped cream and strawberries?"

"Are you thinking of surprising me? I wouldn't mind some maple syrup."

I scoff. "In your dreams."

"Been there, done that," he mutters.

Pushing at his chest, I move to sit at his desk. When I'm shuffling through my bag, I groan. "I forgot my laptop." If Amara hadn't annoyed me earlier, I would have remembered to pack it.

"Use mine." Aiden opens it and puts in his password.

I stare at it like he offered me a dead rat. "And see your porn history? No way."

"You think I just have porn tabs open?" When I only stare back, he shakes his head. "Just use it, Summer."

I make a show of looking defeated, but the truth is, he saved me a whole lot of trouble.

Studying with Aiden would be great if not for his huge, distracting body. He studies shirtless like some sort of male model. He's lying on his bed, annotating the book of the week with his pen between his teeth. There is no way for me to remove myself from this torture now that he offered to read my final thoughts. He's constantly proving hockey stereotypes wrong with every new bit of information he reveals. I read his essay on one of the literature-focused films he was assigned, and I knew I needed him to edit my paper.

"You look like you checked out ten minutes ago." Aiden bookmarks his page and places the book on the nightstand. "Ready for me to read it?"

I run a frustrated hand through my hair. "I can't focus. Can I send it to you later?"

"I'm good with that."

When I'm shutting down his laptop, my eyes catch on his music app. "You have a sex playlist?"

He appears unfazed. "Of course. Some girls are quiet."

"Girls? Do you know how awkward it is when guys don't make a sound?"

He shrugs. "I wouldn't know. I make plenty."

My cheeks heat. If I'm being honest, a man who isn't afraid to moan? *Hot.* I scroll through his music to take my mind out of the gutter. "You have surprisingly good taste, aside from all the country."

He rears back, offended. "You can't hate on country. I'll have to convert you with a playlist."

I close his laptop and turn in his chair to face him. "Don't waste your time. I'm not listening to that."

"Have an open mind, Sunshine."

I glare.

He gives me an apologetic look. "Okay, how about I make you a playlist? You won't even realize it's country."

"Not possible, but you can try."

He appears victorious as he eyes the time on his phone. "What should we do now?"

"*I'm* heading home."

"No, you're not."

I raise a brow. "What are you going to do, lock me in here?"

He lifts his chin in thought. "If it comes to that, maybe."

"Your psychosis is showing."

"Your boring is showing."

My jaw drops. "I am not boring!" The last time I was called boring was by my little sister because I refused to drive her to a friend's house party. She was thirteen, for Christ's sake.

Aiden does a weird exhale somewhere between a chuckle and disbelief.

"What was that?"

Green eyes remain innocent. "What?"

"You exhaled through your nose."

"It's called breathing."

"Don't be a smart-ass. Say what you're so obviously pretending to hold back."

He licks his lips in contemplation before letting out another breath. "When was the last time you had fun?" Seeing my confusion, he clarifies. "Like real, no responsibilities, fun."

What kind of question is that? We aren't kids anymore. It's not like I could tell him the last time I played hide-and-seek. Unless he expected a recounting of a frat party, which I hadn't been to since Amara pressured me to go to the toga party. And that wasn't fun.

"Need the definition?" he nudges.

I speak through clenched teeth. "*No*. I'm just thinking."

"I'm on the edge of my seat." He emphasizes that by scooting to the edge of the mattress.

I know how to have fun. It's just been a little while since I actually did, though that's through no fault of my own. When the course load piles up, I tend to neglect that part of my life and a few others, like my mental health. Not the best practice, but when academic validation is my drug of choice, I can't stop the addiction.

Racking my brain for something fun isn't easy when Aiden's watching me expectantly. "My sophomore year, I got invited to an event by this really smart guy from one of my labs." Aiden listens intently. "He got me to be one of the keynote speakers on his panels that night."

Aiden's interest dissipates when he realizes that's it. "Your idea of fun is . . . *public speaking*?"

From his tone, I gather that he's not impressed. Not nearly as ecstatic as I was when I got the opportunity. "Well, yeah. I'm good at it."

A sigh rolls off his chest. "I bet you are, but that's not fun."

"Maybe not for you," I defend.

"For anyone, Summer. I thought that story was going to end with a storage closet hookup at your nerd convention."

The jab doesn't get far, because if anything Aiden is the bigger nerd between us. "Sorry to ruin your porno fantasies."

"Keynote dude would not be in my fantasy."

I slump back in his chair. "Well, that's all I have. I don't do all that."

"Do what?"

"Hook up with just anyone. I have to like them first."

"Do you like me?" He beams.

I shoot him a deadly glare.

His buoyant look shatters with a laugh. "What? I think a little action could do you a world of good, even if it's not from me."

"It would never be from you." The response sounds defensive, as if Amara can hear me and I'm somehow trying to prove to her how completely platonic this all is.

He locks his arms behind his head. "Then all you have to do is point and I'll be your wingman."

See? Platonic. "You would help me get with someone?"

"Of course. I've seen how hard you work. Clearly, you aren't making use of the handcuffs in your drawer. You need a night of no-strings-attached fun."

"They're not—" I pause, not bothering to correct him about the handcuffs. "The last time I did that, I ended up dating the guy."

His eyes widen in surprise. "I thought Rai was your last boyfriend."

"I dated one guy after him for like two weeks, so I don't count it," I explain. It was back when I thought I was free of Donny's irritable presence. I realized soon enough that breaking up with him didn't mean I got rid of him. He still cast me those judgmental glances whenever he'd see me out and not in my dorm studying.

"And how long ago was that?"

"Junior year."

He makes a tsking sound and shakes his head in pity. "Yeah, we need to amend that immediately."

My skepticism grows. "Why is this so important to you?"

"Because as your friend, I want you to have fun."

"We're not friends, we're friendly," I retort.

Aiden frowns, but he doesn't let me diminish his determination. "*I'm* friendly, you're just you."

"You're making me out to be some grump."

A serious look that I barely ever see settles on his face. "I'm kidding. You're a bundle of sunshine, Summer."

"No need for sarcasm."

"It's not. You really are." Although I'm sure he's still fucking with me, the way he says it is so sincere, I almost believe it. "I want you to let loose so we can see more of that Summer. Not the uptight, scheduled one."

"My strict schedule paid off. I'm on the dean's list." All those nights I spent in my dorm instead of out making friends did mean something. They had to.

"So am I, but I let myself enjoy college," he counters.

"And what's your definition of 'enjoying college'?" Though the answer to that is pretty clear. My first time in this room is proof of that.

"Girls." When he sees my unamused expression, he chuckles. "I'm kidding, but I won't lie, it is a plus. But mostly it's making memories with friends, and not having to ask what the definition of enjoying college is. You just know."

"Then teach me."

The smile that spreads on his face almost has me backing out. "Alas, the student becomes the teacher."

"Don't get ahead of yourself. I'm only giving you a trial run, *Professor.*"

"I'll take it. But only if you keep calling me Professor in that sexy voice."

"Oh my God. Shut up, Aiden." I chuck my pencil at him, only for him to catch it.

FOURTEEN

AIDEN

I DON'T HAVE regrets. Never have, never will. I decided early on that life is too short to let it pass you by. I won't be eighty and unful-filled, wondering what could have been. That's a miserable life to live.

"You're going to regret this."

I move around Kian to snatch my keys off the kitchen counter. "Thanks for your concern, but I won't."

The house is empty because the guys are volunteering. I already have a dozen extracurriculars, so Kilner let me bail. Kian, on the other hand, has to take the team's laundry to the utility center. He's on duty to pick it up in an hour, so I was stuck with his squealing when he found out who I was going out with tonight. The location is undisclosed because he has too much interest in my personal life.

"That wingman title won't bring you comfort when she's leaving with another dude," he calls.

He doesn't know anything about my relationship with Summer. It isn't like that with us. She's focused on her application, and I'm focused on hockey. Balance hasn't been my strong suit lately, so even harboring any thoughts about her would throw me off. Ergo, we're completely platonic.

Ignoring his comments, I head to my car and queue up the play-list I made for her. I sent it to her, but I don't know what she thinks of it yet because I only got a thumbs-up in response.

Iona House is a short drive on clear roads, so I get there earlier than expected. When I text Summer, she says to wait in my truck.

That isn't happening, so I park and head to the entrance. But the view in front of me draws me to a halt.

"You're wearing that?" I choke out when I see her.

Summer runs a hand over the material of her top as she ap-proaches me. "What's wrong with it?"

I clear my throat. "Nothing."

Everything.

The neckline of the red top plunges between her breasts and re-veals her cleavage. She stands confidently in heels that inch her high enough that the top of her head would reach just below my chin now, and her pants hug her hips like I wish I could. My dick stiffens in my jeans, alarmingly quickly. Only this girl could give me a hard-on in the middle of a fucking sidewalk.

I have to swallow before I can speak again. "You look beautiful, Summer."

The compliment melts the crease between her brows, and she gives me the smallest smile I've ever seen before walking past me to hop into my truck, once again not taking my help to get in. Though I have no qualms about it since I get to watch her perfect ass wiggle into my truck. Inside, she zips her jacket, and I hold back from ex-haling a breath of relief.

Get a grip, man.

This is the worst moment to be feeling any type of way. Kian's words float back to me, and I can't help but think that he's right. If I didn't regret it then, I regret it now. Big-time.

Summer is a smoke show, and going out with her only to watch her leave with another guy might be the dumbest fucking thing I've done all year. And that's saying something.

When we arrive at Myth, the converted warehouse bar, we skip the line. I've been here with the guys too many times to have to wait anymore. It also helps that the owners are hockey fans.

"One margarita and a Sprite," I say to the bartender. While she fills the order, Summer shoots me a look. "What?"

"Only a Sprite?"

"I'm driving us home."

Most college students drink a beer to start the night and end up driving home a few hours later. It technically punches below the legal limit, but I'd never take the chance. Especially if I'm responsible for another person. Too much can go wrong in a split second. I'm well aware of that.

"So how do you have all that fun you were talking about?"

Keen eyes find mine, and I like that she's excited. "I usually have a few girls around me for that."

"Sorry, am I cockblocking you?" she asks, tilting her head.

Soft tendrils frame her face, and I can't help but notice how pretty she looks. She would look even prettier on her knees, looking up at me with those pink lips in a perfect O.

Jesus, I need a cold shower.

"Tonight's about you. I'll be your wingman, and if that works out, I can find myself a lucky lady," I say just as our drinks arrive, and I slide hers over.

"You make it sound like an afterthought. It can't be that easy for you."

"It can't?" I look over her shoulder to nod at a group of girls who've been watching me since we walked in.

Summer peers at them, then at me in disbelief. "They see that you're with me. What if we were—you know—together?"

"You haven't done anything for them to believe that." I *really* want her to do something to make them believe that.

"Well, good, because it's the truth." She stirs her drink. "I don't need you as my wingman. You can go over there to entertain your girls."

My brows shoot up. "You don't want my help?"

"I don't need it."

Confidence exudes from every inch of her, and it isn't misplaced. I'm not sure if she noticed the number of heads that turned when we entered.

"This feels like a good time for a bet. You think you can get any guy to leave with you?"

She smiles, all perfect glossy lips and white teeth. "Easily."

"There's that cocky girl I know."

She scoffs. "There's nothing cocky about it. It's a fact."

"Right, of course," I tease.

"You don't believe me?"

I take a long drink of my Sprite, enjoying how she watches me with hot determination. "It's not about believing you. I just think you might be rustier than you think."

Suddenly she stands, eyes narrowed when she comes almost eye level while I'm seated. "It's hot in here, isn't it?"

Summer removes her jacket in what feels like slow motion; my throat grows thick with each sliver of skin she exposes. She pulls it off, and I barely keep my jaw from hitting the floor when I see her outfit up close and under the bar lights. The red top makes her skin glow, and the thin fabric looks like it would be easy to tear off. Her tits are smashed together perfectly, and the skin at her waist beckons for me to touch it.

"Will you hold this for me, Aiden?"

Her smooth voice rolls a shiver down my spine. Hearing my name on her lips has never sounded better. My head feels empty, and I think the Sprite might be spiked. My mouth runs dry, and I get a little dizzy when I hold her jacket and watch her slide her hair around her neck, the intoxicating scent especially strong tonight. The action exposes even more skin, and my jeans tighten. The smell of peaches surrounds me.

It's going to be a long fucking night.

Summer stands between my parted legs, bringing a hand to my biceps, then sliding it up to my shoulder. I watch the movement in a trance, swallowing the thick ball in my throat. *What the fuck is happening?*

"You look hot," she purrs.

I pretend the strangled noise that leaves my throat isn't mine, but she smiles that sweet Summer smile that tells me she heard it. Her expression is all teasing and flirty, making the synapses in my brain fire at random. The only time we've been this close was in the locker room shower, and I could barely handle that. But nothing has felt better than having her close enough that if I leaned forward, my lips would capture her perfect ones.

"What?" I squeak. As if it's the first day of seventh grade, and my balls haven't dropped yet. I clear my throat and try again. "What?"

"I said you look hot." I'm still barely registering her words when her hand strokes my ear. I hold in the shiver that racks through my body. "You're sweating," she says.

Oh. *Oh.* That kind of hot.

Maybe it's because she's closer to me than she's ever been, and I might combust like a fucking teenager. I feel tongue-tied like she's somehow paralyzed every muscle in my mouth, stopping me from forming any coherent sentence.

I clear my throat to regain some motor function. "It's hot in here, like you said."

"Right." She smiles, still stroking my ear until my eyes are tempted to flutter shut. She's found a particularly sensitive erogenous zone, and I'd be content with my life if she did this forever. When she moves closer, I go rigid. Summer's tits are so close to my face, I feel starved to have my mouth on her sweet skin, but then she shifts toward my ear and whispers, "You wanna get out of here?"

My heart stops beating in my chest. My eyes widen when her brown ones meet mine again. Her face looks so fucking pure, I use every ounce of self-control to not carry her into a storage closet and fuck that look off her face.

When I go to pull out my wallet so I can carry her over my damn shoulder, she pulls away and sits back on her stool with an apathetic exhale. "Well, what do you think?"

Her nonchalance is a pure contrast to how electric she was a second ago. "About what?"

"Am I still rusty?"

Rusty?

"That's how I'd get any guy in here." She stirs her drink.

My heart slows when I realize she showed me exactly what I had asked. She was proving she's not cocky, she's fucking confident.

"So, which one?" she says flippantly. "Which guy do you want me to talk to?"

None.

No guy, ever. Jealousy rears its ugly head and hits me like a fucking truck. Her confidence radiates off her in waves.

Fuck. I feel like pure shit that she doesn't even look half affected by our proximity while I'm still reeling.

I eye the bar, recognizing some frat guys and UHart students. "None," I say roughly, my annoyance seeping through my tone.

"Scared I'll win?"

Yes. "It's getting late. You have class tomorrow."

Her forehead creases. "You're the one that's been saying I can't have fun, yet you're reminding me about class? Which isn't until after our meeting with Dr. Toor, by the way."

I knew that, but I needed an excuse to get out of here. She was right. It is getting hot. Hot enough that my clothes feel uncomfortable, and I'd much rather be out of them. Preferably with her under me.

"Why are you acting so strange?"

Maybe because I'm so hard I don't know how I'll stand? "I'm just giving you an out in case you want to leave."

"That's very nice of you, but I'm fine." She flips her hair over her shoulder and scopes the far corner. "That guy's cute."

My eyes meet Kayce Howard, the point guard for the basketball team, playing pool. Our teams don't get along, and it isn't for lack of trying. They're reckless idiots, and they've roped my players into their disruptive behavior too many times.

When he stands to his full height Summer gawks. "And . . . *tall*."

"I thought you don't like athletes." I sound bitter, but I don't bother playing it off.

"I don't like *hockey* players. What does he play?"

I glare. "Basketball."

"Perfect." She takes her jacket from my lap and slips it on. I keep my hands to my sides to prevent myself from reaching out and sitting her ass down on my lap. Suddenly, I want everyone in this bar to know she came with me.

Just before she stands, she licks the salted rim of her glass and downs the liquid. Watching her saunter over to the pool table is like having a hot spear shoved into my chest. Her ass is distracting, so distracting that I barely notice the girl who comes up and takes the seat Summer just occupied.

"You play for Dalton, right? I'm Bethany."

I nod, though my head swivels between this girl and the one who gets Kayce's attention instantly. The slow smirk that blooms on his face tells me she has him exactly how she had me.

"I go to Yale," she says.

I bring my attention back to her. "You're a little far from home, aren't you?"

Bethany shrugs. "The guys here are better."

When she smiles, I finally notice that she's damn pretty. Her blond hair falls in waves around her face. Her blue eyes are so bright and innocent I almost don't see the low-cut top that gives me a full view of her cleavage. "Are they?"

Staying in the moment is hard when there's a girl on the other side of this bar laughing with the douchebag of the century.

"I'm looking at one right now." She takes my hand and runs a finger over my palm. "These calluses would feel so good—"

I stand when Kayce's hand reaches to twirl a strand of Summer's hair. "I'll be right back."

Bethany holds on to my hand. "You're leaving me at the bar?"

I pry away her fingers. "Just need to check on my friend. Give me a minute." The friend who is currently taking off her jacket. Half of the basketball team is watching her like she's putting on a fucking show, and I bite down so hard I feel the tension in my head.

Summer's giggle hits me as Kayce lowers to whisper in her ear.

Without much forethought, I walk up to them and pull her away.

She stumbles. "What are you doing?"

"It's time to go."

Confusion riddles her features when she yanks her arm from my grasp. "You can leave. I'll get another ride home."

"Hell no, you don't know any of these guys. You're coming with me."

"She knows me. I could give her a ride," offers Kayce.

"Stay out of it."

Summer looks at me in shock and drags me away from the pool table. "*Dude.* You're being the worst wingman right now."

I'm so irritated I can't respond. Everything is fucked. She smells so good, her skin is glowing, and those eyes. Don't get me started on her eyes, which have their own gravitational pull.

"Look, you don't have to stick by me. That pretty girl over there looks like she really wants to see what's under all this." She gestures to my body. "And I want to see what's under all that." She points her thumb in Kayce's direction.

He's already talking to someone else, and somehow that annoys me too. Why would another girl interest him when Summer is right here? It's like being given the sun and deciding a light bulb will do.

"You don't know that guy. Trust me, he's not the one you want to hook up with."

"I do trust you, that's why I'm here. He checks all the boxes. He even offered to teach me how to play pool."

I snort. I'm pretty sure every guy in this bar would volunteer for a view of that ass bent over the pool table.

The soft look in her eyes dampens my irritation. "You really want to stay?" I ask.

Say no. Say no. Say no.

"Yes," she says, touching my shoulder. "But you should, too."

"You're seriously going to hook up with him?" My voice sounds fragile, almost insecure.

She laughs. "Do you even know me? I was kidding. I told you I have to like a guy before we hook up."

"And how long does it take for you to like someone?"

She thinks for a minute. "How long have I known you?"

"A month," I say.

"There's your answer," she says, and walks back to Kayce.

I'm left blinking in her absence, unsure of what to make of that. Summer has never said she likes me.

This is uncharted territory.

FIFTEEN

SUMMER

THIS IS NOT a date. Nothing about my outfit or the extra time I spent on my hair means anything. It's two friends—kind of—hanging out in an attempt to learn the ropes of college fun. *God*, when did I become so lame?

When I left the dorm, Amara and Cassie were adamantly referring to Aiden as my date. Something about me not going out for months and saying my vagina is probably shriveling up as we speak. Rude. My vagina is completely fine, I just don't have time to focus on her, though fixing that situation is exactly what I need.

Now that we're here, I've learned that my tongue gets loose when I drink. I say things that I would otherwise keep safely locked up in a fire-resistant safe, and there was proof of that when I told Aiden I *like* him. Logically, my only option after that is to walk back to Kayce Howard in this athlete-infested bar while Aiden's eyes focus like a sniper's on my back.

The attention Aiden gets on campus is staggering. But the attention he gets in off-campus bars is ridiculous. I hadn't even taken three steps from where we sat when a girl from the overeager table approached him. So what if I wanted a taste of what it's like to be the one with all eyes on them?

"Crawford couldn't convince you to stay away from me?" I crane my neck to look up at Kayce. When I said he was tall, it was the understatement of the century. Kayce Howard is six feet, six inches of pure *man*. It's kind of jarring seeing him this up close. The epitome of tall, dark, and handsome.

"I've never been one to do as I'm told," I say.

His eyes spark. "Then lead the way and I'll follow."

I laugh despite knowing we aren't going anywhere. Aiden is worried about something, and I don't want to ruin his night by stressing him out.

"Does your offer still stand?" I point to the pool cue, and his answering smirk is heavenly. When Kayce leans close, his woody scent sends a sharp thrill down my back.

"I'll teach you anything you want, Sunshine," he drawls.

"Don't call her that."

Aiden's rough voice assaults my back like a flame. Kayce's eyes focus above my head and his mouth sets in a tight line. Instead of responding, he heads over to the cues to pick mine out.

With a dramatic pivot, I face Aiden. "Is this a part of your shitty wingman approach?"

"*Sunshine*?" he repeats, annoyed.

I probably should have corrected Kayce. But I mean, what's the point? Telling a guy I just met about my fucked-up relationship with my dad probably isn't the best opener.

When I shrug, he releases a sardonic breath. "I'm just here to play pool."

"I'm sure you are. Go assert your caveman tendencies elsewhere."

Aiden leans against the pool table, arms crossed and biceps popping under his white T-shirt. "Only thing I'm asserting is my free will. How about we play a round? Me and Bethany versus you and Kayce."

Kayce's deep laugh sounds beside me. "Kicking your ass in pool? I'm game."

"I love pool!" A drunk Bethany sticks to Aiden, and his arm encircles her waist to steady her.

"I'm not so sure your aim will be any good," he teases.

She tiptoes to whisper in his ear, but even in the chaotic bar, I can hear her clearly. "Keep your hands on me, and I'll be steady."

Barf. I'm going to need another drink soon.

Kayce racks the balls and hands me the pool cue. He explains the basic rules and I pretend to pay close attention. We order drinks before we start, and the booze hits me hard. I try to aim, but it must be bad, because a hand slides over my abdomen, and Kayce's warm body covers my back.

"Hand higher. Position yourself to the left on the balk line so you can aim at the second ball." Listening to Kayce's instructions is awfully hard when he's so close his minty breath fans my neck. I might as well be getting fucked on the pool table with how the basketball team watches us. Though out of our opponents, Aiden's the only one who looks like he's going to break the pool stick.

When Kayce's hips connect with my ass, I stumble and take the shot. It's a crappy one, but I manage to pocket a solid. That earns me a high five, and I step back with flaming cheeks.

Aiden steadies Bethany but lets her take the shot on her own. Bad idea, because she fumbles and misses, which only makes Kayce's next shot a breeze. When it's Aiden's turn, he easily pockets the stripes, winking at me when he makes my next shot near impossible.

"I can go for you," offers Kayce, as if I'm some measly woman who can't step up to a challenge. I hold my head high, determined to wipe that smirk off Aiden's face.

"I got it." I head over to where Aiden stands, bumping him away with my hip. He lets out a low chuckle, watching me with a cocky smile.

Leaning over, I take one calculated strike for the ball to slam three solids into two pockets. The murmur quells when the basket-ball team, including Kayce, stares at me in shock. Bethany whoops in excitement, but I don't think she remembers whose team she's on. I prepare myself to gloat at a sulking face, but instead, Aiden beams brightly as if this is exactly what he wanted. The smug smile slips from my lips.

"He must be a good teacher," Aiden says, gesturing to Kayce.

My hand tightens around the cue. "Maybe I'm a good actress."

"Is that right?" he drawls. "You like a little role-play?"

His words are like hot liquid cascading down my skin. I bring my pool cue to lift his chin. "You'll never find out."

His gaze only darkens with a determined look that startles me.

"Didn't know you had a hidden talent," Kayce says, snapping me away from Aiden's unsteadying look.

After that, it's an easy win. But instead of wearing a look of de-feat, Aiden's eyes are alight with satisfaction. I have an inkling it's because he got me to drop the clumsy girl act that would have stroked Kayce's ego.

I turn to Kayce, who pulls me into him. But it feels weird. None of it's like I thought it would be. Not the touching, not the whispers about how hot I am, and definitely not the flirting. It feels like I'm forcing it, and I don't want to do that anymore. I don't want to mold myself into something I'm not. Winning at pool might have sparked this awakening.

My eyes gravitate to where Aiden and Bethany stand to find his gaze already on me. She pulls him to the bar, yanking his attention from the heavy hands on my waist. I'm not sure if it's the look Aiden gave me or that weird feeling swirling my stomach, but I detangle myself from Kayce's arms.

"This was fun, but I think I'm going to call it a night," I say awk-wardly.

His disappointment only lasts a second. "I had fun, too, and if you ever want to make Crawford jealous again, you know who to call."

Make Aiden jealous? Kayce walks off before I can dissect the statement. When I look for Aiden, he's whispering into Bethany's ear as she types into his phone. She's laughing, face blushing. There's something about Aiden that turns women into a fawning mess.

Taking my jacket, I exit the bar, bypassing all the drunk patrons loitering by the doors. Outside, I'm trying to get an Uber, but the app reloads, unable to find any available rides. I'm leaning against the brick wall when a hand pulls me back.

"You were just going to leave?" Aiden runs an exasperated hand through his hair. "Jesus, Summer, I thought you left with him. I was losing my damn mind until I found you out here."

His distressed face confuses my drunken brain. "Sorry, you just seemed into Bethany. I didn't want to interrupt that just because I wanted to leave."

He stares at me like that is the stupidest thing he's ever heard. "I'm wherever you are, Summer."

That weight in my stomach sinks. With a hand on my back and without another word, he leads me to his truck. It's a quiet drive, aside from the low hum of the radio that switches between pop songs and new renditions of classics.

We're driving through an unlit area when the first strings of "Tennessee Whiskey" filter through the speakers. Suddenly, Aiden halts the truck. When he chuckles, I wonder if some of Bethany's drunkenness rubbed off on him.

"What's so funny?" I ask.

Somber green eyes search my face for a long second. "This is a newer version, but this was my parents' first dance song."

My smile mirrors his. "Country?"

Although the hockey stereotypes run deep with the genre, Aiden's love for country seems more personal, like it's a part of him he keeps close to his heart. He turns the volume on the radio up and steps out of the truck.

I'm watching him round the truck before my door pops open, and Aiden extends his hand to me. "Come."

"Where are we going?" I ask over the lyrics.

"Just out here." He nods to the front of the truck. I don't know why, but I take his hand and follow him to where the headlights drown us in bright white. When he looks at me, his eyes are as muted as the evergreens surrounding us. There's a sadness to them that I can't quite place, but his sweet smile contrasts that look.

"You dance?" I ask when he lifts my hand onto his shoulder.

"No," he says. "But I want to with you."

There's a lump in my throat when he pulls me closer. "Are you sure you're not drunk?" I ask, attempting to crush the boulder pressing into my chest.

He shakes his head, and the look in his eyes is so intense, I lay my head against his chest to escape it. I let my eyes close as the lyrics wash over us. The cold night air barely penetrates the warm weight of Aiden's arms around me. Either that, or it's the alcohol that heats my blood. But I can't shake the feeling of comfort and safety when I'm with him. I can't deny that he feels like home.

My eyes wrench open at the thought, and my heart runs into overdrive. No. *No.* It has to be the alcohol. It's the only explanation for the ache in the center of my chest and the tingling, warm feeling prickling my skin. When I finally calm my beating heart, Aiden presses a kiss to my hair. It knocks the speed right back into my heart.

Slowly, the song fades, and I pull away. His breath tickles my forehead, and for a split second, all I can think of is his lips on mine.

I abruptly break free of his warm embrace. "It's a good song. I heard it on the playlist," I say.

That melancholy look goes nowhere, but he's smiling now. "I guess I managed to turn you into a country fan after all."

"I wouldn't go that far." I laugh and let him help me into the passenger side.

When we're pulling into Iona House, I'm reluctant to pop the bubble around us. It might be the haze from the alcohol, but the buzz of nerves that tunnels under my skin is aware of the change that's taken place between us. One I can't begin to explain.

My ability to form words scatters, and when I unclip my seat belt, my hands are sweaty. In a quick decision, I lean over the console, and his breath hitches before I plant a kiss on the corner of his mouth.

Then I exit his truck like it's on fire.

SIXTEEN

AIDEN

"WHERE'S MY PHONE?"

The guys are sitting in the dining room when I walk in to locate my phone. Dylan's studying, which is uncharacteristic of him, and Kian's on his phone with his legs up on the table, disregarding that people eat where he puts his nasty feet. Eli walks in too.

"You know that Find My iPhone was invented in 2010, right?" Kian says.

Dylan chucks an eraser at him. "Did you lose it last night? You didn't answer any of our texts."

"I think I might have left it at the bar."

"When Summer friend-zoned you, or when you let her cozy up with Howard?" asks Kian. He follows a few basketball guys on social media and saw us in the background of their videos. So much for keeping things private.

Ignoring him, I grab my keys to head down there.

"Dude, it's two p.m. They don't open until late," says Dylan, stopping me. "Here, use my phone to track it in case it's in your truck or something."

When I enter my information, the compass spins, and I see my phone down south. In the opposite direction of the bar. At Yale University.

The guys all stare at the screen in confusion. Shit.

"Why the hell would you go there?" Dylan looks disgusted.

"I didn't. I gave it to this girl to put in her number, and I never got it back." Bethany was clearly too drunk to remember to hand it back to me. And I was too preoccupied with someone else.

"You might as well get a new phone now."

Except I can't. Summer texts me when she needs me, and not having my phone means not talking to her. There's also this strange feeling that I have something important to do today.

"That's Kappa Zeta. She's probably in a sorority," says Dylan.

I head to the door and pull on my shoes when Eli stops me. "We're leaving for Chicago in a few hours. Are you sure you want to risk pissing off Coach?"

Right. That is the important thing. "I can't leave without it."

"Then we're coming with you," he declares.

"You don't have to do that."

Eli doesn't budge. "If Kilner's going to be pissed, he might as well be pissed at all of us. We're not letting you go to New Haven alone." A blanket of understanding falls over us, and just like that we're headed to Yale.

When we near campus, a sea of blue coats the sidewalks, and it's hard to keep the collective shiver at bay. "Should I have brought garlic?" asks Kian.

"Why?"

"If it repels vampires, it should work on Yalies, too."

Dylan laughs. "Smart thinking. Maybe we can buy some before we head in."

"We won't need it. I'll be in and out. No one's going to notice us." We park and follow the directions on Dylan's phone.

"There's not one person on campus who doesn't know who you are." Kian barely finishes his sentence when we hear my name.

Eric Salinger, captain of the Yale hockey team, appears. "Never thought I'd see you guys here unless you had to be." He laughs. "But it's good I didn't get to apologize in person for trashing your school. My guys won't pull something as reckless as that again."

Eric's a stand-up guy. Like me, he was drafted when he played for A leagues, so his sole focus has always been hockey. His team, on the other hand, are a bunch of air-headed morons.

"Still pretty fucked-up of you. Cap's been paying for that shit for months," says Kian.

Eric shakes his head in pity. "Look, if I knew, I would have stopped it. That shit doesn't fly with me."

"Do dirty plays fly with you?" My hand on Kian's chest prevents him from moving forward. The last thing we need is for someone to see him getting mouthy and retaliate.

"You're good, but your guys still need to learn a lesson," I say.

A hint of amusement lifts his lips. "I'm certain you'll make sure of that at the final."

"You think you'll make it?"

"It's looking that way. Don't know about you, though."

"Guess we'll see." My parting words are more of a courtesy than anything. He definitely knows that we've won nearly every game this season.

We head to the bright yellow house on the corner of the street that screams sorority. Walking up to the white wooden porch, I knock on the pink door. The girl who opens it is bright-eyed and smiling, but her posture is stiff.

"Hey, one of your friends took my phone last night. I'm going to need it back."

Her perfect smile doesn't waver. "I'm sorry, that's not possible. Kappa sisters don't fraternize with Dalton cronies."

Dylan pushes forward. "Look, I'm not trying to get a rash here, so if you just hand us the phone, we can head back."

"Dylan?" A girl from inside charges toward him. "You never called!"

Dylan mutters a curse. I turn to the girl who opened the door as Dylan apologizes profusely to the one he ghosted. "See, it is possible. Now can you just get her?" I ask.

"What's her name?"

"Bethany."

The girls give each other a look. "Wait here."

I think I might have gotten Bethany in trouble. Kian and Eli climb the steps to stand behind us, and that's when we notice the girls staring at us from the windows. I wave, making them scramble behind the curtains.

"I don't know any hockey player—*Aiden*?" Bethany curses and then pulls me to the side. "You need to leave. Now."

I pull my arm from her hold. "I need my phone."

"What phone?"

I show her the flashing location pin on Dylan's phone indicating mine is in this house. "That's probably what's been buzzing all morning," she mutters, running a hand through her hair. "Look, I'm on thin ice here and they're going to kick me out if they find out I was drinking last night. If I get your phone, will you make an excuse for me?"

"You're not exactly in a position to negotiate," I say.

"Do you want your phone or not?"

"Are you blackmailing me?"

She shuts her eyes in frustration. "Please?"

I concede, and she heads upstairs. Her sorority sisters cross-examine me. "How do you know Beth?"

I scramble for an excuse. "We met at a diner last night. She used my phone and must've accidentally taken it."

"A diner? Are you sure?"

"Yup."

Her glare sends me a step back. The guys have already moved onto the sidewalk. Cowards.

"Here." Bethany shoves my phone into my hand. Before I can

thank her, she slams the door shut. What is it with women and slamming doors in my face?

SUMMER

[10:00 a.m.]
Summer: As much as it pains me to admit it, I had fun last night.
Summer: See you at noon!

[11:30 a.m.]
Summer: Meet me at Advanced Imaging. Behind Carver Hall.

[11:42 a.m.]
Summer: Please don't be late. Dr. Toor is going on paternity leave this week.

[11:55 a.m.]
Summer: Aiden???

[11:58 a.m.]
Summer: If this is some type of sick joke, it's not funny.
Summer: I swear to God if you don't show up in two minutes, I won't ever speak to you again.

"Twenty bucks says she socks him in the face."

"I'm thinking knee to the balls."

"Maybe she'll beat him with his hockey stick before Kilner gets the chance."

The guys pop off with their unamusing predictions of my plight. But I know, of all the things she can do, the worst is if she ignores me.

When I spot her crossing the street to her dorm, I tell Dylan to stop. "Don't want to rush you, man, but we're late," he says as I hop out.

To my dismay, Summer doesn't turn when I call her name and instead walks faster. "Summer." I take hold of her arm.

She jerks out of my hold, skewering me with an angry look.

I deflate. "It slipped my mind. I lost my phone last night."

Her gaze flicks behind me to the car full of guys watching us. I hear a bunch of *Hi, Summer*s from the peanut gallery, and she gives them a half smile.

"I made a mistake," I continue.

"A mistake?" She scoffs. "Dr. Toor and I waited an entire hour for you! I've been reminding you about this for weeks. Losing your phone shouldn't even matter."

"I know. I don't want to give you any excuses. I fucked up, and I want to make up for it."

She shakes her head in disbelief. "You're a goddamn headache, you know that?"

"I know, and I'm sorry."

She stares at me for a long minute, something akin to surprise passing before she blinks it away. The light tap of the horn behind me tells me I'm running out of time.

"I have to leave for Chicago, and I won't be back for a few days. I was really hoping we could talk this out."

"You're leaving?" There's a hint of disappointment in the question. "I mean, you should leave, then. You don't want to be late."

Dylan calls my name again, and I want to punch a hole through his head.

"Give me a minute!" I yell back. "Please, can we just talk this through later?" I say to her.

"There's nothing to talk about. I'll figure something else out."

Dejection ripples through me. "I can't leave without making this right."

She shakes her head in disbelief. "You have a whole team waiting for you, Aiden. Don't let them down, too."

I should have expected that jab. "I won't. I just need to make sure this"—I gesture between us—"isn't ruined."

"My project is almost done. It shouldn't matter anyway."

Her sharp words are punctuated by a honk.

I ignore it. "Just tell me I can redeem myself."

Summer bites the inside of her cheek in contemplation.

"Crawford! Kilner's calling. We gotta go, man."

"*Fuck*—One second!" I shout.

Summer doesn't answer. She looks completely withdrawn, and it fucking kills me that I made her feel that way. "I messed up, Summer. I'm sorry."

"Me too," she finally says, turning to the doors of Iona House and disappearing inside.

SEVENTEEN

SUMMER

THE DORM IS dark and quiet when I walk in after my run. I've only taken one step before I see a small box on the counter. The golden bow shines despite the dimness. I gingerly approach the mystery item, and my heart inflates in my chest when I see it.

It's the tea my dad used to buy me, and there's a note attached to the bottom.

For all those headaches I give you—A.

There's a riot in my stomach. I haven't seen or texted Aiden back since he came back from Chicago. I spent my time figuring out another element to add to my project because he missed the test. It's an exhausting feeling when it seems like my work isn't important enough. But the way Aiden looked at me made my chest feel heavy. The way the one apology and his earnest look had me wanting to say it was okay. I never feel like this when someone lets me down, I just learn my lesson.

It's because his eyes were the first thing I noticed about him.

As a kid I was obsessed with my dad's eyes. Gray with tiny flecks of gold, sometimes blue in different lights. I'd constantly ask my mom why I got the boring brown, and my sisters had his eyes. I cried about it for days, and weirdly enough, it still hits me. The realization that it was another thing my dad couldn't give me. Another part of him I couldn't have. Another part that belonged to my sisters and not me. It was pathetic. Pure genetic probability, yet ironically it perfectly explained our relationship.

But Aiden has the same mesmerizing eyes. Eyes that make you forget your words until you make a conscious effort to remember them again. Eyes that tell you with just one look how pure the soul behind them is. He has them, and I hate that he does. Even more, I hate that I noticed.

When my phone glows, Dalton app notifications litter my screen. I don't need to open them to know that the guys probably won. It's hard enough avoiding the game when everyone and their mother is posting about it. Amara and Cassie are there too. They invited me, thinking I could stomach the sport now, but that hope's been incinerated by a tardy hockey player. I'd rather study in my dorm and occasionally freak out at creaks in the hallway.

A knock sounds on the door, and I jump. Hesitantly, I move to answer it, trying to calm my erratic pulse. When I ease the door open and peek through the crack, my heart stutters.

Aiden stands in my doorway in his hockey gear, minus the skates and helmet. Somehow his hair is still flowing perfectly. Helmet hair doesn't exist in his universe.

I open the door wider. "What are you doing here?"

"I'm here for our session."

"We didn't schedule one." I look at the time on my phone. "Your game ended twenty minutes ago, Aiden." How he even managed to make it here in twenty minutes is beyond me.

When my mom used to take me to my dad's games as a kid, most of the night was spent waiting outside the arena after a game. I'd wake up the next morning only to realize I had fallen asleep before I could even see him.

"I know."

"You're still in your gear."

"I can change." That's when I notice the gym bag on his arm. "Do you mind?"

I point to my bathroom, and he stalks inside. "I can bring you a towel if you want to shower."

Shower? Why the hell did I suggest that? He looks surprised by my invitation. Honestly, it surprises me too, but the least I could do is offer.

"You sure?"

I shrug. "Or if you want to be gross and sweaty for the rest of the night, it's your call." My lame attempt to cut the tension doesn't work when he simply nods and heads to the bathroom.

Towel in hand, I knock and hear shuffling before he says, "Come in."

I hesitate. When I open the door, he's removed his shoulder pads, and his body is on full display. My bathroom has terrible lighting, but he still glistens under the fluorescents.

He takes the towel. "Thanks."

The tension between us is thick in my tiny bathroom. The whirring fan and the buzzing lights are loud as ever. "I can turn on the shower for you. It's kind of difficult to get right."

He presses his lips together and nods. The sound of clothes being removed resumes, and I swallow. I turn the faucet with my sweaty hands, and when I face him, he's so close I startle.

If he smells, my brain isn't registering it, because all I can think about is how we're alone, he's half naked, and my pjs aren't leaving much to the imagination.

"It takes a second to get hot," I say, though that statement could apply to me. It doesn't feel like I offered him a shower, it feels like he's waiting to tear off my clothes and take me against the shower wall.

He nods, reminding me that my overactive imagination is playing tricks on me.

"You won," I say. In my defense, the shower does take a minute to heat. I'm being a good host if we really look at it.

"Barely." He looks like he wants to say more. We haven't talked in a week, but I have every right to be pissed. Though the memories of my anger are slowly but surely fizzling away.

When the shower steams, I step away. "I'll be outside."

The sound of running water fills my bedroom. To rid myself of my sinful thoughts, I sit on the furthest side of the living room.

Aiden steps out a few minutes later as I'm editing my statistics paper. He's wearing a tight white T-shirt and black sweats. It's distracting, until I notice the trickling red on his cheek.

I jump in alarm. "What happened to your face?"

He settles on the couch. "You should see the other guy."

"You got into a fight? Can't you get disqualified?" The NCAA has strict rules, and risking the penalty isn't worth the punch most of the time.

"Some Princeton jackass had it out for me. He got the major."

My worry unravels, knowing the infraction wasn't on him. Still, when I get a good look at his cut, it unsettles me.

"I'm fine. Really."

I shake my head. "You should've gone to the team's medic."

"I did, and I'm fine." He shrugs. "I didn't want to be late."

"Late for what?"

"For you," he says. "I feel like shit for missing last week because I know what this research means to you."

Hot coals press harder into my chest cavity. Without another word, I take his hand and pull him off the couch. My tugging doesn't do anything until he lets it.

"Sit," I say when we're in the steamy bathroom.

He gives a tired sigh. "Summer, you don't have to do this."

"Tell me what I can do again," I warn.

He gives me an exasperated look before taking a seat on the toilet lid. I pull out the first aid kit from under the sink, and he parts his legs for me to step between them. Aiden doesn't flinch when I tilt his head and dab alcohol on the cut. His gaze focuses on my face, and my breath splinters. Aiden rests his arms on his leg, and I feel the light brush of his fingers on the back of my thigh. The touch is hot and prickly, and it makes me itchy all over.

"You know, Hank, our PT, is also our team medic. You could totally replace him."

"You really have it out for Hank, don't you?" I chuckle, trying not to look at his lips. "Besides, I'm only first aid certified."

"You fix up a lot of athletes?"

I shake my head.

"Just me, then?"

"Just you." *Why am I whispering?* I clear my throat as I dig into the first aid box to distract myself.

His eyes turn solemn, and the air thickens. "I'm sorry, Summer."

My breath catches in my throat, and I can't meet his eyes. The energy sparking between us gives me whiplash.

"I did the test this morning."

My hands freeze mid-dab. "What?"

"I got in touch with Dr. Toor with Kilner's help, and he referred me to his friend who works at a sports clinic in Hartford. You should get the results of the ACSI-28 test in a few days."

My sunken heart floats to the surface. "You did?"

He nods. "I should have been there in the first place, Summer. Your work is important."

I can only stare at the Band-Aids in my hand. He'd completed one of the most important parts of my research without me having to reschedule or plan anything. My lungs have ceased to work, and I have to consciously recall how humans breathe to get oxygen to my blood again. I drag a clammy hand through my hair, but when he touches the back of my thigh, I jerk back to the present.

I hold up two cartoon bandages. "Barbie or Bratz?"

He looks dumbfounded. If he didn't know before how bad I am

at accepting it when someone does nice things for me, he knows now. Though he did initially fuck up, so is it really a nice thing? *God, who even cares?*

His expression smooths into understanding. "Does it matter?"

I sigh in relief when he doesn't push about the test. "Immensely."

With a curve of a smile on his lips, and his fingers unconsciously brushing my leg, he appears deep in thought. "Bratz, *obviously.*"

I suppress my smile as I put the purple Yasmin Band-Aid on his cheek. The box has neutral bandages I could have used, but I keep that information to myself.

EIGHTEEN

AIDEN

I CUT OFF the power.

It isn't often that I find myself in our cold, dingy basement, but desperate times call for desperate measures. After I showed up at Summer's dorm a few days ago, I thought things were back to normal, but that was a heavily misguided conclusion. She hasn't texted, called, or even emailed. Nothing. Kian is the only one who sees her during class, and he's become mute. His loyalties have clearly shifted. Asshole.

Last practice, I was desperate enough to ask Tyler Sampson about her. He smashed me into the boards. Clearly, her feelings are anything but positive.

So, what do you do when the girl you can't stop thinking about ices you out? You power down an entire house.

With the house plunged into darkness, screams sound upstairs. I make my way back up, innocent as ever. There's no other way to get this many Dalton students out of our house and to Summer's carnival.

"Sorry, power's out, guys." My words are followed by drunk grumbles. "But there's an event on campus tonight. Everyone can head over there." Kian comes into view, lit by the flashlight on his phone. I gesture toward the door, and he gives me a thumbs-up.

"Everyone follow me," he says. "I'm bringing the booze!"

The crowd cheers, and people spill out of the house behind Kian. A flashlight shines on me, and I squint.

"We have a generator," Cole says, buzzed and skeptical.

I shrug. But he's right, I'm lucky it hasn't kicked in. Behind him, Eli shoots me a wink before he heads out.

"You sure are going above and beyond for this *project*," Dylan says when he finds me outside.

"I don't like to do anything half-assed."

"Sure, Barbie," he snorts.

I don't bother correcting him. Since I came back from Summer's with a bright purple Band-Aid on my face, they've been ripping into me.

Turning into the west wing parking lot that's cleared for the event, I can tell from the attendees' reactions that Summer's event is a hit.

"Dylan!" A girl squeals and runs into his arms.

He mouths *Who is this?* over her shoulder. Shaking my head, I walk to where Kian struggles to throw a baseball at a target. He's trying for the stuffed animals, one of them being a tiny cow that somehow looks like it's begging you to take it home.

"This has to be rigged," he complains.

A girl in line gives Kian a sweet smile. "I can teach you the trick."

He perks up. "Just a heads-up, I'm a hands-on learner."

"Yeah? I'm a hands-on teacher," she says.

Taking that as my cue to leave, I go over to Eli, who's talking to Kayce Howard. "Finally took a day off?" Kayce asks when he sees me approach.

"Gotta give the opposition a head start, or else it gets boring."

He laughs. "It's looking like a Frozen Four between Dalton and Yale. You think you'll choke?"

"We'll win like every other year. You, on the other hand, barely got into the final four. Hopefully you don't trip," Eli says.

During the final four competition last year, Kayce missed a free throw when he tripped at the last second. He's proved himself since, but we've been dogging him over it for months.

I bite back a smile at his pointed words because Eli never chirps, on or off the ice, but he always has my back. Kayce gives a bitter laugh, brushing off the remark. It's an unspoken rule that no one steps to Elias Westbrook.

"Your girl did a good job," says Kayce.

My girl.

"She did."

After our night out, it must have been pretty clear to Kayce that Summer wasn't going home with him. That was why he decided to have his fun during pool. I couldn't complain, because my night ended with a kiss. Elementary or not, it was fucking electric.

Scanning the place, I spot Summer at one of the booths. She's wearing those tight jeans that hug her ass, and her white top hangs off her shoulders. The ruffles along the neckline make her look like a fucking angel, and I have a strong urge to find a quiet corner where I can yank it down and have my mouth on her.

I snap out of the thought when I feel my blood rush to my groin, but I can't quit looking at her. Having her inches from my lips and not kissing her that night heightened everything.

When Summer turns, looking as radiant as ever, her eyes meet mine and widen for a split second before she smiles, then turns away. That surprises me because Summer's been anything but nervous with me. Angry? Absolutely. Nervous? Never.

I excuse myself from the guys and head over to her, shaking my head. "That won't work."

Her eyes sweep over me. "What won't work?"

"That smile."

She crosses her arms. "What's wrong with a smile? It's polite."

"Not from you, and definitely not to me."

She pulls her lip between her teeth to hide a smile. "Ah, so you like it when I'm rude to you?"

"Obviously."

"Degradation kink?" She knocks a playful hand to my chest, and the touch zips through me, heading somewhere dangerously low.

"You'll have to find out."

She purses her lips. "Next time Kilner's hocking a loogie, I'll send him your way."

"I'm cured." I laugh. "This is incredible, by the way."

Brown eyes sparkle. "Really? I can't believe so many people showed. Last semester's was a bust."

"It's all you. You need to start believing what you put out there matters."

A blush tints her cheeks. "I'm glad you came."

"Does this mean you forgive me?"

Her laugh fucks with something in my chest. "I forgave you the second you showed up at my door in your hockey gear."

For my whole life, the sound of my skates hitting the ice and the puck sliding into the net were the only things that brought me pure happiness. I was sure there would be no other sound or substance that could rival that feeling of euphoria. Except now I feel like I'm an addict who got his first hit after years of sobriety. Summer's light laughter fills my ears and drifts to a part of my brain that brands it into my memory. Now the thing that brings me peace, what I yearn for like a game-winning goal, is the sound of her laughter and the sight of her smile.

"Summer!" She turns to the volunteers beckoning her.

"I should check on them," she says, glancing back.

A pang of disappointment hits, and I feel the urge to press her against my chest. It's like the further she is from me, the more that string between us strains. My wish comes true when long, wavy hair twirls, and she lunges forward, tiptoeing to hook her arms around my neck. A rough sound of surprise escapes me, but I quickly recover and wrap my arms around her.

It's a long hug, full of the smell of peaches and the feel of her perfect body pressed against mine. My arms tighten around her warm waist, and her breath hitches. Sooner than I hope, she pulls back an inch, lips so close to mine I can taste them. Her eyes draw me in with the force of an ocean wave.

"Save me a ride on the Ferris wheel?" she says.

The boyish excitement that surges through me is embarrassing. "Of course."

NINETEEN

SUMMER

IS IT CHILDISH to feel excited over a carnival ride?

If it is, I don't care.

The rotating wheel calls me like a beacon through the sea of students laughing and playing games. The smell of popcorn is long gone, replaced by the addicting scent of Aiden. Though that may just be my own hallucination.

The concession stands require restocking, the game operators need breaks, and there's a serious booze problem that I'm willing to overlook as long as no one keels over and wrecks the expensive equipment.

The ring toss attendant, Kenna, looks minutes from falling apart, so I tap her out. The couples approaching the booth showcase an uncomfortable amount of PDA, but it doesn't irritate me nearly as much as it usually does. My gaze drifts to the Ferris wheel again.

As I'm cleaning up after the last game, Kian leans against my booth while his date admires a large stuffed animal. "Think you can rig this to make me look good?"

I take his tickets and collect a few rings. "What's in it for me?"

"The joy of seeing your best friend in the embrace of a woman?"

My laugh escapes me without warning, causing his date to look over. I wave. "She's pretty."

"Is that a yes?"

I shrug, then hand him the wider rings meant for children.

"You're awfully nice today," he notes.

"I'm feeling charitable."

His eyes widen like he's uncovered a big secret. "You're getting laid."

My face scrunches in disgust. "Why is that your first guess?"

"It's not a guess. Either you're getting laid, or there's potential for it."

I don't want to dwell on whether he's right or not. "You're the last person who should know anything about my sex life."

"You mean the nonexistent one?"

I glare. "You're one to talk." That only has him sticking his tongue out. "If you must know, I'm just happy."

Kian's expression softens. "Good. I like seeing you happy." Then he steps back, boasting to his date that he's winning her the largest prize.

For once in my life, it looks like everything is going well. The carnival is a hit, my application only needs minor tweaks, and my poisonous feelings toward hockey are temporarily remedied by a certain captain.

A tap on my shoulder pulls me from my thoughts, and Kenna takes the key from me. "Shoo! You've been working all day. Go have some fun."

"I can stay if you need a longer break."

She pushes me out of her booth. "Go find your hockey hunk." She shuts the wooden door.

I guess our hug was on display for the entire carnival.

I make my way through the crowd of drunk students. For the first time in months, I feel light. That night out at the bar with Aiden felt like the beginning of a new me.

"Great event, Summer." Connor Atwood's voice is close enough that I startle. His blond hair flows in the wind as he matches my quick strides.

"Thanks for coming, Connor."

"I wouldn't have missed it." He continues walking with me as I'm nearing the Ferris wheel. "What are you doing now? Maybe we can hang out for a bit."

I'm completely ignoring Connor, but I can't find it in me to care. With a giddy rush of excitement, I slow to search for one tall hockey captain.

"What do you say?" he asks.

"Look, Connor, w—"

My heart sinks into the acid of my stomach when I finally spot Aiden getting on the Ferris wheel. With Crystal Yang. A Beta Phi sorority girl.

Spikes lodge in my throat. Connor's muffled voice mixes in with the noise of the carnival.

Aiden's eyes lock with mine before he sits in one of the Ferris wheel cars. Crystal throws an arm around his shoulders, smacking a kiss on his cheek as she takes a selfie.

In the heat of betrayal—one I definitely shouldn't be feeling—I turn to Connor.

"Hey, Connor?" I cut him off mid-ramble.

"Yeah?"

"Kiss me."

He's clearly not the idiot I thought, because without another word, he lowers his head and seals his lips to mine.

THE SCALDING HOT shower leaves my skin hot to the touch. My feet ache from standing for hours, and even the peach-scented lotion I slather over my body doesn't do much to alleviate the soreness. As I finish running a comb through my damp hair, there's a loud knock at the door. I throw on a long T-shirt and head to the front door, assuming it's Amara.

When I open the door, it's Aiden. A very pissed off Aiden.

"What was that?" he asks.

I lean against the door, trying to appear as if my heart hasn't just lit on fire. "Hello to you too, Crawford."

"You left."

"Because the event ended." I turn to glance at the clock on the kitchen stove. "It's midnight."

"I know what time it is." He steps closer, and I instinctively try to close the door on him, but he holds it open. "Why did you leave?"

"Do you have short-term memory loss? I just told you." I wince at the irritation seasoning my words.

"The truth."

"Look, I have an early class tomorrow—"

"I waited for you," he says, voice low and something vulnerable kissing the words. "She wasn't supposed to be there. You asked me to save you a ride."

"I shouldn't have asked you to do that."

Green eyes darken. "Why did you kiss him?"

I hadn't been sure he saw the kiss, but knowing he did makes something pop in my chest. So, I do the only thing I can. I act clueless. "Who?"

His expression morphs into one of disbelief. "Is there more than one guy you've kissed tonight?"

I cross my arms to regain composure, and he takes the opportunity to step inside, closing the door behind him. It's like he's sealed off the last bit of oxygen I could suck into my lungs to stay lucid. The dorm rivals a cardboard box with every inch of space he steals.

His gaze turns molten. "If you're trying to irritate me, you're doing a good job at it."

"You're the one who barged in here," I accuse.

"Fine. Why did you kiss Atwood? First name Connor, in case you've kissed a few Atwoods on your rampage tonight."

I don't want to answer him. Mostly because I'm not even sure why I did it in the first place. Well, I have an idea, but I'd rather not divulge that.

"Because I wanted to."

He moves forward, making me take an instinctive step back. The dance continues, each step sending me further into the dorm. "Why did you kiss him?"

My chest heaves from the proximity and the hot tug of tension between us. "I just told you."

"The truth, Summer."

With another step, I bump into the couch. The lack of space is hindering any logical thought. "He's a good kisser—"

He punctuates my sentence by pressing his hips to mine and driving me into the back of the couch. Searing, solid weight cages me in, and all my resistance to him goes up in flames when all six feet, four inches of him hovers over me. His scent ignites a fire somewhere low in my stomach.

"That's not what I asked. Try again." He whispers the demand inches from my lips, and I stop myself from letting out an embarrassing whimper.

My body didn't feel nearly as flammable when I kissed Connor, and Aiden's lips haven't even touched mine. The memory of Connor's kiss has long since faded, probably because Aiden has a special power of making my thoughts dissolve into a murky soup.

"I don't know what you expect me to say. It was just a kiss."

"Just a kiss?" he drawls, our lips a hairbreadth apart. "And if I kissed you right now, would that be just a kiss, too?"

His words flush through me like hot water. He's calling my bluff, and damn is he good at it. But he doesn't know me if he thinks I'll back away from a challenge. "Why don't you find out?"

He looks stunned, but recovers quickly, with a smirk that could make me melt into a pathetic puddle at his feet. "Is that a yes?"

"Well, it's not a no." It's actually a loud, resounding yes. But I'm losing control over the situation. It's obvious from the way my legs quiver. I'm not sure my flimsy guard can hold up for another second.

"I'm going to need you to do better than that. Can I kiss you, Summer? Yes or no?"

I'm not sure what possesses me to say it. Maybe it's the way his hard body presses into mine or the way he looks at me with a rawness I haven't seen before. "Yes."

When I'm so desperate for him to claim my lips, he sinks to his knees. The surprised sound that leaves me might have been embarrassing if I could produce any thought, but Aiden Crawford is on his knees in front of me with his breath hitting my bare thighs, so thinking isn't my number one priority right now.

"W-what are you doing?" I stutter.

"Kissing you." His fingers skim along the backs of my thighs, and I shudder. By the rumbling sound that leaves his throat, he knows he has me in the palm of his hand.

This is going south. Fast. "Do you need me to teach you what a kiss is?"

His slow smirk rattles my chest, sending a hot sensation to pool at my core. "I think I can manage."

"You sure? Because Connor could give you some good tips."

Why do I keep talking? And why do I love the way his eyes narrow at my words?

My taunt does the opposite of what I want, because Aiden stands. But instead of leaving like any other guy with a fragile ego, he hooks his arm around my waist and lifts me effortlessly. When my legs hook around him to accommodate his large body, I'm hyper-aware that I'm completely naked under my thin T-shirt. Aiden freezes.

It would have taken him just a small lift of my shirt to realize it when he was on his knees, but I couldn't keep my mouth shut long enough for that to happen. Now I desperately want him back down there, and I don't know how he managed that.

"Is this the only thing keeping me from seeing you naked?" He fists the old, graying shirt, his other hand lifting me. His strength doesn't surprise me, but it turns me on to a whole new degree. It even manages to snatch any witty remark I might make.

I nod, and his rumble of satisfaction bleeds into my veins with an exhilarating sizzle. A restless buzz saturates the air when he sits me on the back of the couch and lowers his head to kiss my neck. His erection digs into my stomach, begging to get out of his pants and right inside me. A strangled noise escapes my throat.

"I want to see you," he rasps, brushing my hair back, his other hand still clutching the hem of my shirt. "Can I take this off?"

"Yes," I breathe. Apparently, I only need that one word when Aiden is in my vicinity.

My entire body is crackling. The draft does nothing to cool my heated skin when he pulls off my shirt in one swift move. The curse that follows sends a vibration through my core. It's so electric, I shiver despite the heat licking my body. My cheeks must be crimson as I sit completely naked for only him to see.

Aiden doesn't waste another second covering my nipples with his hot mouth. I cry out, my back arching in his hold. He runs a thumb over the other sensitive bud and I'm panting. I'm so wet already, and he's barely touched me. I'm not sure how I can handle any more.

Rough hands slide to my waist, holding tight. "Is this how you walk around? Naked under those thin T-shirts?"

"It gets hot at night," I say, my voice barely above a whisper when his hot touch spreads like a fever writhing and pulsing in my veins.

He hums, and his hands eagerly roam every part of me as he kisses my collarbone, down to my breasts, and then my stomach. When he reaches my belly button, my breathing shallows. He goes lower to my navel and finally sinks to his knees again.

"Is this okay?"

Does he even need to ask that? I'm ready to go off like a fire hose. But he's still looking up at me, waiting for an answer, so I nod. *Isn't it obvious?*

"Words, Summer. I need your words." His gentle voice touches a corner of that rapidly beating thing in my chest, but his expression is of barely contained need. I'm shaking when his fingers press harder into my thighs as he waits for an answer.

"*Yes*," I breathe. "It's more than okay."

He kisses my thighs and holds me like a meal he's going to devour. "Tell me to stop and I will. Understand?"

I nod, but he continues to look at me. "Yes, I understand."

He yanks my hips forward and off the edge of the couch, and my hands shoot out to stabilize myself when he presses his face between my thighs. Before I can take my next breath, his mouth seals over me, and I'm pretty sure I'm floating out of state. Aiden's tongue slides over my clit, and my legs tremor. His lips curve in an infuriating smirk, and he drives his tongue inside me.

I throw my head back, and my fingers dig into the couch, almost piercing through the fabric. Amara would kill me if I ruined our couch. Though, if she knew the reason, I'm sure she'd understand.

"*Jesus*." He lets out an amused breath. "I knew you'd taste this good." His words make my toes curl, and his moan races up my spine. I expected dirty talk from him, but experiencing it has goose bumps riddling my skin.

"Fucking beautiful," he whispers, leaving small kisses along my inner thighs. Aiden works his tongue inside me like it's his last meal. Like giving me pleasure is his sole purpose in life.

I've had men go down on me, but I've never had one *worship* me. The grip on my thighs loosens when he brings his fingers where his mouth is, holding me open with his thumbs. The exposed position makes me shiver with an oncoming orgasm.

"Oh *God*," I moan. My hands sink into his hair as he continues torturing my clit. Just when I think I can't take any more, he slips a finger inside me, and I feel the moan in his throat when I squeeze around him.

"You're so fucking tight," he rasps, sliding in a second finger.

I feel so full, my head falls back in pure pleasure. His teeth nip my clit, and I whimper.

"Watch me," he orders. "Watch me fuck you with my mouth, Summer."

He does a twirl and flick that I can't comprehend but my body loves. He doesn't take his hypnotizing green eyes off me, and I can't seem to look away either. Not even when I see that cocky glint, the one that would otherwise make me tell him to fuck off.

My hand sifts into his hair, and I press him into me. His deep rumble tells me he finds my desperation amusing, but I couldn't care less. This smart-ass can tease me forever if this is the pleasure his tongue gives me.

"Don't stop." My needy voice sounds foreign to my ears.

He hums against my core, and it burns through my blood like an inferno. How flammable are humans?

Aiden runs the flat of his tongue over my clit as his fingers move in and out of me. "Is this a good enough kiss for you, baby?"

The *baby* absolutely ruins me. I'm a trembling, shaking mess in his hands, and the writhing becomes unbearable when he hooks one of my legs over his shoulder. If I thought the earlier position wrecked me, this one absolutely demolishes me. His heavy, calloused hand squeezes the soft flesh of my thigh in a rough grip.

"Aiden, I can't—"

"Come on my tongue, Summer. Show me how good my mouth feels on your pussy."

That's all it takes. I come completely undone. Pulsing and squeezing around his fingers until he withdraws them. Aiden kisses up my torso to meet my neck, his hair mussed from my erratic pulling. The need for him gnaws at me like a persistent woodpecker.

Standing, he maps my naked body like he's memorizing it. As if what he just did to me isn't even close to enough for him. Seeing my flushed face, he smiles like he's accomplished a difficult feat. When his tongue swipes across his wet lips, my pulse drifts between my thighs.

Rough hands cup my face, and soft lips touch my forehead in a featherlight kiss. The contrast of what those lips just did between my legs and now to my forehead short-circuits my brain.

I reach for his waistband to undo his jeans, but his half-lidded gaze turns reluctant. Aiden releases a strained breath, and it looks like he's doing everything to hold himself back. When I cup the erection tenting his jeans, he stops me.

Of every possibility of how tonight could have gone, Aiden on his knees in front of me was quite literally at the bottom of the list. But somehow this was even lower.

With his thumb grazing my bottom lip and a pitiful smile on his face, he shakes his head. Aiden moves away from my parted legs, and I feel cold and exposed. The realization of what just happened hits me hard. I close my legs as the sudden rejection pools in my stomach.

Aiden grabs my shirt from the floor and pulls it back over my head. With one last look, Aiden covers me completely. I've never been more disappointed to be dressed.

"Aiden," I say, taking hold of his hands as he's adjusting my shirt. With a rough exhale, he finally looks at me.

If confidence was the reason I found my voice, the look on his face is the reason I lose it again.

"If you want it, you're going to come to me." He lifts my hair from the shirt, pushing it back. "The next time I have you, it won't be to prove something or to win some competition. It's going to be because you know the only guy that can satisfy you is me."

With one last look, he walks out.

TWENTY

AIDEN

I'M A FUCKING idiot.

I might have looked confident when I walked out of her dorm, but it's taking everything in me not to crawl back and give her what she wants. What *I* want.

Finding out what shade of brown her nipples are might be the nail in the coffin. There's no one I can blame but myself for charging into her dorm like I have a right to question her about who she let kiss her.

Instead of getting laid, I just hardwired the object of all my wet dreams into my brain. It hasn't even been five minutes, and I can already count the showers I'll need to jerk off to her. The walk back to the car is a walk of shame.

Did I expect to go into her dorm and make her come all over my face? Not for a second.

Even if I did, I didn't think she would be just as eager for it.

I don't bother with music for my drive because, apparently, I want to torture myself even more. Fortunately, the roads are nearly empty. Trying to focus on my driving is impossible when I can still fucking taste her on my tongue. Her beautiful sounds and sweet body had me dropping to my knees without a second thought. Fucking centerfold worthy.

With her tits in my face and her pretty brown eyes watching me, I could worship her for eternity. I'm surprised I didn't come in my pants like a pubescent teen the second she let me undress her. There was so much to touch, so much to taste that I felt lucky to even be allowed to look at her.

Summer could have anyone pining over her. I've known that since she walked into Kilner's office the first day I saw her. She would have rather slammed my head into a car door than have anything to do with my dick, but now her breathy *yes* plays on a loop in my head. It's a special kind of torture considering I just denied my dick its salvation. I can only imagine how wet and tight she would be taking all of me, so perfectly spread out on the back of that couch. Fuck.

Barging into her dorm to find out if she and Atwood are a thing wasn't my finest moment. Crystal Yang's ego has been bruised since that sorority party, so she thought dragging me to the Ferris wheel would change my mind. It didn't. Especially after I saw Atwood kissing Summer.

I can't remember if I even got an answer about why she kissed him. And I don't know why that kiss twisted a knife so deep in my gut, I couldn't breathe until I saw her again.

Pulling into the driveway, I spot Kian standing by the garage in his boxers as if to tell me this fucked-up night isn't over yet. He's barefoot on the slick pavement. Music spills out of the house behind him, and a few people hang by the front door. Of course they've resumed the fucking party.

There is nothing uneventful about this house. I should have taken Brady Winston's advice more seriously, because being a captain to these guys is like being a full-time babysitter.

I slam my truck door shut. "Ishida, what's going on?"

He falls into me. "She's back. She's back for me!"

His horror-stricken look tells me everything I need to know.

Tabitha. Kian's ex-girlfriend/stalker. "How do you know?"

"This was on my pillow!" He shoves the bride and groom wedding cake topper into my hands, and I relax.

Last year, a few days before Christmas break, a wedding cake was delivered to the house. When we opened it, it read CONGRATULATIONS MR. & MRS. ISHIDA. Safe to say we don't buy cake anymore, and anonymous deliveries are no longer accepted at the hockey house. Except the rest of us know Dylan's behind all this, because he gets a kick out of messing with Kian.

"It's probably nothing, buddy. I'll take a look for you."

Inside, I disconnect the Bluetooth speakers. "Get out. Party's over," I say over the groans and murmurs. There's only so many things I can let slide for the sake of the team. The only reason I allowed a party earlier was so I could get everyone to Summer's carnival. Not so these idiots can get plastered.

Finding Sebastian and Cole in the kitchen, I get them to direct everyone out the front door. I head straight for Dylan's room and hear the moans too late. Knocking would have been smart.

"Donovan!" I can't say I'm shocked when I see him tied to the bed, a blindfold over his eyes and a gag in his mouth.

The blonde turns to wave. "Hi, Aiden."

I throw her a tight smile. "Do you mind, uh, untying him?"

She removes the blindfold and gag. Dylan blinks, adjusting to the light. "Hey, what's up, man?"

Only he could be so cavalier. I toss him the cake topper, and he snickers before he spots my expression, and his amusement vanishes. I might be petty, but if I'm not getting laid tonight, no one is.

"Living room. Now."

By the time he makes it out, he's still pulling up his sweats. "Is this about Kian? That was a joke."

"It's not only about that. You're fucking around while Kilner's coming down on me after the Yale mess. You invited those assholes here, and you're the one who lost the bet to throw the parties." I sift a hand through my hair. "I can't keep doing this shit with you. You miss practice, show up hungover, and get into fights bad enough that you get ejected. When are you going to get it together?"

He runs a hand over his face. "Do I have to listen to this lecture? I'm just having fun. We all are."

"What you do off the ice is up to you, but you're my friend, man. Tell me if something is happening, and I'll help."

"Aye, aye, Captain!" He mimics a salute, making my jaw tighten. "I'm serious."

His smirk slips off his face when he looks away. "Nothing is happening."

"You would tell me if there were?"

He pauses, but then he nods. "Yeah, I would."

Deep down I know he won't. Dylan's ready to share everything in his life unless it has to do with feelings; then he's a brick wall.

The summer of freshman year, we camped out in Hammonasset on a team-building retreat, and that's the only time I've learned anything personal about Dylan. His parents are hard on him about school, and his dad hates that he plays a *barbarian sport like hockey*. His mother, on the other hand, is so caring she stocked our refrigerator for an entire semester with her cooking. Eventually, they moved upstate, so her visits became less frequent, but we got a good look at her relationship with her golden boy.

"Good. And I'm putting an end to that bet you lost. Anyone who has a problem with that can deal with me."

"Works for me," he says, visibly relaxing. "Where'd you come from? You left the carnival hours ago."

The switch in topic only reminds me of sounds I've been hearing on repeat. Her moans. And her whimpers. And her raspy calls for God. "Just checking on something."

Dylan snorts. "Stalking your girl after Atwood kissed her? You know, I never thought you'd stoop to Tabitha's level."

Kian walks in at that moment, the fear on his face returning. "She's here, isn't she?" he screeches, disappearing into the kitchen.

"I liked you better with a gag," I say to Dylan, which only makes him laugh harder.

"You know who else is gagging—"

I chuck an empty Solo cup at him, and he dodges it. Idiot. "I'll have fun with you at practice tomorrow," I say.

His laughter seizes, and he pins me with a glare.

Kian comes back, holding a spatula. "Do you think I can bunk with one of you guys?"

"Not it." Dylan beams, completely apathetic to Kian's fear.

"We can switch rooms, Kian," I offer.

"But I would feel more comfortable with you in the room."

Could this night get any longer? "Fine."

I'll have to sleep on the uncomfortable sponge mattress because Kian will complain all night if he has to. And there is no way I'm sharing a bed with him, because he thrashes around like he's being attacked.

"But you can't keep asking every ten minutes if I'm awake."

"How else will I know if you're asleep or not?"

I don't bother entertaining that response when my phone vibrates. It's Dylan, who's already down the hall snickering to himself.

BUNNY PATROL 2.0

Dylan Donovan: Get your cameras ready. Ishida and Cap are
   sleeping together.
Cole Carter: I'd pay to see that.
Sebastian Hayes: Of course, you would, Cole.
Dylan Donovan: Five dollars at the door. Ten if you want to
   record.

Eli Westbrook: I thought that scream was the girl you have over.
   You scared Kian again, didn't you?
Dylan Donovan: It was a harmless prank, Dad.
Sebastian Hayes: WTF? That's why you dragged me to the dollar
   store at one a.m.?? I thought it was for a project.

"Who's texting you?" asks Kian, trying to peek over my shoulder, clutching his spatula.

"The guys."

"I'm not getting any messages," he says, staring at his smart-watch.

"Maybe the Wi-Fi's bad," I answer, not paying attention because I'm texting Dylan that he's one message away from having his number blocked.

"I'm using data. There's nothing."

I shrug when I look at him, only to find him peering down at my phone to see the chat. I realize it too late, because a look of disbelief and hurt mixes onto his face.

Shit.

"You guys have a group chat without me?!"

TWENTY-ONE

SUMMER

"WHY ARE YOU zoned out?" Tyler looks at me with a weird expression as he enters the private study pod.

A restlessness flares at the memory of last night. The pressure of Aiden's fingers pressing into my thighs and dirty words pressed between my legs sends a heat wave crashing into me.

I unzip my jacket. "Haven't had any caffeine yet."

Or maybe it's that Aiden gave me a mind-numbing orgasm, and I'm pretty sure I've become stupid. That would be the only explanation for staring at my blank computer screen for twenty-five minutes. Nothing like flashbacks to the best head you've ever gotten to distract you in the middle of exam season.

There is a high chance that I'm prone to making bad decisions. Maybe it's a genetic predisposition that should be studied closely, because I know I should have denied the "kiss" and just finished myself off, thinking about the version of him I could stomach, like an accountant with no ties to the wretched sport.

"Here you go." Tyler sets a cup down and sits beside me.

"Thanks," I say, taking a sip. "What are you doing here?"

"I can't hang out with my favorite girl?"

I swivel my head to search. "Where?"

He doesn't laugh. "It's the truth. All the other girls I talk to I've either slept with or am planning on it."

"Ugh!" I gag, putting my tea down. "You're a pig."

He's unperturbed. "You should be flattered that we're genuine friends."

"Only because you've known me since we were kids."

"Nah, I think it's because your dad is one scary dude. That and I've had you throw up on my shoes."

"You're the one who brought booze to a school assembly."

"And you drank to show off," he counters.

"You dared me in front of everyone!"

He shakes his head, wearing a grimace. "Never mind. I think it's because we fight like siblings." He shoves my head away in a playful move, and I flip him off.

"What's up with you and Crawford?" he suddenly asks.

I had plucked Aiden out of my head for a split second, only for the question to drag me back to square one. How do I answer that? *He's helped with my assignment and barges into my dorm to give me orgasms?*

"He's helping me with my research." I feel him scrutinizing me. "What?"

"Why are you blushing?"

I pull out my phone to check my reflection. "Makeup."

I'm not wearing any makeup. Despite the small amount of melanin my mother passed down to me, my cheeks still glow red. Now the guy is making me blush? He is seriously pissing me off, though it's hard to be mad at someone when your body has assembled a choir for them.

Tyler hums in acknowledgment, though I know he sees right through me. "I still don't forgive you for bailing on the Christmas party, by the way. You know those things are torturous."

"I do. That's why I didn't show up."

"You promised. I don't take promise-breaking lightly, Summer."

"I'm sorry. I couldn't stand there in front of all those people and pretend we're a perfect family." Our Christmas celebration is hosted by a rotating handful of families in the league. Last year it was my parents' turn, so our house transformed into a winter wonderland. From the pictures my sisters sent, I couldn't be happier that I didn't attend.

"I get it, but I don't forgive you."

I sigh loudly. "What do you want?"

It doesn't even take him a second to answer. "Set me up with your roommate."

I'm surprised my head doesn't snap from how fast I turn to him. "No way, that's my best friend."

"*I'm* your best friend."

"Amara doesn't like you."

His gaze turns quizzical. "Why?"

"Cause you're a know-it-all asshole. This shouldn't be news."

"I've spoken to her once, like a year ago."

I shake my head. "She also saw you at some party going into a room with four girls."

"So she's slut-shaming me?"

"No, you idiot. Two of those girls had boyfriends."

He smiles like he's recounting the memory. "And how is that my problem? It was completely consensual for all parties."

"Well, it doesn't matter. She likes Eli." The words are out of my mouth before I can shove them back in. I wince when I see the playful expression on his face melt away.

"Westbrook?"

I nod. A shadow crosses his face, but it's gone almost instantly. He's quiet for the rest of the hour, and I don't bother prodding, aside from occasional homework questions.

I finish studying just in time for my first class of the day. Sampson turns to the East Hall, and I walk down to my class.

Kian Ishida drapes his arm over my shoulders, looking sullen. Seeing anything but pure happiness is rare for him. "What's wrong?"

He exhales an anguished sigh. "You think you know people, but they all end up being the same."

What I learned from being friends with Kian is to never ask him to elaborate. I nod, though I have no idea why his mood is so sour. When we pass the student aid center, Dylan comes out with an ice pack on his face. He waves at us, and I notice the new shiner on his jaw. "Ouch, what happened to you?"

"Let's just say I deserve it," Dylan says, heading in the opposite direction.

The last time I saw Dylan, he had a busted lip, and he said the same thing. I thought it was a one-time thing, but it seems like he's made himself an enemy.

I turn to Kian. "Who did that to him?"

"A guy on the basketball team. Dylan slept with his grandma."

I choke on my spit. "You have to be joking."

"To be fair, she's still pretty young. Can't say I wouldn't have done the same."

"You're—"

"Hot? Smart? Extraordinary?"

"Disgusting."

"Not the adjective I would have picked." He shrugs. As we pass by the quad, he makes a weird noise. "I seriously can't believe you dated that guy."

I follow his line of sight to Donny setting up for a chess event. "It was freshman year, and he wasn't always like that."

"So, he just started being a preppy douchebag now?"

"Uh, no, he always presented himself that way. I think it's because his mom still does his shopping."

He laughs. "Then I guess he's your Tabitha."

"Tabitha?"

"You know, like your one dating mistake."

I'm sure there is a story there, but I only shrug. "Yeah, I guess."

"So, are you coming to Aiden's birthday?" he asks as we descend the steps.

"It's his birthday?" He hasn't brought it up, not that we've talked after what happened.

"Well, not really. It's January fifth, but since our games are mostly away at the beginning of the term, we celebrate it later."

"That is an entire month late."

"A few weeks, a month, who cares? Are you coming or not?"

"Of course, I'll bring the party hats and streamers!" I clap.

He's unamused by my fake enthusiasm. "Seriously, you should come. It'll be fun." He tries again when we're seated. "Besides, I thought you and Aiden were getting along. What happened?"

If I think about what happened, I won't get any work done. "Nothing. I just have exams."

"So does everyone else. Just make an appearance with Amara and Cassidy." He blushes at the mention of Cassidy, and I try not to laugh. I think someone's got a crush. My best friends have apparently become a hot commodity with hockey players.

"You seem to have a vested interest in whether I attend."

"'Cause you're my friend, and I want to hang out with you. Besides, I don't know who my real friends are these days."

"What does that mean?" I ask, despite knowing not to.

"Have you ever been betrayed, Summer?"

TWENTY-TWO

AIDEN

MY BIRTHDAY PRESENT is wrapped in a tight pink dress that's short enough that I wouldn't need to unwrap it.

I can feel the blood rushing to my groin as I watch Summer lean against the snack bar. The party, all credit to Kian, is island themed to ring in my twenty-first birthday. I had no intention of celebrating, because I've been twenty-one for some time now. But the guys had other plans. There is no way they would let this day pass, even if the party is a month overdue.

When the glimpse of pink moves again, a wave of something hits me and I have the urge to take off my Hawaiian shirt and wrap it around her. The last time I saw this much of her thighs, I had my face buried between them. That memory doesn't help the growing problem in my pants. Maybe I should have left a few hickeys on her thighs so anyone looking would back the fuck off.

I'm not sure how Kian got her to come, since he's still pissed about the group chat thing, and Summer's been actively avoiding me since last week. Her assignment doesn't depend on me anymore, so I have no excuse to show up at her dorm, and one surprise visit was more than enough. Any more, and I'm certain she'd call security on me.

When a guy approaches Summer, I head over. My chest covers her back, and the warmth from her body sends a thrumming sensation through me. She tenses but relaxes almost instantly. I bite back a smile, finding that she's comfortable enough to let her guard down around me.

"Aren't you going to wish me happy birthday?" I let my lips brush the shell of her ear.

She spins to face me. Fuck, I thought the back of her dress was hot, but the front is an entirely different story. The thin straps sit against her glowing skin, and from my height and I can see the perfect dip of her neckline that makes me clench my fists.

"Is that what all this is? I just wanted a drink."

That drags a low chuckle from me. "Didn't think you would show. A party probably scores pretty low on your fun scale."

She gives me an unamused look. "Your best friend has highly persuasive qualities."

"I bet he does." I have a feeling Kian got her to come to make me feel like a shitty friend. "What did he offer you?"

"He's going to write my notes for a week." She fixes the white flower in her hair. "He also said something about making you feel bad for betraying him, so of course, I had to come."

Someone slaps my shoulder, drawing my attention away from her. "Happy birthday, Cap."

More people come up and say the same. Most of them are friends from freshman year and guys from other teams. I'm sure Kian invited everyone he could find, though he has had a strict rule against anyone lower than a junior since the Tabitha debacle. She was a sophomore who easily fooled him with her southern belle charm, and quickly became his personal nightmare. Now he's decided the older they are, the less likely he is to find a stalker. The logic isn't clear with that one.

I glance over at Summer to make sure she hasn't left. I'm hoping she's being extra nice because it's my birthday. I'm also hoping her charitable mood will finally make her take me up on my offer.

When she moves away from me to talk to Connor Atwood, I try to end my conversation quickly. Connor wears an earnest expression, but Summer looks thoroughly confused.

Uh-oh.

When Connor sees me approach, he gives me a quick nod and scurries away. "Sorry," I say to her. "I haven't seen some of those guys in years."

She pierces me with a dangerous look. "Care to explain why Connor Atwood just told me I'm a nice girl, but nothing can happen between us?"

Suppressing my grin is harder than I expected. "Not really."

She takes a menacing step closer. "Did you threaten him?"

"*Threaten* is a strong word."

Anger flares in her brown eyes. "You told him not to talk to me?"

"No, I told him what would happen if he did." I've never been jealous of anyone, not even in the cocky jock way. But when she kissed him, something green like envy burned through my veins.

"So, a threat," she says.

"Look, I'm only looking out for him. I don't like to see my fellow athletes get used."

Disbelief darkens her expression. "You think I'm using him?"

Man, I love it when she speaks with that fiery attitude. She gets this crease in the middle of her eyebrows. One I know would disappear if her thighs were wrapped around my neck. "I believe it was my name coming out of your mouth a few hours after you kissed him."

Her throat twitches. "Well, I got that out of my system now."

"*I* got it out of your system."

I hope it isn't out of her system. She is the furthest thing from out of mine, and that night just made my itch for her grow. I didn't think she'd care that I talked to Connor after we hooked up. She hasn't outright said she isn't interested, but being upset over another guy is making how she feels loud and clear.

"Whatever." Her mood has dampened, and I feel responsible. I don't like it. I prefer her expressive eyes and her sharp tongue.

"I'm sorry for ruining whatever it is you had with Connor. I didn't know it was serious. If you want him, I'll talk to him." It pains me to even say it.

Her sardonic laugh doesn't comfort me. "I never wanted him."

That statement cuts through my sulking, and joy erupts. "So we're good, then. I did you a favor."

Summer glowers. "No, Aiden, you didn't do me a favor. But it doesn't matter, because letting you decide what he can do makes him irredeemable."

I guess that's a plus, but I still don't like the annoyed look on her face. "You're right. I did it for me," I admit.

"Shocker."

"To apologize for my selfishness, let me get you a drink. We have margaritas."

"Margaritas won't get you redemption, Crawford."

"How about three margaritas?" I smile, but she ignores me. I try my hardest not to seem like a petulant child. "Just talk to me, Summer. That's what we do—we communicate, right?"

"We're talking right now."

Someone taps my shoulder, probably to wish me a happy birthday, but my focus is Summer, and I need for us to be alone. In a brave move, I take her hand to lead her upstairs. We're not even halfway when she yanks it away.

"Talk." Her stubborn stance tells me she's not going anywhere with me. This might be a good thing, because I don't know if I could stay true to my word if we found ourselves alone again.

"Why are you upset?"

She unravels. "Because I'm trying to do what you said, and even when I try, I can't get it right. I want to let loose, have fun, and not stress about everything."

That, I understand. I'm sure that night in her dorm was a catalyst for all this, but it doesn't explain why she didn't just come to me. I could give her all of that and more.

"Connor is your idea of fun?" I ask.

"I don't need to explain myself to you, Aiden."

I stare at my hands in regret. "You're right, you don't. I just want to make sure we're okay."

She huffs. "We are. It's your birthday party, I guess I can give you one free pass for being insufferable," she says with a tilt to her lips. Not a smile, but close enough. Though the way she says *one free pass* only makes my abdomen tighten. I know she's referring to Connor, but images of what she can grant me flash in my head.

Before I can say anything, the guys barrel up the stairs and drag me away to do shots. Birthday shots, which is just a keg stand, and the guys attempting to take twenty-one shots.

Going down the stairwell, I look back at Summer, and she's laughing. It calms an uneasiness in my chest.

EVEN MY BUZZ doesn't alleviate the irritation I'm feeling right now. I was happy with how things were going after we all played beer pong about an hour ago, but now my fists tighten. Summer's dancing and laughing her ass off when Tyler Sampson whispers something in her ear. If I see him smile at her one more time, the team's going to be missing a forward. What could she be laughing about, anyway? I've had the displeasure of sharing a hotel room with him, and he's not that fucking funny.

"Careful, you're going to break that glass." Amara stands beside me, pointing at my angry grip. "Though I'd be all for you channeling that rage into Sampson."

I down the remnants of my drink and leave my glass on the table. "There is no rage."

She nods in response, though it seems disingenuous. "Here." She holds out a shot.

"What are we toasting?"

"Your birthday. And for you to grow some balls." Amara sees my raised brows. "You've been staring at her all night. Go get your birthday wish, Captain. Unless you've lost your charm."

My *charm*? I'm pretty sure she felt every ounce of my charm between her legs the other night.

She clinks our glasses, and the liquid burns my throat along with its bitter taste. "Everclear? Are you trying to black out?"

"Precisely." She seems unaffected by the bitterness.

I'm not sure if it's the Everclear or if time has stalled, but Summer moves in slow motion. The heat that fogs my senses makes my vision hazy. Her tits are tightly wrapped in the thin-strapped dress, and all I can think about is how she whimpered when I took her nipple between my teeth.

Her tight little body isn't feeding only my fantasies. When she dances like that, the attention around her grows heavy, but it doesn't seem like she notices as she pulls Cassie closer. Taking Amara's advice, I move through the crowd. I'm inching close enough to smell her peach-scented shampoo before Eli slaps a hand on my back. The lights dim, and a chorus of "Happy Birthday" begins, but my eyes only focus on Summer, who glows even under the dim light. I don't often drink, so her ethereal state could be a product of alcohol, but there is no doubt she's sparkling. She always does.

"Make a wish," Kian says, snapping me back to the candlelit cupcakes in front of me. I do, and my friends erupt into cheers before the music grows loud again. I'm sure Summer is going back to her friends, but instead, she heads toward me. She swipes a finger over the icing on my cupcake and pops it in her mouth. I hold back a groan.

"Twenty-one, huh? You're practically an old man," she says.

I chuckle. "We're the same age."

"Nuh-uh, I'm twenty until October."

"Ah, forgive me. I must be thinking about your fake ID," I say.

When screams erupt from the dance floor, Summer's friends call for her. "We love this song," she says.

"With the way you were dancing, I'd think you loved all of them."

"You were watching me dance? That's a little creepy."

"Not much else I could look at." I lean in to whisper in her ear. "It was like watching a train wreck."

She tries to appear offended but fails. "I was going to ask you to dance, but I guess train wreck and all, you wouldn't want to."

My blood thrums with an unfamiliar heat. "Ask me anyway."

"Dance with me?"

I take her hand, and she pulls me to the center of the dance floor. I can barely make out the lyrics because Summer presses into me, but I know it's dark and sinful from the way her hips sway. The lights are so dim I can't make out anybody but her. I let my hands fall to her waist, my touch light, but she takes them anyway, snaking them around her body. I feel desperate and on fire to touch every bit of her warm skin. It's a challenge keeping my hands in a respectful place, especially with all these people around. Summer doesn't seem to care, because she hooks her arms around my neck and swivels her ass all over my erection.

"Easy, Summer," I whisper into her ear.

My head feels like it's underwater when the music changes, and she turns, her movements slow and sweet. I can't tell whether I appreciate the change, or if I'd rather have her torturing me with her hips again. No doubt it's the latter. I would choose anything this girl willingly does to me over and over again.

Somehow, I feel both sober and completely drunk out of my mind. Never have I been this achingly desperate for the girl rubbing against me. It might be because Summer is the last person I expected to grind on me in the middle of a dance floor, although I'm assuming alcohol is playing a part.

When the dance floor gets crowded, I pull Summer away to a

more secluded corner. I'm still holding on to her, both my hands resting on her waist and hers locked around my neck.

She fiddles with the collar of my shirt, half-lidded eyes gazing up at me. "What did you wish for?"

I can feel her beating heart, but I can't tell if it matches my erratic one. "I can't tell you."

Summer frowns. "Why not?"

"Can't risk it not coming true." I touch the soft skin of her cheek. "You're so pretty."

She chuckles. "You're so drunk."

"You can thank Amara for that."

She rests her head against the wall. "Everclear?"

I nod and move my hand higher on her cheek. Her eyes flutter with the contact, and so does my fucking heart. "I missed you."

Her voice is quiet. "I saw you a few days ago."

"Not like this. Not with these eyes that tell me you haven't forgotten about my tongue on your pussy either."

Her breath hitches.

"I feel like I can still taste you, Summer." My words leak with desperation.

"Aiden . . ." I'm not sure if it's a warning, but she swallows, and the delicate column of her throat twitches. I palm her tight ass and I wish we were in my room and not down here, but I know if I suggest it, the haze around us will scatter. I need her so bad I can't think straight, but that's exactly why I can't have her.

Summer pushes her hips against mine, clearly feeling the erection that's been rock solid since I first saw her. My fingers skim the hem of her dress and I hold back my groan.

"Do you have any idea what you do to me?" I say roughly against the shell of her ear. She lets me kiss her neck, and we're dry humping against the wall when I slow our movements.

It's at that exact moment that Dylan crashes into the speakers beside us, knocking them over. Summer jumps, and I pull away to help him off his ass, the screech from the speakers only resolving when I lift them back into place. From Dylan's glossy eyes, I can tell he's wasted. It's one of those nights where he won't get lectured for it, and he's taking full advantage.

"I'm going to throw up." Dylan gags as I haul him up.

I glance back at Summer, who watches us with wide eyes. "I'm going to take him to bed," I say.

"Need help?" she asks. There is no way I'd let her care for a drunk Dylan. The shit that comes out of his mouth is too unpredictable. When I shake my head, she gives me a half smile, and before I drag away my blabbering friend, Summer says, "Happy birthday, Aiden. I hope your wish comes true."

TWENTY-THREE

SUMMER

I'D RATHER STAB Cupid with one of his pink arrows than go through this holiday again. Except saying that out loud would paint me as a bitter single loser, so I'm stewing safely in my thoughts. The pink heart cutouts decorating the table, which I've been ripping in half, leave a mess in my lap. This is not a good look.

"Did Cassie do something to her hair?"

My head swivels to Kian, who might as well have hearts for eyes as he watches Cassie perform.

Starlight karaoke lounge has been a regular place for Cassie when she has the urge to sing. Mostly, it's a form of therapy after a messy breakup. I think she's finally over her last situation, but all the Valentine's lore thrown in our faces isn't helping anyone.

That is why I was set on bingeing my comfort show with a heart-shaped pizza from Uncle Frank's tonight. Except Kian Ishida showed up at my dorm and forced me to go out with him. Not to mention he made me change twice. He thinks wearing a sweat suit in public is a cardinal sin. I agreed only because his clean button-up and dress pants made me look like a troll in comparison.

He's using me as a buffer to not seem like a stalker, but I'm pretty sure Cassie knows about his infatuation. I'm not sure what happened between them, but I heard they snuck up to his room during Aiden's birthday party.

"It looks lighter. Did she dye it?"

"I think she just curled it," I say.

He rests his chin on his hands, staring dreamily. "She can pull off anything."

I check the air for the flying baby. If Cupid has Kian obsessed with Cassie, he'll have me doing something just as stupid. And I do not have time for stupid.

As I'm stabbing the ice in my Shirley Temple with the disintegrating paper straw, Kian raises his arm. I look where he gestures, and that's when I see him.

Tall, confident, and looking too good for me to even deny it, Aiden Crawford.

The energy in the room seems to shift, and I realize I'm not the only one looking at Dalton's star hockey player. The entire lounge watches him enter with Eli and Cole behind him. Green eyes search the lounge, and when he spots us, my cheeks burn.

"Why is he here?" I whisper, dusting the paper hearts off my lap.

"I invited him." Kian gives me a weird look. "Should I not have?"

I groan instead of answering, assessing the area for an escape route.

"Did something happen between you two?"

My stomach dips with the memory. A lot happened between us, mostly between his mouth and that sensitive place between my legs. "No. Why would you ask that?"

"Because you're acting like a crazy person."

A loud voice interrupts my eye roll. "Hey, guys!" Cole says, pulling out a chair.

When Eli sits beside me, I sigh in relief. "No date tonight, Sunny?" he asks.

"Nope. This one fawning over Cassie is the only action I'm getting. You?"

He chuckles. "Same, though your company soothes a lonely soul."

I fight the blush his smooth words elicit. "Are you asking me to be your Valentine, Brooksy?" I bat my lashes.

The grin that takes over his face is wide enough to show his perfect teeth, but it's replaced with an amused smirk when his gaze slips away from mine. "It would be my pleasure, but I don't want to step on any toes."

Following his line of sight, I catch on green, and the weight of Aiden's stare makes my throat dry. I know what he's thinking about because I'm thinking the same damn thing. Darkened eyes slide down my outfit in a thorough assessment. I fidget with the thin straps of the dress and hear the quickening thuds of my heart. When Aiden's hungry gaze meets mine again, he smirks. The same smirk he gave me when his hand gripped my thighs, and his fingers sank into me.

It isn't clear how I found myself surrounded by four hockey players on Valentine's Day, but this would get a great laugh out of Amara. Unlike me, she had a date set weeks in advance from a long list of potential guys from her computer science classes.

"All right, let's give a round of applause to our amazing talent, Cassidy Carter," the host says, and the lounge erupts in applause and howls from our table.

"On to a fan favorite segment. The annual Valentine's Day matchmaker!" I'm stealing one of Kian's fries when he perks up, fidgeting with his tie and running a nervous hand over his pants.

"We have our performers joining our game. Let us welcome Amelia, Shawn, and Cassie onstage once again."

Cassie hates blind dates. Judging by the look on her face, she was talked into this by the lounge. "Now we'll take a few hands from our audience. We'll need three lucky volunteers."

Cassie's tortured expression is comical, but before I can bask in the hilarity and enjoy more of Kian's fries, his hand grasps my wrist.

I look in horror at our raised hands. For some reason that I'm sure is orchestrated by the flying baby, the host points right at us. He says something into the mic, but my blood bubbles so furiously I don't hear it.

"What the hell are you doing?" I hiss.

Kian's showy smile goes nowhere as he mutters, "Just trust me?"

"Kian, I swear I will stab you with my heel if you don't let go."

"I'll owe you. Anything you want, I promise." When he sees my glare, his smile falters. "Please?"

There is a split second when his earnest eyes and desperate plea almost sway me into playing this dumb game. But then I catch all the eyes on us, and I snap out of it.

Trying to pry my hand away without making a scene is impossible with his steel grip. Kian pulls me through the crowd and up the wooden steps. The idiot knew about this game, and it's the reason he dragged me down here. It's his only chance to get a date with Cassie, and I'm not just his buffer; I'm his excuse.

While I plan how I'm going to hurt him once I'm off this stage, Kian happily introduces us. Our linked arms make us appear as a friendly pair, but it's more for his safety.

I barely hear the host's stupid joke about joining the game himself to get my number. My expression quickly shuts the laughter down, and he turns back to the crowd to scour for one final victim.

Under the bright lights of the stage, I discreetly elbow Kian, forcing him to duck his head so he can hear me. "You owe me. Big-time."

He nods happily, not at all thrown by my deadly glare.

The crowd is livelier this time. It doesn't surprise me, because Amelia is a catch. Her curly blond hair is pushed back with a brown bandana, and the innocent tutor look is racking up interest. I recognize a few people from campus raising their hands, but only one catches my eye.

"No fucking way," Kian whispers in disbelief, voicing my exact thoughts.

Just like that, our third contestant walks onstage and parks himself beside me. I do my best not to gawk at Aiden as he converses with the host.

He's easygoing and personable onstage, a complete contrast to the raging bitch I'm channeling. He puts an arm around Amelia, who smiles sweetly. His type isn't clear to me, but I didn't expect it to be one of the contestants of a Valentine's blind date game.

The host explains the game called Paper Dancer, where each couple will dance on a square of paper that's folded into a smaller square every round. The objective is to dance without stepping off the paper.

It's a ridiculous game, but I can't exactly run off the stage. And Aiden Crawford volunteered, so the competitive girl in me wants to make him lose.

My blind date introduces himself. "I'm Shawn."

"Summer." I take the hand of the tall, curly-haired singer.

"You know, our stage manager forces us into these, but I would've volunteered after seeing you."

I laugh. "Thanks. Though, I would do anything not to be here right now. Nothing to do with you."

He chuckles. "I assumed so from the way Ishida dragged you up here."

When the lights turn pink, the papers are placed on the floor by each pair. A deep voice pulls my attention to couple number three.

"You play guitar? I've always wanted to learn," Aiden says, smiling at Amelia.

Since when? Not once has he mentioned wanting to be musically inclined. Though I'm certain he'd be good at that, too.

"I can teach you. It's not that hard once you practice a few chords."

"You would? If it helps, I've been told I have pretty good hand-eye coordination." The smile he gives her is as innocent as a boy sitting on a church pew. It causes a sweet laugh to bubble out of her.

I snort, bringing their attention to me.

"You okay?" Shawn asks. I look away from a smirking Aiden and allow Shawn to take my hand. I fix my feet between his on the small paper.

Round one is simple enough that we all pass, which is unfortunate, because the sooner this ends, the sooner I can strangle the idiot I call my friend.

Round two means another fold. Shawn lifts me in his arms to tiptoe onto the paper. I look over at Kian, who has Cassie step onto his shoes as they dance, completely lost in each other. I don't have much time to dwell on the sweet moment because Shawn tries to sway, missteps, and loses his hold on me. A chorus of gasps from the audience hits me just as I plop onto the wooden floor with a screech.

If I just lie on the floor, maybe an angel will carry me away. Or a gremlin under the stage might pull me into his embrace. Anything would be less mortifying than facing the audience.

A large hand is the only thing I see through the bright stage lights. When I don't take it, because I feel so disoriented that I'm not sure I can figure out how to grab it, the hand slips around my waist and lifts me in one swift move. From the utter strength of my savior, I know who it is.

"Are you hurt?" Aiden asks. The bright lights illuminate the green in his eyes and the golden brown of his hair. He looks angelic. Maybe I hit my head too. The hand on my waist tightens. "Summer," he urges.

I snap out of it. "I'm okay."

Aiden doesn't look away and neither do I. His muscular arm sears my waist, and his gaze warms my face. When Shawn lets out a frantic apology, I detangle myself from Aiden.

"I lost my balance, and I couldn't hold on. I'm so sorry, Summer." Aiden's jaw tenses as he lands a scathing glare at Shawn.

"It's okay, it was an accident." This is a stupid game anyway, and the only one I'm mad at right now is the guy unaware of everything but Cassie in his arms.

The host makes sure I'm not going to sue the place for injuries before he thanks us for playing. "We have our winners! Everyone give a round of applause to Kian and Cassie!"

I realize Aiden must have left Amelia, so I made them lose too. The partial victory doesn't feel good, but only because of the bruise forming on my back. When the crowd cheers, I'm off the stage and barreling through the lounge before Kian can rope me into something else. Metal doors screech when I exit through the back, and the February air cools my hot skin.

I'm calling an Uber when the door screeches again, and Aiden steps out. "You really wanted that date, huh?"

AIDEN

BROWN EYES SHOOT me a glare that tells me I'm not on her good side tonight. Not that I ever am, but I thought helping her off her ass might have given me a few brownie points.

"No?" I smother a laugh. "It looked like you were falling for him."

Her glare doesn't go anywhere. "Funny."

"No comeback? Are you feeling all right?" I bring the back of my hand to touch her forehead, but she bats it away. "If it helps, he feels pretty bad about dropping you."

"I don't blame him. I'm probably heavier than he expected," she says. "But dropping me in front of all those people? Great for a girl's ego."

"That says more about his lifting capabilities than your weight. We both know how easily I can lift you."

The reminder of how I held her body in my palms dances in the air between us.

Her gaze flickers before she drops it. "You left your date?"

"Amelia's a beautiful girl, but it's better if we part ways," I say dramatically.

"Why? You were flirting with her the entire time."

Summer's magnetic pull brings me an unconscious step closer. "Focused on me, were you?"

"Hard to ignore that blinding douchebag smirk."

"You're really feeding my ego here."

"My life's purpose."

"Aren't you supposed to be nice? You're giving a bad rep to Canadians." With another step, I'm treading on thin ice.

Her back hits the wall this time. "Right, we have to be the nice ones so you can have free rein to be assholes."

"I'm not an asshole."

"I specifically recall 'Fine, I was an asshole' coming out of your mouth," she says pointedly.

"That was to get on your good side."

"You're not on my good side."

"Really? Because I think eating you out for so long my jaw was sore should bump me up on your list."

I bask in the way her breath hitches. "You're . . . vulgar."

I assess the conflicting reactions she gives me. "You know, I don't think you hate hockey players as much as you say you do."

She raises a brow, cheeks pink with heat. "And why's that?"

I still haven't touched her, and it's beginning to feel impossible to keep my hands away. She only has to appear in front of me for my fingertips to inevitably find her skin. What puzzles me is that she's always accepting my touch, and leaning into it as if she wants this as bad as I do, but she does everything not to come to me, not to let herself touch me like she did that night in her dorm. I allow my hand to hover over the material by her thigh. "Because I have a feeling if I slipped my hand under this tiny dress, I'd find you wet. For me."

"What makes you think your hand will get the privilege of going there?" Her voice shakes, the confident words not acting as the facade she hoped.

"The last time I touched you, you begged me not to stop. I'd say I have a pretty solid chance."

"That was you? Huh, I totally forgot about that."

Yeah, right. There's no way she forgot. I've been going mad thinking about how she moaned my name.

"Is that right? So, I wouldn't find anything that says otherwise?" Everything in me needs an agreeable answer. I'm not sure how much clearer I can be about wanting her.

"You'd find me drier than this conversation."

My knuckles beg me to skim the soft skin of her thigh, but I only allow myself to hover over the warm center that's calling my name. Despite her nonchalance, I know what I would find. I've *tasted* what I would find, and there is no denying that she's attracted to me, no matter how she spins it.

The pounding of the pulse point on her neck becomes prominent as a shiver dances along her skin. "Cold?" I tease.

Blazing eyes pierce mine, but no words leave her mouth.

"Ask me to touch you, Summer."

I hope to God the next thing that pushes past those beautiful lips is a moan, and not an insult. Though it turns out anything this girl says turns me on.

"T—"

An annoying screech breaks through the lavender haze, and Summer instinctively pushes me away. Kian finds us standing there like culprits in a major crime. "What are you two doing out here?" He shakes his head when he doesn't get an answer. "Second and third place get a prize too. Come on, we're waiting for you."

"I wouldn't step foot on that stage again even if they were giving away college degrees," snaps Summer. "Besides, my Uber's here."

"You're leaving? We came together. I would have taken you."

"You also tricked me into playing that stupid game. Forgive me if I'm not your biggest fan right now."

"Sunny," he says, defeated.

"Keep that *I owe you* ready, Ishida. You're going to be working overtime to make it up to me."

Kian runs a frustrated hand through his hair and looks at me for assistance. I shrug. I'm annoyed that he interrupted us, so watching him struggle is pure entertainment.

"Let me at least take you home," he tries again.

She rips her focus away from her phone. "It's in your best interest not to be alone in a car with me right now."

Not being the subject of Summer's rage for once is a welcome change. A white Tesla lights up the road.

"I'm sorry, okay?" Kian says. "But even you know this was my only shot at a date with her."

The gravel crunches under her heels when she pivots. "I never said I didn't get it, Kian, and I'm happy you won. But you could have just told me the truth."

"You wouldn't have come."

"And I wouldn't have wanted to strangle you either. You decide what's worse." She ducks into the Uber, leaving us in the dark alley.

Kian runs a frustrated hand over his face. "How forgiving is she?"

My pointed look must convey my answer.

"I guess I have my work cut out for me, then."

TWENTY-FOUR

SUMMER

"LIKE A STIFLER'S mom situation?" Amara asks, shoveling a spoonful of cereal into her mouth.

"More like Stifler's grandma," I say, zipping my bag.

Amara chokes, mirroring my reaction when I found out about Dylan's escapades. "Somehow, those guys continue to surprise me," she says through a bout of coughs. "So, what's your decision on the captain?"

I shrug. "I'm thinking about it."

"What's there to think about? He made you see stars. I'm pretty sure that checks all the criteria."

I put my mug in the sink. "I don't usually do this kind of thing."

"Hooking up?" she supplies.

"We're not hooking up."

"You rode his face into oblivion. Sorry to break it to you, but that screams hookup to me."

"I specifically remember you saying you floated off the couch," Cassie chimes in when she enters our dorm.

"Great timing, Cass." Amara smiles. "We also can't forget how you two were stuck together like glue at his party." Her knowing eyes tell me she saw more than I hoped.

"I was drunk."

"Uh-huh, right," she mocks. "So, let me get this straight. There is a superhot hockey player that makes you laugh and gives you mind-altering orgasms, yet you still don't want to fuck him?"

Cassie lifts her fingers as if to count something that doesn't add up. This is not the intervention I need this morning. I was hoping more for a long list of reasons why this is a bad idea.

"Because we hooked up one time, and he pretty much ran out the door right after," I try to explain.

"That was *after* he left the ball in your court. Or the puck in your . . . rink. Whatever, you get it."

"Time to net the puck. Pretty straightforward," says Cassie.

I shake my head in disbelief. Are these girls my friends, or are they praying for my downfall? "What do you want me to do? Go over there and ask him to fuck me?"

"Yes!" they exclaim in unison.

I blame Kian for this. If he hadn't invited me to the party or dragged me to Starlight, I wouldn't have these thoughts. I wouldn't be thinking about how quickly Aiden lifted me off the ground when I fell or how close he got outside the lounge. If he'd just let me rot in my dorm with a box of pizza, none of this would be happening.

"Take my car."

"I have class. I'm not going there for a nine a.m. booty call."

Amara places her keys in my palm. "Do us all a favor and let that man do unspeakable things to you."

Cassie high-fives Amara, then they shove me out the door.

Five minutes later, I'm sitting in Amara's car, making a mental pros and cons list that somehow only fills up the pros side. If I were well rested, I could make a more logic-driven decision.

Ten minutes have passed in my contemplation, which leaves twenty minutes until my class. I won't be able to sit through 180 minutes of the most coma-inducing lecture on the planet without fixing this situation. The carrot dangles in front of me as I drive to the hockey house.

I make my way up the steps and see Eli in the driveway. "Back for more?" he asks.

"Huh?" Is it obvious what I'm here to do? Maybe there's a big dick with Aiden's name drawn on my forehead that I didn't see.

"More research. Your paper is about hockey, right?"

Right, that. "Oh, yes, it is. Can't get enough of that research!"

He chuckles. "He's in the living room."

The house is quiet, and keeping my heart from falling out of my throat is a challenge when I see the back of his head.

"I'm here."

Aiden lifts his head in surprise, then eyes me from his seat on the couch. "I see that," he says, turning back to his laptop.

I close his laptop, forcing him to remove his hands from the keyboard. "I'm here because I want you." I push the words out with great difficulty.

His expression flashes before it's neutral again. Aiden shifts to get comfortable on the couch, delving deeper into the cushions. "Want me to . . . ?"

"You're going to make me say it?"

He smirks at me. Like a fucking prick. I want to walk out, but I've been battling my head for days. There is no more denying that this is what I want. Also, because I don't want to hear the lecture Amara will have for me if I chicken out.

I stand straighter. "I want you to fuck me."

Aiden scrambles to sit up and give me his full attention.

"Never thought I'd ever hear Sunny say that." Our heads whip to the archway that leads into the living room, and I see four wide-eyed juniors and one very amused Dylan. "You gotta start sharing your secrets, Cap," he snickers.

"*Oh my God.*" My face flames from my neck to my ears. Mortification tickles my bones and pales my skin.

Aiden curses under his breath when he sees my blanched face.

"I-I'm going to go." I make a beeline for the door, ignoring Aiden calling my name. When I'm halfway down the steps, he catches my arm.

"Wait."

I try to wrangle away my arm. "Spare me the humiliation."

He doesn't let go, but turns me to face him.

I groan. "Do you enjoy embarrassing me?"

"I've never embarrassed you. You do that all on your own." He smiles.

"What do you want?"

"You." A part of my chest melts. "Trust me, that's not even in the top ten embarrassing things to happen in that house."

"It was in front of your entire team!"

"It was the juniors. Who cares?"

"I do! Now they think I'm some girl who would do anything for dick."

His brows raise. "Are you?"

Is this really the guy I wanted to have sex with? *Yes.*

I hit his arm, but that only makes him bark out a laugh. Which would be a pretty hot sound if I wasn't so irritated right now.

When warm fingers reach to lift my chin, my stomach flutters. "Did you mean what you said?"

This is no time to be a coward, Summer.

I swallow hard. "Yes."

His tense shoulders relax, and he grins. "Say it again."

"Hell no."

"Come on. One more time," he goads.

I shake my head more seriously now. Aiden shrugs and turns to leave. I fight the urge to roll my eyes when I grab the sleeve of his T-shirt to pull him back to me. He comes easily, not even trying to hide the big smile on his stupidly smug face.

I breathe a dramatic sigh. "I want you to fuck me."

Aiden's eyes light like a kid's on Christmas. "Was that so hard?"

"Extremely," I say. Then the awkward feeling starts to creep back in, and my brain tells me to neatly resolve this situation before it slips from my fingers. "So, like a friends with benefits thing. People with benefits? Or fuck buddies, I guess."

Aiden's jaw ticks. "Right." He rubs the back of his neck, and his bunching biceps momentarily distract me. "Now?"

The word sends a hot burst through me, but I shake my head. "Uh, no." I take a safe step away. "I have class, then I'm going over my paper with Donny. But I'm free Friday."

He tenses at the mention of Donny. "I have practice till seven. How about eight?"

If anyone were to hear us, it would sound like a business meeting, but the ease of the conversation is the only thing keeping me from wanting to wipe myself from the face of the planet.

"Your place? The guys will probably have a party they're not supposed to have here," he says.

"Sure. Amara's out on Fridays."

"Works for me."

I turn to leave but stop. "And can we keep this low-key? I know the guys in there heard me, but I'd rather everyone else not know."

"Embarrassed?" The question is probably meant as a joke, but I'm confused by the prickly contempt that slips into his tone.

"I just don't want everyone in our business."

"Yeah, I get it. I'll see you later, Summer."

TWENTY-FIVE

AIDEN

FORTY-EIGHT HOURS AGO, I was a much happier man. Summer said she wanted me, and I was seconds away from letting a tear of sheer joy fall before we were interrupted by the guys. If it hadn't been for them, I'd have taken her right there on the couch.

When I gave her the choice to find me if she wanted me, this isn't exactly how I pictured it. Mostly because the only thing I've been able to picture this past week is her naked body.

Now I'm waiting for her text to confirm we're meeting tonight. I've taken three breaks since practice started to go to the locker room and check my phone. Coach let it slide, but I'm sure he's going to ream me for it next time. Plus, the punishment I'm opening myself up to is useless because I'm zero for three. Summer hasn't so much as sent a thumbs-up or a simple *K* to any of my texts.

"Crawford."

I toss my phone back in my locker, slamming it shut with too much urgency. "Sorry, Coach, just checking on my grandma."

"You know, I've been a coach for so long, I've heard just about everything. Sometimes I think you kids forget I've lived the life of a collegiate athlete, too. Lies don't interest me."

I release a resigned breath. "I was waiting for a text."

"Shower girl."

Summer would kill me if she knew that's her nickname. I nod, even though it isn't a question. Coach is like an all-knowing wizard, and lying to him has never been something I've accomplished. Though I won't reveal that shower girl is also Summer Preston.

"You gotta get your head on straight, boy. You're never like this. You've been showing up to all the kids' lessons, you've completed your part in Summer's project, and the team has been playing great. Do you wanna lose your balance for a girl?"

"She's the reason I've been on top of all that. It's just . . . different today." Different because I think I might combust if I don't have her under me tonight. And on top of me, and on my face. My heart thumps in my chest like I'm going to lose my damn virginity. This girl clearly has my balls in her fist.

A calculating look passes through Coach's eyes. "Get your ass back on the ice, or I'll have all of you on bag skates for the rest of the week." He walks out of the locker room.

The remaining hour of practice flies by, and I manage not to focus on one girl. The time shifts closer to eight, and my phone is still as dry as ever, aside from texts about a party and a few sorority girls letting me know they'll be there.

"You good, Cap?" Kian runs a towel over his hair as he watches me carefully.

"Fine. Just thinking about an exam I have tomorrow."

"Same. Summer and I have been cramming for psych."

My head snaps up. "You talked to her?"

"Nope, she's still pissed at me. But I see her in class." He scrutinizes me. "Why? You in the doghouse again?"

The proverbial doghouse would be an appropriate appraisal if I'd seen her. "Nah, just wondering."

He nods, slinging his hockey bag over his shoulder. "Are you gonna be at the house for the party?"

This time the party isn't due to the bet. I put an end to that immediately, and because the guys have been on their best behavior since, I'll let one or two parties slide before quarterfinals.

"I'll be out. I'm not trying to be the designated Dad tonight." I follow the guys out of the locker room and pull Kian aside. "Watch him for me." I nod toward Dylan, who sits in his car.

His drinking is getting out of hand, but since he's playing at his normal level, there isn't much I can bring up with him. He's been controlling his anger on the ice, and he doesn't come to practice hungover anymore, which means our talk helped. I care about being a good captain, but being a good friend is more important.

Kian groans. "I don't babysit for free."

"You do now."

He grumbles before shoving his things in the back of the car.

"Aiden, you're not coming?" Dylan asks, lowering the window.

"Nah, I've got something to do."

"I bet you do." He winks, and my answering middle finger has Kian's eyes narrowing in suspicion. Summer is adamant that we keep this a secret, so my lips are sealed. I head to my truck, chucking my bag in the back and checking my messages yet again.

"Your truck is easy to spot."

I startle at the sound of the voice that's been haunting me for days. Summer leans against the door, arms crossed, and dressed in one of her impractical outfits. The skirt is short, and her sweater is entirely too thin for this weather. But she looks so good I find it hard to swallow. Fuck, even if I wanted to be mad for being ignored all day, I know I wouldn't deny her a damn thing.

"You didn't answer my texts." The words come out accusatory.

"My phone's been dead since this morning, so I couldn't tell you that my place isn't available tonight. I came straight here from my lab. Been waiting for twenty minutes."

The elation that melts over me from her words excites something in my pants, too. She waited for me. I fail miserably at keeping any grudge toward her, once I see her sincere face.

"Get in. You're probably freezing." I unlock the doors, and instead of going to the passenger side, she pulls open the back door and climbs in.

"What are you doing?"

"You ask too many questions." She smiles seductively, patting the seat beside her. I scan the deserted parking lot before climbing in, too. This isn't the best place to be alone, considering Coach is a few feet away inside the arena, and we're near a busy street.

Summer fists my shirt and pulls me toward her, eradicating any concerns of possible onlookers. "Aren't you going to kiss me, Crawford?"

I palm her face. Beautiful plump lips that have haunted my every thought are so close, my mouth waters. From the moment I walked out of her dorm, I've been thinking about her lips. Wondering why I hadn't claimed them like I did her pussy.

"I've been dying to taste these lips," I whisper before I capture her next breath in my mouth. It's explosive, a crackling fire that sparks to life. Her soft lips melt into mine, our mouths fusing in a desperate battle. The first glide of her tongue strikes me like a lance of fire. A pulsing sensation caresses my body as I sweep my thumb over the delicate skin of her jawline.

Her kiss is dangerous. Addictive. Part of me is glad I didn't kiss her until now, because if I'd tasted her sooner I wouldn't have held out so long.

I pull Summer to my lap so she straddles me. The instant rock of her hips makes me voice a tortured groan, and she takes the opportunity to slip her tongue inside my mouth. With every dance of her tongue against mine, a quiet shiver rolls through me and blinding fireworks burst behind my eyes. Summer grinds harder, feeling exactly how turned on I am, and I'm trying every trick in the book to not come fast.

She places my hands high on her hips, allowing me to slide them up to touch the silky skin beneath her shirt. Her whimper vibrates against my skin when I touch the lace of her bra, sending a shudder rocking through me.

Summer pulls back to take a breath, her full lips swollen and eyes as dark as night.

She's fucking pretty. Like really pretty. Just being this up close feels like a violent hit to the chest. I can feel this image making a home in every part of my brain.

Soft tendrils frame her face, and when I brush them away, brown eyes glimmer. We're both breathing hard, and my body feels wound up like a toy as I stare at her parted lips.

Desperate, I pull her shirt up until the lacy white bra that barely covers her heavy tits is on full display. The air grows so thick I feel like I'm suffocating. I fist her hair to pull her back to my lips. She doesn't miss a beat as she falls into rhythm, sliding her hands down my abs and hooking them around the waistband of my jeans. Her movements are quick, and I'm dying to free myself and sink into her. But for some fucked-up reason, even with every ounce of blood in my body rushing to my dick, I want to go slow.

I want to hear her voice, to make her laugh, to make her scream when I slowly bring her to her climax. I want all of it all night long. But with the pace she's going, she's ready to get it over with on the cold leather seats of my truck. We've barely spoken a word since we got inside, and I have the clawing need to hear her voice, or her insults, *anything*.

"Did you wear this for me?" I ask as her lips skim the base of my throat, igniting a line of fire, and I absently glide my fingers along the material of her bra.

She pulls back as if trying to figure out why the hell I'm talking. "Yeah, and then I got your name tattooed on my ass."

I laugh, and she smiles. Instantly, I'm vindicated when her raspy voice turns me on to a new degree. I explore the bare skin of her stomach as I glide my lips along her neck in open-mouthed kisses.

"Oh my *God*," she moans when I nip the area just below her ear. I make note of that reaction for future purposes. When she pulls at my waistband again, the whoosh of car tires against the slick pavement outside distracts me from my intoxication.

It snaps me back to reality, and I hold her hands. "Wait."

Wait?

My cock stands still, as if telling me how much I'm going to regret this. "I don't want our first time to be in my truck."

Her eyes soften, but she blinks, clearing away any vulnerability. "Who cares? It's not like I was picturing flowers and candles."

The shitty part is, I would have gotten her those if I wasn't sure she would throw them back at my face. "You deserve more than a quick fuck in a parking lot."

Despite the very disrespectful images running through my mind, I would much rather do all those things to her in my room. Or hers. Anything with a bed and four walls.

Her throat bobs, and I can't tell whether her expression is understanding or annoyed. Summer doesn't look at me as she moves off my lap and fixes her shirt back in place. She doesn't say anything for a long minute, allowing the tension to grow thick enough to taste.

"This nice guy act is starting to get annoying."

Annoyance it is, then.

I sigh. "You can't be mad because I think we shouldn't do this in my back seat."

She finally looks at me, and something frigid settles in the once electric air. "No, I'm not mad. Because unlike you, I'm not letting my emotions get involved in this." Her laugh isn't friendly. "You seriously have to be the first jock to turn down a girl in his lap."

Summer throws open the car door and jumps out, slamming it shut behind her. In the cold secluded air of my truck, I mutter a curse and slide out with an uncomfortable erection in my pants.

She's already halfway across the parking lot before I process what's happening. How the fuck did this go so wrong?

"Let me drive you home," I call after her.

"I have legs. Call me when you're not pretending to be a gentleman."

Banging my head against my car frame doesn't help ease the weight of my stupidity. What was I thinking? A girl like Summer doesn't give an opportunity like this easily, and I let it slip from my fingers in minutes. I seriously need to be evaluated, because she's right. I have to be the first guy to turn down the girl he's been dreaming about. This could have ended with her peach scent rubbing all over my body, but I know despite everything that I would still make the same decision. She deserves better than the view of the arena and the smell of leather.

I sit in my truck and follow behind her to make sure she gets home safely.

This nice guy shit really is annoying.

TWENTY-SIX

SUMMER

I'M SECONDS FROM tossing my five-year plan in the trash and dropping out. How important is it to pursue dreams anyway? Living a life that rivals a crash on the I-95 can't be that bad.

"You've totally disregarded the basis of your original proposal," Donny continues berating my work.

"My research can differ from my proposal. That's the whole point," I argue. This conversation is making my eye twitch. After storming out of Aiden's truck two nights ago, I haven't slept. I couldn't stop thinking about the way he kissed me. Or the moan that left his lips when he rolled his hips against mine. Until his damn conscience became a cockblock.

"The final paper should still be based on it," Donny states.

"I changed a few things in my methodology and literature. That's bound to happen." Arguing with Donny is impossible.

He tightens his jaw and turns to our professor. "Don't you think what I'm saying is correct, Lau—Dr. Langston?"

Donny averts his eyes, and a weird tension looms in the air of her office, as if I'm missing a large piece of a puzzle. The slipup isn't significant, but no one calls Langston by her first name unless you're a colleague. She made it very clear the first time I met her to call her *Dr.* Langston. I guess that's one way of getting your money's worth for a Ph.D.

"Donny has a point. We want to keep the methodology close to your original plan." She reads over the paper. "You're almost done, Summer. I'd hate to see you lose sight of your goal now."

Those words sound a lot like Donny's. When I pack up to leave, he doesn't move. I'm not sure why he still needs her guidance if he got early acceptance to the program.

"I'll send you the edited version," I mutter. Donny doesn't make a move to leave, so I head out alone. I'm halfway down the hall when the door clicks shut.

The odd thoughts in my head burst when I see Shannon Lee parked outside the annex.

"Shannon," I call, waving as she carries a large box into her car. "What are you doing?"

She slams the car trunk shut. "Packing my things." She fidgets with her keys. "Turns out the program's more competitive than I thought."

"Shit. I'm sorry." I pull her in for a hug and she squeezes tight. "They have no idea what a mistake it is letting you leave."

"It's fine, I got into my backup. Go Tigers!" She smiles weakly. "What about you?"

"Just finalizing my application. My backup is waiting for my answer." Stanford University sent me an offer weeks ago, and I'm hoping I'll get to deny it once my Dalton application goes through.

"If I've learned anything, it's to make your own decisions before someone else makes them for you," says Shannon.

THERE ARE TIMES when I let my irritation about one thing trickle into other parts of my life. Today, I feel it happening when I wake up to a stuffed animal sitting on my desk.

A fucking cow plushie.

"Who left this here?" I demand, stepping into the living room clutching the plushie.

Amara shrugs. "Maybe someone enjoys leaving you gifts."

The box of tea Aiden left for me also miraculously made its way inside the dorm. I'm starting to think loyalties are shifting around here. It's pretty clear how this tiny thing sat itself on my desk and watched me while I slept. It's probably the reason I woke up with a start. It's one of those Palm Pals, and the ridiculously adorable cow gives me the urge to rip it in half but also to safely tuck it into bed. The extreme mood swings ravaging my mind are because of one guy.

With a vengeance, I call an Uber, head straight to the hockey house, and ring the doorbell.

"We don't want your cookies!" Cole opens the door, brows pulled tight in irritation until he sees me. "Oh, I thought you were a Girl Scout. You good, Sunny?"

"Can I come in?"

He nods, moving to the side. "Cute cow."

I push past him, climbing the stairs two at a time, heading straight for the door on the left, not caring if he has a girl in there. Strawberries and whipped cream on a pair of tits are the least of my worries. Plowing through the door, I'm hit with his familiar scent, sparking a topsy-turvy feeling deep in my stomach.

The door to his bathroom opens and Aiden steps out, halting when he sees me. He's shirtless and wearing low-riding sweats. He looks unsurprised, which tells me he's noticed the Palm Pal in my hand. He leans against the bathroom door, arms crossed.

"What's this?" I ask, rounding the bed to show him the cow.

"A stuffed animal?"

My eyes narrow. "I know that. Where did it come from?"

"If it's in your possession, shouldn't you know the answer?"

"I'm being serious."

He sighs and moves to sit on his bed. "I won it at the carnival. I was going to give it to you on the Ferris wheel, but . . ." He trails off. The heavy reminder of that night pulls at my gut.

"Why?"

From the way his eyes flare with annoyance, he doesn't like that question. "It's a toy, Summer. It doesn't need to mean anything."

Who wins you a stuffed animal as a token from a carnival without it meaning something? It felt awfully sentimental. From the look on Aiden's face, he's not going to elaborate.

Not wanting to argue, I turn away and head to the door. But impatience lights my skin, and I pause before I can twist the doorknob to exit. "I guess you're still on that nice guy shit, huh?"

Aiden moves so fast I don't register it until his palm is flattened against the door. He hovers over me, green eyes glowing like kryptonite. "You don't like nice guys, Summer? Won't that disrupt your little five-year plan?"

Annoyance tightens my throat. "You're such an asshole."

"Yeah?" He leans in. "Does that make you wanna fuck me now?"

"Screw you."

"I'd rather you do it."

My chest heaves as his breath tickles my temple. "I don't like you."

He takes a suffocating step forward and my heart flips. "Good to know."

I lick my lips, drawing in his weighted attention. "You don't like me either."

His expression softens with an unexpected warmth. "I never said that. I'm pretty sure it's impossible not to like you."

Frustration claws through me, and I react by crashing my mouth to his, either to shut him up or because I've been needing this ever since I got a taste of it in his back seat. When a satisfied moan parts my lips, he reacts quickly, and I feel the wet glide of his tongue as if it were between my legs. The pressure spreads a feverish ache to my core.

I grip his hair when he cups my ass. My back hits the door as we devour each other, his hips on mine and a hand on my throat. The kiss is nothing like the last time. This time it's carnal, almost animalistic the way we go at each other. Like the small taste left us thirsty and impatient.

"You're so fucking stubborn." He smacks my ass.

"Only because you're so irritating."

His hand dips into my leggings and he fists my panties. My desperate sound breaks our kiss, and Aiden's lips find my neck. My entire body flames, and I need him to ease the burn.

My hand cups him through his sweats, and he groans, his face drawn up in pure pleasure. "*Fuck*."

"Can I?" I ask against his lips, and he nods, watching me drop to my knees. "I need your words, Aiden."

"*Yes*, Summer."

My breath hitches as I drag his sweats and boxers down his legs and see all of him. Most importantly, the spider tattoo that sits just below his hip bone. My attention is snatched from the ink before I can question it.

"Tell me you want me in your mouth."

"I want you in my mouth," I say, completely thrown off by the view of him.

Aiden tightens his fist around the thick base and pumps it a few times. My eyes flicker from his hard length to his face when he slaps it against my cheek. "Open."

It's one of the rare times I do as I'm told. I bring my half-lidded gaze up as I take him entirely in my mouth. Aiden grips my jaw and slides in so deep, I have to regulate my breathing to keep up. My lips suction around his shaft, and his hand sinks into my hair.

"Just like that, baby."

Tears spring free from the corners of my eyes when I take him deeper, hitting my throat. Aiden's head falls back on a groan, and I take that as my cue to cup his balls and give them a gentle squeeze. The deepest rumble vibrates against my core, and his hold on my hair is so tight it almost hurts. He pushes me forward to take all of him, and I brace myself with a firm grip on his thighs.

"So perfect. So fucking good, Sum."

My belly flutters, and I squeeze my slick thighs together.

"Fuck. I'm going to come," he chokes out when I take him so deep, I splutter. "In your mouth?" he asks.

When I nod, warm release trickles down my throat, and I swallow his satisfaction. With a low curse, he bends to press his forehead against mine.

"You're going to be the death of me," he says, bringing me to my feet with a tender kiss.

Aiden's hands stay firm on my face, but my burning skin is pleading for his heavy hands. "Touch me," I whisper.

I can feel him smile against my neck when he cups me between my legs, and my breathy noise of approval soaks the room.

Suddenly, I'm tossed on his bed, and he pulls off my leggings, lifting one of my legs to kiss a path to my inner thigh. Soft lips kiss the scrap of fabric until his finger hooks on the waistband. Aiden's hands tremble, as he drags my panties down my thighs. This confident athlete who could have anyone on a golden platter is *trembling*, and it drives an entirely new heat to my core.

I squirm when his gaze warms my skin, and just as quickly his face disappears between my legs. His fingers dig into my flesh, lifting my hips off the bed as his mouth covers me. I grasp his hair as he tortures my clit with painfully good suction.

"You taste so fucking good." His warm breath makes me so hot that my breasts ache with pressure. When he slips his tongue inside me, accompanied by two thick fingers, my eyes squeeze shut, and I swear a tear stains my cheek. He continues at an intense rhythm that rips my breath from my lungs and makes me come so hard I don't have a single thought for several minutes.

I only regain focus when he's kissing my stomach, lifting my shirt higher until his eyes meet mine to ask for permission. I chuckle, pulling it off myself. He removes my bra next and doesn't hesitate to relieve the budding pressure. His thumb caresses the distended nipple on one as his tongue swirls and sucks the other.

I bring my hand to his face, making him look up so I can kiss him again. I love the way he kisses. Slow and attentive, like he's reading exactly what I want. The sweet kiss incinerates any inhibition, and my body lights up with a specific need. The desperation sends a shiver cradling my body, and when Aiden pulls away, he's already smiling.

"That good?" he teases.

I roll my eyes and pull him closer. "Can you fuck me already?"

TWENTY-SEVEN

AIDEN

IF MAKING HER angry ends with her naked and in my bed, I don't think I'll ever stop. Looking at Summer's flushed face and soft skin beckoning for my mouth, I'm thanking the little cow that sits discarded by the door.

Can you fuck me already?

She doesn't need to ask me twice.

Her gaze follows my hands as I stroke my dick, pretty brown irises flaring.

"I hate you," she mutters.

A chuckle escapes me as I move closer. "You're going to hate me even more when you can't walk tomorrow."

"Is that a promise?"

"It's a guarantee."

I press my lips against hers before she can say anything else. If she keeps talking, I'm pretty sure I won't last more than half a second. She lies flat on her back and parts her knees, showing me her sweet pussy wet and ready. Reaching into my nightstand drawer, I take out a condom and roll it on.

My body buzzes, and I kiss her again, tasting her sweet tongue.

Her desperate whimper breaks our kiss, and her back arches on a breathless moan when my knuckles brush her sensitive core.

"Don't be a tease," she chides.

I pull back with a wide grin. "Not a tease." I drag my cock along her pussy and watch her writhe with a soft sound of pleasure. "I just know what you like." I press only the tip inside, and she moans so loud I'm forced to put a hand over her mouth.

"The guys are still sleeping," I whisper, my lips brushing her ear. "And I really want to keep your sweet moans to myself."

She moves her hips against mine, searching for my cock to fill her. Giving her what she wants, I slide in and watch her eyes roll backward. She's so fucking tight I can barely move without feeling the resistance. I try to relax her by removing my hand from her mouth to press it against her clit, the other on her perfect tits.

"Come on. Take all of me."

Her forehead creases. "There's more?"

I hold back my chuckle when I see her disbelieving face. "You can take it. You're doing so good, baby."

I'm holding the back of her head, hovering over her lips. She relaxes in my hold, and I thrust, feeling her fingers dig into me as she muffles a cry into my shoulder.

"Don't stop," she says breathlessly.

I could be having a damn heart attack, and I still wouldn't stop.

"Harder," she demands, and I hesitate at the throaty command but do as she says. I move her legs over my shoulders, holding her firm against me. Her legs stretch when I move forward.

She whimpers, fisting the comforter, mouth parted, her body moving with each thrust. "Oh my *God*, right there."

Hearing her voice her satisfaction gives me a fucking god complex. This might be my favorite time to hear her voice, and I never want her to stop. I lean forward, bringing my hand to the back of her head to lift her mouth to kiss me. She hooks her arms around my neck, so far gone she can't even reciprocate the kiss.

"How are you this flexible?" I ask, seeing how she's folded. Her breathless laugh answers me before she does. "Shut up, Crawford."

Summer wraps her legs around my waist, kissing me with a desperate pull. It surprises me how much she wants to be face-to-face since missionary isn't my go-to. I'm the only one thinking that, because she holds me so tight, her tits crush against my chest, and she bites my shoulder. With how big her personality is, I almost forget how much smaller she is than me. It's obvious when I'm hovering over her, and her small form clings to me.

She shakes around my cock. "Can't. Too much."

I apply just a touch of pressure and watch her shatter. Her muffled high-pitched moan sends a voltage to my dick, and I'm so close I can feel every muscle in my body tighten.

"I'm going to come." My words are hoarse on their way out. With her pulsing around me, I ride out her orgasm as long as I can. Then with strength I didn't know she possessed, Summer flips us around to sit on top of me.

Dark eyes brighten. "You're going to come when I tell you to come."

Fuck.

I'm doing everything in my power not to, but her tits are sliding across my chest, and I'm entranced. Absolutely fucking mesmerized. When she sees my desperation, she smirks. She fucking smirks at me and lifts higher, pulling me out, my erection begging to go back inside her.

"I need to come," I beg.

She leans in, her mouth inches from mine. "Say please."

"*Please.*"

The quick answer must satisfy her, because she holds the base and sits down all at once, buried to the hilt. "Summer . . . Oh fuck, that's it, baby."

With one lazy roll of her hips, I see a flash of white and the pearly gates of heaven through the dizzying array of lights behind my eyes. I would go a happy man.

"Fuck me, Summer," I order, my fingers digging into her flesh when she does, slow, then all at once. It's almost amusing that the only time she's listened to me is when my dick is inside her. Though I don't voice that thought because Summer's palms land on my chest as she works me inside of her so slow, I think I might pass out. Her complacent smile tells me she's holding back.

"Now who's being a tease?"

She rolls her shoulder. "Seeing you suffer brings me joy."

"You won't succeed."

"I think I already am." She smiles, watching my abs tighten with each gyration of her hips.

"Only one of us is winning at this game, and baby, I never lose."

Whether she intends to agree or shoot back a rebuttal, I don't hear it. In one quick move, I clasp both her wrists and flip her on her stomach. She kneels as I pull her up to lay her head against my shoulder, mouth parted in pleasure. I don't think I've ever been this hard in my life. With the way every nerve in my body ignites, I'm sure I could replace a bonfire at a campsite.

"I don't like you," she says through bated breaths.

"Tell me again when I'm not inside you." Her pussy squeezes around me, and when she tries to move her ass into me, I hold her still with a moan stuck in my throat. "I like you in charge, but let's be clear. This pussy is mine, and I'll take care of it."

Those must be the only words she needs, because her face tightens in ecstasy, and she comes apart when I angle myself to hit her G-spot. The deep position triggers my own release.

My forehead falls in the crook of her neck when she drops onto her stomach. I rest my weight on my forearms so I don't crush her. A sheen of sweat covers my body, and her sweet smell hugs every inch of my skin. My high hasn't worn off, and pleasure skips along my bones, wanting more. Flipping away, we're shoulder to shoulder as I stare up at the ceiling and she looks at me.

"That was . . ."

"Yeah," she exhales.

When my heartbeat settles into a steady rhythm, I turn to her. "Five minutes, then we can go again."

"Five minutes?" She stares in horror. "I'm going to need like one to three business days and some serious electrolytes."

I chuckle. "How about ten minutes, and I'll bring up some Bio-Steel?"

She only makes a face, probably because she is happily distracted by my naked body. I roll off the bed to discard the condom and pull on my sweats only for her to boo at me. Unlike Dylan, full frontal this early in the morning isn't my thing. I toss her a shirt for good measure.

"Not very productive if it's coming off in a few minutes," she teases.

"Preventative measures in case one of the guys walks in."

She wears it immediately. Summer's hair is messy, her face flushed and lips swollen. She looks hotter than ever.

"Hungry?" I ask as she slips out of bed to head into my bathroom. She thinks for a minute and shakes her head, but I don't buy that. "I'll get you some breakfast."

TWENTY-EIGHT

SUMMER

I ALWAYS THOUGHT the whole "You won't be able to walk tomorrow" thing was a lie that men who talked a big game often said to inflate their own egos. It's a credible conclusion considering no one has ever been able to make a promise on their word.

But Aiden Crawford has a knack for proving me wrong.

Six times. He made my limbs jelly and sent my body orbiting into space, *six times*. Aiden is a sex god, and it brings me a great deal of pain to admit that.

Damn hockey players and their stamina. Because it's a ten-minute walk across campus to my first class, and I'm thinking of crawling there instead. My body is clearly basking in the stupid and wonderful decision to sleep with Aiden. I didn't even need an alarm this morning with all the singing from my ovaries.

"Need a ride?" Donny stares at me through the window of his black G-Wagon.

"Not from you."

"Come on. You know I'm only trying to help."

"Help? I have to redo an entire section of my paper."

When Donny came over Thursday night, he said my paper needed even more work, and that Langston agreed. Now I have to redo it to add limitations that I had no idea even existed.

"I'll help you with it. Just get in."

Because of my uncomfortable walking situation, I hop in. The royal blue interior that his parents customized when he got into Dalton is spotless. The Ralph Lauren sweater and dress pants he wears look so preppy I have to hold off rolling my eyes.

"Water?" He pulls out a Fiji water bottle from the console.

I take it with a quick thanks, downing half of it. Yesterday's activities left me parched. There wasn't time to recharge, because when Aiden fell asleep, I got into an Uber. There is no reason for me to know that he likes to cuddle or that he doesn't snore.

"Were you out last night?"

When I nod, he glances at me from the driver's side, but I don't elaborate. Donny likes to pretend we're old friends who gossip about our personal lives when that has never been the case.

"You know, partying won't help you get into the program."

Here we go. "I'm not partying."

"You're moving like you're hungover. I'm just looking out for you, Summer. I've known how much you wanted this for so long. I just hope you don't lose it by being careless."

"I know what I'm doing."

"Your paper says different."

A hot spike jabs into my stomach. "You said it was good." I hate the insecurity that laces my words.

"It should be excellent."

I despise his constant patronization, but he's right. "I know. I'll work on it and send it over."

He pulls into the parking lot, and we both head in the direction of our classes. I have no classes with Kian today, which is a pro and a con. A pro because I just spent yesterday with his best friend and if I accidentally slipped up and told him, I wouldn't hear the end of it.

And a con because without a distraction, Donny's words continue to replay in my head.

On my way to the cafeteria, I stop at food services to check my card balance for the month. All the money I have in there is from my savings and the odd jobs I did at the beginning of freshman year. The cashier swipes the card and hands it back.

"It's full. You're good to go."

I stare at the plastic card, checking if it's the right one. There is no way the three meals a day I buy on campus didn't drain every penny. "Are you sure? Can you check again?"

The woman swipes it again, twisting the screen to show me. "You could buy the cafeteria with that much money," she says.

Stepping out of line, my breaths are shallow as I dial my father.

"Morning, Su—"

"I don't need your money."

Lukas Preston has a bad habit of using money to buy love. It may have worked on my sisters, but it won't work on me. I have money in my savings from waitressing the past three years, and the rest is covered with my scholarship. Aside from the money my mom is adamant that I use, my dad has always been my last option.

"It's not about the money, Sunshine. I want to make sure you're doing okay over there."

A resentful scoff rises in my throat. "You should have spent it on someone who could be bought, because it's not me."

"Summer, that is no way to speak to me," he scolds, and a spike of guilt hits. The feeling is so instinctual it's hard to feel vindicated by my behavior. "I'd still like to have dinner when you're free."

"I called because I don't want you spending a penny on me. And no, I'm not available for dinner." I hang up, still feeling that dark twist in my stomach. It lasts for days after I speak to my dad, but I've learned to live with it.

Defeated, I swipe the card for my lunch and find a spot in the lounge. Kian Ishida walks in holding a pink gift basket and wearing a bright smile, pulling me out of my pathetic reverie. His presence is lifting, but I still ignore it.

"Oh c'mon, anything but the silent treatment." He groans like he's in physical pain. "Did you get the Uncle Frank's pizza? And the handmade card? In case you're not a fan of those, I made you a gift basket all on my own. I even included some bruise cream."

If falling on my ass wasn't enough embarrassment, then the bruise cream would do the trick. The basket Kian places in front of me is wrapped with a neat pink bow. Through the poorly taped cellophane, I can see snacks, tea, and skincare items.

It's been days since Kian embarrassed me at Starlight, and he's been working overtime for my forgiveness. The handmade gift pulls at my heartstrings. "I'm not giving you the silent treatment."

"Good, but I'd do this forever if I had to," he says. "You're my best friend, Summer, and I don't take hurting my friends lightly."

I glance at him. "I thought Aiden was your best friend."

"Yeah, and all the guys, but you're my best and only girl friend."

"Wow, what an achievement," I mutter.

"I'd call you my sister, but I don't want to draw that hard line just yet in case Crawford fucks up."

The joke might have been funny if I was in a better mood. "Hey, you never told me what it was like."

"What?"

"Being dropped on your head as a child."

He scowls.

As stupid as Kian is about ninety percent of the time, hearing him call me his best friend feels like a warm hug. It's rare that I get this close to anyone, but with him, it feels natural. I won't tell him now, but he's one of my best friends, too.

TWENTY-NINE

AIDEN

HOW SOON IS too soon to text someone after a hookup?

I'd say I'm well versed in post-hookup etiquette, but when it comes to Summer Preston, all my experience is out the window.

I'd be lying if I said I wasn't expecting a text from her the morning after she left—snuck out in the dead of night—to tell me she had fun or to schedule another romp in the sheets. That's usually how morning afters work for me. But of course, this girl is going to be different.

Last night in itself was different. It was the best sex of my life, and I don't really know how to move on after knowing that. With itching impatience, I pull out my phone and text her.

SUMMER

Aiden: Get home safe?

It's a cowardly move, but I'm not confident I'd get a reply if I texted her anything else. I'm not sure if caring about her safety will get me one either, but it's worth a try. I'm banking on her feeling bad about disappearing. The last thing I expected this morning was seeing the right side of my bed empty, especially since it still smelled like her. Since *I* still smelled like her.

> **Summer:** If I didn't there would be cops at your place right now.
> **Aiden:** You think I'd be a suspect? I guess yesterday's noise complaints wouldn't help my case.
> **Summer:** I have no idea what you're talking about.
> **Aiden:** Maybe I can remind you. When are you free?

The grin on my face is embarrassing, but the memories replaying in my head definitely aren't. Checking my phone three times a minute doesn't seem to garner a reply, so I put it away. The desperation to touch her or hear her voice is debilitating. Not ideal because I have a meeting with Kilner today.

Our first-line defense has been slacking, so Kilner wants to pull someone up. As captain, I've been given the responsibility of compiling names, despite the guys being pissed about the sudden change.

Downstairs, I see Kian slip on his shoes. "Where are you going?" I ask.

"You're kidding. Even my professors know about tonight."

Seeing his outfit, I recall, "Your date with Cassie."

It took Kian three days to choose an outfit. Summer helped finalize one because apparently, she forgave him. Which is annoying as hell because she's never forgiven me that easily.

Kian fixes his tie and nervously heads to his car. I do the same, except my night is going to be spent with an angry Coach Kilner, who won't be happy that I can't help but zone out every few minutes.

PEACH-SCENTED SILK SLIPS through my fingers. "You have amazing hair."

Two days after my first message, Summer finally texted me her schedule. Two whole days. It was absolute torture. But we managed to carve out a few afternoons and the rare morning. She's firm on her no sleepover rule because it treads too close to the relationship category. I don't care as long as I get to see her.

"You can thank my mom for that. She used to oil my hair growing up and now I'm addicted."

"Oil?" I ask curiously. This is my favorite part. When we talk about anything and everything. Things I'd never get to know about her otherwise.

"You've never had oil massaged into your scalp?" she asks, eyes wide with surprise.

I shake my head. "Can't say I have."

"You're missing out. It used to be my favorite thing." She lies back, and I run my hand over the smooth skin of her arm.

"You don't do it anymore?"

She lets out a nostalgic breath. "I do, but having someone else do it is a whole other feeling."

"I can do it for you."

It's the silence before she bursts into laughter that has me furrowing my brows. She catches her breath, losing it again when she tries to talk. "You did not just say that."

I frown. "What?"

She laughs again, bewildered as she stares at my blank expression. "*I can do it for you*? No guy just offers to oil hair. I've literally never heard that before."

Is that a weird thing to say? Fuck, maybe I should google serial killer tendencies again. "Well, you said it's your favorite thing. If it makes you happy, I'd do it."

All the residual humor dissipates, and her eyes lock with mine. All my senses focus on her.

Then her gaze drops, snapping the tight string between us. "That's a bit much for fuck buddies."

Her words are a grimy knife to the gut. But before she can say something else that digs a hole out of my chest, I lean in and kiss her.

"Ow." Summer rears back, breaking our kiss.

"What's wrong?"

"Your beard," she mutters, rubbing her chin. "It's scratching me."

My growing playoff beard is at that awkward length that leaves the friction burning Summer's skin whenever I kiss her. She hasn't said much about it, but I can tell she's not its biggest fan.

"You weren't complaining when it was scratching the inside of your thighs."

She rolls her eyes, and when I go in for another kiss, she stops me. "I have homework."

"You kicking me out, Preston?" I settle for a kiss on her cheek. Trying to spend an extra second with her is nearly impossible lately. She was with Donny this morning, so I expected her to be a little distant. It's become obvious she feels guilty about what we're doing.

Summer steals my hoodie from the end of the bed. I have a T-shirt, so I don't care if she takes it; it looks better on her anyway.

"Yes." She tries escaping my hold, but I pull her back to stand between my legs.

"I'm starting to feel used."

She raises a brow. "Try being bent in ten different positions."

"Come to my game tonight." Summer makes a face and I sigh. "Give me one good reason why you won't." I have never invited a girl to a game, but having Summer sitting rinkside feels right.

"One: I don't like hockey. Two: I'm not sitting in the stands wearing your jersey to fulfill your weird fantasy."

A sliver of humor rises up my throat. "One: You like *me*. Two: I think Crystal wears my jersey anyway."

"What?"

I examine her incredulity with delight. "The guys noticed she's been wearing it ever since the carnival."

The look is replaced with indifference. "When you hooked up with her."

I glower. "*No*. Nothing happened. She's just trying to get my attention now."

"Does she have it?"

"What?"

"Your attention. Does she have it?"

The question catches me off guard. I didn't think Summer even cared where my attention was. *Is she jealous?* "If you haven't noticed, I've been a bit preoccupied." I pull her in for a kiss that she finally reciprocates. "So, are you coming or not?"

"Not." She releases herself from my hold and heads to the bathroom. "I have work to do."

I follow her to block the door. "You're mad."

"I'm not."

"Fine, then you're jealous."

I must be enjoying her reaction too much, because she glares. "You wish."

"Then why is this here, hmm?" I press a finger to the crease between her eyebrows. "Contrary to what you believe, I know you, Summer."

"You know my body, Crawford. You don't know my mind."

"I bet I can figure it out just as quickly." She tries to close the door, but I don't let her. "I don't even get to shower with you?"

"I'm taking a quick one."

"Me too, just a quickie." That splinters her annoyed glare. "Don't you at least want to wish me luck before my game?"

"We both know you don't need luck."

"Yeah, but I do need this." I reach around to grab her ass, and she yelps before melting into my arms. Walking backward into the bathroom, I kick the door closed.

TUESDAYS ARE MY favorite. Why? Because Summer has no classes and I'm free after my coaching session. Another plus is not worrying about the guys throwing parties, because we have practice on Wednesdays, and hangovers don't mix well with Kilner's voice.

Walking into Summer's dorm, I drop my bag by the couch. "Those little tyrants know how to wear me down."

"Don't complain. You love it," she says when I crash beside her with a groan. "Admit it. You do."

I shrug, but I can't suppress my smile. "Yeah, I do. They're pretty amazing. I get to see their passion, and it reminds me how much went into getting me where I am today."

Admiration flits through her eyes but then her face scrunches. "God, I bet all your kids are going to be hockey buffs."

"Definitely. They'll learn to skate before learning to walk."

"Sounds torturous. What if they want to play soccer or . . . basket-ball?" She adds the latter suggestion purposely, but her smile is so pretty I have a hard time focusing on anything else.

"I'll support them no matter what." I wasn't pressured into sports, so putting an ultimatum on a kid never made sense to me. People are naturally drawn to their talents, but to get to the top it takes hard work, and that doesn't come from force.

"How magnanimous of you."

"What can I say? Our kids will be lucky to have me as a dad." The words spill like water, and I freeze.

The awkward air hovers for only a second before she laughs. "You're crazy if you think I'd ever carry your big-headed children. Your wife better have a wide birthing canal."

That eases the tension drilling my chest. "I'll add it to my list. A wide birthing canal for large-headed children."

"Don't forget, willing to suffer through your idiocy."

"Is that what you do? Suffer?"

She nods, not paying me her full attention until I lean over to move her laptop. She doesn't protest when I wrap my hand around her ankle and tug her to me, homework abandoned. Contentment skips my bones because Summer never abandons her books, but right now her only focus is me.

She smells so good I dip my head to kiss her neck, burying my nose in her sweet smell. "Is this considered suffering?"

She sits on my growing erection. "Yes," she breathes. "Complete torture."

I slide up her white tank top, looking at her for permission. She doesn't waste time, removing it herself. Braless tits are so close to my mouth that I have to shift her on my lap to keep a semblance of control. I push her hair behind her bare shoulders, touching every expanse of skin except where she wants it. My hands run along the outline of her body, only grazing her full tits, which pulls a frustrated noise from her. Summer's fingers dig into my shoulders, and when I look at her, her eyes are ablaze.

"I'm half naked in your lap, Crawford. It doesn't take a genius to figure out what I want you to do."

I move just a hairbreadth away from her strained nipples. "I know what you want. It's always clear what your body wants from me, Summer, but I know you like it like this. When I tease you, make you *suffer*." My breath blankets her goose-bumped skin as I leave gentle kisses between her tits. The hand squeezing my shoulder moves to the nape of my neck.

"Don't tell me you want me to beg, because that's never going to happen," she declares.

Slapping the side of her breast, I watch it bounce. "Only good girls get rewarded. And you're not being a very good girl right now."

"I'm a brat, you've said it yourself." She moves closer so she can whisper in my ear, her tits pressed against me. "Now make me come, *Captain*."

I swallow so hard I'm surprised my tongue doesn't go down.

Games are my thing. I'm good at them, good enough that I always win, but here, Summer wins. Every time. There's no chance I could ever refuse her, especially when she smiles like that or draws her bottom lip between her teeth with a deceptively innocent look. The sweet tits in my face are also a plus.

My hands fly to the buttons of her jeans, and hers to my belt. We're fumbling, trying to shed our clothes as quickly as we can. She shifts from my lap to peel her jeans off. The eagerness is almost animalistic as we focus on one goal.

"I want you like this. Want you to ride me," I say when she's naked and back on my lap.

She takes me in her hand, giving me a slow pump. I shift to angle her perfectly, my hands spanning the entire width of her waist, and I revel in how much smaller she is than me.

"*Fuck*, wait," I grit out before she lowers herself. "Condom."

But when I reach over to grab my bag, she stops me. "I'm on the pill."

It takes everything in me not to choke and form a sentence. "Okay . . . I'm clean," I say, clearing my throat. When she nods, there's no hiding my shock. "Are you sure?"

"Yes," she says. "I trust you, Aiden."

With warm pleasure blanketing my chest, I take hold of her hips and sit her on my cock so slowly, my head lolls. Every inch of her squeezes me like a tight, wet fist with three simple words fluttering around us.

Summer's fingers tighten in my hair when her ass slaps my thighs. Her face scrunches in half pain, half pleasure as I move her up and down my length.

"You're so tight, Summer. Fuck, I can't get enough of you."

She closes her eyes and rests her forehead against mine, but I can't take my eyes off her. Her face, her tits, her taking me so well. She's mesmerizing. Nothing I've imagined holds a candle to the reality of her. When I kiss her, her pace slows, and she rolls her hips, causing me to let a rough moan into her mouth.

"You feel so good," she praises, leaving kisses all over my face.

"You like my cock? You like that only I fill you up?" My throat is tight when she nods. "Then be good and take it all."

Her eyes brighten. "Who said I'm a good girl?"

"We both know you are when you're riding my cock. Now make me proud, baby."

She shifts back, bringing her hands behind her to rest them on my thighs. She slides down until I'm buried deep, her nails digging into my skin. I lose my breath at the view of her naked body taking me bare inside her pussy. I'm living a wet dream, and I can't remember how to function.

She smiles when she sees my tight jaw and wild eyes, then moves high until only the tip throbs inside her. I groan.

"Am I being a good enough girl for you, Aiden?" I lean back to look between us and bask in the wet sounds of her arousal. "So fucking good, Summer. So good."

She hums and lowers herself again. "Then don't touch me."

My eyes are so focused I barely process her words. "What?"

"I want you to watch me. No touching."

"Fuck no." My grip tightens. But she stops, sliding up until my dick threatens to bob out of her.

"Your choice."

"*Okay*," I concede, pulling away my hands. "Okay."

Her wicked smirk matches her rhythmic movements, threatening my sanity. With her face inches away, she buries me to the hilt, and I struggle to keep my eyes open.

"I'm going to come." The words grate against my throat. "Tell me to come inside you." I whisper the demand against her lips as my hands dig into the couch, itching to touch her.

A heavenly sound leaves her and she whispers, "Come inside me."

"Then let me touch you, baby," I beg. "*Please.*"

She must take pity on me, because she takes my hands and brings them right to her full tits, and I squeeze. She's so wet, I can feel it all over my thighs. My thumb presses her clit, and I pinch it between my fingers. She cries out, slumping forward, and the tremor and the tight grip of her pussy make me come too.

It's her sated smile when she drops her forehead to mine that cracks my chest wide open.

Fuck.

THIRTY

SUMMER

IT'S THAT TIME of the month when everything starts to make sense. Crying over a car commercial about International Women's Day, wanting to tear a certain hockey player's clothes off, and eating everything in our emergency snack drawer. It all makes sense when I get my period.

It's an unwelcome surprise, because I had written off my aches and pains to hunching over my laptop and pulling all-nighters at the library. I sent in my final draft last week, and it received a reluctant stamp of approval from Langston. I expected relief to sink in and that tornado in my stomach to settle, but instead, I've become more fraught. Because this is it. I'll soon find out if I've worked hard enough to make my grad school dreams come true.

The thoughts are depressing, and the unrelenting torture from my uterus isn't helping. Amara asked if I needed something before she left, but I told her not to worry. Now, after a few hours of rotting in my bed and throttling the life out of my poor stuffed cow, I could use some serious painkillers. Crying and moaning haven't subdued the pain, so I'm hoping she comes home soon.

Over my groaning, I hear rustling in the kitchen. "Amara, is that you? Will you break into the pharmaceutical sciences building and get me some morphine?"

But when my bedroom door opens, Aiden is standing there.

He's wearing a gray suit, crisp white dress shirt, and royal blue tie. You can tell how large his arms are even under the jacket, and he looks so *hot* I can't contain myself. He leans against the doorframe with a smile. "Hi, Summer."

I think I might be drooling, so I turn to press my face into a pillow. "I'm out of commission," I say, my voice muffled.

He chuckles. "You know that I like seeing you even when we don't have sex, right?"

That is mostly true, I suppose. This past week we hung out more times than I can count, and it ended with us talking for hours or watching a Turkish show instead of our original arrangement.

He looks so handsome in that suit, and it's confusing the hell out of my ovaries. I'm so hot for him it's concerning. "Why are you still here? Don't you have the Ohio State game?"

"Home game. Wanted to stop by and see you first."

"Don't think you can win without me at your game? Don't worry, I'll be there in spirit after I die from these cramps."

He shakes with laughter. "Amara told me you weren't feeling well, so I brought you something." He leaves my room and comes back with a bed tray. There's steam clouding out of my favorite mug, a box of chocolates, a warming pad, and best of all, some extra-strength ibuprofen.

I sit up, allowing him to lay it over my lap. My eyes begin to sting. "When did you do this?"

"While you were screaming into your pillow."

"I was not screaming. Just gently cursing Mother Nature." I take the warming pad and place it over my stomach. I eye the mug with suspicion, bringing it to my lips. It's perfect. Aiden even added ginger, and my heart burns a little, this time not from the overuse of cinnamon. "You've been practicing?"

"Dylan's been teaching me. He used to make it for his mom."

The thought of two hockey players hovering over a stove to make the perfect chai makes me smile. "Thank you."

"Anything for you," he says softly. "Want me to get your laptop so you can watch something?"

Still stuck on his words, I slowly shake my head. "The only way I'll get my mind off the pain is by taking a nap."

He nods and leans in to kiss my forehead. Once, twice, three times. Each kiss causes a devastating flutter to erupt in my stomach. He shouldn't be playing with my emotions like this, especially not right now.

"Stay," I blurt because apparently, I'm an idiot. He pauses halfway to the door, and my dumb request makes my heart twist like a coiled spring. When his hooded gaze meets mine, I'm breathing so hard I might be panting.

Aiden stalks over to me, pulls my chin forward, and kisses me so thoroughly that butterflies ravage my uterus. When he pulls back, he stares at me with a thunder of emotions behind light eyes.

"I have that game."

"Right. Obviously. I don't know why I said that." Do cramps also make you stupid?

He watches me for so long that I think there might be something on my face. He reluctantly pulls away, like leaving right now is bringing him a great deal of pain.

But then he says, "Give me a few hours."

I watch his broad shoulders and hard back exit my bedroom with a soft click of the door.

I STIR FROM deep sleep when my mattress dips and a warm body sneaks under my comforter. A heavy arm drapes over my waist, relieving the sparks of pain that still flare there. Aiden's clean scent envelops me in a comforting hug, and I think I might be dreaming.

He pulls me so close our bodies curve together like two puzzle pieces, his legs tangling with mine. With a deep inhale, he buries his head in the crook of my neck and plants a featherlight kiss there before he starts massaging circles just below the waistband of my sleep shorts. It's as if he senses the tightness in my body, and his magical hands unravel it within seconds.

I hum in pleasure and absentmindedly move my hips into him. He grunts a sound of disapproval, and when I try to turn, he doesn't let me.

"Go back to sleep," he murmurs. His warm breath dusts the shell of my ear, and a shiver erupts. Aiden takes that as me being cold and pulls the comforter higher under my chin. Honestly, I'm kind of burning in the heat of his body, but I'd rather have a heat stroke than tell him to move.

"How was your game?" I ask anyway.

"OT win. I was dying to get back here," he admits, kissing my temple. "Now go to sleep, baby."

I smile at the wall, wrapped up in everything Aiden. His smell, his body, his words. Everything is mine at this moment, and I don't want it to end.

MY FIRST ALARM should have been when I woke up smelling Aiden. My second alarm should have been Cassie's loud voice on the other side of the door.

Unease tickles into my stomach when I feel hard muscles underneath me and open my eyes to Aiden's sound-asleep face. It's peaceful, and smooth since he shaved the stubble. But just seeing him here sets alarms blaring in my head. We've explored every part of each other's bodies, but we've never actually *slept* together.

"Donny! You're here early," Cassie's voice drifts over again, and my heart drops. His name disintegrates the remaining fog in my brain. I completely forgot we were meeting today.

I twist away from Aiden, but he's holding me so tight I can barely move. The heavy weight of his hands relieved my residual pain, and I will be forever grateful for that. But right now I need him gone.

"Aiden," I whisper, but he doesn't stir. When I jostle him, his grip tightens as he stretches. Sleepy eyes find my face inches away.

Then he smiles.

He's so content I wonder if he realizes it's me he's looking at. His large hand comes to my face, letting his thumb smooth across my cheek. The touch is so delicate that I hold my breath when he tucks a strand of hair behind my ear and leans in.

I should move. I should really move.

When footsteps sound outside my door, I jerk, tumbling out of his hold and onto the floor.

"You good?" Aiden's deep voice is laced with sleep as he stares at me over the edge of the bed.

I'm already pulling a hoodie over my head. "Great," I mumble, fixing my hair.

Aiden's still lying there, propped up on an elbow. "Summer, what's going on?"

I sigh. "Donny—"

Rap rap rap

"Summer, Donny's here."

"Give me a sec, Cass." I frantically fix my hair and turn back to Aiden. "You need to climb out the window."

"Excuse me?"

"Now!" I urge.

"I'm not climbing out of a four-story building, Preston."

I run an impatient hand through my hair. "Why not? Isn't that what all those muscles are for?"

He releases a tired breath. "We don't need to hide from him."

"I don't. You do."

His jaw ticks. "That asshole is not going to dictate how I spend my time."

"Aiden, I can't do this right now. Can you just hide in my bathroom?"

Rap rap rap

"Summer?" Donny's voice filters through the door.

My heart catapults to a different dimension when Aiden still hasn't moved. "Please?"

He grumbles but disappears into my bathroom. Guilt pricks at me, seeing the wounded look on his face, but I don't have time to dwell.

I yank open the door, and Donny pierces me with a suspicious look. When he looks at my clothes, I stare down at the dark blue hoodie. Aiden's hockey hoodie. Shit.

Donny raises a brow, and his eyes sweep the room behind me. I wait for his know-it-all attitude and his slew of questions. Instead, he hands me a paper and gestures to the living room. "We should talk about your analyses."

I follow him out of my room.

THIRTY-ONE

AIDEN

SITTING ON A toilet lid in this tiny bathroom is not my ideal Saturday morning. It's a rest day, so I would have preferred spending it in bed with Summer on top of me, but she didn't stay long enough for that. Any possibility of making that a reality burst when Donny fucking Rai became our full-time cockblock.

When her bedroom door creaks, I take it as my sign to head back out. I will need a serious stretch after sleeping on her bed and then being shoved into her bathroom. Summer runs a hand through her hair before collapsing on her bed.

"How'd it go?"

She jerks. "Shit, I forgot you were here."

"Yeah, I'm still here," I mutter. "What did he want?"

"Something about the scale I'm using," she mumbles, putting her hair up. "I need to focus on some work. I'll text you later?"

I don't expect the jolt of irritation that hits me at her words. Being locked in her bathroom for an hour might have eaten at any patience I had left. "Why do you always do this?"

"Do what?" She's barely paying attention as she makes her bed.

"You talk to him, and then you're completely withdrawn."

Her movements pause. "That's not true."

"Don't pull that shit with me, Summer. Why are you letting him control your life?"

She doesn't make eye contact. "I'm not."

"Really? Because you were just about to kick me out."

"Because I have work to do." She's still fiddling with the sheets when I approach her. Slowly, she brings her eyes to mine, and the guard she keeps so high starts to slip.

"You can tell me."

There's an exasperated breath before she speaks. "Fine, yes, I pull away. But it has nothing to do with him. Every time I remember the project, I'm reminded of everything on the line, and I hate that I let myself get distracted."

"You think I'm a distraction?"

"It's not the insult you think it is, Aiden." She sits on her mattress, defeated. "I don't want either of us losing focus or shifting priorities."

"Priorities change."

"What are you saying?"

That I'm falling for you. "That I can focus on hockey and you."

Turns out Kilner was right. Finding the balance depends on figuring out the things I consider priorities. She has quickly become one of mine, and that isn't changing anytime soon.

"That's not true. You can only focus on one thing effectively." She drops her hands in her lap. "If this is about sex, I'm sure any girl on campus would happily give it to you."

The words sound simple enough, but the damage they do makes me take a step back. I can't even think about another girl when this stubborn one is the one I want. "This isn't about that."

"Of course it is! That's all we do. It's all we agreed on."

My eyes narrow. "Then when's the last time we had sex?"

"What do you mean? It was—" She falters, unable to find a reality where our relationship amounted to one thing.

"Exactly. Even you know our relationship isn't only about sex." I take a step closer. "We've been together every day for the past few weeks simply because we like to be around each other. Why can't you just admit that?"

She bites the inside of her cheek, eyes set on her lap. "That sounds like more than I signed up for, Crawford."

"Admit it."

She releases a shaky breath. "I can't, okay?"

"Why not?" I prompt.

"Because you're a *hockey player*." She says the last two words with disdain, like every other time.

My frustration grows heavy. "What do you have against us?"

"Nothing." Her expression shadows with reluctance. "It's not a very interesting story."

"I don't need it to be." I sigh. "Come on, you know I would never judge you. You can tell me if it's an ex or—"

"My dad."

"Your . . . dad?"

"My dad was a hockey player." She gauges my reaction. "I know, a psychology major with daddy issues. Big surprise, huh?"

"That's not at all what I was thinking. I had no idea he played."

"He's played my entire life."

"So, he's the reason you hate the sport?"

"I don't *hate* it." My blank stare makes her release a breath. "Okay, maybe a little." She glances at me. "Fine, I don't like it because it reminds me of everything my dad chose over me."

I sit beside her on the bed, speechless. Finding out her dad is a hockey player is more shocking than finding out Kian slept with Tabitha even after she stalked him and all of us.

"My parents had me when they were young. My mom was in college, and my dad had just gotten drafted. Getting pregnant flipped everything they knew. My mom really stepped up, and my dad got to play like he didn't have a daughter waiting for him to come home.

So, I knew early on that to him, this sport was way more important than the kid who ruined the life he had planned."

"Summer, that's terrible."

She shrugs. "Anyway, that's who called that time at the pool. My dad is the interim coach for Boston."

"Boston's coach is Luk—" I pause. "*Lukas Preston* is your dad?"

She nods.

"Number one draft pick, two-time Stanley Cup, and Art Ross winner, Lukas Preston?"

"Yes." She watches me as I try to contain my shock. From the looks of it, she's been through this before.

"How did I not know this?"

"I don't particularly advertise it. I'd rather not think about him." She falls back on the bed, hands resting on her stomach. "That's why it's so hard for me to do this. Us."

I lie down beside her. "Because I remind you of him?"

She sighs. "Because you remind me of everything he loved more than me. He's dedicated his life to hockey."

I feel like complete shit. "I'm sorry, Summer. I had no idea."

"Don't be. It's not like I told you."

I intertwine our hands. "You can, you know. Tell me, I mean."

"Thanks, but sharing my daddy issues with the guy I'm sleeping with isn't exactly my idea of unwinding."

Reducing me to the guy she's sleeping with feels like she's tossing my heart into a blender. I do my best to chuckle, but it's hoarse. "Well, the guy you're sleeping with is also your friend. So you don't need to keep everything bottled up."

"I don't. Sampson obviously knows, the girls too, and I've had pretty intense therapy sessions."

Everyone knows that Tyler Sampson's dad was in the NHL. Not because he advertises it, but because he's never bothered to hide it. Summer grew up with him; it's only reasonable that it's because she's from a hockey family, too.

"And now I know," I add.

"Right, now you know."

"You're not going to tell me not to tell anyone else?"

"Nope. There's this super weird thing called trust that you've seemed to earn a lot of."

My smile is impossible to suppress. The last time she said it, I was bare inside her. But this time it feels like she's finally showing me all of her. "You trust me?"

"We're friends, aren't we?"

"I thought I was just the guy you're sleeping with."

She gives a playful shove to my chest. The touch sends an electric rush rippling down my spine. "For your information, we actually haven't done that recently."

"Are you keeping count? I would never." I put a hand to my chest in mock offense.

She nods, pointing down. "I think someone is."

"We can't upset him."

"Definitely not. We should rectify this immediately."

I pull her on top of me and kiss her. The content sigh that leaves her warms my skin as I cup her face. "I mean it, by the way. We're friends. You can talk to me anytime about anything. I'll always listen to you."

"I know you will, Aiden." Her thumb grazes my jaw before she slides down my abdomen. "But I need you to be very *un*friendly to me right now."

I smile. "Whatever you say, Summer."

THIRTY-TWO

SUMMER

SPRING BREAK IS only a few weeks away, but at Dalton, it isn't really "spring" or "break."

It's in this awkward stage during the last week of March when the frost still covers the ground, and we only get a week off from classes. For the last few years, I've spent the break at Amara's house. Partly because I didn't want to fly back home to even colder weather, and mostly because I didn't want to see my dad. However, this year my parents are in Boston, which means my mother has bombarded me with a dozen calls on how excited she is that I promised to have dinner with her.

Never promise your mother anything while you're in a rush.

My excuse of spending my time in Texas with Amara's family is a flimsy lie now that she's not going home for break. She and that big brain of hers got invited to a tech conference in San Francisco, and although she invited me to go with her, I don't want to invade her experience. I'm leaning toward spending a pretty penny on a nice hotel accompanied by a suitcase of books.

But right now I push aside those thoughts when I hear the guys downstairs, and a flutter of nerves erupts in my stomach. Aiden doesn't know I'm here. My hands are so clammy, I've washed them with his peach-scented hand soap three times. The last text I received from him was a picture of his group of mini mites winning their scrimmage this morning. Aiden was carrying one of the kids on his shoulders as she proudly held up her medal. It was so ridiculously cute, I made it his contact picture.

The door opens, and I almost dive to the ground and make a home with the monster under his bed. He hasn't even seen me yet, and I already regret this. I should have just gone to the library.

Before I can contemplate, he steps inside. He looks like the stereotypical hockey player, in his gray sweatpants and overgrown hair peeking out of the baseball cap. Even the outline of his sculpted abs is visible under his tight long-sleeve.

He makes a sound of surprise seeing me sitting on his bed. His eyes ping around my face, down my outfit, and again to my face. He's stunned, and I feel like an idiot.

He runs a hand through his hair. His biceps momentarily distract me from the nervous friction in my stomach. My heartbeat gallops, and I try to control the rapid rise and fall of my chest, but Aiden sees it. He must also notice my indecent top, judging by the way his Adam's apple bobs.

After I told him about my dad, I expected things to get weird. That's usually how it goes when people find out your dad's an NHL legend. But Aiden never brought it up again. He didn't ask for an autograph or to put in a good word for him, though he doesn't exactly need it. It's like I opened a jammed door, and now the moths have cleared, and the cobwebs are dusted. It leaves all the nerves I had about letting someone in a little easier to cope with.

Kneeling on his bed, I barely reach his height. "I didn't mean to drop in like this. I just—"

"Stop." He smooths his hands over my arms. His expression is tender when he kisses my forehead. "I'm just surprised."

"Good surprised?"

"*Very* good surprised."

My erratic pulse doesn't slow, but his words calm the dark feeling in my stomach. His approval skates between my legs. I move forward hoping he'll kiss me before I malfunction, but he pulls away.

"You smell too good for me to ruin that." He moves to grab a towel. "I'll shower first."

I nod, even though he doesn't smell. Not to me, at least. It's odd, because the last time Kian hugged me after practice, I all but launched him across the room for touching me while smelling like a rotting pair of socks. Since then, he's been extra cautious about even walking by me after a game.

Aiden drops his stuff by his closet. His phone pings, and when he checks it, the drop in his mood is palpable. He stares at the phone for a long minute.

"Is everything okay?"

He ignores me and types out a text. Trying not to pry in what isn't my business, I stay quiet. For all of two minutes.

"Am I keeping you from someone?" The question is harsher than I intend, but he's starting to irritate me. The slow lift of his head and those piercing eyes bring an unknown heat to my neck. "If I am, I can see myself out."

I drop my eyes and climb off the bed. The temperature in the room rises to a degree that makes my clothes uncomfortable. But I don't dwell for long, because when I walk past him, he stops me with a hold on my wrist. A conflicting emotion clouds his features, and another I can't quite pinpoint.

"You want to leave?" he asks.

"You seem preoccupied, and I don't like to be ignored."

With a sigh, he releases my wrist and moves to sit on the edge of his bed. My anger puffs away like smoke, and there's a pull that forces me to follow, and it also spurs me to put my arms around him. I'm hugging his left side because he's huge, and my arms aren't that long.

Another long minute passes in silence. I sheepishly pull away. "You looked like you needed a hug."

He pulls me back into him. "I do."

The eruption in my heart feels so massive, I'm sure he can see it. With my face planted on his chest, I bask in the comfort of his arms.

"Here," he suddenly says, placing his phone into my hand, without letting me go.

"Why?"

"So you can dampen the jealousy."

I try to lift off his chest, but he doesn't let me. "I'm not jealous. You were just being an ass." I shove his phone back into his hand.

"We're playing Yale tomorrow."

That is not what I expected him to say. The Yale-Dalton hockey rivalry is a long and contentious one, but it's unlike Aiden to be worried about a game.

"You don't think you'll win?" I ask.

He chuckles with a shake of his head. "It's not that. The game's just hard to play."

"Why?"

"It's an away game."

Being off home ice is a disadvantage, but Dalton hasn't lost an away game this season. Our school support is also high at away games because sororities make a point to represent gold and blue.

"You're not a fan of New Haven?"

"My parents died there."

My head snaps up in shock, and my heart crumbles into my stomach. "What?"

Aiden stares at his hands. "I was thirteen, and they were coming to see me play at a scrimmage. The roads were icy, and the sun had set when a drunk driver hit them out of nowhere."

Pain sears me in half. "I had no idea, Aiden. I'm so sorry."

His hold tightens. "That's why Yale's a tough one for me. The guys know, so they try their best when I'm off my game."

I slide my hand against the smooth skin of his jaw. "I can't imagine how hard that must be."

He covers my hand with his, the warmth tingling my skin. "It's better after all these years, but it's just something about that locker room."

"Is that where you found out?"

With a faraway look, he nods. "My grandparents showed up, and I knew something was wrong." My heart feels like it's disintegrating in the acid of my stomach when I imagine a scared little boy having to deal with that. "Sometimes it feels weird to continue playing hockey because I can't shake that feeling of guilt."

Confusion riddles me. "Guilt?"

"I was the reason they were even driving on that highway."

"Aiden, that's—"

"I know, it's not healthy. Every therapist has told me that."

I shake my head. "No, it's simply not true. Someone made a stupid, reckless decision, and it took two very important people from you. In no way is that your fault." He stares at me for a long, fragile minute. "What were they like?" I whisper, not wanting to shatter the glass of vulnerability.

Shadowed eyes flicker with an emotion I can't place. "No one has ever asked me that."

I blink in surprise. "Why not?"

"Eli and I grew up together, so he knew my parents well. The guys have heard stories, but I guess a fatal freak accident makes the topic unapproachable."

He laughs, but I see his hesitation. "So, tell me."

"You don't have to—"

"I do. I want to know," I insist.

He lets me take his hand. "My dad did everything to get me to be the best player I could be. He wasn't one of those overbearing fathers who would punish me if I didn't become a pro athlete. He just wanted me to be passionate about something. If I'd quit hockey after ten years, he would have thrown out my skates for me."

Knowing he has fond memories of his parents creates a deep warmth in my chest. I'm not surprised because Aiden is the most caring guy I've come across, but when you grow up in a place where that kind of love isn't given freely, finding out others have it feels foreign. "He seems like a really great dad," I say, softly. "And your mom?"

His smile is tender. "She was electric. Fun and so full of energy, it was like she was one of the kids, and my dad loved her all the more for it. All the moms at practice would complain about our grueling schedule and the dangers of hockey, but Mom didn't care. She trained me on being safe, but she'd say 'You have one life, Aiden. It's okay if you get a few bruises. They'll make for good stories.' All while showing me the stitches she'd gotten from playing."

"She played hockey too?"

He nods. "She's the reason I got into it."

"She seems badass."

Green eyes lock with mine. "Yeah, she was."

THIRTY-THREE

AIDEN

INSPIRATIONAL SPEECHES TRAPPED in long-winded threats are Kilner's pregame specialty. By the time he's done talking so animatedly that spit covers most of the guys up front, everyone is on edge. That's my cue to give them actual words of encouragement. But losing isn't an option tonight, and I make sure everyone knows that.

Today is Dalton Royals versus Yale Bulldogs, and we've never been more prepared. We watched game tapes and corrected our failed strategies from our loss to Brown. I'm content with the plays we ran during practice, and although I still have that dark feeling in my stomach, it dampens as game time approaches.

"All right, get your heads on straight before we get out there." The collective agreement fills the locker room. Just when I'm starting my centering exercises, there's a tap on my shoulder.

"Summer's here," Dylan whispers. I'm out the door in an instant, hoping Coach doesn't catch me. With skate guards on, I head down the hall and spot her instantly. She's like the beam from a lighthouse in a dark sea.

"You came."

Summer turns, peach scent filling the air. She looks unimpressed with the atmosphere of the arena. "You owe me compensation."

"My compensation is all yours." When I gesture to my crotch, she glares like she'd like to knee me.

"You're lucky I'm still here."

She's right. I'm a lucky bastard. "How about I score for you?"

Her nose scrunches. "That is so cheesy. Is that what you offer all your fuck buddies?"

That lights an uncomfortable fire in the pit of my stomach. I want that damn word out of her vocabulary. "No." My jaw ticks. "The offer is exclusively for you."

"I'm honored," she says dryly. "But no, you can make that in your sleep."

"Aw, is that a compliment?"

She shoots a scornful look at me. "Don't act humble now. I heard you comparing yourself to Crosby the other night."

When I laugh, she finally does too. The soft melody is a symphony to my ears and a much-needed contrast to her previous unimpressed expression. "Then how about a bet?"

Intrigue lifts her head. "Stakes?"

"Two goals, and we go on a date."

"What?" she sputters.

In all honesty, I didn't plan to say that, but now that it's out there, there's nothing I want more than to be alone with her without the excuse of school or sex. Not that I'd mind if the date ended with the latter.

I level her with a serious look. "I want to take you on a date."

"Why?" The look of repulsion on her face should be off-putting, but I'm a determined man.

"You're the first girl to sound disgusted by the proposition."

"You've never dated. How would you know?" she counters.

"Actually, I've been on plenty of dates. I just haven't been in a relationship."

Her bored look is amusing. "And let me guess, those 'dates' ended in hookups?"

I purse my lips. "That's not important. So what do you say?"

"No."

Can't she pretend to think about it? Jesus, this girl is something else. "Didn't take you as someone who backs out of a challenge."

"Seriously? You're trying to reverse-psychology me into this."

"I don't think you can use that as a verb."

She mutters something under her breath. "It's too easy for you, no."

"Pumping my ego already? Are you sure you don't want this date?"

She stares blankly.

"Fine. What's your counteroffer?" Going on a date with this girl would need a high-stakes presentation and a lot of balls.

"Three."

I shoot her a questioning look.

"Make a hat trick, and I'll go on your date." She grimaces. "No hat trick, and I get your truck for a week."

"Had that one ready to go, did you?"

The joyful look on her face tells me she expects me to sink. It isn't lost on me that she once referred to my truck as a jock-mobile.

"Then it's settled. If I win, I get a date."

"And when I win, I get your truck. No tricks," she warns.

"Only hat tricks, baby."

My cool, confident smile is as much of a facade as it can be. Yale has had us on a losing streak over the years, and we don't have a home-ice advantage either. I'd have to get the guys on board to set a potential play for it beforehand.

When I'm about to head back, I notice her shirt. "A jersey? I thought that lifestyle wasn't for you."

She looks at it with disdain. "It's not, but Cassie said going to my first college game without a jersey is a cardinal sin."

"I have to agree." I will be forever indebted to Cassie for making Summer Preston wear my name on her back. It's doing serious wonders for my ego. She's definitely leaving it on tonight.

"Are you sure?" The question borders on mischief, and when she turns, I see why.

Summer is wearing Sampson's jersey.

"Yours was occupied." She gestures to the concession stand, and my eyes follow to where Crystal Yang watches us, wearing my number. I don't even pause before I grab the back of my jersey and pull it over my head, leaving my shoulder pads exposed.

"What the hell are you doing?" Wide eyes trail down my bare torso.

"Take it off," I demand. "You're putting this on."

She stares at the jersey. "Aiden, you're playing in a few minutes."

"I know. Now put this on, Summer." Our equipment manager has extra jerseys, and her wearing Tyler Sampson's felt like a jinx. She doesn't argue and pulls off the jersey, exposing the tight long-sleeve underneath. The low-cut neckline has me looking away. Getting hard before the game would not be ideal.

When Summer pulls my jersey over her head, it engulfs her. It's big enough to fit over my padding, but it still makes me smother a laugh when it comes down to her knees.

"I look ridiculous," she mutters.

"No, *that* made you look ridiculous." I point to Sampson's jersey.

"At least it fits me," she argues. "You know what? I just won't wear one."

I shake my head and hold her arm straight to fold the fabric up to her forearms. Pulling her toward me, I tuck the back of the jersey into the waistband of her skirt. "Better?"

She straightens the jersey, a small smile on her lips. "I'll give Sampson's to Amara, but she said she'd rather get hit with a puck than wear any man's name on her back."

"I can burn it for you," I offer.

"That sounds sacrilegious."

"Trust me, I've seen his jersey in more sinful places."

She shivers in disgust, stepping back. "Good luck, Captain."

I stop her before she can walk away. "Come here and kiss me."

She looks around the packed hallway. "Not happening."

The team shuffles, gathering before game time, but all I see is her. "Kiss me or I'll kiss you, and it won't be PG."

"There are children here, Crawford," she hisses.

"It's your decision, Mother Teresa."

"I hate you," she grumbles, closing the space between us. I don't duck, so she places her hands on my shoulders to rise on tiptoes. The kiss is an absurdly short peck, but I palm her face to pull her back.

"You don't hate me." Then I tilt her head to take her in a deep kiss, one that elicits a surprised moan from her. The wet heat of her mouth sends a cascading pleasure down my spine.

I need the hat trick, and the team needs to win. Not only because it's Yale, but because I'll do anything for a date with Summer. That motivation alone tells me we've got it in the bag.

WE DO NOT have it in the bag.

With a burst of speed, I enter the offensive zone, eyes fixed on the net. The crowd hushes when I release a slapshot, only to be denied by Benny Tang. I bite back a curse as I take off with the puck, gaining possession again to pass it to Sampson. Stationed to the left of the key, he snipes in a wrist shot that sounds the buzzer.

The next shot is mine, and my backhand flips into Yale's net, getting us another goal. Skating across the rink, I can't keep from smirking when I bump into the glass where Summer sits.

When I point at her, she glares and flips me off. She actually fucking flips me off.

I bark out a laugh just when Dylan skates into me. "Really want that date, huh?"

Of course I want it. I want *her*. Alone and all to myself.

As the last minutes of the game trickle on, I net another goal and we're tied. At three seconds to the buzzer, Cole Carter is our saving grace with a wicked shot that shocks the crowd and gives us our first Yale victory.

It's ages before I step out of the madness of Ingalls Rink. "Two goals, and an assist. Plus, we won," I say when I see her smug face.

"Rules are rules, *baby*." Summer holds out her hand. I drop my keys into her palm, and she beams, clutching them tightly. From the looks of it, she won't waste any time picking my truck up from the parking lot back at Dalton. It'll be tough living without my truck for a week, but I like that Summer's using something that's mine.

"Preston. You coming for the next one?" Coach's voice makes us turn. "We'll need you to fight the refs on a bad call."

The faintest blush of pink dusts her cheeks, and being able to spot it feels like a superpower.

"I'll try," she says.

Coach nods, slapping my back before heading to the bus.

"Not a fan, huh?" I tease her.

"That one referee sucked, and I only threatened him once," she explains. I'm laughing when she glares. "I'll meet you at the house. Gotta pick up my prize from the rink first," she muses.

She follows Amara to her car, and I get on the bus. The forty-minute drive back buzzes with contagious energy, and I feel high off the win even as we hop off the bus and get in Dylan's car.

After I take another shower, Summer is lying on my bed, and the buzzing energy I'm feeling shifts. Summer eyes me staring, and her cheeks tint a shade deeper. Her face looks so warm and comforting, it stirs something in my chest.

I gravitate toward her, cupping her face to bring her lips to mine. I kiss her so hungrily, she gasps when she falls back on my pillow, long brown hair fanning around her face. The pillow is going to smell like her, and as happy as that makes me, it'll also make me miserable as hell when she's not here and I have to smell her even when I'm sleeping.

"Your hair's wet," she whispers. Man, I love her fucking voice. I kiss the warm column of her throat up to her jaw. "Aiden."

"Hmm?"

"You're getting me wet."

"I'd hope so."

She groans against me. "Your wet hair is dripping on me."

Placing my arms on either side of her head, I pull back, and sure enough, water droplets cover her cheeks and the hollows of her collarbone. I can't stop smiling when I see her annoyed glare. I kiss her again for good measure, and this time she pushes harder. I allow her to flip us over so she can straddle my lap.

"Towel?"

"You're sitting on it."

She looks at the towel wrapped around my waist and lifts up, her hair in my face as she pulls it. She pouts. "Who wears boxers under a towel?"

I laugh. "I wanted to wrap your present."

She rolls her eyes, bringing the towel up to my hair to dry it. She's thorough with her movements, fully concentrating on the task, her plump bottom lip between her teeth. I watch her work through my wet hair, my focus drifting to her thin white shirt. To my dismay, she's taken off my jersey, but when I see the perfect swell of her breasts so close to me, I don't care.

"My eyes are up here, Crawford," she scolds.

Those words don't do anything to ebb my thoughts. Arousal lights her irises, and I take it as my signal to move forward. Pulling down her top, I'm greeted with her braless tits. I drag a hand over her tight nipples and her soft whimper makes me harden to stone.

"Come here," I say. She does, her hands still in my hair, gripping it tighter when I draw her nipple deep into my mouth. I bring one hand to her ass and lift up her skirt. "Your panties are probably soaked, huh?"

"I wouldn't know," she says breathlessly when I grip her thighs.

"Why not?"

"I'm not wearing any."

A zip of electricity jolts my dick. "*Fuck*. Turn around."

When her ass is in my face, I lift her hips to position her bare pussy right where I need it. Shocking me, she pulls down my boxers to curve her hand over my length.

"You don't—"

"I know," she says, looking over her shoulder. "I want to."

Then she takes me entirely in her mouth, and I have to regain focus so I can taste her sweet center. The noises she makes as she suctions her lips around my cock don't help me last longer. The competitive side of me comes into play when I swirl my tongue in a whimper-inducing combination. It's not long before she's grinding down on my face, and I'm teasing her toward an orgasm.

"Please, Aiden. I need to come," she begs. I don't budge, ignoring her clit entirely, bringing her to the verge of imploding, then sneaking away. My balls draw up so tight, I have to use every ounce of willpower to not explode into her mouth.

"Jesus," I groan as she applies a tantalizing touch past my balls in retaliation.

"I'll use teeth, Crawford," she threatens.

That draws a laugh out of me. "Nah, you won't injure your favorite little man."

"You did not just refer to it as that."

"What do you prefer I call it? My hockey sti—" She takes me deep in her hot throat, making my hips buck. Her gag vibrates against my shaft, sending my body into a spiral. "Fuck. You need to stop that before this is over too soon."

"Two pump chump?" she teases with fake sympathy. "Happens to the best of us, buddy."

I take that moment to insert two fingers so deep inside her, my knuckles press against her sensitive core. Summer's high-pitched moan tells me I've hit her G-spot, and when she writhes on top of me, still driving me crazy by swirling her tongue along my tip, I seal my mouth over her swollen clit.

She comes just as I do, releasing every bit of the built-up tension into her mouth. Summer flips away, and the post-orgasmic flush on her face is so hot I have to look away.

A knock on my door makes her scramble to fix her clothes.

"Dinner's ready," Eli calls.

"I'll eat later." His footsteps retreat. When I try to kiss her, she pulls away.

"You didn't eat after your game?"

"I just did."

She makes a face and moves farther away. "I'm serious."

"Me too. And I'm still hungry, so get your ass back here." Despite my pull, she doesn't come.

"You should eat. I didn't realize I messed up your schedule." Before I saw my truck in my driveway, I didn't think anything could make me happier than our win against Yale. But knowing Summer drove back to my place instead of her dorm lit me up with deep satisfaction.

"You didn't mess up anything. I'm fine."

"You're not. You can't burn that many calories and not eat anything. It depletes the—"

"Summer, don't give me a science lesson," I say, and she frowns. "Fine, but you're coming with me." I move off the mattress and pull on my sweats. We're both looking at her indecent top when she stands. So, I toss her a shirt and sweats.

Eli's the first to spot us when we're downstairs. "Hey, Sunny."

Dylan's icing his ribs when he looks up, smirking.

"Why is your hair all messed up?" Kian yawns after his postgame nap. His low-riding Twilight boxers are the only thing he's wearing when he saunters over with a carton of orange juice.

Eli puts out an extra place setting. Kian wipes his mouth with the back of his hand, and his eyes bounce between us. "You didn't answer my question."

"You ask stupid questions, Kian," retorts Dylan, shooting Summer a sympathetic smile.

"As my very hot sixth-grade teacher Ms. Marple once said: There are no stupid questions, even if Kian is asking them."

"Didn't she quit teaching after our year?" Dylan retorts.

Kian shrugs. "No one can prove it was because of me."

Unintentionally terrorizing his middle school teacher is on brand for Kian.

Before I can sit beside Summer, Kian occupies the chair. Mildly irritated by the action, I sit on the other side of the table beside a very loud-chewing Cole, who digs into his plate like it's his first meal of the day. The kid stays locked in the basement unless he's on the ice. He doesn't look away from his phone except when he acknowledges my presence.

Kian's still trying to play Sherlock Holmes, eyeing Summer with suspicion.

She stares right back. "What?"

"You seem different."

"Fuck off, Kian," I say.

My warning only incites him. "Am I talking to you? She doesn't need a guard dog."

I'm going to cause him serious bodily harm, and from the way he avoids eye contact, he knows it. "I'm going back to sleep." Just before he turns the corner, he stops. "Try keeping it down this time. The walls are too thin to drown out your moans."

The guys shake with laughter, and Summer turns red, dropping her face into her hands.

THIRTY-FOUR

SUMMER

MY TAPPING FOOT annoys the hell out of my lab partner. Our professor is lecturing over class time, and I'm itching to leave.

So, I check the time on my phone again and sneak a text.

AIDEN

Summer: My lab's going to run late tonight, but I can probably make it to the second period.

Aiden: It's okay if you can't. Don't rush.

Summer: I'd speed through every traffic light just to see you play, Crawford.

Aiden: I'll hide the keys to my truck before you even think of speeding.

Summer: What are you? A cop?

Aiden: Kink?

Summer: No. But if you're down to dress up, a firefighter would do it for me.

Aiden: I guess almost burning down your tenth-grade classroom
   has its perks.
Summer: I regret telling you that.
Aiden: Promise me you'll drive safe, and if your lab runs late
   you'll go home.
Summer: Promise.

I smother my smile and shove my phone back into my pocket. Once I'm out of here, I have to head to the library for one last check on my application. Today, Langston gave me the green light to submit it, and with one press of a button, my lifelong dream will dangle slightly closer to my reach.

When our professor dismisses us, I don't linger. When I arrive at the library, I don't expect Donny to be there. I guess an extra pair of eyes can't hurt, so when he asks to review it, I let him. Except I forgot his presence is equivalent to eating rocks.

"Have you checked your limitations? You were missing some things last week."

The trickle of doubt is hard to ward off. "Langston signed off already. It's good."

"She can't hold your hand through it. You have to identify what's lacking."

I pinch the bridge of my nose and exhale a disgruntled breath. "Do you not want me to apply or something? The deadline is in a few days. If I don't send it now, I might as well not do it at all."

He laughs, a weird, awkward one that has me scrutinizing him. "Of course I want you to apply. It's not crazy to want to double-check."

"You don't need to. I know my work, and I know it's good. I'm not changing anything."

Contempt coats his features. "Why are you being so difficult? I'm only trying to help."

"Thanks for all your help, Donny, but I don't need it anymore." I press submit. "It's done."

His jaw tightens just a smidge before he gives me a tight smile. "Good, I'm glad you don't dwell on all the imperfections. It adds character; maybe that'll set you apart."

I let the remark roll off my back. I have more important things to do than sit here and listen to his snide comments. If I leave now, I'll be able to catch the game after the second intermission.

"Where are you going?"

I lift my bag onto my shoulder. There isn't any obligation to tell him, but I do. "I'm watching the game."

He halts. "The hockey game? Why? You hate hockey."

"I never hated the game." I used to love the sport itself. It was everything that was attached to it that I hated as I grew older. Now I'm finally able to let myself enjoy it again. I haven't missed any of Aiden's games since I went to the one against Yale.

"You were pissed when Langston gave you this assignment."

I shrug. "Guess something changed my mind."

"What could change—" He lets out a derisive laugh. "Holy shit. You're into him." I slow to see the look of disgust he aims at me. "I don't know how I didn't realize it before. I mean it's obvious you two are hooking up, but you actually *like* him."

My face burns red-hot.

"The texting, the late nights, the way you lost track of the only thing that has ever mattered to you because of him. *God*, I've been so fucking clueless."

"What are you saying?"

"Crawford?" He spits his name like venom. "Out of anyone, you chose Crawford. A fucking jock. A *hockey player*?"

Donny has never cared who I'm with, but that's because I don't particularly flaunt anyone around him. "You don't—"

"Don't start that bullshit with me, Summer. What are you going to say? He's not a jock? He's more than that? I don't know him like you do?" His laughter irritates the hell out of me.

"It isn't like that," I say quietly.

"It's not? Don't you think I would know what you look like when you're into someone?"

My annoyance bubbles to the surface. "No, because you don't know me anymore."

"Wow." His expression makes me feel smaller than the pebble by my foot. "This entire time I thought you were busy with the one thing you sacrificed so much for, but turns out you were just fucking around."

An unexpected shameful itch covers my neck. "How can you say that? You've seen the hours I've put in. My personal life has nothing to do with you or any of this."

"Once upon a time, it did have something to do with me. You can't blame me for looking out for you."

Irritation skewers my chest. "No need to look out for me. Aiden and I aren't together, not that it's any of your business."

He pauses, eyes trying to detect a lie. "You're not?"

I shake my head. "No."

"Let me guess, the captain doesn't do relationships? He's probably never had a girlfriend either." Despite his words having a bite, I can't deny the truth. "You would have never made a stupid decision like this if I was looking out for you."

"I don't need your constant judgment. I'd be better off if I'd never met you."

His face tightens. "Don't come running to me when he swaps you out for someone less emotionally wrecked. Though, if you want him to stick around, tell him who your dad is. That'll make your baggage a lot easier to digest."

His words are like scalding water to my face, but I feel frozen, almost paralyzed when he walks away.

TRYING TO STAY under the radar isn't easy when you have snitches for friends. Amara let Aiden into our dorm, so when I came back from my exam, he was waiting for me.

Now I'm in the kitchen pretending to clean as he drinks a glass of water I poured him.

"Sorry I couldn't come to your game," I finally say when he's rinsing the glass in the sink. He's apparently decided to go mute until I break the silence.

Aiden dries his hands, and when he leans in, I panic, turning so his kiss hits my cheek.

He stares for a long minute. "I just assumed your lab ran late."

I busy myself with cleaning the countertops, which are already spotless thanks to last night's anxiety-driven deep clean. It's more for my sanity, because after Donny spilled his poison into my thoughts, I've been on an infinite merry-go-round.

"Is there a reason you're trying to wear down the countertop?"

His words make me pause my aggressive movements. The surface does look like it's beginning to erode. "Just some pre-spring cleaning."

He steps in front of me. "You didn't answer my texts. Not one in the past two days." He pulls the rag from my hand. "Are you going to tell me what happened?"

"I'm just worried about my application."

"You shouldn't be. You did great. Müller even said so." He takes another step and my resolve crumbles. "It's something to do with us, isn't it?"

When I swallow instead of answering, he knows he's on the money. It feels like I have a rat infestation in my brain, and I'm left with sparking, chewed-up wiring. Last night's thoughts form into half-baked words and slide to the tip of my tongue. "We should see other people," I blurt.

There. It's done. Like ripping duct tape off a hairy arm.

Aiden doesn't move a muscle. He doesn't even blink, and if I hadn't seen the rise of his chest, I would have thought he stopped breathing too.

"Why do you say that?" The words are calm and drawn out in a voice that is so unlike his heated expression it gives me whiplash.

"Because we're not exclusive," I say matter-of-factly.

His eyes cloud like thunder. "You're right, we're not, but that's because you don't want to be."

My throat tightens. "That's not fair. We haven't been exclusive because that's what we agreed on. We're supposed to see other people, too."

He laughs. A sardonic, low chuckle that flips my stomach. "I don't give a shit about what we're supposed to do. We're the ones making the rules here, Summer."

"I know, and that's why we're fu—"

"I dare you to say *fuck buddies*." Warning swims in his forest green eyes.

I sigh. "Look, I've never done this before, but I'm pretty sure not being exclusive means seeing more than one person."

He shakes his head in disbelief. "This is what, a regular fling for you?"

I chew the inside of my cheek, unable to answer him.

His long fingers comb through his hair. "For someone who looks down at athletes and sees them as players, you're being pretty fucking jock-like right now."

"I'm not playing anyone."

"Really? Because when you're in my bed, your words are a lot different."

A cramped sensation blooms into my chest. "I'm not saying I don't mean them. I would never lie to you."

His eyes flicker. "I thought you trusted me."

The words settle like rocks in my stomach, and I have the need to reject them. "You think because I told you about my dad, I need you to prove something to me? That's not what this is, Aiden."

Tension crackles when he sighs. "Talk to me, Summer."

"I am! I don't know where you've been for the past few months, but I've been in reality. The reality where we're having a good time, but it would be beneficial for us to see other people, too."

Just when I think he might walk out, he pierces me with a heavy look. "You were with Donny yesterday. It's him, isn't it? He made you feel this way."

As much as I try not to, I can't help thinking that I'll be left with nothing if I continue this. There is no going back if my heart takes that reckless leap. Especially with someone who won't even be here in a few months. "He's not wrong. I can't let what I've worked so hard for be on the line for—for this."

"For *me*," Aiden says. "What are you telling yourself? That this is just a fling and we're just *fucking*? Because you know damn well that's not all it is." My words are stuck in my throat. That's when Aiden grips my chin to make me look at him. "Tell me you know that."

His touch breaks a barrier, and I cave like a sandcastle. "I do. But I'm scared that if I don't get into the program, it'll be because I let myself be distracted by you, and Donny will be right."

"Summer, you're the most focused and determined person I know, and I'm constantly surrounded by guys who are headed to the NHL." He steps closer. "Just forget him for one second and tell me how you feel about us."

"I like what we have, Aiden," I admit.

His expression smooths with relief. "Good. That's good, I can work with that."

"But we shouldn't keep all our eggs in one basket."

His forehead creases as if I'm speaking a foreign language.

"We should explore our options," I clarify.

Everything slows when green eyes meet mine. "You want me to fuck other girls?"

My shrug makes the crease between his brows deepen.

Aiden takes several steps away from me. "I haven't even looked at another girl since I've been with you."

I bristle.

"I'm not sleeping with anyone else," he says, making it even clearer. My logical thoughts scatter like pigeons. "I don't care about metaphorical eggs or what we should be doing. I already know what I want." His eyes flicker with an intense emotion, and a wash of panic floods through me. Aiden searches my face, and his heavy expression changes. "But you're right. We're not exclusive. So, if you want to explore your options, you should." His words are as rough as sandpaper.

My panic drains, but the sudden switch in his demeanor makes me skeptical. "You're okay with that?"

"It's not for me to be okay with. It's your life, Summer. You make the decisions."

The details of our amended arrangement flutter in uncertainty, but I straighten with renewed confidence. "Right. You're right. Maybe I will."

He plasters on a smile, and there's a split second where I wonder if he's tricking me.

"Good," he says.

"Good," I affirm.

THIRTY-FIVE

AIDEN

SUMMER SHOULD HAVE just punched me in the face, because every word out of her mouth was salt on open wounds. For some reason when I'm around her, everything stops being logical and clear-cut. Instead, it blurs into a turbulent storm.

She wants to see other people.

Why the fuck did I agree to that? I couldn't exactly throw a fit and demand we become exclusive. Her panic when I told her I know what I want was enough for me to reel in the caveman act. I'm clinging on to her *maybe* like a rope from a cliff. But if I've learned anything about Summer, it's that she'll set her own path. Pushing her into something would only hurt me in the long run.

Yeah. I'm thinking about the long run now.

No ice time today means I can bury my feelings under a bench press. When Kian enters the weight room, he holds up a neon green helmet that has a dozen modifications. "Ta-da!"

"What is that contraption?" Dylan drops his weight to look.

"It's protective headgear. Got it custom-made after that brain dysfunction seminar."

"Doesn't seem like you've made much use of it," jokes Cole.

Kian aims a sharp eye at him. "Watch it, Carter."

Cole's shoulders slump, the joke not holding up in a group of seniors. I would have found it funny if I wasn't sulking.

I zone out when Kian explains his helmet, and I don't realize I'm simmering until Dylan stands in front of me.

He tilts his head in observation. "You're a mess."

"Thanks," I say dryly.

"All this over some girl?"

I'm hoping my middle finger conveys my thoughts on him boiling Summer down to *some girl*.

"Jeez, I thought I'd never see the day you were off your game. You're Aiden fucking Crawford, man. There isn't a girl on campus who doesn't have you as her hall pass."

His useless pep talk only reminds me of Summer's sordid words. "Keep running your mouth and see what happens."

He raises his hands in defense. "And moody too. I'll run to the store and get you some tampons. What kind do you like?"

"You'll need them when I make your nose bleed."

"Heavy flow it is," he snickers. "I'm kidding, man, I can see why you're so bent out of shape. If it makes you feel any better, I'd consider monogamy for her too."

His words are comical because monogamy for Dylan is as repellent as bug spray to a mosquito.

"I mean, she's smokin—"

"Fair warning," I say. "I will punch you in the face if you finish that sentence."

He barks out a laugh, going back to lifting his weights.

Kian approaches. "Not to make you feel worse, but she's going on a date," he says gently, like I'm a fragile toddler getting news that my favorite blanket has gone missing.

The flare of heat in my chest can't be healthy. Everything in me wants to ignore him, but curiosity is a dangerous emotion.

"With whom?"

"Some accounting major."

That's a stake to the heart. Her five-year plan is nearing reality, now that I'm not disrupting it. Fuck, what I would do to disrupt all her complicated plans and keep her mindlessly in bed with me.

"How do you know that?"

"I overheard Amara when I was studying at her dorm," he says.

Unlike me, Kian's been spending time with Summer because of exams. Would it be crazy if I transferred into her class? *Yes.*

"What are you going to do?" This time all the guys crowd me. Even Cole and Sebastian approach, probably aware of everything because of Kian's big mouth. Though they're well acquainted with Summer's presence in my bedroom over the past few weeks.

"Nothing."

Curious faces fall, and they stare at me like I've gone crazy. "Your girl is going on a date with another guy, and you're going to do *nothing*?" Cole asks incredulously.

Kian starts, "If I were to give my two cents—"

"Don't," we all say. His face contorts with shock.

"I have more experience with complicated relationships than any of you," he defends.

"Your stalker doesn't count as a complicated relationship, Ishida. That was just complicated. Period," says Eli.

"Okay, but what I've learned is—"

"Don't duplicate house keys and give them to someone you just met?" I offer.

"Don't leave your car in the driveway for someone to siphon gas from it?" Dylan adds.

The guys shake with laughter. I'm sure we could provide a dozen more examples of things Tabitha did to him, but he pouts. "You know what? You don't deserve my wisdom."

I groan when he does that wounded puppy thing with his face. "Sorry, buddy, we're joking. What did you want to say?"

"I don't want to tell you now."

"Fine with me." Dylan stands and the rest of the guys agree.

"Okay, okay." He blocks them. "Girls are like buttons—"

Coach clears his throat, cutting him off. "Ishida, what have I told you about gossiping in the weight room?"

"That it fosters healthy connections among growing boys?" He smiles, white teeth on display.

The glare Kilner sends his way is sharp enough to make everyone stand straighter. He's got that angry vein in his forehead that usually pops when Kian's involved. "One more word from you, and I'll make sure you never see that ice again."

Despite the threat, Kian opens his mouth to speak, but Eli elbows him with a sharp look.

"Coach, what would you do if the girl you want is going out with someone else?" Cole asks.

I shoot him an irritated look. The last thing I need is Kilner in my business. Though he is happily married with four kids, so he must know a whole lot more than I do.

Coach eyes me. "Shower girl?"

"Summer," I supply.

His brows knit, and his small smile is almost undetectable. "Only a matter of time with you two," he mutters. "You know her better than anyone else does. But I know she's got a good head on her shoulders, and she thinks hard before committing to something—or *someone*. Still, you gotta let people come to their own decisions, even if you think you know what's best."

I consider his words. While I want to stop Summer from going on that date, I know I was right in what I said to her. But that doesn't mean I'll let her forget about my existence in her life.

THIRTY-SIX

SUMMER

THE SMELL OF bitter liquor and fried food wafts through Porter's. It's Friday night, and ever since I told Amara and Cassie about my talk with Aiden, they've been hell-bent on taking me out. Apparently, they think telling him we should see other people means I should actually go out and see other people. I don't know how to break it to them, but I can't even look at another guy without comparing him to Aiden. Turns out they're all pretty lackluster after him.

"Uh-oh." Cassie halts and chuckles nervously. "I forgot to mention a very tiny inconsequential detail."

Nothing from that sentence sounds tiny or inconsequential. When I turn, the bar is swarming with Dalton's hockey roster.

"They won tonight."

I knew that because I watched the game on TV. Aiden dominated the ice and my heart did little flutters every time the cameras focused on him. He hasn't texted me to hang out after our talk, so I'm taking the newfound space to do what I want.

My only option is to leave the bar, but Cassie stops me. "The old Summer would never let hockey stand in the way of anything. Come

on, we're here to have fun, and there are plenty of other people here.
We can avoid them."

I haven't seen Aiden yet, so I guess that's a good sign.

"Sunny!"

As soon as I hear that voice, I squeeze my eyes shut.

"Worth a shot," mumbles Cassie as she and Amara head to
the bar.

Kian's smiling wide, and he's definitely drunk, judging by how he
sways. His suffocating bear hug envelops me in the smell of beer.
"I've missed you around the house. How have you been, stranger?"

"I saw you in class the other day."

"Oh right, Aiden had me reporting ba—want a drink?" he di-
verts.

"I'm good for now, thanks. Congrats on the win, by the way."

"Thanks, but it was all Aiden tonight. He was electric. I don't
know what has gotten into him lately."

I raise a brow. "Practicing more material for your best man
speech?"

"Yup. You'll have to hear it twice."

I'm barely paying attention to his slurred words as I try to find an
escape. He doesn't let me go even as our conversation dwindles, so I
nudge him. "Go back to your friends."

"But you're so much prettier than them."

I roll my eyes. Finally, he saunters back, but not before giving me
a sloppy kiss on the cheek. I don't watch his retreat because I'm a
coward, too afraid to see Aiden back there. But when an electric tingle flutters down my spine, and my heartbeat slows to little thumps,
I know he's got me like a spotlight.

On shaky legs, I head to the bar. Knowing that Aiden is here
makes me highly sensitive to flirting, so much so that my stomach
flips anytime a guy looks my way.

Like clockwork, I feel a warm presence hover over me. The way my heart starts to palpitate, you'd think I'm going into cardiac arrest, but then I smell the cheap cologne rubbing off on my skin.

It's not him.

"Pretty girl like you must not have come here alone." The man is too close for my liking, and his breath is worse than the cologne. But his smile slows the uneasy feeling jittering through me.

"I'm here with my friends." I point to the dance floor. The subtle nod I give Amara dampens her worry.

"Wouldn't want to interrupt your girls' night, though it would be a shame if I didn't get your number."

I laugh. "I don't even know your name."

"I'll get you a drink, and I'll tell you everything about myself."

"Already have one coming. Though if you can guess what it is, you can buy me another."

He takes a seat at the bar. "I'm not much of a gambler."

The response is disappointing, but before I can say anything, an abrupt shove from a drunk girl sends me crashing into his lap.

That spotlight from earlier just got hotter.

He slithers a hand around my waist to hold me in place. Despite my determination not to scope the bar, I look to where the guys are talking loudly, and my eyes collide with green. Aiden leans against the wall, eyes on me as he takes a slow swig of his beer, ignoring his teammate talking to him. His casual stance is a picture of calm, but something cold leaks into his eyes.

The sharp ache in my chest threatens to rip me in half, and I swallow the lump in my throat. Suddenly, the idea of a drink from this stranger or even touching him makes me itchy.

"I have to go." I scramble off his lap to head to the bathroom. I release a shaky breath as I stare at my flushed face in the mirror. My hands are clammy, so I run them under the sink.

I'm drying my hands when the bathroom door creaks open, and Aiden steps inside, a dark shadow covering his face. I swallow so hard that his eyes drop to my throat. When I step away from the sink, he closes the door.

A storm brews in my belly. "You're in the wrong bathroom."

"I'm not." He twists the lock, and the *click* echoes in my ears. "Is that the accountant?" he asks.

"What?" The word wobbles off my lips.

"The guy at the bar. Is he a part of your five-year plan?"

It takes me a second to process what he's saying, but when I do, it irritates the hell out of me. "I don't know. I'll have to get to know him better."

His tongue runs along the inside of his cheek, his gaze dragging down my body. "Didn't have much of a conversation when your ass was on his lap?"

"Wasn't really focused on talking." I sound unbothered, though I'm sure he notices my heaving chest.

He shadows each of my slow steps. "Who is he?"

"It's none of your business."

"Another guy touching you is very much my fucking business."

"I thought we were giving each other space to—"

In one swift movement, he cages me against the wall. "Is this enough space for you, Summer? Because it's too much to fucking bear for me."

My heart constricts in my chest. "But Donny—"

"*Fuck* Donny," he says through gritted teeth, pressing his hips into mine. "I want to know what you want."

"I don't know what you mean." My voice trembles.

"Yes, you do," he says. "Either tell me you want this just as bad as I do or tell me to leave."

"Aiden . . ."

"One word." His thumb runs along my jawline so delicately, I shiver. The caress tightens the twine suffocating my heart. "Either I'm in, or I'm out, Preston." His usual confidence is loud, but tonight he sounds vulnerable. My mind teeters, but I know that I need him close right now.

"In," I say breathlessly. "You're in."

"Good answer."

My pulse drops like a weight between my legs, and I wonder how much longer I can stand. As if he's reading my mind, or maybe just my body, one of his hands slides to my waist, searing my skin through my dress as he lifts me off the floor. His mouth covers mine, and he breaks me open with hungry, desperate kisses.

My dress rides all the way up, my back hits the cold tiled wall, and his hard body spreads my legs open.

"Fuck, I missed you," he whispers, nuzzling my neck.

He didn't miss this. He missed *me*. The small detail wrenches my heart. Aiden pulls the straps of my dress and bra down, baring me to him. He kisses me everywhere, pressing the flat of his tongue along my skin. He nips, licks, and sucks my nipples until they're impossibly hard in his mouth.

"I'm hoping you wore this dress for me," he murmurs.

"I didn't even know you'd be here."

His lips glide along my buzzing skin. "We both know I'm the only one taking it off."

"I don't know," I pant. "That guy at the bar was pretty close." I'm not sure why I'm trying to incite him, but I can't help myself.

"Hmm, how close?" He yanks up my dress.

"Judging by how his lap felt—*Ah*!"

He interrupts me with a pinch to my clit. "You're going to get fucked hard for that." The clanking of his belt might as well be a singing church choir with how close I feel to heaven.

"Just to be clear." He yanks my panties to the side. Cool air brushes over my exposed skin, but the heat of his gaze warms my core. "The only one filling you up is me." He presses the head of his length along my wet core, and I shudder, every muscle in my body contracting. "The only name you're screaming is mine—"

"Screaming is a bit of a hyperbole," I interrupt.

"—and the only lap you'll be sitting on is this one." He looks down to where our hips meet and thrusts so deeply inside me, a scream rips from my throat. "Hyperbole, my ass."

I try not to bite the hand that covers my mouth when he thrusts in again with too much force, causing too much pleasure. The firmness of his hold sends my heart aflutter.

"You love it, don't you?" His stormy eyes lock on mine. "You love when my eyes are on you while I fuck you."

I nod, just as he hits a spot so deep my eyes roll backward, and his soft moans light up my body.

"You're making a fucking mess, baby, dripping all over my cock." He's so deep, only our filthy noises soak the bathroom air. "Did you miss me, Summer? Miss feeling me buried inside this tight little pussy?"

Too far gone to answer, I kiss him. But he fists my hair to pull me away so our foreheads touch, making me watch where we're connected. He brings his thumb to rub over me, and my head falls back, grazing the tiled wall.

"Watch me, Summer. Look at what you do to me."

I whimper, and Aiden grips the underside of my thighs and edges them back to my stomach. My calves touch the backs of his hands when he lifts them higher. The display of strength must be unintentional, but it gets me wetter than ever. I drop my head in the crook of his neck when he thrusts into me.

"Please don't stop." I bite down to keep from screaming.

"I won't." The slapping of skin echoes around us, and I squeeze, feeling my orgasm build to the point of no return. "Show me how much you like it, baby. Come on my cock."

I come so hard I feel like I'm floating. Aiden's strong arms hold me up, and I'm astonished how he still has strength. Then, with a low, guttural moan, he finishes inside me.

The click of my heels against the tiles is the only sound I can hear over my heavy breathing. I lean against the wall, watching him clean himself off and zip his pants. Then he grabs a paper towel and crouches to clean the wetness dripping down my thigh.

When he brushes over my sensitive core, I flinch and his touch gentles. He moves my panties back in place before tossing the paper. When he grabs my face to pull me high on my tiptoes for a kiss, I feel it between my legs. As if what he just did to me wasn't enough, I need him again.

"When you're too sore to walk tomorrow, remember that only I can give you this. Bar guy wouldn't stand a chance with your needy pussy."

His words cling to me like leeches as he unlocks the door and walks out.

THIRTY-SEVEN

SUMMER

A MANDATORY LUNCH date with my mom is something I try not to schedule until I have every ounce of mental energy available to deal with her questions. However, crappy luck seems to be the theme for this afternoon, because when I enter the formal restaurant, my parents are seated at the table.

I halt a few feet from the table, making the server behind me stumble with the tray in his hands. I debate whether my appetite is more important than protecting my sanity. I don't get to decide because my mom stands and pulls me in for a tight hug.

"It's so good to see your face. Come, I ordered your favorites."

I'm so stunned, it takes me a minute to hug her back. I can't help but melt into her warm embrace. Avoiding my dad has been my main objective, but that means I barely see my mom.

"I missed you too, Mom." I pull back. "You should have told me he was coming."

"And listen to your excuses?" She raises a brow. "Your father did call, but you never answered."

I walk over to the table, where my dad pulls out my chair. "Thanks," I mutter.

"No problem, Sunshine."

The nickname guts me, and it hurts when I try to breathe again. "Where are Serena and Shreya? Didn't they come with you?"

My sisters, although much younger, are the only buffer I have between my parents and myself. Without them, I tend to suffocate.

"They couldn't make it. Your grandparents are staying with them in Toronto."

I nod, knowing they must be exhausted from all the training. My sisters are training to qualify for the Olympics in figure skating, so they don't have much leisure time.

When the food arrives, the sound of utensils scraping against plates is our only conversation. My responses to my mom's questions are limited to yes and no. My dad doesn't ask me much, and I'm grateful for it.

When my phone vibrates with a text, I grab it like a life raft.

AMARA

Amara: How's it going?

Summer: I'm being held hostage.

Amara: It can't be that bad. Divya Preston is anything but boring.

Summer: My dad's here. He's spoken two words to me.

Summer: Maybe I should tell him I'm pregnant to get a reaction out of him.

Amara: Brutal.

Amara: But when he finds out his grandbaby is the spawn of a hockey player he might rejoice.

Summer: Never say that again.

Amara: Why? Unless you're finally sleeping with someone other than Dalton's pride and joy.

Amara: I have the perfect baby names. What do you think of Puckerton? Or Rinkerella?

I snort at the text and put my phone back in my purse. But when I look up, my parents are watching me expectantly.

My mom gives me a nosy look. "So, anything new at Dalton?"

"Nope."

"Any new friends or *boy*friends?" The wiggle of her brows only makes my eyes narrow.

"Not really."

She clasps her hands. "Sampson's mom said you and him have been quite close."

I drink my water, hoping I'll drown. "We're friends, Mom."

"Leave the girl alone, Divya. You weren't telling your parents about us when we got together."

She smiles sweetly, putting her hand over his on the table.

"That's because you two were having unprotected sex."

"Summer!" They both scold in unison.

I laugh, seeing their blanched faces. "What? It's not like it's a secret." I point to myself.

The shake of my dad's head and the glare from my mom fills me with contentment.

When the server takes my plate, I push my chair back. "Well, this was fun, but I need to get back."

"I'll take you," my dad says.

I freeze. A girl can only handle so many awkward interactions in one day. "I already called an Uber."

"Cancel it. I'm taking you."

Not having to take an Uber, as a girl traveling alone, is a relaxing option, but sitting in my dad's SUV makes my chest wind tighter. I knew I should have brought Aiden's truck, but parking that massive thing is a pain. Staring out the window isn't helping the time go any faster. Neither is counting each rain droplet that pings against the window.

He turns on the radio, and of course, it's tuned to a couple of announcers arguing about last night's regular season game.

"Did you watch?" he asks.

"I don't watch hockey."

My dad chuckles. "Are you kidding? You would paint your face and make sure I had rinkside seats to every playoff game."

I swallow the thick ball in my throat. "Anymore. I mean I don't watch hockey anymore."

The silence after that is so loud, it rings in my ears. Thankfully, my dad feels it too, because he turns up the radio volume. The hosts switch to D1 hockey to discuss Dalton versus Dartmouth.

"We got lots of talent coming in from Dalton on this year's roster. With their star player going pro, Toronto's never been luckier to be getting a powerhouse like Aiden Crawford." My stomach has no business dipping the way it does at the mention of his name. "They'll be talking about this kid for years to come, and I can promise you that."

My dad glances at me. "You know him?"

Can he hear my heart rattling inside my chest? "Like I said, I don't follow hockey."

He sighs. "Right."

The phone battery is nearly dead, so I can't bury myself in a doomscroll, leaving me staring out the window for an escape.

"You missed Diwali, Thanksgiving, and Christmas," my dad says, breaking the running silence again.

"I was busy with my application."

"How is that going?"

"You should already know, considering you're a trustee." He tenses. I found that tidbit out sophomore year, and my dad received a very angry text about it.

"I told you I'm going to make sure my daughter is cared for."

"If you ever bothered to listen to what I wanted, you'd know that is the last thing you should have done." I pause, controlling my volume. "I worked hard to get my scholarship. I don't need you acting as my safety net. But you don't know that because you haven't spent a day getting to know me since I turned eight."

"Summer, you know that I love you."

I scoff. "You have a hell of a way of showing it."

"Your sisters have seen me show up."

"That's great, Dad. I'm glad you're finally showing up for your daughters, but I guess it's too late for me, right?"

"That's not how I meant it."

My blood boils. "I am genuinely happy they got the dad I've always wanted. I truly am. But I'll always remember that you chose not to be there for me. You treated me like a mistake."

"Summer!" my dad yells, pulling over when the campus comes into view. "You know damn well you are a blessing to me and your mother. We were young and scared, but we have never blamed you for anything. We made a choice when we had you."

"Yeah, and then you made a choice between your career and your family. Take a wild guess on which one you chose." I unclip my seat belt and open the car door. "Next time you want to help, try being a dad instead of a cash register." I slam the door shut.

Rain mixes with the hot tears that pour down my cheeks, soaking my achy chest.

When I cry over my father, I wonder if eight-year-old Summer, the little girl who thought that if superheroes existed, her dad had to be one, ever feels disappointed.

THIRTY-EIGHT

AIDEN

HAVING A GAME at noon means not being able to focus on any assignments afterward. It also doesn't help when there's a knock at my bedroom door.

"Busy," I call out.

I've already sat through Kian's thorough tattoo tour. The new one on his thigh is an intricate red snake. It was cool until he went on a long tangent. We're going easy on him since he and Cassie fizzled after talking for a few weeks. Unsurprisingly, he was in it a lot deeper than her. Now managing to get him out of my room long enough to write this paper has been a chore.

When the knocking doesn't stop, I let out a resigned breath, pushing back my chair and swinging open my door.

"I said I'm bu—" Before I can finish my sentence, arms wrap around me, and a head of brown hair burrows into my chest. Frozen in place, I'm surrounded by her sweet scent and her trembling rain-damp body.

"Summer?" She sniffles and my heart cracks in two. I rub her back, feeling her sobs become more frequent.

"Come." I close the door, and she lets me lead her to my bed. She's still shaking. "You're scaring me, baby. What's wrong?"

When we sit, I pull her head away from my chest, and the sight of her wet cheeks is a rusty knife to my gut. "Is it Langston?"

She shakes her head as I brush her hair away from her face.

I think for a minute. "Your dad?"

Her bottom lip quivers. Then she does it again—that thing where she notices my concern, and becomes a vault. She pulls away, sitting stiffly as she wipes her flowing tears. "I don't know why I came here." She sees my open laptop and textbook. "You're obviously busy."

"I'm never too busy for you."

Drowning brown eyes search my face before she exhales a deep breath, standing to pace my room. "How many times can you beg someone to love you?"

The heavy weight on my chest grows, making it hard to breathe. I follow, wrapping her in my arms again.

"It's the one thing a parent is supposed to do. The only thing he had to do." Her words muffle in my shirt.

"He does, Summer. It would be impossible not to."

"But why is it according to his timeline? When he's ready, I have to accept him with open arms as if my happiness depends on his willingness." She sobs again. "It's not fair."

"I know, baby." I rub her back, letting her cry it out. "I know."

She inhales a broken breath. "I told myself I'd never get there again. I thought I was over it. But one fucking talk with him, and it hurts the same."

Everything in me wants to run into action mode. To figure out how to help and make the tears stop flowing. Her puffy eyes and tiny red nose prick at me, and I have the urge to call her dad. Which is something I never thought I'd do, because Lukas Preston, as much of an inspiration as he is, is one scary motherfucker.

Not wanting to self-insert, I opt for just listening to her.

Summer aggressively wipes her cheeks. "I feel so stupid for crying about this."

"Don't." I hand her a tissue. "It's been so long, you're bound to have a reaction."

She wipes her eyes, and her expression turns regretful. "I think I might have said too much. He looked really hurt, Aiden."

"And what I'm seeing right now is that you're really hurt. That's not okay, Summer. You don't deserve to be treated like this, and I won't let you feel bad for finally saying what's on your mind. Tell me you understand that."

Her eyes drop to my chest, and she toys with the strings of my hoodie.

I lift her chin, not letting her get away with taking the blame for this. "He hurt you, and for the first time, you didn't bottle it up. Be proud of yourself, because I am."

She blinks away a tear. "I am, and I know it was right for me. But I can still feel bad about it."

This girl is fucking sunshine embodied, and she has no clue. "Of course you can. It's who you are. You're kind and compassionate. And a little stubborn."

She hiccups and hits my chest, only to have tears follow immediately after.

"Come on, I'll make you some tea, and then we can lie down."

LAST WINTER ELI'S family invited me on their annual trip to Whistler. The Westbrooks own a cabin up north that can accommodate a small village. We did every winter-related activity up there, including hockey on the secluded frozen pond and helicopter excursions. But the most memorable—and terrifying—part of that trip was the Coffin Ski Run, which felt like plummeting into an unknown abyss at sixty miles an hour.

That's how it feels to hold Summer in my arms.

She fell asleep a few hours ago after fighting her hardest to stay awake. We talked about everything from our first pet—hers, a goldfish named Iggy, and mine, a cat named Benji—to our life's philosophy, which wasn't that concise considering one of us was half asleep. Pins jammed my chest at the sight of her droopy eyes and slurred responses, as she tried her absolute damnedest to stay up because she said she liked the sound of my voice.

I don't think she meant to say it, or that she would have ever said it if she was fully conscious. But I know it's the truth, and damn, does it feel good. I'll be her white noise machine as long as I live if that's what she wants.

The terrifying feeling, though—that's what keeps me wide-awake. Because just before Summer knocked out, she whispered, "I forgot how much you feel like home."

Home. She thinks I feel like home.

There's no way I could sleep after that. Summer trusts me. She doesn't trust a lot of people, so the pressure feels like I might collapse beneath it. Which is unlike me, because I'm used to pressure. I'm the fucking captain, for Christ's sake. The entire school relies on me. Everyone relies on me. But this feels different.

She snuggles closer, and the movement stirs her awake. I don't bother pretending like I'm sleeping. I've pretty much surpassed the creepy stalker territory in her head. When she tries to move away, I don't let her. "Don't go."

She shifts to meet my eyes. "I'm just going to the bathroom."

My breath of relief has her studying the reaction. Summer's never stayed over long enough for me to see her face in the morning. I once thought handcuffs could keep her here, but knowing her, she'd break my headboard before she'd oblige. It's like trying to cage a butterfly in an open field.

She may think I'm some clingy weirdo, but letting her be more than a few feet away from me right now feels so utterly wrong I'm willing to look desperate.

My hand glides across her cheek. Everything about her feels like it's one in a million. Being able to be this close to her makes me feel like I'm one in a million. "You're so beautiful."

Her breath catches and with a kiss to her temple, I loosen my hold. She rolls off the bed and straight into my bathroom.

I hear a muffled, "Oh my God!" from the opposite side of the door. Then Summer peeks her head out of the bathroom. "You could have told me I look like a raccoon!" She points to the smudged mascara that paints her under eyes.

She looks so fucking radiant standing there with messy hair and my T-shirt on, I can't help but smile. "You're so beautiful, Summer," I say again. All that gets me is an eye roll and a door slam.

Laughing, I text Eli to see what he's made for dinner. He could seriously attend culinary school with how much he enjoys cooking.

ELI

Eli: Two pans of baked ziti tonight. As per our child's request.

Aiden: Kian's still sulking over Cassie?

Eli: Poor kid saw her on a date with Julia Romero. An ice skater.

Eli: He's been listening to Folklore on repeat, and watching The Cutting Edge.

Aiden: I know, I can hear it from across the hall.

Aiden: I'll be down for dinner later then.

Eli: Safest option, you don't wanna risk running into him. I'll leave yours in the oven.

Eli: More than enough for your girlfriend, too.

I ignore that message, and Summer comes back out. It's as if going to the bathroom popped our comfortable bubble, because she stands there awkwardly.

I drop my phone on the nightstand and hold up the comforter. "Come here."

She does. Crawling back into place like she never left.

"How are you feeling?"

"Better," she whispers, burying her head between my neck and shoulder. "I think I've drained all my energy from crying."

"Stay here tonight." The offer makes her stiff. The only sounds between us are my heartbeat and Kian's music. There is no reason for her to leave tonight, and I was serious when I said it felt wrong to let her go. "I know you can take care of yourself, but let me do it. Just this once."

I need to feel useful for her. Summer likes to carry all her problems under a heavy rain cloud.

"I don't know . . ."

"Yes, you do," I say, lifting her chin to hold her pensive eyes. "Will you stay with me tonight?"

She nods.

THIRTY-NINE

SUMMER

THE HOUSE COULD have lit on fire, and I'd have been fine just lying there in his arms. Because that is what Aiden does—he makes me feel safe even in moments where I've never felt more alone. After dropping me off this morning and making sure I was okay, he finally went to practice. Aiden didn't complain, but I suspect Coach is having an aneurysm right about now.

"Where have you been?" Amara asks when I step inside.

"Got into it with my dad. I finally let it out. Not everything, but I didn't stay quiet this time."

Worry mars her features. "Shit. Did he take it well?"

I snort. "Not in the slightest. I haven't checked my phone since, but I'm sure I have voicemails from my mom."

"Well, I'm glad you feel better." She hugs me. "But that doesn't explain why you're coming home in the middle of the afternoon in an oversized hoodie." She pulls at my sleeve to inspect it. "Oh, and what's this? Number twenty-two, *Captain*. Interesting."

I yank it out of her grip. "I slept over at Aiden's, Nancy Drew."

Amara lifts herself onto the counter. "Tell me everything."

"I cried. He held me. And when he asked me to stay so he could care for me, I said yes."

She makes a face like she's going to cry. "This is monumental. You stayed over at a guy's place. *You!* Ms. I don't do anything relationship-y."

"I don't know, Amara. It feels like a huge step because I've stayed away from everything hockey for years, and I've been hurt before. It's like I opened a jammed door and Aiden walked through and uncovered every nook and cranny." I feel vulnerable, and more naked than I've ever been.

"I know, and I get that letting yourself be with him, without the whole friends-with-benefits thing to fall back on, is a huge leap, especially with everything that just happened with your dad."

Emotion clogs my throat. "He's the only other guy I've actually been with since Donny, and we know how that turned out." Donny was sweet at first, but his true self showed eventually.

"Donny's old news. As far as I know, his preppy ass doesn't exist." She grimaces. "And he's a terrible reflection of other guys out there." Her gaze turns inquisitive, like she's calling a bluff. "Maybe that date with Oliver will help."

Crap. I completely forgot about my date with Oliver. Oliver is in Amara's elective, one of the hardest at Dalton. She may or may not have given him my number because she's trying to befriend him for the course. I gave her the go-ahead, but it was before Aiden held me as if letting me go would physically hurt.

The gears in my brain spin, and I find Amara awaiting my answer. Aiden's words about making my own decisions float back to me and I know what I need. "You're right. Maybe it will."

Her smile tightens as if she's kicking herself for the suggestion.

WHEN I WAKE up late Friday morning, I don't expect Aiden to be at my front door.

"Hi," I say awkwardly. The energy between us feels like it's shifted, and I don't really know how to act.

"Hey." The look on his face teeters between longing and caution. "I finished practice and came to see how you're doing."

"I'm great. Why wouldn't I be?"

His face falls. Probably because you don't cry in a guy's arms, then act like it meant nothing, especially when it meant too much.

"Sorry, I didn't mean for it to sound like that. I'm okay. I haven't cried, so that should mean something." It's been two days since I felt like even if the world collapsed, I'd be okay if I stayed in Aiden's arms. I haven't seen him since, but he has texted me random things about the guys that make me laugh. Mostly about Kian and how he's been coping with the Cassie situation. Apparently, Dylan's teaching him how to figure skate.

"I'm making breakfast. You want some?" I ask.

He's surprised, and when he steps back, I think he'll refuse. "My truck's just out front. Let me park in a proper spot."

Giving his truck back was bittersweet, but I felt bad he had to carpool with the guys or take an Uber to the rink.

I'm in the kitchen washing fruit when he enters again. He focuses on the tablet I have set up on the counter. And just like that, we're sucked into our show, and the awkwardness is gone.

"So whose kid is that?" He steals a grape from the bowl.

"It's his, he just doesn't know it yet."

"That is so fucked-up."

We're discussing the show when Amara walks in. "Sum, when's your date? I need the dorm tonight." Her gaze shifts to Aiden in mock surprise, telling me she already knew he was here. "Oh, hello, Aiden."

"Hey, Amara," he greets, sounding a little stiff.

"So, when is Oliver picking you up?" she innocently asks. I am so going to post her number on a Craigslist singles ad.

"Seven," I grit out.

She brightens, stealing one of my strawberries. "Right, you told me that, but good to know. I'm going to head out, see ya."

The door slams, and we're left in prickling silence. Even the buzz of the lights can't penetrate this ticking time bomb.

I continue chopping, trying to ignore the gaze on my face. Aiden leans against the counter, waiting for me to break.

After everything, I can't call us fuck buddies. But I've had this date set since before the restroom at Porter's when we . . . yeah.

Every sound is heightened. The knife hitting the cutting board feels like sensory overload. I finally turn to him. "What?"

His relaxed demeanor is a front. "Nothing."

I point the knife right at him. "You're not fooling anyone. You want to say something."

"Nope." He bites a strawberry, ignoring the dangerous object.

"You're pissed."

"I'm not," he says. "You can see whoever you want."

"I don't believe you."

"If you want me to be the toxic guy who tells you I'll fuck up anyone that comes near you, I will. But that's not the kind of guy you deserve, Summer. I won't dictate how you live your life."

I'm always on edge about every decision I make. Every turn feels wrong, but Aiden's conviction cushions that feeling.

I meet his eyes. "So, you don't care?" I ask. My life would be a whole lot easier if he doesn't, or if I can convince myself that I don't. But the truth simmers like a pot ready to overflow.

His jaw tightens, and that once calm expression slips from his face like melted ice. "Oh, I care." He steps forward, and his palms rest on either side of the counter to cage me in. "The thought of someone else getting to see your smile." His thumb leaves a warm imprint on my lip. "Making you laugh or touching you. Drives me. Fucking. Insane."

He steps back to lean against the counter like he didn't steal every ounce of my personal space. "But I'll deal. Because I know you're only going on dates to distract yourself. You can pretend all you want, Summer, but we both know it'll be me in the end."

My pulse pounds. I bite my lip, drawing his attention to my mouth. "And if he kisses me?"

The pad of his thumb tugs my bottom lip free. "Then when you finally come to me, I'll make sure there isn't a memory in your head of any other guy's kiss or touch."

The words settle in my stomach like rocks. "You're wasting your time."

"You don't get it, do you?" I give him a blank look, and he smiles. "Well then, let me make it really clear. You could strip me of every championship and every award I've ever earned, but if I had you, none of it would matter." He stares at me for a long minute. "Besides, we both know your cyborg accountant wouldn't be able to handle you in bed."

"And you can?" He can. He definitely can.

"I think I've proven myself many times. But if your memory is a little hazy, I can provide a thorough demonstration." He makes a move to sink to his knees, but I push him away.

"And how do you know I'm going on a date with an accountant? He could be another athlete, for all you know."

His smirk only sends unease flooding through me.

DID YOU KNOW yellowtail snappers are nocturnal predators?

Oliver Benson, an accounting major with a passion for agriculture studies, as well as my date for the night, has been droning on about his trip to the Florida Keys. My eyes glaze over with boredom as I mentally organize my schedule, but a familiar voice interrupts my calendar debrief. *Two* irritatingly familiar voices, headed straight for our table.

I purposely chose this diner for my date because it's off campus. It's a twenty-minute drive just to get here, and it's usually not full of Dalton students.

Dylan falls into the booth beside Oliver, and Kian tries to slide in next to me, but I stay rooted in place so he can't fit. We have a silent stare down until he hip-checks me, sending me sliding across the leather to make room for him.

Kian brightens with mock surprise. "This is crazy! What are the chances of us seeing you here?"

"You don't mind if we join, right, man?" Dylan asks Oliver.

"Friends of Summer's are friends of mine," he says slowly.

I try not to roll my eyes. These two are interrupting our date, and he's inviting them to stay?

Dylan extends a hand to Oliver. "I'm Dylan."

"Oliver."

"Nice to meet you, Ollie. That's Kian," he says, pointing to a beaming Kian. "By the way, you left this in Aiden's bedroom, Sunny." Dylan pulls something out of his pocket and places it in the center of the table.

Oliver eyes the hair clip, and I hope I'm doing a decent job of looking neutral even as I clench my fists. "That's not mine."

Kian's head tilts. "You sure? You're wearing an almost identical one right now."

Before I can lie again, Oliver chimes in, "Are you talking about Aiden Crawford?"

Could this date get any worse? I suppose this is karma for not actively listening to Oliver's fishing story.

"Yeah, Summer was getting that vitamin A with a side of that D, if you know what I mea—ow!" Kian yelps when I elbow him.

"We did an assignment together," I explain. "You know, the one on athletes and burnout."

Oliver hesitantly nods, but it doesn't take a genius to understand what Kian is getting at. Just as I'm about to throw the stupid hair clip at Dylan's smug face, the waitress pops in.

"Oh! Is this a double date?" she asks, looking between us.

"Yup," says Dylan, putting his arm around Oliver. "I think it's love at first sight."

Oliver's eyes widen in alarm, and he shrinks in the booth. Kian and Dylan have personalities the size of the campus. It's hard to be around them if you can't keep up. This date will leave Oliver with some serious post-traumatic stress issues.

"Fantastic. What would you like to order?"

Before Kian can speak, I push him out of the booth. "Actually, there's been a change of plans. Come on, Oliver."

Dylan doesn't budge for an uncomfortably long minute until he sees my scathing glare and concedes, letting my date out. I walk straight out of the diner, taking Oliver's sweaty hand in mine. We're about to cross the street when someone calls my name.

Connor Atwood.

Haven't I suffered enough? I throw a sheepish smile at Oliver. He's gawking at the quarterback. I might as well have run into the entire Dalton roster.

"Haven't seen you in a minute, Sunny. What's up?"

Apparently, the damn nickname is catching on. "I'm good."

Connor runs a hand through his blond hair. "Are you coming to the charity game?"

"Not today, I'm kind of busy. Maybe next time."

He cocks his head. "Really? I thought you and Crawford would for sure come together."

My teeth grind. "Don't know why you would think that." Either he's being purposely obtuse, or he hasn't seen Oliver's hand in mine.

Connor's eyes shift toward him. "Who's this? Cousin?"

"*No*," I grit out. "This is my date, Oliver. Oliver, this is Connor."

Connor scrutinizes the poor guy. "My bad. What's up, man?"

Oliver smiles and politely shakes his hand. "What game are you talking about?"

I almost groan out loud. Why must he engage Connor? "Football. You don't watch?" Connor asks.

"I'm not really a fan of sports."

Connor gives me a look as if saying, *Seriously, this guy?*

Squinting past the heavy rain, I mark my exit. "We have to go. I'll see you around, Connor."

In the car, the rain pours harder. The parking lot is secluded, just me and this guy who has been on the weirdest date ever. The only sound between us is the water droplets hitting the windows. When he starts the car, the suggestive lyrics that spill from the speakers make my skin itch.

"Sorry about that," I finally say, scattering the hush.

He pulls onto the main road toward Dalton. "Don't be. Your friends seem nice."

I suppress a snort. Those assholes were not trying to be nice. "I feel like I ruined our date."

He puts his hand high on my thigh. Touching isn't something I expected him to initiate, but his bravery is shining through in his car. It's obvious what he's hoping for when he faces me at a red light. I guess my accountant hypothesis has been proven null. A car honks behind us, and he accelerates but doesn't remove his hand. "I have you now, don't I?"

Does he?

My eyes dart to the window to watch the familiar streets run by. It isn't an SAT-level question, and I'm sure he meant it more in the literal sense, but I can't shake the strange feeling in the pit of my stomach when the campus finally approaches.

I find myself nodding, keeping the plastic smile perfectly poised. The only plus to the situation is the heat that blows through the vents, warming my freezing limbs. When he parks outside Iona House, I pry my eyes from the windshield, and the face staring back at me is expectant.

The heavy knot in my throat doesn't go down when I swallow.

I shove away every thought of Aiden. Every kiss and touch, all the ones he said I wouldn't forget, I desperately try to push it all out of my head when Oliver asks, "Can I kiss you?"

FORTY

AIDEN

KIAN'S HOWL PIERCES my ears as he flips off Eli in a celebratory dance.

When he strolled in a few minutes ago, he snatched the controller out of my hand and started playing the game. I didn't put up much of a fight when he took it because there's only one thing on my mind tonight. Rather, one girl.

Don't go.

I won't pretend that those two words didn't slide to the tip of my tongue when I heard about her date. Luckily for me, Kian had already told me about her plans.

Now it's impossible to pull my mind off her date, especially when the animated hockey player on screen is Lukas Preston. Talk about kicking a man when he's down.

The doorbell rings loud enough to be heard over Kian's shouting and my depressing thoughts.

"It's the pizza guy." Eli makes a move to get up.

"I got it." I'm up before he can leave me with a hyper Kian. The bell goes off again as I pull the door open.

A soaked Summer stands on the porch.

"You were right," she says, resting her hands on her hips, chest heaving. I'm speechless, staring at her drenched figure. "My date tried to kiss me."

The heat that radiates off my body feels charged with violence. Apparently, my little speech to her didn't dampen my jealousy.

She rolls her eyes. "Calm down, nothing happened."

When I swallow, my throat feels stripped raw. "Why not?"

"Because I couldn't stop thinking about you. Because every time he complimented me or touched me, I wished it was you. Because when we were in his car and he leaned in, I told him there's someone else, and I ran straight here."

The revelation grips my heart. "You ran here in the rain?"

She nods, droplets falling from her eyelashes onto her cheeks, making her look like a wet dream. I take a step closer to her because I'm pretty sure I'll combust if I don't touch her right now. I slowly brush away the water droplets on her cheeks.

"Are you done pretending, Summer?"

"You tell me." She takes hold of my shoulders, and our lips collide with a burst of fireworks.

I waste no time lifting her up, allowing her to wrap her legs around my waist. Pressing her against the doorframe, I devour her mouth in a reverent kiss, the sound of rain and the whipping wind becoming a faint background noise to the sweet sounds that fill my mouth. She tastes like *mine*. She always has.

She reciprocates my desperation, clutching me tightly when my hand sinks into her hair, angling her perfectly against my mouth.

"Aid—Oh—that is definitely not the pizza guy." Dylan's voice fills the entryway.

"Finally," Kian mutters.

Summer pulls away and looks over my shoulder to glare. "Your cockblocking worked, assholes."

I turn to the two idiots grinning from ear to ear. "What did they do?"

"You don't know?" Her eyes are round with surprise. "They crashed my date."

Dylan grins. "You were moping around like a lovesick puppy."

"And since you weren't going to do anything about it, we took it upon ourselves. You're welcome," Kian says proudly.

I shake my head. I realize these reckless and loyal friends of mine have my back like no other.

"Lovesick puppy, huh?" Summer teases, planting an affectionate kiss on my cheek.

The doorbell rings, and Kian shoots past us, reappearing with the pizza boxes. "You staying, Sunny? We got plenty of food."

"I should probably get home." She gestures to her soaked clothes, shivering ever so slightly.

"Fuck, you're probably freezing. Come on, I'll get you a change of clothes." I take her hand and lead her to the stairs.

"You two better be quick, or I'm eating your food," Kian says.

"There's no way they'll be quick," answers Sebastian, passing us in the hall to head to the kitchen.

"I'll take their share," says Cole, making his first appearance of the day.

Upstairs, in the quiet of my bathroom, Summer stands behind me as I set the shower temperature.

"I think I can work a shower, Aiden."

"Let me feel useful."

"Be useful over here," she says, peeling off her wet top.

I crouch in front of her, unzipping her skirt. "You wore this for him?" I ask, tugging it. The insecurity in my voice is embarrassing.

"You're the one taking it off, Crawford. I wouldn't be complaining."

A chuckle escapes me as I kiss her stomach. She's right. The last thing I should do is complain when she's half naked.

"I'll leave some clothes on the bed." My hands linger on her soft skin, and I have a hard time pulling away. Though I don't get far because she pulls me right back. I search the brown eyes that stare up at me so innocently.

"Will you shower with me, Aiden?"

"You sure?" I'm trying not to look like a puppy offered a treat. She just confessed how she feels, which is a lot for her, and I don't want her to feel suffocated.

"Are you choosing now to be a gentleman?" She takes a step back and unhooks her bra, dropping it to the bathroom floor, then pulls down her panties and tosses them at me. "I'm yours, Aiden. Treat me like it."

She's mine. And she's perfect. "You are," I say, my throat thick.

"So it's only right that you get the Summer Preston girlfriend experience."

I'm rock-hard. "Girlfriend? Is that the word we're using?"

"Mm. I figured you'd like it." She eyes my pants with a demure smile. My hands itch to touch her, so I pull her toward me.

"And what would that make me?"

Her hands glide up my biceps, causing a tremor to run through me. "My boyfriend. My hot, sexy, kind boyfriend."

A fire ignites somewhere foreign. "You don't need flattery to get into these pants, baby."

Summer's hands snake around my shoulders to the nape of my neck. "Then why aren't they off yet?"

I make quick work of shedding my clothes, carrying her straight underneath the showerhead. Her squeals fill the bathroom, and this time I don't tell her to keep it down. I want to hear every sound, every word, and every laugh.

FORTY-ONE

SUMMER

COLLEGE IS A lot more fun when you're not buried in textbooks.

When I left my dorm this morning, anxiety was eating at my bones, but just entering the hockey house has eased it.

"You wear glasses?" I ask Dylan, who's in the living room reading a book.

Dylan lowers his glasses. "Why? Is it turning you on?"

I give him a blank look. "How could you possibly come to that conclusion?"

"You didn't answer the question."

"Neither did you."

He smiles. Damn it, he does look good in those glasses. "Nah, just put them on because you were coming over. I heard you like romance books." His brows raise suggestively.

My face feels hot. "I am going to kill Aiden."

"For what?" Aiden descends the stairwell, wearing a white tank and black dress pants, his hair damp from a shower.

"Somehow, Dylan here knows about my book collection." I narrow my eyes.

"It's not like you hide it. You left one of your books on the couch. He's literally reading it right now."

What? When I see the blue illustrated book cover, I blanch.

Dylan rolls his eyes. "Don't be a prude. You two are not as quiet as you think you are." Mortified, I turn to Aiden, who only shrugs. "Besides, it's a good book. I got Kian to buy a copy. We might have to raid your library for more once we finish."

The words process slowly in my brain. "You and Kian are buddy-reading a romance book?"

"What? Men can't read romance? Selfish of you to deprive us of this gold mine of information. Aiden, you gotta read one too, she's onto something."

"I have."

That shocks the hell out of me. "When?"

"Babe, you fall asleep twenty minutes into every movie, and you made me promise not to watch them without you. I have to do something to keep occupied."

"So you've been reading my books?"

"Yup. I'm a big fan of the ones that have all the red tabs." My eyes widen when he smirks and drops a kiss on my lips. "Let's go upstairs so I can show you what I learned."

Hypnotized, I follow Aiden. When I hop on his bed, I sit with my legs crossed to watch him get dressed. The view doesn't get better than this, especially when his back muscles flex to show all those rolling hills and valleys that make me want to drag my nails down the smooth skin. Though when my eyes catch on something yellow beside me, my thoughts pivot.

A bouquet of sunflowers wrapped in paper and tied with a small bow sits on his bed. Something in my chest rattles, and my eyes sting. I stare at his back; my bottom lip quivers with a river of emotions. My breath is wobbly as I try to gain composure and not show my lunacy over getting flowers.

"Sunflowers? You don't think I'm a Venus flytrap?" I ask.

Aiden turns, smiling when he sees the flowers in my hand. My eyes must still be misty, because he watches me with a look so soft, I'm afraid it might break me.

"They were sold out." He grins when I glare. "You're my sunflower, Summer."

The light kiss he leaves on my nose sits heavy on my chest. "These are a step up from your funeral flowers," I say, making him chuckle. "I'm surprised you've never been in a relationship with all the cheesy things you say."

"Only for you." His earnest look has me lifting my head for a kiss. He kisses me until I'm flat on my back, still clutching the flowers. They'll have to pry them from my lifeless hands.

Our heated kiss leads to wandering hands and heavy breathing until it's cut short by his ringing phone. Aiden kisses me a final time before twisting to grab it off the nightstand. From the immediate smile on his face, I can tell that it's his grandma. I move to sit up as he leans against the headboard to talk to her, eyes still dark around the edges.

It's a short call, and when he hangs up, he asks, "Have you decided what you're doing for break?"

The question catches me off guard, but last week, Aiden asked if I wanted to come home to Providence with him. My original plans were to spend spring break in a hotel with room service and books. I'm hesitant about Aiden's sweet offer because meeting his family is a big deal. Especially if they're normal and not as dysfunctional as mine.

"I don't know." I take a breath. "I'm nervous."

"Summer, they already love you," he says. "If you feel uncomfortable, we'll leave. We can get a hotel, and I'll take care of you all night."

My heart swells. "As amazing as that sounds, I'm not going to make you miss time with family."

"So is that a yes?" he prompts.

"Yes, Aiden. Any place that made you who you are has to be the closest thing to heaven on earth."

He grows quiet for a long second. "Shit, you're making me blush, Preston." He chuckles. "You're getting spanked for that."

"It's a compliment! I can be romantic too."

His pitying look is irritating. "Babe, you are not the romantic one in this relationship."

I shrug. "I guess I can't have too many talents."

"I can." He rolls me onto my back but taps his phone to text his grandma that I'll be coming with him. Slowly, the reason I've been so anxious all day flutters back into my mind when he's not distracting me. Aiden seems to notice my nervous fidgeting, because he lifts my chin, forcing me to look up at him. His eyes do all the asking, and my words spill out automatically.

"My dad invited us to dinner."

The silence that follows the statement has me on edge. "Lukas Preston wants us to come over for dinner?"

"You don't have to say his full name every time."

He throws me a sheepish smile. "Sorry. Habit. Are you okay with this?"

"No, but I figured if you're there, he'll just talk to you about hockey all night."

"Babe, I don't want to intrude on your time if you need to talk to your dad."

I fiddle with my flowers. "You're telling me you don't want to meet a Hall of Famer?"

"That's not what this is about. I'm meeting my girlfriend's dad. How you feel is the most important to me."

There goes that heartburn-y feeling again. "It's fine. I only agreed because of my mom."

He nods, though he doesn't voice his opinion on my nonchalance. "When is it?"

"Next week."

Two rapid blinks tell me he's freaking out, but he masks it quickly with an impressively calm smile. The action makes my heart melt a little. "Okay. I'll pick you up after practice. Is it at their house in Boston?"

"Something like that." He stares at me for a better explanation, but I'd rather not discuss my parents' extravagance. "Let's go. It's our first official date, and I want to soak up every minute."

"Are you sure it's not because you want to hurry back so I can show you what I learned from your books?"

"Definitely not." I smile. But I file away that information to thoroughly explore later.

"NOW THAT I think about it, it's cold, and Ferris wheels aren't my fondest memory."

The surprise location for our date that my very ridiculous boyfriend had in mind is the Hartford Spring Fair. The event takes place the week before break, and it's usually filled with locals and college students. As I stare at the stupid rotating wheel, my insides go for a slow churn.

I successfully dragged Aiden to every game and even onto the teacup ride for toddlers he barely squeezed into. The attendant gave us some serious side-eye when I shoved Aiden's legs inside, but luckily, we got away with it. We went to every food stand I saw, in hopes that a warm, sugary funnel cake would make him forget about the ride, but none of it worked.

"Think of it as exposure therapy."

"Great idea. Except you're not my therapist, so it's just torture." I try rooting myself in place when Aiden pulls me forward. My strength is no match for him, and he easily drags me to the steps.

"I can sweeten the deal," he whispers, wrapping his arms around me from behind. There isn't much he can do about the outdoor temperature, but man do his arms make a huge difference.

"How?" His firm hold sends goose bumps traveling down my arms. "This isn't exactly what I pictured when you mentioned a date, Aiden."

"You're not having fun?" His expression swims with worry. It's kind of endearing, and it makes my heart hurt.

"Of course I'm having fun. I'm with you, aren't I? I feel like we're finally a real couple." The worry on his face melts away. "But this is pushing it." I point to the evil ride.

"I told you I'd save you a Ferris wheel ride. I always follow through on my word, Preston." He presses an index finger between my furrowed brows to relax the tension in my face. "We're creating a new memory. I promise by the time we touch the ground again we won't remember any of that."

Seeing Crystal all over him tainted the memory for me, but he saw Connor kiss me. We're both in the same boat about Ferris wheels.

I let him take my hand and seat us in one of the cars. The cold metal stings my thighs, and I shiver as the ride attendant gives a thumbs-up and pushes the lever. The car swings, and Aiden's hand intertwines with mine.

"See, this isn't so bad," Aiden says. "I'll have you warmed up in seconds." His warm hand skims my leg, going beneath my skirt to let his knuckles graze the thin fabric between my legs.

"There are people all around us, Crawford." My words are too breathy to hold any weight.

"I can make you finish before we even hit the ground."

He talks a big game, but I would be stupid to think he couldn't do it. As he watches the answer float around my head, he removes his letterman jacket and drapes it over my legs. The stolen warmth of his body kisses my cold skin, and I hum in pleasure. Aiden takes the moment to press his fingers against me, the fabric of my panties wet from just the touch.

"I can already feel you heating up, Summer. Let me between these pretty thighs, baby."

You'd think he was getting a blow job with how desperate he sounds. He kisses me slowly and thoroughly. Pulling away to catch my breath, I look around to see if anyone's watching, but none of the other riders are visible in their small pods.

I wrap my arm around Aiden's biceps, snuggling closer as he nuzzles my neck. The sun sinks into the Hartford skyline, and I whisper, "You're missing the view."

He focuses on my face, and his smile makes my stomach dip. "No, I'm not."

He kisses my nose and sends my heart into a frenzy. I part my thighs and Aiden's smirk grows as his finger hooks my panties to pull them aside. We rise higher into the atmosphere, and before I can prepare myself, he slides two thick fingers into me. A strangled moan flutters past my lips.

He threads his other hand through my hair and pulls my mouth against his. "Come on. Let me hear those pretty moans. Tell me how good I feel."

Stubbornly, I keep my jaw locked. He's too good at this, and I won't give him the satisfaction of proving me wrong about this ride. He moves his fingers slowly, going so deep I can feel his knuckles. The atmosphere feels much warmer up here. I'm so far gone my surroundings wilt away. I could be launched into the clouds for all I care. Every nerve ending in my body focuses on the hand between my legs.

My body jolts when our seat swings, sending my heart racing. The fading carnival music gives way to the wet sounds of Aiden's fingers pumping in and out of me. Soft lips dust kisses on my blazing hot skin. Whether it's a cool spring or a scorcher in the middle of August, I have no idea.

"I'm going to . . ." My words flutter away with the wind when his hand cups my breasts over my sweater.

He continues to pepper innocent kisses on my jaw as if he's not making me delirious. "We're not even halfway, baby. I have all the time in the world to make you come all over my hand."

My orgasm floats right at the surface, and I'm desperate to reach it. Like a fish out of water, I need to go under his spell again. "Crawford, do it or I'll do it myself."

"Say please."

There are times when I don't mind begging. Usually on my knees with Aiden's hand wrapped around my neck. But right now I feel stubborn. The orgasm that will likely rock my fucking world can wait.

"*You* say please," I counter. His brows raise as a low chuckle spills past his lips. "I might take pity on you and let you make me come."

My reverse psychology tactic doesn't work as I hoped, because he scissors his fingers in retaliation, then curls them, causing my nails to scratch the metal bench to keep from giving him the satisfaction. I swear I could tear through it at this moment. "You're not going to win this one, Summer."

"Try me."

He dips his head, and his lips find the sensitive spot between my neck and ear.

"That's cheating!" I gasp.

"It's winning," he whispers.

The sensory overload all but fries my brain to a pea. He continues palming me through my sweater and flicks a thumb over a sensitive nipple. His tongue swirls a pressure point on my neck that I'm sure only a ninja would know existed, and the throaty groan that vibrates against me is so deep I think it may be a loose current in my body.

Aiden sucks and bites until I'm panting so hard, I'm sure the other riders can hear me. I don't care if they witness my wound-up expression as long as I can find my release.

The wheel moves again, and I manage to open my eyes to see that we've reached the top. Aiden whispers, "Make a mess on my hand, Summer. Let me taste you off my fingers."

I shatter with his dirty words pressed roughly against my ear. Then he slides his fingers out of me and sucks each one clean.

"Did I change your mind?" he asks.

Have I mentioned how much I love Ferris wheels?

FORTY-TWO

SUMMER

"THAT'S IT. I'M quitting school and becoming a stripper." A fuming Amara slumps beside me.

It's a rare occasion that Connecticut gives us nice weather, so I'm taking full advantage by sitting outside by the statue of Sir Davis Dalton. The spray-painted devil horns and superglued pitchfork are long gone, though red stains linger on some parts.

I'm guessing Amara's meeting didn't go well. "I thought you said you didn't have the core strength for that."

Sampson slides onto the bench beside me. "I wouldn't mind a private show from you, Amara. No core strength required."

Amara scoffs. "Like you could afford me, Sampson." She abruptly stands. "I'll meet you at home, Sum, far away from the scum of the earth."

I watch her retreat, and when I turn back to Sampson, he grins. "I think she likes me."

"What do you want?"

He eyes me. "Someone's snappy today."

"Make one period comment and say goodbye to your hand."

He waves his fingers in front of my face. "You'd be depriving many girls of this magic."

"Or saving them from misery," I mutter.

Sampson stares at me with a curious look. "How are things with your application?"

"You're looking at a potential Stanford grad student," I mutter.

Last week, my social media was full of students celebrating their acceptance to Dalton. I haven't received anything, and when I talked to Langston, she said co-op applications take longer. If patience is a virtue, it's not one I possess.

"Look at the bright side, you could be in sunny California instead of Connecticut," he says.

Hopelessness clings to me. "My entire life is here. Every professor I've spent time getting to know, all my friends." I pause to hold the emotion clogging my throat. "Aiden."

"And me." He smiles, failing to scatter the dark cloud looming over my head. "But Aiden is going to be in Canada. You wouldn't be in the same place regardless."

"Except now I could end up on the West Coast instead of a few hours away."

"You're going to get into Dalton, and if by some fluke you don't, I'll transfer to Stanford Law to keep you company."

My heart feels like it's no longer inside my chest. "You'd do that for me?"

"Say the word, Sparkle."

A laugh bursts out of me. We first used that nickname in third grade after watching *My Little Pony*. I was Sparkle, and Sampson was Dash. "Knowing you, you would get accepted the moment you applied. But I didn't spend my entire life hearing you talk about a Dalton Law degree for you to not get one."

When someone calls my name, we turn to Cole Carter sprinting toward us. He slumps against the statue to catch his breath. "You are going to freak! I just saw Donny Rai."

Seeing Cole exhibiting this much emotion is rare. He's usually holed up in his basement with his eyes glued to a screen.

"Yeah, he goes here, buddy," says Sampson.

Cole shakes his head. "He was at the new diner, Lola's, in West Hartford this morning."

"How is that news?"

"He was with Langston." He says it like it's a huge reveal. I glance at Sampson to make sure I'm not the only one witnessing Cole's mental decline.

"She's his advisor. They're probably discussing coursework," I say.

"Sure. If the work required his tongue being down her throat."

I choke on my spit. "By *tongue down her throat*, do you mean kissing her?" I ask, my voice hoarse as Sampson pats my back.

"We both know you're not inexperienced, Summer." He throws me a deadpan look, but the embarrassment doesn't even register over the revelation. "Yes, they were kissing."

"Aren't there policies against that?" I ask.

"Dalton banned professor-student relationships. That's why I stick to the TAs," says Cole. We stare at him, but he only shrugs. "So I guess this means she's been giving him special treatment."

Suddenly, everything starts to make sense. "He's trying to get the co-op. That's why he made it so difficult for me to finish my application. Both of them did."

"And Shannon Lee is at Princeton now, so he doesn't need to worry about her," adds Tyler.

A trickle of contempt leaks into my bones. "So his only other competition is me."

"If you need proof, I took a picture." Cole pulls out his phone to show us. They're fully making out, and although the picture is grainy, it's clear what's going on. "What are you going to do?"

My head feels heavy with indecision. Reporting this to the dean needs to be anonymous. But I can't afford to be involved in this mess so close to when grad school decisions come out.

I drop my head in my hands. "I don't know."

Sampson stands. "I have a plan."

I peek up at him through my fingers. "A plan?"

AIDEN IS ASLEEP.

In the silence of the room, it's easy to hear his soft breaths and the faint sound of music playing somewhere in the house. I'm assuming it's Kian's since he just bought a new vinyl for his record player. He made it a point to tell me it was his way to block out noises coming from Aiden's room.

My eyes catch on my glowing phone screen sitting on the night-stand, but the heavy arm over my stomach bars me from reaching for it. After dinner, Aiden dragged me upstairs, and we celebrated his game-winning goal before he fell asleep.

It was Dalton's second game against Brown University tonight, and we had the home-ice advantage. Amara came with me, though she spent most of the game taunting the Brown students. It ended with her chucking a fry at a frat guy and him simmering in anger.

Now, hoping Aiden is as exhausted as usual after a big game, I carefully lift his arm and scoot away. When he doesn't stir, I roll off the bed and snatch my phone to send a quick text.

I shuffle around for my clothes, but they're strewn across the room. Giving up on the futile search, I pull out my overnight bag stashed in Aiden's closet.

With the time ticking, I get dressed and creep toward the door. The floorboards creak under my weight, sending my heart shooting out of my chest. I watch Aiden to make sure he hasn't been awakened by the ruckus, but his even breaths fill the room without disruption.

Easing open the door without the loud creaks waking the entire house is a difficult task, but I manage it. The house is devoid of light, so I pull out my phone flashlight as a guide. I relax as I reach for the front door.

"Where are you going?"

I jump. My phone slips from my grasp and slides across the floor to land by Eli's feet. The flashlight illuminates his face.

I clap a hand over my erratic heart. "Holy shit! You scared me."

"Sorry." He holds my phone. "Why are you sneaking around?"

"I'm not. I was just going for . . . a walk."

He raises a brow in suspicion. "At two in the morning? Why are you dressed like that?"

"This is how I always dress."

"Summer, you're wearing gloves and a beanie. In all black."

I forgot I stole the toque from Aiden's dresser. I should have put it on outside. "You mean my toque?"

His eyes narrow. "Don't try to distract me with your Canadian words. Why are you sneaking out?"

"What about you? Is there a reason you're awake right now?"

He rubs his neck. "This isn't about me. Where's Aiden?"

"Asleep." When his suspicion doesn't ebb, I sigh. "I have to do something, and I can't tell Aiden, or he'll try to fix it himself."

"What do you have to do?"

"I can't tell you either."

"You're not leaving the house in the middle of the night without telling anyone where you're going."

I check my phone, seeing the texts from Amara and Sampson light my screen. "I swear I'll tell you later. I really have to go."

I turn to the door, but Eli slaps a palm over it. Trying my luck, I pull on the handle, though it's no use because the six-foot-four defenseman's pinky is stronger than my entire body. I let go of the door, feeling like a toddler who's barred from playing outside. Eli's impatient look tells me he's seconds away from waking Aiden to tell him his girlfriend is sneaking out in the dead of night.

"First, you have to promise not to tell Aiden."

"I can't do that," he says.

Sometimes his honesty is seriously annoying. The heart of gold under all that muscle makes it impossible for him to lie. I thought giving him my most doe-eyed look would make him bend his rules a little, but I should know better.

"Fine. My advisor is hooking up with Donny Rai, and he's rigging acceptances with her help."

A look of disbelief clouds his features. "Did you tell the dean?"

"The dean is on sabbatical. He's gone until the end of the month, but we're exposing the truth from Langston's computer."

"Let me guess, you're sneaking into her office to do that?"

"Allegedly."

Concern weighs heavily on his features. "You realize that's breaking and entering, right? You could get expelled."

"She's put me through hell, Eli. Not only me but so many other great students. She never had any intention of letting us succeed."

Students fought to be mentored by her. Finding out that she put her selfish needs above aspiring sports psychologists makes my blood boil. I trusted her, and she stomped on my life's work.

He pins me with a sympathetic look, and when I turn, he stops me. "Let me grab a hoodie. I'm coming with you."

Before I can protest, he's gone. Only to reappear in a black toque and a hoodie to match mine. I frantically shake my head. "No. Nope, sorry. You can't."

"Aiden would want me to."

"Eli—"

"It's either this or I tell him."

He looks at me as if I'm the one who's being dramatic.

My nerves itch at me the entire ride to campus. When we arrive, two figures stand by the building watching our approach.

"This isn't really a plus-one event, Summer." Sampson looks annoyed, and Amara's blush grows when she sees Eli.

"He caught me on the way out. It was either him or Aiden."

Eli waves with an easy smile. "Hey, guys."

Amara greets him and I've never seen Sampson look this vexed.

He slows to match my stride. "Your overprotective boyfriend would have been preferred," he mutters, and stops in front of us. "There are cameras on the north side of the building. This is the only entrance without any. If we're quiet, we'll be fine."

"Two huge hockey players are anything but inconspicuous," Amara says, eyeing the building.

"Good to know you're thinking about my physique, Evans."

"Only in my nightmares."

I break up their stare down before they bicker the entire night. "Do we have a key?" I shuffle through my coin purse and pull out my student ID. "If not, we can try jamming this in there."

Amara shakes her head. "That won't work, it's electronic. We'll have to break it." She slides a mini crowbar from her sleeve.

We all take a step back.

"We are not using weapons." Sampson snatches her crowbar. "Unlike you three, I came prepared." He waves an access badge.

"Where did you get that?"

"Some postdoc student. She worked for admin." An administrative badge won't alert the school systems like a student badge would.

"She just gave it to you?" asks Amara.

"No one is immune to my charm."

"I must be an anomaly, then."

"Or in denial."

The scanner flashes green, ending their back-and-forth. "I'll get into her computer," Amara whispers. "You guys search for Donny's file to see if there's anything in there we can use."

Eli stands by the door. "I'll watch for security. You guys get what you need."

I stop him with a hand on his shoulder. "You can still bail, Eli."

"Not a chance." He disappears down the hall.

When I think back to my therapist's words, I realize she was right. I was missing out on having caring friends. The foreign feeling settles into the warmth of my stomach.

When we're inside Langston's office, Amara goes straight for her computer. It's only a few minutes later that she beckons us over. "I got it," Amara whispers.

We huddle around the computer as she navigates to Langston's email. The plan is to write an email from Langston's account to all the undergrads, and one to Dean Hutchins. Amara attaches the picture Cole supplied to both emails and sets it to send out on Monday morning.

She populates a new document and types out another paragraph. "Who is this for?" I ask.

"Dalton's gossip page." She smiles. "It'll go live when the email is sent out. Just in case the school tries to hide this."

Sampson looks impressed, and when Amara sees his expression, she rolls her eyes. But I don't miss her blush.

When she powers down the computer, a cool feeling of vindication drips into my system.

We sneak out of Langston's office, and Eli signals for us to duck when flashlights pierce through the windows. My breath gets stuck in my throat until the security guard passes by the building. We scurry to the alley we parked in and trickle off in silence.

At three a.m., Eli and I sneak back into the house. I engulf him in a grateful hug before I head upstairs. Slipping under the covers, I curl up with Aiden, who unconsciously pulls me closer. He looks so peaceful, I'm glad I didn't burden him with this risky plan.

Aiden tends to carry everyone's problems. As much as I love him for being a protector, I never want to be another person he risks everything for. He's already done enough by taking on his entire team's punishment for the trash fiasco. Once this is all settled, he'll be the first person I confide in.

In the meantime, I just need to swallow the doomed feeling trying to crawl out of my throat.

FORTY-THREE

AIDEN

"YOU KNOW, I'VE never had sex on a boat before."

I stiffen at the sound of Summer's soft voice in my ear. Any logical man would rectify that without a second thought. But I am clearly the dumbest man alive. "I would love to cross that off your bucket list, babe, but your dad is on this boat, and I still want to have a career when we touch land again."

We're staring at the boat—or *yacht*—that is getting docked in Boston Harbor so we can board. Now I understand why she's been evasive about the location of this dinner.

"Come on, we'll go to one of the cabins. I promise I'll be quiet." She holds up her pinky.

God, she's fucking adorable. "You can never keep that promise, Summer."

She kisses my neck, and I swallow hard when she hums. "You can put something in my mouth to keep me quiet, then."

My resistance is already paper-thin, and she's not making this easy on me. But I know what she's doing. She wants a distraction from the nerves she has about tonight. Summer's been lost in her thoughts a bunch lately, but she says it's because of her application, and I let her have that excuse for now. I know she'll tell me about whatever's on her mind when she's ready.

Her nails run along the nape of my neck, causing a shiver to crawl up my spine. "You smell *so* good."

Her eyes shine under the moonlight. Before I can speak, she kisses me. Hard, rough, sloppy. I kiss her back, unable to resist. I palm her ass and inch my fingers below her dress when someone clears their throat.

I yank Summer away from me so fast she almost stumbles off the deck. I hook an arm around her waist to balance my dazed girlfriend to my side.

Lukas Preston is staring right at me.

Calculating. Murderous. All appropriate reactions to what he just saw.

"You must be the boyfriend," he says with disdain.

My hands are sweaty, and I actually hear the buzz of nerves on my skin. I extend my hand. "Aiden Crawford, sir."

His eyes flash with recognition. "Crawford. Fastest collegiate player in the country. Toronto is lucky to have you." He turns to Summer and my grip on her tightens. "Sunshine?"

Summer stiffens, and Lukas Preston's eyes swim with a softness I didn't think he possessed.

"Hi, Dad." She looks past him. "Where's Mom?"

The hope in his eyes extinguishes. "Up there. She's excited to see you."

As soon as we climb the steps to the front of the boat, a woman comes into view. Her tan skin glows against the red dress, and I see her striking resemblance to Summer.

"Oh my goodness, meri jaan! You look gorgeous," she gushes, giving Summer a tight hug. "And this is that handsome boyfriend of yours? Aiden, right?"

"Yes, ma'am. It's so nice to meet you." I hand her the bottle of wine. Summer said I didn't need to get something so expensive, but we are on a yacht, for Christ's sake.

"Don't be so formal. Call me Divya. Come sit, you must be hungry."

Divya brings out multiple dishes, and from what I can name, chicken tikka masala, butter chicken, naan, biryani, and sweets cover the table. Then two identical girls walk in, eyes glued to their phones. Summer's twin sisters.

Serena and Shreya introduce themselves before they sit down.

"How did you get our sister to go out with you? She hates hockey players," one of them asks.

"Shreya," Summer warns.

I chuckle. "Trust me, I know. It wasn't easy, but it was all worth it." I take Summer's hand in mine.

"Are you two being safe?"

Summer chokes on her water, and I pat her back.

"Shreya. That is not an appropriate dinner conversation," Divya scolds.

The girl's eyes narrow. "Why not? We learned all this in class. I'm just making sure they don't pop out a kid any time soon. I'm way too young to be an aunt." When Shreya sees her dad's warning look, she shrinks in her seat and stabs at the salad on her plate.

The rest of the hour goes by with questions about me. About hockey, my future plans, and the occasional interrogative questions from Summer's sisters about my intentions.

After dinner, there's a stuffy strain in the air when Lukas Preston starts asking about school. Summer's easy body language shifts, and I can't react fast enough to do anything about it.

"Did you buy tickets for graduation? Your grandparents want to come too," says Divya.

Summer shifts uncomfortably in her chair. "Not yet. I'm focused on grad school decisions right now."

Her dad makes a noise, and the scraping of utensils stops.

"What?" Summer dares to ask.

"More school," he tuts. "You'd be better off if you stuck to figure skating like I said. I could have made you a star by now."

I place my hand over Summer's, trying to ease her tension. "Actually, Summer just held an event on campus that was a huge success for the psychology department. She raised way more than the target for her initiative."

Gray eyes turn cold. "Success in school is fine, but it's the real world that matters. Your options are limited after you graduate, and even after a master's, you'll spend more time in school. It's a misuse of valuable time."

Summer stands. "Thanks for your input, but I didn't come here to hear about how disappointed you are in me. I like school, I'm good at it, and I know that I want to be a sports psychologist."

He shakes his head. "That's not what I meant. You had the tools to become the best. I mean, look at your sisters, they're first in every competition."

Summer's eyes fill with sadness. "And I'm proud of them, Dad. But it really fucking sucks when nobody's proud of me." She tosses her napkin on the table and disappears down the hall.

I stand to follow her, but I can't just leave. "I don't mean to disrespect you, sir, but Summer has done nothing but work her ass off to get where she is. If you want to show her that you care, just be supportive of her decisions. How you're acting now is doing nothing but hurting her, and I won't stand by while my girlfriend can't have a conversation with her father without him overstepping."

Gray eyes grow frigid. "You know nothing about my family."

"I know enough." I see red, and I'm pretty sure he does too. "I know how she's cried about you choosing your career over her and how you haven't bothered to get to know her even after you retired. It's a shame, but I'm proud to say that she's the greatest woman I've ever met, and it's no thanks to you."

There's a murmur from Summer's sisters. I expect them to be angry that I'm speaking to their father this way, but they smile. Like they've been waiting for someone to have Summer's back the way she's always had theirs.

Serena pipes up. "He's right, Dad. You put so much pressure on her to mold into what you want."

"Now that she's doing what she enjoys, she's bound to feel like you don't care," Shreya adds.

Lukas Preston simmers in his seat. "Girls, go to your rooms."

Without another word, the twins shuffle away.

I turn to Summer's mom. "Divya, I apologize if—"

She lifts a hand. "No, this needed to be said. There's only so much of this I can take, Luke, it's been years. You need to fix this."

His lack of response only makes me angrier, and I know I need to leave before I do something stupid.

I meet Divya's embarrassed gaze. "I apologize for interrupting dinner, but I need to take Summer home. Thank you for dinner."

Walking through the hallway, I find the door locked. "Baby, it's me. Open the door."

It takes a minute before the lock clicks. Summer sits back on the bed, holding a photo frame. I take a seat and put my arms around her. It's a picture of their family Christmas.

"We were so happy here," she whispers. "He could have been a good dad. He would've been the best, but he chose not to."

"I think he does know, and that's why he's acting like this."

She sighs. "He's being selfish."

"I know."

Three beats of silence pass before she looks at me again. "You shouldn't have stood up for me. I don't want it to affect hockey."

"I don't care about that right now. I care about you. If you can count on one person to be on your side no matter what, it's me. I don't ever want you to think you're alone, because there isn't a second that goes by when I'm not thinking about you."

Tears rim her eyes when she kisses me. I kiss her back, and in an instant, she's all over me. Straddling my lap and pulling my tie.

"Summer . . ." I groan, mostly because my self-control has been withering since I saw her in this dress.

"Come on, check it off my bucket list."

"Your parents are right outside."

"They won't come in here. Please? I don't want to think right now." She starts undoing my shirt buttons, and her ass grinds over my erection, forcing a choked moan from me. She never needs to say please, but hearing it fall from her lips makes me want to fulfill her every desire. Before I can speak, she pulls down the straps of her dress, baring her breasts. I have no resistance as I grab her hips and grind her down. She moans in pleasure, kissing my neck.

I'm so fucking hard I can't remember why I thought this was a bad idea. "Take me out—"

"Sunshine." Our heads snap to the door where Lukas Preston's voice filters through.

Right, that's why.

I spring up, pulling Summer off my lap. I barely have my buttons done when he knocks again.

"Can we talk, Summer?"

I'm tucking in my rumpled shirt as Summer just sits there. Smiling.

"Have I told you how hot you look in that suit?" She's not even remotely alarmed by the man on the other side of the door.

"Summer," I warn, taking it upon myself to pull her straps up and fix her hair. She's holding back a laugh as I make sure nothing is askew, but my glare finally makes her sit up straight. Her eyes still flare with mischief. "*Jesus*, don't look at me like that."

"Like what?"

"Like you want my cock in your mouth."

She smiles wider when I say it, and I step away before I do something reckless. I open the door to Lukas Preston, who surveys my clothing. My lipstick-stained collar, to be exact. Shit.

"Aiden, would you mind giving us a minute?"

His voice is tight, but his neutral face is commendable, considering he wanted to rip my head off just minutes ago. I want to refuse, but Summer comes up behind me to give me a reassuring nod, and I squeeze her hand before leaving them alone.

FORTY-FOUR

SUMMER

TONIGHT IS A clusterfuck of emotions, and the situation before me is the last thing I expected.

"I was wrong," he says.

I lift my head to look at my misty-eyed dad. I've never seen him cry. Not when he lost a championship game, not when he fractured his ribs, and definitely not when his dad died. Never.

"I've been thinking about what you said to me, and I'm beginning to understand how you feel. You're not a prize to be won, Summer. You're a person, my daughter, and you need my love just as much as I need yours."

I take a deep breath, trying to stay strong. I recall everything my therapist allowed me to practice with her. "You're right. It's not okay, Dad. You treated me like a last priority, like hockey meant way more to you than I ever could."

He winces but lets me continue.

"Sometimes I wonder if I even enjoy what I do or if it's to spite you. Swimming? I did it because you wanted me on the ice. Psychology? I dove into my books because getting your attention seemed impossible, so I stopped trying."

"I had no idea you felt that way."

"Because you never cared enough to ask!" I can't keep my voice low. "I couldn't wait to get out of the house so I wouldn't have to see your disappointment every time you looked at me."

"Disappointment? Why would I ever be disappointed in you?"

"Because I stopped skating and playing hockey. I stopped caring about the one thing you loved the most in the world."

"It's my fault. I knew something was wrong, but I didn't bother asking you. When you said you thought we felt that you were a mistake, it broke me." He releases a shaky breath. "At eighteen, when we found out we were pregnant, our parents were pissed, and we were terrified. But none of that mattered when I saw you. I had no idea I could love anything more than I loved hockey. There was your mom, of course, but then there was *you*. The sweet, brown-eyed girl that called me dada."

I have to blink to keep from bawling my eyes out.

"As for your sisters . . . I love all my children equally. But you, Sunshine, you're my firstborn. My baby girl who taught me what it was—what it is—to be a father."

I can't help the tear that slips down my cheek.

"I loved you the moment I held you in the palm of my hand, and that'll never change, kiddo."

These are the words I've been dying to hear. They wash over me like the first drops of rain in a drought.

"But when I got signed, I had to play to provide for my family. My rookie season was tough, but your mom held us together. After that, it was like an addiction. I was living and breathing hockey. The league was different than anything I'd ever done. That's when your mom threatened to leave me."

The revelation startles me. "What?"

"She saw how neglected you were. How neglected she was. My family was slipping through my fingers, but everything was moving so fast, it was hard to get my feet on the ground."

"That's when her parents came back into her life?" I remember when I met my Nanna and Nanni. My dad wasn't around, and my mom was constantly stressed. Having their support was like a weight lifted off her. Grandparents weren't something I knew I was missing, but now I wouldn't trade their love for the world.

He nods. "By the time I grounded myself, your mother and I had gotten to a better place. But I couldn't figure you out. I thought we could share our love for hockey or skating, but you switched directions so quickly I didn't know what to do."

"I didn't want to compete for your attention."

He nods, Adam's apple bobbing and gray eyes softening.

"All the money stuff? I'm grateful, but none of it gave me you."

His tears fall in a stream. "You are the best thing to ever happen to me, Summer. I'm sorry that I didn't show it these last few years or that I seemed judgmental. I would have loved for you to skate, but I can't force passion. Your passion is psychology, and I am proud of you for all you've achieved. Truly." He wipes at his face, red eyes determined as he takes my hand. "I don't deserve your forgiveness, but let me earn it, please."

The sincerity in his voice sears my heart. I don't know if I forgive him, but telling him how I feel makes everything lighter. My therapist would be so proud.

I nod, and his face lights up so dramatically you'd think he won the Stanley Cup again. "Do you want to finish dinner?"

"I think I want to be alone with Aiden."

He gives me an understanding nod, but I don't miss the hint of disappointment in his eyes. He stands. "You love that boy?"

"A lot," I say, shocking myself. But I really, really do love him. My heart feels so full it might burst.

"Captain of the hockey team, huh?"

"Don't even say it."

He holds back a laugh, and I roll my eyes, suppressing a smile. We find Aiden and my mom out on the deck. She's laughing as he tells her something, but I only notice how handsome he looks in his suit. It's such a contrast from the usual tight T-shirts and hockey gear that I find myself entangled in wisps of heat just from the sweet look he gives me.

His hand intertwines with mine. My eyes might still be puffy, but the tears are long gone. Now all I can think of is the question my dad asked, and how easily I gave him the answer.

But those words feel like weights on my tongue now that I'm standing next to Aiden.

His lips press against my temple. "How are you feeling?"

"Better now." I lean against his arm.

He searches my face to reassure himself. Before we leave, he promises my mom another dinner, and I snicker at his naivety. When we're in the car, he turns on his music and drives us home with one hand on my thigh, his thumb making soothing movements on my skin. He hasn't said anything the entire ride, and I know he's trying to give me space, but I can't help but feel embarrassed.

"If you run now, I won't blame you," I say, breaking the silence.

Aiden glances over at me, then back to the road with a tick of his jaw. "Why do you say that?"

"Because you just saw that shit show back there. No one wants to be attached to that."

He shakes his head but doesn't speak until we pull into his driveway. He turns off the car and faces me. "Telling you about my parents was the first time I've talked about them in years."

I hesitate. "Why?"

"I was afraid to feel the emotions that would hit me if I did. But with you, it felt almost therapeutic, like I don't need to carry the weight alone. I can share my memories, so it doesn't feel like my parents are completely gone."

"Because they're not gone, Aiden. Your memories keep them alive, and when you share them with me, I want to keep them alive for you too."

His bright smile surfaces. "Can't you see how lucky I am to have you?"

A burst of fireworks explodes in my chest. When he looks at me like this, I forget about all my problems, and I wish I could see myself through his eyes. Then maybe I could become that version of me.

He captures my hand. "As much as I love your body, your mind trumps everything. I can't understand how someone so fucking amazing is bound up into one human being. You make everything so much brighter, Summer, and it drives me crazy that you can't see that."

I drop my gaze to our intertwined hands. "You make it sound like I'm perfect."

"To me you are. You're beautiful, strong, kind, and so deserving of love that I hope I can prove it to you in this lifetime. Because that's how overwhelmingly perfect you are to me."

His perfection has made me speechless time and time again. Every word he says is one I want to say right back to him. But my tongue weighs heavy as the feelings pin me down.

"How can you be so sure?" My chest fills with a raw emotion that scratches my throat.

"Because I love you," he says, and I freeze. "Anyone would know it. They only need one look at me when you walk into a room to see it. I love you, Summer." His thumb strokes my cheek, and when he touches me, I feel like one of those lava cakes that oozes warm chocolate from its center. "I want to do everything with you, and I want you to do everything with me."

I blink away the tears. "Sounds possessive."

"It is." He pulls me by my jacket and claims my lips. "You and me, Preston. That's the only way I want it."

That's what cracks the center of my chest and allows the river of warm honey to flow through. This fucking guy. He's ridiculously attractive and sweet. I didn't stand a chance.

FORTY-FIVE

SUMMER

CLUBBING ON A Thursday isn't usually my go-to form of self-pity, but here we are.

I probably should just head to the library and study for my upcoming exams, but reading anything psychology-related will set me over the edge. It also doesn't help that I can't find my student ID. Without it, I can't access any of the private study pods. So, logically, clubbing it is.

Amara stares at me wide-eyed as I show her my outfit. It's black, short, and silky. The perfect combination for my newly adopted reckless persona.

A wary look crosses her face. "What's wrong?"

"Does something have to be wrong for me to have fun?"

"Summer, the last time you had fun was sophomore year when we went to that frat kegger, and you played Scrabble with the pledges. So, yes, something had to have happened."

She's right. Something did happen. The moment I've been waiting for, for all these years, was delivered to my inbox this morning, and I've been in denial ever since.

"I didn't get in."

The words slip out so fast Amara jerks like I slapped her. "How? You probably read it wrong." She snatches my phone from my hand and opens my email app.

"I didn't. I got waitlisted. I guess Donny didn't even need to compete with me for co-op," I say with a bitter laugh. Our plan to get Langston out hasn't worked. The dean's still on sabbatical, and although word is getting around through students, no one with authority has done anything. It's maddening and has me jerking awake with anxiety in the middle of the night. It's getting worse because whenever there's a knock at our front door, I expect it to be the police coming to arrest me for burglary. That's why I've been spending most of my days at Aiden's house.

Amara scrolls through the sugar-coated rejection. "You said Dr. Müller loved your report. This can't be right."

"He did, but he's not my advisor, and he's not the one on admissions."

"But you can't wait; that leaves you with no choice but to take a gap year."

I swallow. "I know. That's why I accepted my backup."

The gasp that leaves her is a bit dramatic. "You're leaving Dalton? You've been dreaming about this program for years. Your mom said you were eight when you decided you were attending this school or nothing at all. Honestly, I was surprised you didn't have a shrine of Sir Davis Dalton in your closet."

"That would be overkill."

"Not for the girl who's been on the dean's list year after year. You're a go-getter, Sum. You don't let anything stand in the way of your dreams. Especially not some terribly wrong decision."

"I have no choice." Tears prick my eyes. "Can we not talk about this tonight?"

Amara gives me a tight hug. "If you need me to ruin Langston's life, just say the word," she says. I exhale a watery laugh because even though she says it like a joke, I know she's serious. "Okay, now give me a few minutes to match your slutty vibe."

Twenty minutes later, we're outside a Hartford club. The line is longer than the ones leading to the bookstores during textbook season. "We're going to freeze out here," I say, my teeth chattering.

Amara flips her hair, takes my hand, and leads us directly to the front of the line. The bouncer's eyes land on her chest, then mine. "This is a private event. You need an invitation."

"I see you staring at my two invitations right now, big guy," she says, and I swear his cheeks tint pink. "Look, I just broke up with my boyfriend, and I want to have fun tonight. A lot of fun." Amara emphasizes the lie with a finger trailing along his jaw.

He swallows but remains resolute. "You have to be on the list."

"Is there a substitute for a name? Maybe a *number*?" She waves her phone, and he perks up.

Before I know it, he has Amara's number—a fake one—and we're inside. A minute later, the bartender plops four shots of tequila in front of us. "From the guy at the end of the bar."

A middle-aged man who looks married with children winks at us. Amara sends him a flirty wave and hands me a shot.

"Who is that?"

"Who cares?" We clink our glasses and throw back the shot. She hauls me to the dance floor, and for the first time since I submitted my application, I have fun. Unfortunately, most of that fun is found at the bottom of a tequila bottle. The music bumps through the club and although a few guys try to dance toward us, Amara's sharp glare sends them away.

I'm parched when we move off the dance floor, and when I order water, it's accompanied by another shot. I'm about to decline but decide to down it anyway. I'm not in the mood for self-preservation tonight.

"I gotta go to the restroom," Amara says. "Come with me?"

Inside, the bright fluorescents attack my vision as I stumble into one of the stalls. I'm sure I fall asleep on the toilet for a split second because when Amara calls my name, I jolt.

"Didn't you tell Aiden about your plans tonight?" Amara asks.

"No, he had a game," I say, reaching for the tap.

"You didn't tell him you were going to the club?"

I focus hard on scrubbing my hands. "My phone died before we got here. It's not a big deal."

She jumps off the counter, heels clicking against the tiles. She shows me the six missed calls and four texts, all from Aiden.

"Shit."

"Yeah." When she brings up the phone to call him, I stop her. "What are you doing? He's worried."

"I haven't told him about the application."

Her face drops in disappointment. "Summer . . ."

"I swear I will, but it just happened today. I didn't want to get in his head before the game." The team was gone for an away game, so I haven't seen him since yesterday.

"He's worried."

I shake my head, eyes stinging. Aiden is my comfort through everything, but I don't want this news to feel like reality. "I can't talk to him without crying."

She nods and texts him instead.

Before I know it, we're too many tequila shots deep, and my feet ache so bad I have to remove my heels.

"Ready to go?" asks Amara, finally peeling off her dance partner. She was adamant that there would be no men tonight, but when an attractive guy approached her, I urged her to him.

"My liver's broken," I groan, recalling why I don't go out. I nod to the guy staring at her. "Are you taking him home?"

"I don't know. He has to earn it."

Judging by his expression, he'll do anything to earn it.

Heels in hand and arms linked, we wobble out of the club. Looking past the UHart students, I spot a black truck and a very familiar hockey player leaning against it. My heart stops.

My backstabbing friend wears a sheepish smile. "He insisted."

A few people recognize him, but he focuses on me. I swallow because although he looks serious, he also looks hot as hell. His black shirt accentuates every mountain of muscle, and his weighted look doesn't help the rising temperature in my body.

"You're not wearing shoes," he says when he reaches me.

I look at the pink polish on my toenails. "My feet hurt."

He hums and turns to Amara. "Thanks for texting me." From his neutral tone, I can't tell if he's mad. It's all mixed up in my dizzy head. The dead phone in my purse feels like a heavy brick. "You two need a ride?" Aiden asks Amara and the guy.

When he whispers something to her, she immediately nods.

It's when Aiden starts walking closer, almost right into me, that I stumble back. "What are you doing?"

"Carrying you."

I shake my head. "I can walk."

"I know you can." He lifts me anyway. I make a squeaky sound that isn't much of a protest as I anchor my arms around his neck. His tight hold is warm, coaxing me to lay my head on his chest and breathe in his clean scent. The truck flashes when he unlocks it, and it feels criminal to leave his warm cocoon.

"I missed you," I whisper.

He plants a kiss in my hair. "Missed you too, baby."

FORTY-SIX

AIDEN

DRIVING MY DRUNK girlfriend, her roommate, and some random dude home at two in the morning is not my usual postgame routine. Amara and her date jump out, and Summer sleeps soundly in my passenger seat.

I touch her cheek to nudge her awake, but she swats it away and burrows further into the seat. "Summer, wake up."

She mumbles something again, most likely a threat.

"If you want to sleep in my truck, I'm all for it, but we'll have to move to the back seat. I'll keep you warm back there."

Summer blinks herself awake. "Do you enjoy irritating me?"

I chuckle, retrieving a water bottle from my glove compartment. She takes it, downing the entire thing.

"Why did you wake me? My dreams are so much better than reality, full of little fairies braiding my hair."

"I could braid your hair."

She stares blankly. "You don't know how to."

"I'll learn," I say. Summer smiles, rests her head against the seat, and her eyes flutter shut again. I can't shake the notion she's hiding something. "Why are your dreams better than reality?"

She shrugs.

"Do you want to talk about it?"

"I want to sleep." Summer tries opening the passenger door and groans when it doesn't budge. "If you're trying to kidnap me, I have two thumbs, and I'm not afraid to use them."

"Stay at my place."

"Why? So you can hold me in your stupidly large arms and coax everything out of me? I'm not falling for your tricks, Clifford." She points a finger at me, eyes narrowed to the point that they're basically closed.

The name change tells me she's more drunk than Amara let on. "You can come with me, or I'm staying with you."

"Nope. That's a bad, bad idea. Sober Summer is screaming at me right now."

"Tell her not to, or she'll wake up with one hell of a hangover."

She groans in frustration. "Stop making sense! Just let me sulk in my dorm."

"Sulk with me. No questions asked," I lie. I need to know why she wants to sulk and why keeping it from me is so important to her. "Please?"

She shakes her head more vigorously. "Don't give me those eyes."

I hold back a smile. "What eyes, baby?"

"Those! All green and innocent looking. You can't fool me, buddy." She closes her eyes, trying to stay firm.

"Summer, you can barely stand, and Amara's up there with her date. Let me take care of you."

Her eyes fly open, and I'm sure she's about to argue, but she pauses instead. "You want to take care of me?"

"As long as you'll let me."

It doesn't take much persuading after that to get Summer to come home with me. When I carry her inside, the house is quiet, and I'm relieved there isn't an impromptu party. After my talk with Dylan, he's banned from attending or throwing parties until further notice. But that isn't stopping him from getting blitzed like he's at one.

Summer strips out of her dress and pulls on one of my T-shirts before diving under the comforter. I do the same and slip in beside her. She abandons the mattress to lie on top of me. The way she kisses my chest sparks a hot sensation on my skin. My hands are firmly set on her waist, unmoving despite her protests. She's drunk, and as much as she wants to, I know the only thing we'll be doing tonight is sleeping. And figuring out why the hell she went and got wasted.

"You're boring. Should we go see what Kian's doing?" She tries to climb off me, but I tighten my hold. Apparently, drunk Summer is adventurous.

"I'd rather not get another lecture about tarnishing the sanctity of his room."

"He's so dramatic! We only mistook his room for yours once."

Kian made me buy him new bed sheets and wash his old ones, twice. We weren't even completely naked. Last week, Summer and I were both so lost in each other that we didn't realize we turned right after the staircase instead of left. Kian locks his door now.

She's quiet for a moment, allowing her fingers to draw shapes on my chest. "Why did you come get me tonight?"

"I'll always come get you, Summer. Even when you don't want me to."

She makes a face. "You're nauseatingly perfect. I think I really like you."

Drunk Summer likes to reveal her feelings too. Though I assume the prerequisite to dating is liking each other. "Is that a good thing or a bad thing?"

Her mouth twists in thought. "I'm still deciding."

"Can I do anything to speed up the process?" I tuck her hair behind her ears, and she shivers.

I wrap her in my arms, and she pecks my chin. "You being you is enough."

"So you're nice when you're drunk, eh?"

"Don't make me regret it," she grumbles.

She turns away to lay her head on my chest again. I can feel the shift in her mood. Times like these, I wish I could see the problems swirling in her head and sort them out for her.

Summer rolls off me to lie on the mattress, but I don't let her get far. When I cup her face, the thread of indifference snaps, and vulnerability spills into her expression. The action draws the tears she's been fighting to soak the pillow.

My heart squeezes to an uncomfortable degree as I wipe the wetness. "What's wrong, baby?"

She shakes her head.

"Will you tell me why you got drunk tonight?"

"For fun." She sniffles.

"The real reason, Summer."

"A lot of people get drunk for fun."

"People? Yeah. You? No."

She doesn't speak, and I know I shouldn't push her, but I can't stand seeing her like this. If it has something to do with Donny again, I'm not confident I can hold myself back from driving my fist into his face. Probation be damned.

Her eyes brim with more tears. "I'm leaving Dalton. I didn't get into the master's program." Her voice cracks.

My heartbeat goes into overdrive, and I'm sure she can feel the storm that brews below the surface. Words scatter and I barely form a sentence when I see her anguish. I hold her tighter, attempting to fix the broken look she gives me.

"Fuck, I'm so sorry, Summer. Is there something we can do? Maybe an appeal? We can talk to admission or get Dr. Müller to vouch for you."

She shakes her head. "It doesn't work like that. Besides, I don't think I can fight for this anymore. I'm just tired."

Summer's resilience through the entire assignment had me in awe of her. Knowing she feels depleted by the one thing she wanted most tears at my chest.

"And Stanford is the only other place with a comparable program. It was my backup, and their offer acceptance deadline was tonight."

Stanford? I'll be in Canada after this semester, but I never thought she'd be more than an hour's flight away. Let alone on the opposite side of the country. A headache blooms, and I try to keep from saying something stupid as I stare at the ceiling. "So, you're going to California?"

"Yup." Her shaky inhale tells me she's trying not to cry. "Know any Stanford hockey players?"

"That's not funny."

Her sigh is heavy and full of despair. "I know. I'm sorry."

"So that's it. You're just going to leave?" It's hard to keep my tone from being harsh. I can't fathom that this is reality.

"It's not like I have a choice. If I can't get in here, I have nowhere to go. Everything I've been working for will be gone, just like that."

"What about your five-year plan?" It's a stupid question. That much is clear from her reaction.

"Aiden, I'm in bed with the captain of the hockey team. My plan is obsolete."

I raise my hand to skim her jaw, rubbing my thumb on her smooth skin. "My sincerest apologies for ruining your plans."

"Worth it," she beams, soothing the rubble in my chest. "I've never done long distance."

Realizing that Summer is thinking about us too relaxes me more than I expected, and my headache eases. "Me neither."

"Do you want to? Do long distance, I mean."

My neck almost hurts from how quickly I turn. "Are you kidding? You're not getting away from me that easily, Preston."

She grins. "Damn, I thought I'd finally found my window."

"I'd board up all the windows before you thought about it."

"You're bordering on psychosis."

"Does that get you going? I can turn it up a notch."

"No." She laughs. "I think we need to evaluate you again."

"Evaluate away." I strip away the covers, causing her to squeal when the cold air touches her skin. She clings to me, stealing any warmth she can.

"I meant psychologically," she mutters.

I plant a kiss on her cheek. "We'll make it work, baby. We would have to for my rookie season anyway."

Brown eyes glow with surprise. "You've been thinking about the future?"

I'm not surprised by her question because when we first met, I was adamant about not having a plan. At the time, hockey was my only priority. But now that I have her, I want to balance her into my life. It'll be the easiest thing I'll ever do.

"*Our* future. You make it hard not to want you in every aspect of it."

Her perfect lips pull into a heart-wrenching smile. "Are you proposing?"

"I'm positive if I asked you to marry me right now, you'd kick me in the balls."

She laughs, and the sweet sound strikes the heart that belongs to her. "I'd never hurt Aiden Jr." Teasing fingers flutter down my abs. I let her do it, though it's complete torture knowing I won't act on the impulse. When her fingers dip under the elastic, I grab her wrist to stop her.

Her annoyance is clear when she huffs and slaps her hand on my chest. "You're doing that thing where you're trying to be a gentleman, aren't you?"

"No, I'm doing that thing where I take consent seriously."

She rests her head on my chest. She's quiet for so long that I think she's asleep, but she jerks. "You can't watch our show without me. We'll have to figure out a schedule."

"Can't we just watch, then discuss it later?"

Her gasp startles me. "That is so sick and twisted. Of course we can't do that!"

"Okay, okay, we'll figure out a schedule."

She sticks out her pinky. "Promise?"

"I promise, Summer." I curl my pinky around hers.

We grow quiet again as reality sets in. "This sucks," she says, and I couldn't agree more. "I'm going to miss you."

"Me too, but let's think about now. I'm here." I pull her closer. "You're here too, right?"

She nods. "No place I'd rather be."

I'm all in. Mind, body, and soul, or whatever the fuck that movie Summer made me watch said. Down to my core, I'm hers. "I'll just have to leave my mark, so you keep coming back for more."

Because she's already left hers, and it's right in the center of my chest.

FORTY-SEVEN

SUMMER

MY PARANOIA ABOUT the break-in doesn't ebb until we've left Connecticut. It's been eating away at me, but I've managed to stuff it somewhere deep in my conscience for our week off school. The ninety-minute drive to Aiden's grandparents' house in Providence, Rhode Island, is spent with me changing every song that Aiden suggests. But when I put on one I like, he sings it with me, and I can't keep the smile off my face even when it starts to hurt my cheeks.

When we pull into the driveway of the beautiful brick house, an emptiness settles in my stomach. The last time I spent spring break with my family was when we watched my dad play, and we skated with him after the game, but now the memory forms a dark pit in my stomach.

When Aiden's warm hand pulls my attention to him, that pit shrinks. "You okay?"

I nod, and although it doesn't look like he believes me, he smiles tenderly, kissing my knuckles.

Edith and Eric Crawford glow like Christmas lights when they open their front door. Their love radiates off them like light from a flickering candle, and I feel some of it when Edith squeezes the life out of me.

Since I'm the first girl Aiden's brought home, they want to know everything about me. An hour after I've given my entire autobiography, we head upstairs to get settled.

"Summer, you can stay in the guest room, and Aiden, your old room is just the way you left it."

Aiden gives his grandma a weird look. "She can stay in my room."

"You can't sleep on the couch, bean. Your coach will be upset if I send you to school with back pain."

He laughs, but she's not making a joke. "I meant we can stay in my room together," he explains.

She doesn't say anything, bewildered. Uh-oh.

"The guest room is perfect," I interrupt before Aiden can give her an answer.

"Summer," he starts.

"Seriously, Aiden. Why would you want to sleep on the couch?" My warning look only makes his face screw in confusion.

Edith's face relaxes into a bright smile. "Great, you two get settled, then, and I'll start on dinner."

I smack his arm when she's out of earshot. "Are you crazy?"

He clutches his arm with a wounded look. "For wanting to sleep with my girlfriend? I don't think so."

"In your grandparents' house! I'm trying to make a good impression here, Aiden."

He chuckles and takes my bag. I grab the handle, and we play a childish game of tug-of-war in the hallway until he lets go, and I stumble back.

"You're serious," he says. Aiden looks exhausted. He was probably looking forward to just falling asleep with me. "This is ridiculous. Don't be stubborn."

"It's one weekend. Your balls won't shrivel up."

Aiden frowns, running a hand over his face. "Summer, my

grandma doesn't care." I still don't budge, so he continues. "She's the same woman who filled my bag with condoms when I left for Dalton. And the one who told me if I got you pregnant, she'd kick my ass, but if we got started early, we could fill an ice rink. Trust me, she's messing with us."

I shift on my feet. "I still don't think it's a good idea. This is your childhood home. I'm not tainting its sanctity."

"It's not a church, babe." He takes a step closer. "Come on, I'll even read your porn to you."

I clutch my bag tighter, a hot flush rising to my cheeks. "I don't need you to narrate my porn. I have apps for that."

When his brows raise, I realize I've said too much. But Aiden doesn't fight me further, because I put my things in the guest room.

Dinner with the Crawfords revolves around stories about Aiden's childhood and his parents, Lorelei and Aaron. My cheeks start to hurt from smiling so much, and when I ask his grandparents to reveal his embarrassing stories, Aiden squeezes my thigh in retaliation.

If I could look inside my chest, I'm sure it would glow tonight.

After dinner, I race up the steps before him and lock my door. But I regret it as soon as I'm thrashing around, unable to sleep.

When my phone buzzes with a text, I know who it is.

AIDEN

Aiden: I miss you.

Summer: You just want me to feel bad, so I'll sleep with you.

Aiden: Not true. I want you to feel bad, so you'll come spoon me.

Summer: I'm screenshotting this and sending it to the guys.

Aiden: Go ahead. Tell them how much I love to beg on my knees for you, too.

Aiden: I'll rub your back until you fall asleep.

Summer: Nice try.

Aiden: I can bring up some tea.

Summer: Not gonna work. Good night, little spoon.

WAKING UP EARLY the next morning is easy because I didn't sleep. Downstairs, Edith's in the kitchen, and when I try to help, she bats me away.

"Is Aiden still asleep?" I ask as she fixes me a plate.

"You didn't sleep in his room?" When she sees the look on my face, she bursts into laughter. She places a hand on my shoulder to catch her breath. "I'm sorry, honey. I was just trying to mess with Aiden. I'm not that old-fashioned."

"Oh," I chirp, feeling stupid.

She's still chuckling when she heads to the stove. "Aiden's out with Eric to check on the diner. They're probably on the frozen pond now, though."

I drink my orange juice. "Does Eric play too? Aiden's never mentioned it."

"Not at all. But Aiden's parents used to take him, so Eric's learned enough to hold his own."

Tenderness colors my heart. "You know, Aiden would love for you guys to come to a game."

The suggestion drags a sad look to her face, and I don't know if I've said something wrong. "We want to come, but it's hard with the diner and Eric's knee. The long drive is almost impossible."

Knowing how much it meant to Aiden that I went to his games, I could only imagine how thrilled he'd be to see his grandparents there. He'd never put them out by asking them to make the trip, but that didn't mean I wouldn't try. "If I could arrange something for you guys to come to the Frozen Four in Boston, do you think you could work around the diner schedule?"

It's a long shot. I'd have to ask my dad for help, and the qualifying games haven't been played yet. But I have faith in the team.

"That would be great, but we don't want to put you out."

"Trust me, you'd be doing me a favor." If there's anything I can do to make Aiden's eyes shine brighter, it's a win for me.

A chilly kiss on my cheek makes me jump. Aiden's flushed from the cold, and his hair is messy from playing on the ice. Eric breathes hard, pulling out a chair.

"Need an inhaler, old man?"

Eric laughs. "Let's not forget I almost outskated you."

"I was taking it easy on you."

Edith brings Eric an ice pack for his knee. Despite his winces of pain, Eric looks like he'd do it again just for Aiden.

"Were you taking it easy on me when I outskated you?" I ask.

Aiden's gaze cuts to mine in a narrow-eyed look. One that sends a chill of heat down my spine. He looks really good in the dark green sweater his grandma knit him. Not seeing him last night or this morning pulls at a sensitive part of me. In retaliation, Aiden places his cold hands on my neck, forcing a squeal from me.

Edith bats his hands away. "You beat him, Summer? We've got to hear about this."

His grandparents tease, and Aiden rolls his eyes. When they pull out the photo album, he groans and excuses himself to take a shower while I gush over his baby pictures. Apparently, Aiden was blond like his dad until he was about four years old, and his hair turned the brown it is today. I don't hesitate to send it to the guys.

SUNNY'S ANGELS

Kian Ishida: Is that Cap in a Little Bo-Peep costume? I'm posting this to my story.

Dylan Donovan: No fucken way. I love you for sending these.

Eli Westbrook: I've been waiting for these pics to see the light.

Summer Preston: Eli why didn't you tell me you two took the same girl to prom?

Eli Westbrook: Actually, I asked her first. Then she asked him and suggested a throuple.

Dylan Donovan: It's only right that you take Summer from him now.

Eli Westbrook: You're obligated to marry me, Sunny.

Summer Preston: I would have to decline, though may I suggest a . . . throuple?

Eli Westbrook: You're evil.

Dylan Donovan: Third time's the charm, buddy.

After eating just about everything Edith gives me, I head upstairs with a food coma. Curiosity pulls me into Aiden's room of deep blue and hockey posters. There's a wall of achievements, too, but most of his awards are in the trophy case downstairs.

"Snooping?" Aiden closes the door behind him.

"Just trying to get a read on you."

He falls onto his bed. "Come over here and you can read me like one of your books, baby."

"So confident, yet I just saw a picture of you dressed as Little Bo-Peep."

His laugh is low and addictive. "I was blond, and my mom thought she was having a girl."

I chuckle, then turn to his awards again. "You're really good, huh? The awards barely fit."

"Are you just realizing that?" His easy confidence makes me gravitate toward him. "You know what else I'm really good at?" He pulls my arm, and I fall into his lap. "Kissing you."

His mouth glides down my neck, and my breath hitches. "This was just your way to get me in your bed, wasn't it?"

Aiden's dark chuckle only ignites my skin. He pulls me to straddle his lap, and as his lips skim mine, his phone vibrates.

"We should go," he says suddenly, shifting me off his lap. I don't get to ask questions because he's already descending the stairs with our bags. Aiden hands me my jacket, and I slip it on with questioning eyes.

"We'll visit soon," he says, giving his grandparents a hug.

I'm engulfed in hugs, and Edith hands me a tin of cookies. "There's more where that came from if you visit again."

"Bribing her with cookies? That's genius, Edith," says Eric.

They wave as we pull out of the driveway, and Aiden intertwines his hand with mine. "They like you."

"I like them," I say as he merges onto the freeway. "Where are we going? I thought we were staying for another day."

"I'll have nonstop games when we're back from break, and I want us to spend time together. I've got plans for you, Preston."

"Sexy plans? Or are you leaving me in the woods because I locked the bedroom door last night?"

"I'll have you over my knee for that." My cheeks flush with heat when he gives me a look that weakens my knees. "Shit, you're into that, aren't you?"

"You'll have to find out."

He forces his eyes back to the road. "I intend to."

FORTY-EIGHT

AIDEN

SUMMER'S BEEN CRYING for eight minutes. When I pulled into the hotel parking lot, she was ecstatic that her original hotel plans were coming true. But when we came up, and she saw the rose petals and candles, she started to sob. Even the hotel staff who wheeled in the champagne asked if she was okay.

"Summer, the staff is going to think I kidnapped you."

We're sitting on the couch as she hiccups, wiping her eyes. "Sorry, I'm just really emotional, okay?"

"Why?"

"Because your grandparents are so sweet, then you surprise me with this. And let's not forget the homemade cookies. Was she trying to make me sob like a child?"

"I'll be sure to tell her you appreciate them."

"I already texted her." I can't help my smile. Of course she's texting my grandma after only meeting her once.

I wipe a tear off her cheek. "Babe, the only time I want to see tears in your eyes is when I'm hitting the back of your throat."

"How romantic," she mutters, but her smile shines through.

"It made you smile, didn't it?" I smile at her glistening eyes.

"Are you laughing at me?"

"No, but you do look pretty when you cry."

She pushes me away, and when her eyes hit the clock on the nightstand, she gasps. "It's 11:11. Make a wish!"

Her eyes close, and when they flutter open, a smile lights her face. "What are you doing? Make a wish."

I blink. I can't think of anything more I would want. Not a single wish populates in my brain. "I don't have one."

"Of course you do. Just think of something you really want. Anything. Quick!"

I pause for a long moment, and I realize why my mind is blank. The reason sits in front of me with a special smile and shimmering eyes. There's nowhere else I'd rather be than right here with her.

"Summer, I already have you."

I see the moment my words register, and her eyes start to water again. "You're such an asshole!" she exclaims, smacking my arm. Only this girl could go from sobbing to angry.

"What the hell?" I take hold of her arms. "What was that for?"

"For—for being so you!" she huffs. "Of course you would say something like that. You just had to be everything I wanted."

"I'm pretty sure dating a hockey player was last on your list."

"So was falling in love with one," she says, freezing. "That—"

I kiss her before she can continue. "I know." I rest my forehead against hers, cupping her face. "It's okay. I know."

"I didn't—"

"I have you forever, Summer. If those words come tomorrow or ten years from now, I'll still be here to hear them. I love you enough for the both of us."

She shakes her head. "No."

My heart stops. "What?"

"I don't need years to realize how I feel about you. I already know, and I wanted it to be perfect, but then I just kept talking and—" She stops abruptly when she notices my expression, then takes my hands in hers. "I love you, Aiden."

The words don't quite click in my head fast enough for me to speak. I know she loves me, but hearing the words feels like so much more. My chest is tight, and a wash of serenity sails through my veins.

She inhales a shaky breath. "You're the only one I want. It was always going to be you, even if I never thought I would get with a hockey player. I mean, it was quite literally my last option. I probably should have chosen anyone else—"

"You're not selling this, Preston," I interrupt.

She clamps her mouth shut and seems to rearrange her thoughts. "I love your patience and how ridiculously sweet and caring you are. The way you make me feel like what I want matters. I feel lost without you, Aiden." She smiles wide. "I want to do everything with you, and I want you to do everything with me."

My smile breaks free. "Sounds possessive."

"It is." She lunges to wrap her arms around my neck. I hug her so tight I don't think I'll ever let her go. Summer doesn't say things she doesn't mean, and knowing she loves me, despite everything in her head telling her not to, carves a deeper place for her in my heart. "You and me, Crawford, that's the only way I want it."

"Good. Because I love you, and I'm not letting you go."

My life before Summer revolved solely around hockey. I lived and breathed it with no breaks because it felt like the only part of myself I was okay with. But with her, I want to unravel all the parts of me I've hidden. The parts that drifted when my parents died. The parts that became silent when I went from a thirteen-year-old kid to an adult in one night.

Summer's presence is luminescent. She's the last fragment of sunlight in the overwhelming darkness.

SUMMER

OUR BUBBLE BEARDS have dissolved into soapy residue. In the jacuzzi, I sit between Aiden's legs with bubbles overtaking us.

"You seriously haven't ever had a girlfriend?" I ask.

Our shower was filled with things that didn't require much talking, so when Aiden ran a bath, we made up for the lack of conversation. Our game of Twenty Questions has gone beyond that number, but neither of us seem to mind.

His fingers intertwine with mine. "Unless you count Cassie."

My head whips to him so fast, my neck tenses. "*My* Cassie?"

He chuckles. "No, my Cassie. From elementary school."

"Oh, so she's *your* Cassie?"

Aiden shakes with laughter. "Your jealousy is always a turn-on, babe, but we were nine."

I lay my head on his shoulder to stare up at the ceiling. He takes the opportunity to kiss me. A hot, lazy slide of his tongue that makes my thighs squeeze together.

"You've had boyfriends, right?" he asks.

"Plenty."

"Uh-huh," he says, his tone disbelieving. He already knew about Donny, but other than him, I've never mentioned the guys I was with in high school. I don't think I ever will. I like him thinking he's the only athlete I've been with, even if he's cocky about it.

"You don't believe me?"

"Your delusion is cute."

I sigh. "Fine, I've had two. I guess the rest were just a string of meaningless hookups."

His fingers tighten around mine, and I wrench my hand away. "Right. That's why you were so blasé when we hooked up."

I shrug. "What can I say? It's a regular occurrence for me, you know, big strong men just falling at my feet."

He chuckles. "Ishida begging for forgiveness doesn't count."

"He was on his knees, wasn't he?"

"I guess I'm at the top of that list, then."

I laugh. "That would count toward a very different category." I bring our palms up, and the size difference makes my eyes widen. "First impression?" I ask.

"That I'd totally bang you if you didn't look like you would kick me in the nuts." His smirk makes my eyes roll. "You?"

"That you were an asshole."

He scoffs and nips my ear in retaliation, making me yelp.

"But you had really nice eyes," I add.

"Really nice eyes," he repeats dryly. "That's it?"

"You just said you would bang me. That's not a compliment."

"Are you kidding?" He turns me to straddle him. "I didn't even want to like you, but I couldn't take my eyes off you or your ass."

I try to ignore the hardness nestled between my thighs. "When were you looking at my ass?"

"Every chance I got." He grins and smacks my ass.

"You're such a guy." I fiddle with the overgrown hair at the nape of his neck. Curling the wavy brown hair around my fingers. "It really was your eyes."

"Yeah? What about them?"

I stare into the green that tugs at my chest. Sometimes I can't believe he's all mine to look at. Especially when he looks at me like I'm the most precious thing he's ever laid eyes on. "They're so pretty that I kind of get lost in them. They make you look innocent, but then you open your mouth."

"It's only open when I'm pleasuring you."

I groan. "Precisely my point."

He pecks my nose affectionately. "I have my mom's eyes."

"That explains it. There's a warmth to them. Like whatever's be-hind them is all good."

Nestling into my neck, Aiden kisses a point that always makes me squirm. I can feel his smile against my skin. "You think I'm good?"

"The best."

"Do good boys get rewarded?" His hands run up my sides as he shifts, bringing the upper half of my body out of the water.

I squeal when the cold air touches my wet skin, my nipples sen-sitive to the air. I'm forced to pull him close, so our chests are flush. "You're lucky I'm cold."

Aiden grips my chin. "Do you think I can't feel the way you've been grinding on my dick this whole time?"

Fire scalds my cheeks. "That was unintentional."

"Mm-hmm, of course it was." He lifts me until we're both soak-ing the towel he places on the tiles. In quick movements, he dries me off, then hands me a robe while he dries off.

The way Aiden cares for me is something I've never experienced. I've complained about my dad to him constantly and not once has he told me I'm lucky to even have a dad. Or that there were people who had it worse—him, for example. Never did he make my feelings seem less than because of his own experience. No one has ever under-stood me like he does.

Aiden lays me down gently on the bed, kissing the water droplets on my cheeks. His body feels so right against mine, I can feel my own heating and writhing in need. Warm lips cover my neck, my cheeks, then my lips. His large, calloused hand travels up my bare leg until he's under my robe. We've done this so many times before, but tonight it feels different. The air feels charged with something new.

"Take off your robe." He moves to sit up against the headboard. Slowly, I drop it, feeling his hot gaze pinning me to the mattress.

"Come here." Those two words send a weight dropping between

my legs. I crawl over to him to touch his hard length. "Not yet. Move up higher." He lies flat on the bed, waiting for me to follow his instructions.

"What are you doing?"

"Getting comfortable." I eye him with suspicion. "Higher, Summer," he demands.

I move high enough to straddle his abdomen. He smiles watching my uncertain movements. "Sit on my face, baby."

Surprise lights up my features when he takes hold of my hips and yanks me forward until I'm hovering over his mouth. "Aiden," I moan, feeling his hot breath on my pulsing core.

"Sit."

I do, and immediately Aiden's mouth is on me. I clasp the headboard for a semblance of control.

"All the way, Summer. I want you to ride my face."

A high-pitched moan escapes my throat when I move my hips and meet every smooth glide of his tongue and every press of his fingers. With one hand on the headboard and one sinking into his hair, we say every word that settles in the air around us with our bodies.

FORTY-NINE

AIDEN

SLEEPING ON THE bus is a rarity when your teammates are impossibly annoying.

The three-hour bus ride back from Princeton has my head in knots. Quarterfinals, semifinals, and the tournament have been my only focus for the past three weeks. It paid off, because winning regionals means there's only one more game until the Frozen Four in Boston.

The only downside is that we'll be up against Yale. And although we've beaten them once, they're not to be underestimated. After a loss to them, Kian gets so drunk that he makes decisions he'll regret for years. Tabitha was his last post-Yale mistake, and the year before he was suspended for streaking across Michigan's campus. The aftermath never goes over well with Coach, so he's understandably desperate for this win.

When we hop off the bus and head into the locker room, Coach hands me a paper.

"You're done with community service." Today he allows a smile to sit easily on his face. "As much of an idiot as you are for taking their fuck-up on your shoulders, I'm glad you stuck it out. Your research partner had a lot of good things to say about you. And so did I."

I skim the paper. "They're clearing it from my record?"

"Yes. But there will be a notice in your sealed file. If you or the boys even think of doing something like this again, I'll make sure you never play again."

"I won't." That is for damn sure.

He nods, pausing to pick up a towel from the floor and tossing it at an unsuspecting Kian. "Clean up around here, Ishida. This place is a fucking mess."

Kian collects the dirty towel and tosses it in the bin. "I haven't talked during practice for an entire month, and he still won't relieve me of laundry duty."

"It'll happen soon enough, buddy. Only up from here," I say, just as a jockstrap flies past his face.

Kian's death glare has our goalie backing away. He uses a hockey stick to toss the rotten thing in the bin, and I laugh. "You should be the last one laughing, Mr. Community Service."

"Actually, Coach just handed me this." I show him the paper that exonerates me.

"No fucking way. You're done? I'm happy for you, man."

"You should be. None of this would have happened if it weren't for you and Dylan."

"Hey, we said we were sorry. Plus, I think this is more than enough punishment." He points to the large hamper. I agree. Having to launder those items was much more severe than teaching kids how to play hockey and working with a girl who's the best thing to ever happen to me.

Dylan and Eli toss their things in the bin, saving Kian the job of collecting them.

"You just watch," Kian says. "He'll be begging me to speak when he realizes how boring it is around here."

"Don't hold your breath," says Dylan. "Or, actually, do."

"Watch it, or I might just forget to do your laundry."

Dylan flips him off as we exit the building. "Is anyone heading to Boston tonight?"

I make a face. "For the Harvard party? Hell no."

"I'll come with you," Eli offers.

I look at him as if he's spawned a second head. The last place Eli Westbrook wants to be is at a party, especially one in Boston. "You want to go to Harvard? Didn't you send their defenseman to the hospital?"

"It was a broken clavicle. He's fine now."

"Let me guess. You sent flowers to his hospital room and kissed his boo-boos?" Dylan taunts.

"No. I just paid for his medical bills."

We're laughing when we're halfway through the parking lot, and I hear my name float behind us. I turn to see Donny Rai, dressed in a black sweater over a white collared shirt and perfectly pressed gray dress pants. I gesture for the guys to go ahead.

"You look too happy to have gotten the news," he notes, and his face fills with pleasure.

This can't be good. "If it has something to do with you, you can save your breath."

"As much as I love talking about all my achievements, this is much more entertaining. There was a break-in at the psychology building just before spring break. Turns out it's being investigated, and there are a few suspects. In fact, they've made a list of Dalton students who could be responsible." He stares at me as if I should care. "Would suck if they got caught."

"What does this have to do with me?" I ask.

"You're right, it has nothing to do with you. Unless you know whose ID I found on the floor of the building entrance." He holds up a Dalton student ID.

Summer Preston. Fuck.

"Even someone like you might understand that breaking and entering is grounds for expulsion. Or worse." The fucker is smiling, content with my reaction.

"You snitched?"

"I'm dropping by the dean's office after my debate meeting. Just thought I'd do a good deed so you two can say your goodbyes." His *good deed* is as transparent as plexi.

He walks off, and I jog to my truck, passing the guys. "Think you guys can hitch another ride?"

They exchange looks. "Yeah, no problem. Is everything okay?" asks Eli.

"It will be." Before they can ask more questions, I'm speeding out of the lot. On the drive to the administrative center, I realize I am so embarrassingly in love with my girl that I'm certain if she knew the things running through my mind, she would laugh at me. It's the kind of love that makes you do shit like run straight to her dorm after an exhausting ninety-minute game or power down an entire house full of people. Illogical and impulsive.

Now I'm on my way to do another illogical and impulsive thing, or at least that's how she would see it.

I barrel inside the administrative center, straight to the front desk. "I'd like to speak with Dean Hutchins," I say, startling the secretary.

She assesses me. "I'm sorry, we can't—"

"It's about the break-in." I cut her off.

Hesitantly, she calls to ask about a last-minute meeting and then looks at me. "You have five minutes."

FIFTY

SUMMER

THE FIRST FEW weeks after spring break are my favorite. My professors are relaxed, the students are off Adderall, and the sun is out. Except this year, we're two weeks in, and I'm losing my hair.

It doesn't help that Aiden is miles away playing hockey every weekend and practicing on weekdays. On top of that, the school is investigating the break-in after Dean Hutchins received the email about Langston's professor-student relationship.

Now, lying in bed while Amara is out and the guys are coming back from a tournament, I can't sleep. However, my lucky stars must be aligned, because when my phone rings, it's Aiden.

I answer his video call, seeing the tired smile on his lips. "Hey. I tried to keep up with Kian's short vlogs, but they were cut short."

"We advanced. And Kilner confiscated Kian's phone when he tried to make him do a dance."

I chuckle, feeling lighter with just Aiden's voice in my ears. "Weren't you supposed to get back earlier?"

"We did, but I had something to do first," he says quickly. "Are you coming over?"

"Do I look like a booty call to you, Crawford?"

"Depends. What are you wearing?" He smiles innocently. "We can even extend the booty call and get breakfast in the morning."

"How thoughtful," I say dryly. "But I'm a bit tired tonight." There is too much on my mind, but I can't tell Aiden about the break-in until it's resolved, or he'll try to run into action mode.

"Want me to come over instead?"

"You look exhausted; you'll probably fall asleep at the wheel."

"Then come to me. I can send you an Uber." When I don't answer, he sighs. "Come on, Summer. I'm tired, and I missed you all weekend. I just want you in my bed tonight, please."

Guilt bites at me. "I'll be over tomorrow, I promise."

"You'd tell me if something was wrong, wouldn't you?"

That stings. "Of course. Nothing you need to worry about."

The look on his face is thoughtful. "You don't have to deal with everything alone, Summer. I'm here. For you. No other reason. I'd like to prove it to you sometime."

I do what I can without breaking down: I nod.

He scans my face before smiling. "So, my booty call canceled. How about we stay on video?"

This is dangerous territory. If we keep talking, he will pry everything out of my head. But Aiden doesn't need more stress with their final game coming up.

"I think you might have attachment issues, Crawford."

"As long as you're the one I'm attached to, I wouldn't call that an issue." The ruffle of the covers sounds as he settles into bed.

"Whatever you say, *Captain*."

"Say that again."

"Captain?"

"Yup, that's it. Talk dirty to me, Summer."

I laugh. "Shut up."

"You're right. I'll shut up, you keep talking." He smiles, and when I think he's asleep, he moves again. "Your mom called me this morning."

Divya Preston has a saying: *Clutter in your phone is clutter in your life*. Finding out Aiden made the cut is oddly satisfying. "What did she say?"

"They'll be in Toronto soon, so I should visit when I'm there. She even offered me your room to stay in."

"She's trying to replace me because you answer her calls."

Aiden chuckles. "Don't worry, babe. Eli and I already have an apartment. But I will check out your childhood bedroom."

"Remind me to have all my posters taken down."

"Don't tell me you were a teenage fangirl."

"Don't ask questions you're not ready for. That room holds some dark secrets," I warn, and he chuckles wearily. "Go to sleep. I can see the dark circles forming."

"Not true, I'm flawless."

He actually might be. "Goodnight, my Sleeping Beauty."

"Night, baby," he murmurs, sleep overtaking him.

THE CHIMING OF emails hitting my inbox jolts me awake. My call with Aiden must have disconnected, because my phone is sandwiched between my mattress and the wall. Groggily wiping my eyes, I fish it out, and when I open my email, I hear a knock.

Amara's already at the front door, looking at Sampson's phone. Squealing, she almost hugs Sampson but turns to me. "We did it!"

I have been mentally preparing myself for being taken away in handcuffs since the break-in. "We did?"

Sampson beams. "Someone I know from the committee said she's fired. They're talking to Donny now."

"You think he'll get expelled?" asks Amara.

The spark of guilt is unexpected, but Donny used to be someone I cared for. It's too bad he had to let his greed win.

Sampson slides his phone back into his pocket. "His parents are loaded, and Langston had all the power in their relationship. But he'll be punished because students read the article on the gossip page, and they're pissed," he says. "And I talked to Müller. If Langston approved your application and you've been denied or waitlisted, you can reapply with the dean's approval."

Leaving my dreams and all the people I love for Stanford was so painful that I shoved my feelings deep down—until right now, when hope bubbles up. "But what about the investigation?"

"Someone confessed. Müller didn't say who it was."

Relief doesn't set in, and I hope whoever confessed won't get in too much trouble. Part of me knows that letting someone else take the blame will eat away at me until I make it right.

Amara jostles me into a hug again, distracting me from my thoughts. "You're not leaving! I was totally getting an army ready to hack admissions for you."

I hug her tighter. "I should tell Aiden the good news, too."

"Definitely. You should surprise him. Wear something sexy!"

Sampson groans.

"He has practice. I'm not going to walk in there in lingerie."

"Wear a trench coat," she offers.

"She's going to look like a flasher. Please don't do that," says Sampson, looking worried about our decision-making skills.

Amara gives him a look. "What do you suggest then, Tyler?"

"My jersey." He grins. "Kidding. But you should tell him, he'll be happy."

Amara and I exchange a look. "You want him to be happy? Since when?" I'm stunned by the new discovery.

"Since he started making you smile," Sampson admits. My awestruck expression makes him roll his eyes, but he allows my hug. "Okay, that's my quota for hugs." He moves out of my grip.

"Go already." Amara pushes me, and I'm out of there before she realizes she's alone with Sampson.

When I arrive, I'm looking through the plexi to find him on the ice when I catch Dylan walking in late.

"Hey Dylan, I need to talk to Aiden. Is he late?"

"You don't know?" he asks, and I stare in confusion. "Summer, he was kicked off the team this morning. Kilner didn't want to, but he's out for the rest of the season. He's done."

My heart drops, and shock swirls in my chest. "Is he okay?"

"He's fine. Well, as fine as he can be after being told he's missing his last Frozen Four." He must see my confusion, because he goes on. "Donny caught up with him after we got back from Princeton the other day. Aiden confessed to the break-in."

My mouth feels dry, and my bones feel weak when I lose my footing and stumble forward.

Dylan catches my arm. "You good?"

"It's my fault."

Dylan's strong hold gives me enough energy to stand on my own. "He would never let you go down for it, Sunny."

Anger sears my chest. "Why the hell would he do that?"

"He would do anything for you, you know that. Honestly, if he didn't, one of us would have." He squeezes my shoulder. "Look, I gotta go practice, but he's at the house if you wanna talk to him. Think you'll be okay to get there?"

I nod and head out of the arena, pulling out my phone.

AIDEN

Summer: You are so dead, Crawford. I'm going to strangle you!

Aiden: Yeah? What else?

Summer: Don't play with me! I'm coming over.

Aiden: Pants on or off?

God, he is infuriating. But before I can head over to the hockey house, there's something I need to do, so I text Amara.

AMARA'S RAGE IS palpable as she storms over to one oblivious guy who startles when he sees her. "Rai! You fuck with my best friend again, and I will crush your skinny little bones with a pillowcase full of your textbooks."

He smirks. "Bodyguard? Surprised it isn't your jock."

"She can call him too," threatens Amara.

I move forward. "You did all this just to take my co-op spot? There were students whose futures depended on getting into the program. Shannon Lee left because of what you did!"

His face is a mask of indifference. "Last time I checked, Shannon made her own decisions. Besides, with her gone, you had a shot. Though we both know you'll always come second to me."

"Really? Because I'm pretty sure you're the one who had to fuck our professor to secure your spot."

His jaw tightens. "Maybe I just wanted to have some fun."

Anger spreads through my blood like poison. "You did it on purpose, didn't you? Instead of threatening me, you went to Aiden. You're a fucking coward, Donny."

"Coward or not, I'm the one who got into the program. Have fun in California, Summer. Maybe you can find another hockey player to fuck your way through your assignments."

My slap ricochets off his face, sending a sharp sting to my hand. But the pain doesn't register because of the rage that boils through me.

Donny steps forward, but Amara blocks him with a hand on his chest. "I wouldn't do that if I were you."

His rough exhale is angry before he takes off.

I turn to Amara. "Can you drive me to Aiden's?"

"After a slap like that, I'll give you anything," she laughs.

AIDEN

YOU DON'T KNOW your girlfriend's strength until she's absolutely livid. As soon as I open the front door, I'm pushed back. "How could you?!"

I have to take hold of Summer's frantic arms. "Listen—"

"No, Aiden!" She yanks her arms away. "You told me not to mess up my dreams, so why can't you do the same?"

Her anger is burning hot, and to balance some of that heat, I stay calm. "Because I know how hard you've worked for this."

"So have you! You're missing your final game because of me."

Her eyes swim with the hurt I can't bear to see. The whole point of this was to avoid that. To never see her cry like she did that night in my arms. "Baby," I start.

"Don't *baby* me, Aiden. You overstepped." She jabs a finger at my chest. "This is my problem!"

I take hold of her violent finger. "My girlfriend was crying in my arms, and you expect me to stand by and do nothing? Fuck no. Your problems are my problems too."

She lets out a heavy groan as if I'm the one being difficult. "You could have been expelled."

"But I wasn't. A suspension isn't that bad."

"It is when you're the captain! Why am I the only one concerned about this?" A look of exasperation takes over her angry one. "You have to retract your confession."

I move to touch her, but I think better of it. "I can't do that."

"You can. Come with me, we can explain. They'll understand."

"I'm sure they would, but I stand by my decision."

She appears indignant. "This could ruin things with Toronto."

"I'm already signed. But if they want to take action, I'll deal."

The crease in the middle of her brows and her glare are hard enough to crack me in two. "You're being ridiculous. Think about what you're doing for one second."

"I don't need to because it's the right choice. I'll be okay."

"This isn't—" She inhales. "You can't make decisions on my behalf because you want to save me. I can save myself without putting you in jeopardy."

"And I think if I can help my girlfriend with a problem, I will."

"You're being stubborn."

"And you're not? Summer, I did this because I wanted to. Because I love you, and I don't want anything messing with your dreams."

She blinks away the moisture welling in her eyes. "What about your dreams? I care about those too, you know?"

It's hard not to grab her and kiss the lights out of her. "I know, and thank you, baby, but this won't affect my future as much as it would have affected yours."

She pushes me again, not nearly as hard as before. "You're crazy. I'm dating a crazy person!" she exclaims. "Who does that?"

"Your boyfriend. Your hot, sexy, kind boyfriend." I grin, making her glare harden. "Yell at me all you want, Summer, but I wouldn't change what I did."

"This is your career!"

"And you are my future."

Summer falters, eyes searching my face.

"I told you that you come first. That hasn't changed. It won't ever change."

"But you've worked for this your whole life. You don't potentially fuck that up for a girl."

A pang of irritation hits my chest. "Why are you fighting me on this? I'm not changing my mind."

"Because you can't miss the final. Coach is probably pissed."

"He is. I've been getting angry voicemails all morning because he was too pissed to speak to me in his office. But we've already won a Frozen Four. It gets boring after a while."

"You're just saying that to make me feel better."

I take a step closer. "Is it working?"

"I'm mad at you, Aiden," she says, trying to keep her distance.

I clasp her wrists. "Okay, but come a little closer and be mad at me where I can hold you." She doesn't protest when I tug her forward, and her hug makes the burn in my chest cool. "You smell like me," I say, noticing she's wearing my hoodie.

"I'll have to shower immediately, then," she mutters.

"What's the point if I'm showering with you?"

She groans, pulling away. "Where is your hockey stick?"

"Why? You wanna test out a new kink?" I smirk.

"Yeah, let's experiment by shoving it up your ass."

"Eh, I'll have to pass on that one. Though I do have plans for your ass." I pull her in, and she rests her head on my chest. A perfect concoction of peach scent and me. "I'm sorry I didn't tell you, but I don't regret a thing if it means you're happy," I say.

"I am happy. Always happy with you." She tiptoes to meet my lips. "But I don't like that you have to suffer to make that happen."

"I'm not suffering. The team's doing great, and Sampson gets to captain a final."

"You're okay with that?"

"He's not so bad." Finding out he helped with the break-in had pissed me off for all of three seconds. Eli told me about that night, and I couldn't blame them. They all had Summer's back when I couldn't, and that alone is reason enough to take the blame.

"That's not what you were saying a few weeks ago."

"People change."

"Not all people," she mutters, and I raise a brow. "I slapped Donny. But he deserved it," she admits.

The reveal isn't nearly as shocking as it should be. The guy had it coming; he's just lucky it wasn't my fist. "I don't doubt that."

Her head tilts, assessing me. "What happened to never losing?"

"I'm fine with it if you're the one winning."

She sinks her hands in my hair and kisses me deeply. "I'm sorry, too. I should have told you about the plan," she says sheepishly.

I rub my nose against hers. "It's fine, my little criminal."

She rolls her eyes. "So, you forgive me?"

"Do you even have to ask?"

"And you still mean all that stuff about the future?" she asks, toying with the strings of my hoodie.

"I fully intend to spend the rest of my life with you, Summer."

"I love you." She scrunches her nose. "Like, a lot."

"I love you, too, Preston. Like, a lot."

FIFTY-ONE

SUMMER

I NEVER THOUGHT I'd watch a game where Aiden wasn't on the ice, but last night Dalton versus Michigan happened. Aiden was able to witness how passionate I get during a game. Instead of telling me to calm down like most people would, he only sat back and watched proudly. We won by one, which isn't anything to be proud of because we're headed to finals, and playing like that won't win us a national championship. Aiden's words, not mine.

"Why are you sitting all the way over there?"

I glance at Aiden, who sits on the opposite end of the couch. If there were a picture for the word *sluggish*, it would show Aiden and me watching movies with our spread of junk food. "Why? Do you usually cuddle with Kian while watching TV?"

He gives me a blank stare. "Come here, Summer." He grabs my ankle and drags me to him. Our days usually start and end like this, and although I'm upset he isn't playing, I wouldn't trade this time for the world.

He's not allowed to get on the ice for practice either, so we've been spending every free second together. Most of the time, we're planning our schedules for after graduation, but we spend plenty of time watching Turkish shows and tangled together in his bed. I've basically moved into the hockey house, and the guys don't seem to mind because I cook them dinner, mostly Indian food that my mom taught me—though Eli's still got the title of the best cook in this house.

Occasionally, Aiden and I sneak into the pool or head to the community rink because he still needs to stay in shape. I'm sure all the cardio we do is helping with that. Between my dorm and his place, Aiden and I have fallen into a comfortable routine. One that I know I'll miss when he leaves.

Amara and Cassie have been coming over too, so we spend most of our time with the guys. They're all finished with classes, and I wrote my last exam this morning, which means the semester is over. It's been a relief, especially because I haven't seen Donny in any of the classes we shared. Sampson told me he was put on distance learning, so he will complete all work off campus for the remainder of the semester. He's been given the option to transfer to another school before he's expelled. Aiden thinks he got off easy, but he's glad Donny won't be at Dalton anymore.

"Have I told you how proud I am of you?"

Aiden's words cause a blush to run down my neck, making him chuckle. Reapplying to the master's program had my hands shaking, but yesterday, we were eating dinner when I got the acceptance email. The leftover cupcakes with graduation caps that Eli made still sit on the coffee table. Aiden disappeared for a little, and when he came back, I found out he drove the hour to Boston because my mom wanted to congratulate me with her homemade gulab jamun. I was a little hysterical after that, but I felt less crazy when Kian shed a tear too, though that might've been because he ate ten of the syrupy sweets.

"Thank you. I don't think I've even processed that I got in. I spent years pouring my blood, sweat, and tears into this one thing for so long, and now that it's reality, everything feels unsteady."

He nods. "I get that. But you deserve it; don't let the voices in your head tell you any different."

Bliss. That's what I feel with him. "I'm proud of you, too, even if I don't agree with what you did. I know you'll never admit it, but not playing is killing you. I just wish I could do more to help."

"You're doing plenty," he says, kissing my shoulder. Aiden trails a path up my neck to my lips, and I sift my hand through his soft hair. In seconds the unsteady thoughts are forgotten, and his kiss pulls at my heartstrings, which only strum for him.

"You two are bordering on Dylan's level of disregard for the other people in this house."

Aiden pulls away to look over my shoulder, where Kian covers his eyes like a child avoiding a kissing scene on television. "He's subjected us to full frontal on this very couch. Don't compare us."

"Gross!" I scramble off Aiden. "I've slept here!"

"Not too far off from what Dylan was doing," Kian says, and I find it hard to keep the acid from crawling up my throat. "But seriously, it's too early for all this." He waves a hand in our direction.

"Is there a specific time you would prefer to watch us?" Aiden counters.

Kian makes a gagging sound before grabbing a controller and starting the gaming console. He sinks a spoon into a container of peanut butter on the coffee table and shoves it into his mouth.

Aiden catches my eye. "My room?"

I shake my head. "We need to get out of this rut." I start piling junk food wrappers into a trash bag.

Aiden stops me and cleans it up himself. "What do you suggest we do, Summer?"

"If this is your idea of foreplay, can you do it somewhere else? I already hear enough of it upstairs," Kian mumbles through his spoonful.

"Shut up. You can't hear anything anymore." Aiden and I have taken serious soundproofing precautions. We even tried to get Cole to switch rooms, but he is very protective of his hobbit hole.

"*Oh Crawford, yes, yes, yes!*" Kian mimics girly moans.

When he goes to dip his spoon into the peanut butter again, I snatch away the jar, making him scowl. "I do not sound like that."

"Want me to record you next time?"

I lunge at him, but Aiden bars me with a hand on my waist. "Watch it, Ishida," he warns, and Kian rolls his eyes and focuses back on his game. Before I can chuck the tub of peanut butter at his head, Aiden pries it from my grip and carries me out of the living room. "You're right. We need to get out of this rut."

AN HOUR LATER, we're parked in front of the dockside restaurant in Hartford. Inside, I stumble when I spot Connor Atwood and Crystal Yang making out in a corner booth.

"My ex-fling and your ex-fling. What are the odds?"

Aiden tugs me to our table. "He was not your fling. She wasn't mine either."

"Should we go say hi?" I wouldn't dare, but it's fun messing with Aiden, especially when he gets all worked up like this.

"Sure, we can make this a double date," he deadpans, taking the seat in front of me.

"Ooh, we could be swingers!" His glare sobers up my laugh. "I'm joking."

"Yeah, good joke. Come here and tell me another," he drawls, and when I roll my eyes, he abandons his seat to sit beside me instead.

"What are you doing?"

He settles in. "You were too far away."

"For what?"

"For this." His hand snakes up my thigh, high enough that my breath hitches. When he squeezes my goose-bumped skin, I squeak.

I slap my hand over his, preventing him from reaching higher. "You can't just move. The server's going to be annoyed."

"It's not like I moved tables. It was such a pain when customers did that."

Occasionally, Aiden drops random bits of information about his past that always manage to surprise me. "You worked as a server?"

"At my grandma's diner. Only for a summer when I was sixteen. She fired me pretty quick."

"Why? Did you start playing hockey with the breadsticks?"

"I locked Eli in a freezer."

I laugh. "Working with your best friend? That must've been fun."

"For me. Not so much for him. It was our family's way of teaching us about hard work. As if we hadn't spent every last bit of our energy on hockey already."

When he absently squeezes my leg again, I grab his thigh in retaliation. It reminds me of the ink just below his hip bone. The spider tattoo has been on my mind since the first time I saw it. "What does your tattoo mean?"

He doesn't look the least bit surprised by the question. "Pulled it from a hat," he says.

"Huh?"

"When we all moved in together, we came up with a hat of consequences if one of us did something that pissed the other off. We wrote two consequences each and tossed them in a hat."

"And you pulled that." I've never seen a man with a tattoo in that spot, but on Aiden, the black spider is so hot I can't help the heat on my neck when I think about it. "Did any of the other guys get one?"

He shakes his head. "Nope, the other consequences have been pretty tame . . . except for the piercing."

That catches my attention. "The piercing? None of the guys have any." I've seen them shirtless enough times. I'd know if they did.

"None that you've seen." He pauses. "Or that you'll ever see."

"What does that mean?" My mind spins with possibilities. "*Oh my God*, is it a dick piercing?"

Aiden's neutral face gives me zero clues.

"Who has it?"

He chuckles at my curiosity. "Can't say. It's against the rules."

"Is it Kian? Wait, no. Dylan?" Our food arrives, and my questions stop until the server leaves. "Eli?"

"Eat, Summer," he says. I stab my fork into my plate. But I'll get it out of one of them later. Probably from Kian.

"Summer? Aiden?" Connor Atwood smiles brightly, standing by our table with a grimacing Crystal.

"Hey, haven't seen you in a while. Why don't you guys join us?" I offer. Aiden's hand squeezes my thigh in warning.

Much to my pleasure, Connor accepts.

I guess this is one way to get out of a rut.

FIFTY-TWO

AIDEN

"CRAWFORD! GET YOUR ass up. We're going to be late!"

Hearing Dylan's voice from downstairs so early in the morning makes me unwrap myself from Summer.

"Bus is leaving in fifteen," he shouts, rolling out his suitcase.

"What are you saying, D? I'm suspended."

"Check your phone, man. You're in. Hutchins approved." A half asleep Summer comes up behind me with my phone. Messages clutter my home screen, and when I look at my email, it sure as hell says I'm playing. Summer reads it too, and squeals.

"Oh my God. You're playing!" She stands on tiptoes to pepper kisses all over my face. I'm still processing, trying to make sense of it, when Summer slips back into my room as I get a text.

COACH

Coach: Not sure how you pulled this off, but I will drag your ass to Boston if you are not on this bus in twenty.

BUNNY PATROL

Kian Ishida: Coach said I can talk if Aiden gets here. Pls hurry!
Dylan Donovan: Weird. I think my car just ran out of gas . . .
Sebastian Hayes: Just get here. Kian's been whining for 20 mins.
Cole Carter: Can you tell him to shut up?? I'm trying to nap here.

I can barely comprehend what the conditional reversal of suspension entails, but as long as I'm playing, I don't care. All the campus community hours I put in must have paid off.

"You're still not dressed? Let's go, man," Dylan urges as he runs down the hall with another bag. Driving to the rink on his own is part of his pregame ritual, so he leaves later than the team.

Summer comes in, carrying my heavy bag. "I packed everything I could think of. You just have to check if it's all there."

What would I do without this girl? No matter how many times I've told Summer that watching the game with her would be just as good, she was still upset that I wasn't playing. Sometimes, I even caught her whispering on the phone and sending last-minute emails to try and get me cleared to play. When that didn't work, she got a petition going. Coach made her shut it down because my expulsion wasn't unwarranted.

Summer's rummaging through my things when I stop her. "I love you," I say, tilting her head for a kiss. I deepen it until she abruptly pulls away.

"Yeah, yeah, you too. Now go! Your bus is leaving." She tosses me a change of clothes and runs out of the room. I take the quickest shower of my life and change before heading downstairs.

Summer's standing by the door with a brown bag. "Here's a poorly made sandwich for your carbs and a snack for your low fats. Don't forget to eat your banana."

"Thanks, babe." I kiss her again. "You'll come?"

"Of course. I'll catch a ride with Amara."

"Who are you, and what have you done with Summer?" I tease.

"She fell in love," she says like it's a big inconvenience.

I know then that whatever the outcome of the game, those words sound like sweet, sweet victory.

SUMMER

WAKING UP TO find out I didn't ruin my boyfriend's life makes today a good day.

These past few weeks have put me through the wringer.

I spent this week meeting with Kilner and the dean's secretary to see if an exception could be made for Aiden's suspension. None of it worked, and I felt defeated. Even my mom was upset he couldn't play, but mostly she was mad at me after I confessed to her about the break-in. Her perfect Aiden could do no wrong.

So, when I read that email this morning, I didn't know if it was me or Coach who got Aiden in, but none of that mattered when I saw the smile on his face. He could say all he wanted that sitting in the stands with me is just as good as playing, but I knew he was born to be on that ice tonight.

Turns out the guy Amara took home from the club a few weeks ago, Bennett Anderson, goes to Harvard, and his dad's a dean. He's also coming from Cambridge to Hartford to drive us to Boston for the final. It didn't surprise me because Amara could have any man at her beck and call.

"I'll get some drinks and meet you guys inside," Bennett says once we're inside the TD Garden arena. Walking through the double doors, I spot a small crowd by the entrance.

"Dad?" Lukas Preston is surrounded by fans asking for an autograph, but he slips away from them.

Amara waves. "Hi, Mr. Preston."

"Good to see you, Amara. How's school?"

"Oh, you know. Just representing women in STEM every day of the week," she says. "You guys catch up. I'm going to go find Bennett."

"What are you doing here?" I ask.

"Watching a hockey game with my daughter. Someone told me being a dad has nothing to do with spending money and everything to do with spending time."

I smother a smile. "Sounds like a very smart person."

"She is."

There's a twinge in my chest. "How did you even know I'd be here? Aiden only found out this morning that he's playing."

"Lucky guess."

"Preston." We turn to Dean Hutchins's deep voice. "Want to grab a beer in the box? I got your favorite."

My dad clasps his hand with a smile. "Another time. I got my sports buddy right here."

"Of course, Summer Preston. Great fundraiser last month."

My eyes bounce between them. "Thank you, Dean Hutchins."

"Call me Cal. Your dad and I go way back. I bet Divya can tell Summer some of our stories."

My dad chuckles. "Probably better if she doesn't."

Cal shakes with laughter. "Well, you're both welcome to join us in the box whenever you like."

"Thanks for the offer, but rinkside is the place to be if Summer's going to give the refs hell."

I smile. We might not be as close anymore, but he remembers how I am at hockey games. Cal pats my dad's shoulder before heading for the box. The friendly gesture makes the cogs turn in my brain. "It was you."

"Hmm?"

"You got the suspension reversed after I called Mom."

My dad turns to me with a smile.

"You did!" A warmth settles over me. "Thank you."

He looks taken aback. "Don't thank me, honey. I know what a big deal this is, and if that boy was willing to miss one of the biggest games of his college career just so my daughter would be happy, I could pull a few strings."

I lunge to hug him so tight I feel like I'm trying to soak up all the years we missed out on. Our relationship is far from perfect, but this beginning feels monumental.

When we make it to our seats, I almost trip when I see Aiden's grandparents. "You made it!"

"When Lukas Preston calls to invite you to a hockey game, you don't refuse. Thanks for setting this up, Summer," says Eric.

Calling my dad after spring break took a bite out of my ego, but if it means Aiden's grandparents can see him play, I don't mind. When I asked my dad to send over a driver for them, he was more than happy to provide one. What I didn't expect was when I called my mom to tell her we didn't need the car anymore, my dad heard about it and got Aiden on the ice tonight.

"He's going to be so happy to see you."

"Coach Kilner let us surprise him in the locker room." A ring of happiness expands in my chest, and I hope one of the guys got it on video so I can cry happy tears later.

When the Dalton Royals make their entrance, Aiden skates along the boards, and we bang on the glass as he glides by, his white teeth gleaming through his cage. The rest of the guys are behind him, and of course, Dylan starts to figure skate. The home crowd loves it, and cheers consume the arena when he spins a double axel. It doesn't last long because Coach shoots him a glare that drops him back to stretches.

When the game starts, I try not to drool over how hot Aiden looks since my dad and Aiden's family are beside me. But Amara elbows me like an excited schoolgirl whenever he passes by us or bangs into the boards. Sitting rinkside means the referees hate me, but I don't let that keep me from speaking my mind.

Aiden scores two goals, and we almost climb over the damn glass

in excitement. Each intermission raises everyone's blood pressure because the game has been tied since the start of the second period.
When we resume, it's a brutal start for Dalton because Sebastian
Hayes gets cross-checked badly enough that he's carried off the ice.
The Yale player gets a five-minute major, leaving his team short-
handed, and everyone cheers when he's sent to the sin bin. By the
third period, my dad and I are on the edge of our seats.

Aiden glides across the ice with an ease only he possesses. Every
time the puck is in his possession, it's clear why he carries the title of
the fastest NCAA athlete. There's nothing I love more than seeing
him do what he's passionate about. Even as the last seconds drain and
the result is a toss-up, I know he'll be happy either way.

FIFTY-THREE

AIDEN

I'M CRUSHED AGAINST the glass by heavy hockey players, and I couldn't be happier. Madness ensues as the final buzzer sends the arena into a frenzy. We won 4–3 with an overtime goal by yours truly. Going from not playing to winning the game with the people I love watching in the stands feels surreal.

"Let's fucking go!"

"We're national champions!"

The ice is covered in royal blue as we line up to congratulate Yale on a good game. Eric Salinger shakes my hand. "Well played, Crawford. See you out there."

I nod, patting his back and moving down the long line of players. Eric signed with New York on an entry-level contract, so facing off again is inevitable.

I spot Kian inching the tub of BioSteel closer to Coach, who takes a postgame interview. They wheel out the trophy, and right before the camera's call for us, we lift the tub and drench Kilner in the blue liquid.

"Pains in my ass," he shouts, though his genuine smile and blood-shot eyes tell us a different story. He pulls me in for a hug. "Don't know how I'll handle these Neanderthals without you. Gonna miss you, kid."

"I'll miss you too, Coach."

"Do I get a hug?" Kian interrupts with a hopeful smile.

Kilner pulls back. "You're talking again?"

"You said I could!"

Coach cracks a smile. "Get over here, Ishida."

Letting him have his moment, I move through the crowd, throwing hugs and congratulations around as I search the area.

"Aiden!" Summer jumps and swings her arms around my neck. "You killed it! I'm so proud of you, Captain." She attacks my face with kisses. Our eyes lock, speaking a million things that words can never do justice. When I bring her to my lips, she pulls away too quickly. "My dad is watching us."

That bursts the bubble, and I let her climb off me. Lukas Preston approaches us with a serious look that turns into a shockingly wide smile. "Now that's what I call a game."

I relax and shake his outstretched hand. "Thank you, sir. And I appreciate you talking to the dean." Coach told me about him helping with the suspension lift, and I'm grateful. Especially since we didn't end on the best note.

"It would be a disservice to hockey to not get you on the ice tonight. You did good, kid," he says. "And call me Luke." I freeze, and Summer laughs at my starstruck expression.

My family makes their way down. "We're so proud of you, Aiden. You were amazing out there." My grandparents' embrace feels warm and comforting. It echoes the feeling I'd get when my parents would attend a game. I'll be forever grateful to Summer for making it happen. Her five-year plan has been thoroughly dismantled, but mine has just begun, and she is its focal point. Summer is my sun, and I'm the simple planet revolving in her orbit.

"Well, your mother expected me home hours ago," *Luke* says. "You need a ride back, Sunshine?"

"I can get a ride with Amara." When he turns to leave, Summer stops him. "Hey, Dad? Maybe we can meet for dinner again. Like a redo."

A grateful smile spreads on his face. "I'd like that."

Summer's smiling when I snake my arms around her waist. "I'm proud of you."

Her cheeks blush. "Me? You just won a championship. All I did was talk to my dad."

"Both equally important victories. We did good today, Preston."

She smiles brightly. "We did."

When cheers erupt, my attention follows the team heading to the locker room. "I gotta head in. Meet me at the hotel?"

"Actually, I think I have a better plan."

IT'S PAST MIDNIGHT. The postgame celebration went on for hours, not including the time it took to shower the champagne off. I tried to stay sober, but being the captain means celebration is necessary. This time Kilner even indulged, but he left soon after because he didn't want us to see him drunk. The way he slurred his words and allowed a stray tear to slip down his cheek during his heartfelt speech told me he's an emotional drunk. Kian recorded the entire thing to watch later.

"It's a surprise!" Summer says, trying to focus on driving.

When we exited the arena, Summer rounded us up, and we shuffled into a car. The guys, Cassie, and Amara piled into the back. Apparently, Amara's date, Bennett, said we could borrow his van. Summer invited the rest of the team, but they were still getting wasted. Our bus back to Dalton leaves tomorrow afternoon, so we have tonight to celebrate.

"You can give me a hint. Come on, I'm too drunk to even remember it long enough to spoil it for anyone," Kian says loudly, even though he thinks he's whispering.

Summer blows out a breath. "You'll see it with everyone else. I'm not playing favorites."

"I'm your favorite? I knew it," he whispers excitedly. "Did you hear that? I'm Sunny's favorite, you all can suck it."

The car erupts in grumbles, most of them telling him to shut up or threatening to throw him out the window. Which I'd be all for because he's been jabbering the entire drive. An exhausted Eli made us pull over earlier because Dylan placed the godforsaken wedding cake topper on Kian's seat. He managed to separate them, but that meant Kian was directly behind the driver's seat, annoying us.

"I feel like a bad boyfriend for making you drive."

Summer glances at me, probably noticing I've sobered up a great deal, because two hours ago at the arena, I was singing her love songs and holding her tight.

"You're my passenger princess. Just look pretty and tell me the wrong directions," she says, patting my thigh.

I intertwine our hands. "Are you sure your parents are okay with this?"

"Yup. My mom loves you, so I didn't even have to finish asking before she said yes. She even watched your game on TV. Divya Preston is a big fan."

"That's sweet. I should probably check my phone, but I glanced at it earlier, and it gave me a headache."

"Just relax today. You can go back to being a disciplined captain tomorrow."

"And tonight?" The heavy look I send her makes her blush and turn to the road.

When we arrive at Boston Harbor, everyone gawks at the vessel. Summer shoots out instructions that go over poorly with our drunken group. But somehow, we manage to get everyone into cabins.

"Lastly, this is our room." Summer kicks off her shoes and lies flat on the bed.

I notice a box beside her. "And what's this?"

"For you." She smiles.

Opening it, I pull out the black lingerie. The sheer fabric of the tiny one-piece is butter smooth. "If this is my reward, I don't think I'll ever lose."

"I thought you'd want to check it off my bucket list."

I drag her mouth to mine and kiss her hungrily.

"Wait." She pulls away. "There's one more thing." She pulls an envelope from the box. I'm still opening it when she blurts, "It's tickets to Toronto."

I'm stunned. "You're coming with me?"

"For two weeks. Before I have to come back for my program start date. I thought I could show you around, and we can start this long-distance thing off right. It's not too much, is it?"

"It's perfect. Thank you, baby." She blushes as I lower her onto the bed. "Now, put this on so I can fulfill your bucket list." As I un-buckle my belt, I feel a metal object in my pocket. I almost forgot I had it.

I pull out the fuzzy pink handcuffs. "Can't forget these."

She giggles between my kisses, tugging off my sweater. "I brought something for you too."

"Hmm?"

"Maple syrup," she whispers.

I groan, hastily trying to remove her top. A hard knock startles us. "Is your dad here?" I ask in horror.

"What—No, why would he be here?"

Right. That would be crazy. The knocking intensifies. I lift off the bed to answer the door with Summer behind me.

Dylan peeks through his fingers and exhales when he sees us. "Good, you're still dressed. Kian just fell overboard."

"What?" we both exclaim. A nonchalant Dylan leads the way to the commotion in the main room.

"Well, that definitely sobered him up," says Cassie. She's sitting next to Kian on the couch.

"That totally killed my buzz," Kian grumbles. "Can someone get me another drink?"

My worry drains when I hear his voice. The last thing I need is one of these idiots dying on me. "Never thought I'd feel peace from the sound of your voice, buddy."

Kian flips me off as a shiver racks through him. Eli tosses him a robe, and I find the switch for the fireplace.

"I'm pretty sure I saw the afterlife down there," Kian says to Cassie. Amara and Sampson roll their eyes from their place on the couch.

"You were in there for two minutes before Eli pulled you out," says Dylan.

"The afterlife doesn't have a specific timeline."

Dylan groans. "Say *the afterlife* one more time, and I'm drowning you myself."

Kian gasps.

"Okay, that's enough. No one is drowning anyone. Kian and Eli are going to change, and then we're all having a nice dinner." A shivering Kian throws Summer a salute, and everyone finally goes to their rooms.

Three fights and two flying utensils later, we've had dinner and settled into board games. Amara was close to biting Sampson's head off, so we put them on the same team. That didn't work as expected because now they're bickering about who won the game. Dylan and Kian sang karaoke with Summer while they drained an unlabeled bottle of alcohol that worried me.

But it makes Summer extra nice, especially when Cassie calls us outside to watch the fireworks, and she wraps us in a blanket before settling in my lap.

"They're a handful," she whispers sleepily, resting her head on my chest. She even brought the stuffed cow I won her at the carnival, tucking it between us.

"You're telling me. I've been fathering those children for years."

"You make a great DILF," she says with a kiss on my chin.

I laugh. "So, I suppose you can say it now."

"Say what?"

"Aiden Crawford, you are the one to tear down my ice fortress and show me the ways of a hockey player."

"Not happening," she mutters. "But you are pretty damn perfect, you know that?"

I brush my lips over hers. "Only when I'm with you."

"You're stuck with me, Crawford."

"Good, because I love you, Preston. Like, a lot."

"I love you, too. Like, a lot." Summer burrows deeper into my embrace. Her warm, peachy scent swirls around us, a soothing concoction that has me pulling her closer. When I hold her like this, I realize my entire world fits in my arms.

And I wouldn't have it any other way.

EPILOGUE

Nine Years Later
Toronto, Ontario

I'M MAKING MICKEY Mouse–shaped pancakes when a little voice calls for me.

"Mommy?" Aurora, our three-year-old, climbs her chair, her bright pink tutu flowing like a cloud. Her blond hair is in a messy braid that Aiden did for her last night. She refused to let me redo it for her this morning.

"Yes?" I ask, plating her breakfast.

Today is the opening day for my new sports clinic. It took slaving over my Ph.D. and then burning myself out while working for Team Canada for me to settle down in my hometown. I'm still on retainer with the Olympic Committee, but it's on a contract basis. Traveling all the time and barely seeing my family was depressing. With Aurora in our lives, it didn't feel right to be gone so often.

I got pregnant with Aurora with a year left on my Ph.D., and as tough as it was, it helped that she was born in the offseason.

Aurora bites a strawberry. "Are you and Daddy fighting?"

I freeze. They never tell you how perceptive kids are. I slide her plate across the island. "What makes you think we're fighting?"

"You didn't hug yesterday."

I'm living with a CIA-level spy. How she deduced that just from mere seconds of interaction last night is beyond me. She's right, though. Daddy and I are fighting.

The other day, Aiden watched all the episodes of our favorite show while I was at my clinic. It was his recovery day, so he spent it with his legs in his compression technology, sitting in front of the television, betraying me. It didn't help that my hormones were out of whack, so when I cried over it, he felt terrible. Not terrible enough for me to let him sleep in our room, though.

"We're not fighting, sweetheart," I lie. Daddy's little girl doesn't need to know her hero is also a dumbass.

The devil himself walks into the kitchen. He slept in the guest room last night and slipped out early this morning for his workout. Now he strolls in, hair damp from a shower, gray sweats and a tight shirt hugging every muscle. The years have been nothing but kind to my husband, his face and body aging like fine wine. He looks so *hot* I have to stop myself from staring as he goes over to Rory and kisses her. She giggles, and I bite down my smile.

Aiden comes to me as if he's forgotten that I'll stab him with a butter knife if he gets too close. Aurora watches us, waiting for the interaction to prove her analysis. She knows Aiden's routine. He always kisses her first, then comes to me.

"What were you asking Mommy, Rory?"

"If you're fighting," she mumbles through a mouthful.

"And what did she say?" His gaze holds mine hostage.

"You're not."

He hums in acknowledgment, eliminating the space separating us. "Is that right?"

The big brown eyes watching me across the island force me to give Aiden a tight nod.

His smirk is infuriating. "Then how come I haven't gotten a kiss?"

"Crawford," I warn, using my favorite name for him in college.

His lips tip into a smirk. "*Crawford*," he shoots back. Suddenly, I remember why I stopped using it. "I'm sorry, baby," he whispers, trying not to alert the hawk watching us.

The icy exterior that he melted away years ago is too flimsy to hold up anymore. Just one of those earnest looks, and I'm ready to forgive him. Especially when he looks so damn sexy while he's saying sorry. What am I mad about, again?

He lifts my chin, and when my eyes meet his again, he smiles, kissing me so thoroughly that I almost don't hear the gremlin squealing across the island. I pull away to see her covering her eyes.

"She's getting too smart," I say to him. "And I don't like that she's always on your side."

"Someone's gotta be, or you'd have me on my knees day and night," he says. "Not that I'd complain."

I'm hoping my face isn't red when Rory pipes up. "Daddy, are we seeing Nanna and Nanni today?"

She's talking about my parents. My family and Aiden's fawn over her like I've birthed the Stanley Cup. Which is saying a lot, because Aiden has won an actual Stanley Cup, and so has my dad.

"We are. Finish up, and we'll take the big truck today," he says.

She beams, gobbling the rest of her food. Much to Aiden's and my dad's pleasure, Aurora loves hockey. So, they play at my dad's rink every week. They both say she's a natural-born star, but they might be a little biased.

Aiden steals a stack of pancakes and sits beside Aurora, who licks her plate clean. "I'm done! Let's go play hockey."

"Uh-uh, you still have to clean the playroom, remember? That was our deal," I remind her.

She deflates, looking at Aiden, who is hyper-focused on his plate. One glance at her, and he's going to be cleaning the room. "Daddy," she says in that sweet, sweet voice.

Aiden closes his eyes for a brief moment. "Aurora, you have to do what you promised."

She pouts, doe-eyed and blinking up at him. Damn, she's good. Better than me.

He sighs in defeat. "I'll come to help you if you get started."

She lights up, running out of the kitchen and to her playroom. I shake my head in pity, laughing at the poor guy.

"She has your eyes, you know," Aiden says. He gets up to put his plate in the sink.

"Oh, so it's my fault she has you wrapped around her finger?"

"You do too," he says matter-of-factly, loading the dishwasher. "How are you feeling? Still no appetite?"

I shrug, trying to cling to my residual annoyance. Just when I think he'll let me get away with it, he wraps his arms around my waist, pressing my back against his chest. "I'm sorry. I promise it'll never happen again. We can rewatch it or find a new show."

It almost makes me laugh that he's treating this so seriously. If I was thinking more clearly, I wouldn't have had the reaction I did. But knowing he cares about the little things melts my heart. "I slept horribly last night."

"Me too. My workout was rough. Even Eli said I was off."

I knew that. Only because Eli texted the group chat a picture of Aiden looking disheveled this morning. Kian and Dylan found it especially funny, and happened to guess that he probably pissed me off, because that's the only time he's grumpy.

Aiden's palms flatten against my stomach, and I place my hands over his, skimming his diamond-studded band. He had both our rings engraved on our first anniversary with *I love you, like a lot*.

"I don't like sleeping away from you." He rubs my belly, though it's still too early to have a bump. "When are we telling the rug rat about this one?"

"Maybe when I'm further along. She really loves being an only child right now."

"She'll be a great big sister," he says, turning me in his arms. "I love when you're pregnant."

I raise a brow. "That's just because my hormones give me the sex drive of a horny teenager."

"Well, yeah, but also because we made something with our love." His cheesiness makes my insides mushy. "Would've never thought the stubborn psychology student would willingly carry my children."

"Me neither," I snort. He glares until my smile breaks free. "But I wouldn't have it any other way." His hands move lower, and it's like a switch when his lips brush against my neck.

His hips press against mine. "Want me to take you right here? Nice and slow, Sum."

I really did miss him last night. "Y—"

"I'm done. Let's go!" We break apart when Aurora runs straight to us, and Aiden lifts her in his arms.

"Okay, I'm going to check the room, though. If it's not clean, we can't go," warns Aiden.

She gasps, sliding out of Aiden's hold to run off again.

I'm shaking with laughter when he hugs me, sighing contentedly. "You think this one's going to be as wild as she is?"

He rubs my belly. "Nah, I think this one will be more like me."

I scoff. "You can't seriously think Rory has my personality."

"I don't know. She's stubborn as hell." He leans in, and my eyes narrow. "She's the most beautiful girl I've ever seen." I soften. "And she's got me wrapped around her finger." I lay my head on his chest, and like this, I can hear the calming beat of his heart, as well as Rory's toys clattering down the hall.

"I'll take care of you tonight," he whispers, and a hot rush of electricity zips through me. Aiden is always attentive, but when I'm pregnant he's on a whole other level. Foot rubs every night, moisturizing my belly, and lots of hot baths.

When I groan, he pulls away. "What's wrong?"

"You're a hockey player."

"Babe, I thought we were over this."

My eyes widen. "That means if this one is a boy, he's going to be huge. How am I going to birth a hockey player's child?"

"You already have."

"She was tiny! God, why did I let you trick me into falling in love with you?" I whine.

He laughs and kisses me again. "You'll do great, and I'll be there, just like always."

"You better be."

There's no doubt that he will. Because when I look into his eyes, all the years of unwavering love come fluttering back, and I know for certain that he's the best decision I ever made.

BONUS SCENE

Aiden: When are you landing?
Summer: Late. But don't worry, I'll get a cab.
Aiden: Send your flight details.

I ROLL MY eyes but send the flight number anyway. Aiden wouldn't let a stranger pick me up, even if he could barely walk after a game.

The bustle of Vienna Airport drowns away when I hear the intercom calling for my connecting flight. The World Figure Skating Championship held in Prague was a huge success for Team Canada, and even though I'm only an intern sports psychologist, I know this is what I've always wanted.

This and maybe getting more than four hours of sleep.

Heavy exhaustion tramples my body, and I sleep for the entirety of the flight. Hours later, I exit Toronto Pearson Airport to find a pitch-black sky and a sheet of snow covering the ground. Only in Toronto can you find snow in late March. Through the faint white, I spot a bright red sports car parked out front.

Aiden bought the car on his twenty-third birthday, thanks to the very unhelpful encouragement from Kian, who regretted the same purchase only a year later. It was impractical, with two doors and louder than anything I've ever sat in. During Thanksgiving, my dad eyed the car in the driveway, but instead of disapproving as I hoped he would, they went out for a ride, only to come back hours later.

When Aiden approaches with a shake of his head, the overgrown waves of brown flowing in the wind, the light stubble, and the perfect curve of his smile tell me I'm home.

"Only you would look this good after a nine-hour flight." His hand snakes around my waist, and he kisses me. Short and sweet but somehow deep enough to touch the parts of my heart that belong to him. My entire body hums with pleasure, and a chorus of *finally* rings through me.

I eye his sports car again. "Only you would bring *that* while knowing I have two suitcases."

He chuckles. "I missed you." Aiden tugs me along, somehow stacking my luggage in the limited space.

"Your place?" I ask when we veer onto the highway.

Something flickers through Aiden's eyes before he nods and we drive back to his downtown apartment. It's right by the water, and so high up, I spend most afternoons by the fireplace staring at the city. He's asked me to move in on multiple occasions, but I didn't see a point because I was traveling so much for work, and my place is closer to the airport. But now that Worlds is out of the way, there's no reason to stay apart.

When we arrive in the warmth of his apartment, I slump on the couch, and Aiden disappears into the kitchen just as my phone rings. I answer the group FaceTime call and listen to the life updates I missed because of the shitty hotel reception.

Though Dylan attended Worlds, so I didn't feel completely homesick, because we had dinner together almost every night.

Aiden reappears with a plate of pasta. Something he can actually cook without it tasting terrible. Sometimes, I think he sneaks over to

Eli's to steal what he's made for dinner. The chatter of our friends' FaceTime call fades into the background when he feeds me the first bite. My grateful moan lights a smile on his face, and he immediately ends the call and tosses my phone away.

We finish our dinner, which is more difficult than I expected because Aiden interrupted every bite with a kiss. I didn't object because spending weeks away from each other was something we haven't had to do since my master's degree. Neither did I object when he carried me to the shower and showed me exactly how much he missed me.

Now, with the heat from the shower and his lips still warming my skin, Aiden lays me on his mattress.

"Is that a mirror?" My eyes lock on my reflection staring back at me on the ceiling above his bed. My pulse flutters at the sight of his rippling back muscles and me underneath him.

"I know you like to watch," he whispers, in a gravelly voice that makes my cheeks flush. It isn't long before I'm praising him, over and over, for the new addition to his room.

AIDEN

THE LAST THREE weeks of my life felt like an eternity. Even as I watch Summer sleep soundly in my arms, there's a pull at my chest that hasn't left since that first night without her.

As I glide my thumb over the smooth skin of her cheek, she stirs, her hands searching her surroundings. There's a split second of disappointment when she touches the cold mattress, but when she opens her eyes to me, she lets out the heaviest sigh of relief and burrows into my chest.

"I thought I was still in my hotel room," she mutters.

"Nope. I finally have you."

"You always have me," she says as her wandering hand snaps the elastic of my boxers, and I catch her wrist to pull her on top of me.

"I thought about you every day, every minute. I don't think I can stay away from you again."

She runs a soft hand along my jawline. "Me neither. I like knowing that I can wake up to you in the morning."

I bring a hand to the nape of her neck to pull her down for a kiss. Flipping her over, I find every part of her sweet skin with my lips, memorizing the way she feels under me.

"Let's get married," I whisper against her lips.

"Mm-hmm," Summer mumbles, completely lost in the haze of my touch.

The nonchalant response tells me she didn't hear me. I pull away to get her attention. "Summer. Let's get married today."

She freezes, blinking once, twice, then one more time. "I'm severely jet-lagged. I'm going to need you to repeat that."

"Let's go down to the courthouse and make this official." I cup her face. "I want you to be my wife. I want you in my bed every night. I want *you*."

She swallows. "I could just move in for that."

"Are you saying no?"

"What? No—I mean yes." She lets out a breath. "I want to marry you. Of course I do. But my mom wants a traditional Indian wedding, your grandparents have to attend, and Amara will be pissed if she isn't my maid of honor."

"Call her. I'll pay for her flight. Her and Eli can be our two witnesses at the courthouse. Your mom will still get the big wedding she dreamed of for us with all our friends and family in attendance, but I want to do this now."

I'm sure when the rest of the guys find out, I'll be shelling out for their tickets too, but I don't mind as long as I get to finally call her my wife the next time we wake up together.

Brown eyes water. "Are you serious?"

I pull her out of bed, so she's standing in the middle of the room while I head into my closet, returning with a velvet box.

"My grandma gave me my mom's ring. I had it customized for you, and I even asked your parents for their blessing. I was going to do this with flowers, candles, and everything you could've wanted. And I still want to give you that, but right now there's nothing more I want than to be your husband and for you to be my wife."

She exhales a shaky laugh, blinking away the tears. "You're crazy."

I lower to one knee. I'm in boxers, and Summer's in her pink slip dress, in the middle of my bedroom with the sound of rain pinging against the windows.

"Summer Preston, will you marry me? Today?"

"Yes. Obviously yes!" she squeals as I slide the ring on her finger before lifting her in my arms. Just like that, the tightness in my chest unravels when I feel her heartbeat against mine.

ACKNOWLEDGMENTS

Publishing is a daunting process and I'm so grateful for everything I've learned. Though none of it would be possible without the connections I've made along the way.

Nina, for being my first reader and self-appointed PA. Thank you for always answering my late-night "this or that" texts and every single anxiety-driven FaceTime call. I'm so beyond grateful for your friendship. This book would be nothing without you.

Shayla, for hyping me up. Jenny, for being right there with her.

BLGC, for being so supportive. Monse, for inspiring that *one* scene. Carlyn, for being as unhinged as me for fictional characters.

My author friends, for saying writing this hockey romance is my "birthright."

Leni, for this amazing cover that's more than I could imagine.

Leigh, for putting up with the tight deadlines and giving me invaluable knowledge.

Lastly, my readers, you are the reason I'm motivated to write anything. Thank you for your kind words.

Turn the page for a sneak peek at the
next romance from Bal Khabra!

ONE

ELIAS

TORONTO THUNDER'S GOLDEN BOY KEEPS THE ICE COLD AND THE WOMEN HOT!

Being a rookie in the NHL is as bad as you expect it to be. But being a rookie in the NHL who's constantly in the media and hasn't scored his first career goal is even worse.

The hotel lobby has a selection of magazines to choose from, but the one on the coffee table has my name on the cover. It's a blurry picture of a woman leaving the club, with me right behind her. The rare time I could be persuaded to celebrate a win is when they catch me with a woman. If they bothered to do some research, they'd know the woman is Brandy, our team photographer. I had offered her a ride home and didn't expect someone to snap pictures.

Avoiding parties and outings isn't something I do intentionally, but it's difficult to celebrate something you had no part in. I prefer going over the games and analyzing my mistakes to find what's preventing me from getting that first goal. So that's exactly what I have planned for tonight.

Except, we're in Los Angeles, and I'm still waiting in the hotel lobby for my room to be ready. Despite knowing not to, I take a closer look at the magazine, reading the smaller headlines.

IS WESTBROOK LOSING HIMSELF TO FAME? ANOTHER BAD MOVE FOR TORONTO?

"Mr. Westbrook?"

I drop the magazine as if I'd been caught reading something illicit and head to the front desk. When I thank the concierge for the key, he shoots me a not-so-discreet wink that confuses me. Ignoring the weird interaction, I head up in the elevator to my room. Sliding my keycard in the door, I waste no time heading straight for the shower.

The hot water unravels the tense muscles in my back and the thoughts of the stupid magazine. Steam wafts out of the shower behind me as I wrap a towel around my waist and run another through my hair. I've been dying to get into bed and turn on the game highlights, but I stop dead in my tracks when I see what's in my bed. Or rather *who* is in my bed.

What the fuck?

Clutching my towel, I take several steps back. "Sorry, did I get the wrong room key?"

I didn't. I'm sure of that since my luggage is only two feet away from me. Suddenly, the concierge's wink makes sense. The woman's long blond hair falls in waves around her face, red lips and perfect teeth forming a smile. She's lying on the king-size bed in one of the hotel-provided robes with half-eaten snack wrappers from the mini bar strewn across the covers.

"The key seems perfect to me." Her mischievous smile as she sits up makes me uneasy.

"I'm not sure who you're looking for, but it's definitely not me."

"Trust me"—her eyes map every inch of my torso, lingering on the wet droplets slipping down my abdomen—"it's definitely you, Eli."

If this is a prank, I'm killing my teammates.

"I thought you'd want to celebrate tonight's win," she purrs, taking a step toward me.

The only reason I'd celebrate is if I scored, and that hasn't happened yet. I take several steps back and toward the door. "I'm sure you can find someone else who's interested."

Her brows jump so high I can tell she's never been turned down. My refusal doesn't have her putting her clothes back on and leaving as I'd hoped. That gives me no option but to turn and walk out.

In the hall, naked in only a towel, I head straight for the neighboring room. Aiden and I are only a few rooms apart since the rookies are paired together, and I'm hoping he's still awake.

Aiden Crawford, my best friend and teammate, isn't like me. He got his first career goal the moment he stepped onto the ice in our very first game. His second goal came that next night with an assist by me. His stint here is nothing short of stellar, and I couldn't be more proud. But Aiden's not one to throw a party for each goal. His ambitions extend beyond a single game, a drive he's had since he led us as captain at Dalton University.

So right now, I'm hoping he's also bailed on celebrating, because hotel guests are walking in the corridor, and one has taken a particular interest in my half-naked state. If they recognize me, I'm sure cameras will start clicking.

"Aiden!" I knock harder than I should, earning even more looks when the elevator opens to a new batch of hotel guests. *Fantastic.*

Mid-knock, the door swings open, and Aiden eyes me with a curiosity. "What's up?"

Before I can explain, the reason for my escape strolls out of the room, scanning the hallway for me. "That is." I gesture to the girl and barrel my way inside his hotel room.

"Again?" Aiden chuckles, closing the door behind him. I see the phone in his hand, with his girlfriend, Summer, on a video call.

"Hey, Brooksy." She waves at me through the screen, and I wave back, clutching my towel a little tighter. Although, Summer's probably immune since she's seen way more than she signed up for when she and Aiden started dating earlier this year. We've become great friends, and there's nothing I wouldn't do for her.

"You need security, man," Aiden says. "I'm pretty sure those people in the hall took a picture of you."

I sit on his bed and drop my head back against the headboard in defeat. All I ever wanted was to play hockey, and now that I have it, it feels like it's slipping through my fingers. The extra attention and opinions wouldn't bother me if I could shake off the pressure to perform, a weight that conveniently snatches my ability to do the one thing I've always been good at.

"Did Eli just virtually cockblock us?" Summer asks.

Aiden shrugs and smirks at his phone. "I'm still down if you are."

I groan out loud. You'd think them being in a long-distance relationship would give me some reprieve from the PDA.

"I think I'll pass." Summer laughs. "Have fun at your sleepover!"

I drop my head in my hands. "How am I supposed to focus on playing when I know this is the stuff that's hitting the headlines first thing tomorrow?"

Aiden tosses his phone on the nightstand and gives me a pitiful look. One he does every time something stupid like this occurs. "This is some pretty shitty luck, man. It seems like people are buying into the whole golden boy turned playboy narrative."

In an unexpected turn of events, a video posted by our team went viral. I had hesitantly agreed to film a day in the life of an NHL rookie, and people loved it. I'm not sure if it was the bloopers they found endearing, or maybe my workout routine was just that inspirational.

"It's my fault. I should have turned down the extra press when I had the chance." When our social media team approached me with ideas for more content, it was up for my approval. Thinking it would benefit my game rather than dampen it, I stupidly agreed.

"They would have talked you into it regardless. They need eyes on the game, especially with the ratings dropping last year."

I sigh. "Pretty boy hockey player who can't score for shit. That'll be the next headline."

"You've had plenty of assists. Trust me, you'll get the goal too," he assures. "Just find something that lets you breathe. Something that takes away the pressure you're feeling."

"Easier said than done. We can't all have a Summer," I mutter.

He smiles. "True, but they only leave me alone because of her dad. He'd shut that shit down before they tried anything."

Summer's dad is in the NHL Hall of Fame, and we were all pretty starstruck when we met him at our last Frozen Four. "Maybe I should date him," I suggest.

Aiden laughs and tosses me an extra pair of his sweats. "Good luck with that."

When I'm changing into the sweats, my phone vibrates with a text from Coach. That is his sixth reminder about tomorrow's event. We have to be ready for bidding since the team is auctioning dates with players. "You going to the fundraiser tomorrow?" I ask Aiden.

"It's mandatory. The whole Thunder organization is going to be there."

Great.

THE COLLAR OF my dress shirt suffocates me as we enter the venue.

Our flight back to Toronto this morning had been more uneventful than anticipated. No new headlines and no more surprise visits from fans. The hotel even apologized for letting the woman upstairs, but they couldn't have known since she introduced herself as my fiancée. Apparently, she attends every game, whether home or away. Her dedication to the cause would be commendable if it wasn't so creepy.

"Relax, man." Aiden nudges me, forcing me to quit pulling at my collar. "It's only a few hours, then we can head out."

"You're only saying that because you're not the one being auctioned off."

The auction happens every year, and since the older women in the crowd are the ones bidding, our PR team thought it would be great to throw me into the mix. That, or it's a bit of hazing for a new rookie. Aiden got to bow out by using his girlfriend as an excuse.

"I got your back, but just know you'll make someone's grandmother very happy." He chuckles.

I roll my eyes just as Coach comes to stand by me, his presence alone raising panic in my chest.

"Westbrook. A minute." He gestures toward the bar.

It doesn't take a genius to figure out what this is about. When I join him by a table, he places his phone on it, revealing an article and a photo of the girl from last night with my face under yet another headline.

TORONTO THUNDER'S ROOKIE IS OUT FOR THE COOKIE.

Seriously? Are they hiring an intern to write these?

"I don't make a habit of reading this shit, but when the GM questions why my newest rookie is seen covering more magazines than he is covering the ice, I have no choice."

Crap. The general manager, Marcus Smith-Beaumont, is the hardass of hard-asses. If he's heard of this, I'm sure I've become the talk of the board of directors—the ones who decide whether I'm worth the advance they've paid me.

When I first got recruited, I had heard a rumor that he was against my draft to the Thunder. It isn't a norm to draft two players from the same college in one year, but it's not exactly groundbreaking either.

"I have a few magazines from this month alone if you want to do some light reading." His words come out less angry than they should. I'm single-handedly tainting the rookie image, and the organization can't be happy about that. "Another scandal and another game without a goal. I don't know how many press meetings we can control if things like this continue to surface."

The bartender offers a drink, but I refuse. "It's all fabricated. I have no idea why they're spinning it this way," I say.

"Because you're popular. That social media video of you went viral, and the people want more. It's great publicity, but not if you become the next playboy."

"That's not who I am."

"I'm sure, but the only perception the league cares about is the fans'. You need to pick up your game and keep your hotel rooms empty."

I run my hand through my hair, feeling a headache pounding at my skull. "I understand."

"Get that first one out of the way, and I can hold off on the press we're getting about you. Don't make the organization question whether they should have signed you. You're a strong player, I can vouch for that, but I can't do it unless you back it up with some proof."

He takes the drink I had refused, downs it in one go, and walks off. The echo of his advice and a fading clink of emptied glasses circle my thoughts. The pressure is overwhelming.

If it stay in here another second, my head might explode. I don't stick around to find out and head for the double doors, signaling to Aiden that I need a break.

And maybe a solution to all my problems.

TWO

SAGE

BROKE BALLERINA.

It kind of has a ring to it.

"Auditions will be held again in the spring. We do not need any more background dancers," Aubrey Zimmerman dismisses as he barrels through the rotating glass doors in a flurry.

Next *year*? That's an entire dancing season gone. Another year older. Another stack of unpaid bills. Another has-been.

Broke washed-up ballerina.

Not so catchy.

"Mr. Zimmerman, I'm here to audition for Odette."

Either he hears the desperation in my voice or my statement is so bewildering that it stops him in his tracks. My focus lands on the back of his balding head that glistens under the sunlight. He isn't old in terms of years, but he looks rough for a thirty-something-year-old. I guess that's what years in this industry do to a person. Some days, I feel halfway there.

When he turns, his lips tip in a curve that makes me tilt my head to assess it. But then the sound that comes out of his mouth drops my shoulders.

Aubrey Zimmerman is laughing at me.

"*Odette*? You've stopped the executive director of the American Ballet Theatre to declare *yourself* as the lead for *Swan Lake*?"

Well, when he says it like that, it sounds laughable. But even with the disdain dripping off his words, I stand tall. It took me three hours to get to this audition. *Three*. The man sitting next to me on the bus had a fever that I'm sure I caught when he sneezed on me. As if on cue, a cold chill runs down my spine, though that might be the product of Zimmerman's cold gaze.

"Yes," I squeak. I hope my posture is doing enough for my confidence because my expression has dropped into the depths of hell.

He chuckles. "When I start taking orders from nobodies on the street, I'll let you know. But thanks for the laugh. I really needed that today."

Zimmerman answers his phone, dismissing me as he mutters something about never holding auditions in the crack of New York. Buffalo was the closest audition city I could attend coming from Toronto, and I didn't meet the cut-off time. Arriving two hours early meant waiting in the line that wrapped around the building, and by the time I made it to the door, we were cut off. They didn't even bother auditioning the rest of us waiting outside.

Irritation flares in my gut as I watch his retreating figure. His bald head and straight-set shoulders burn into my memory. At least I'll have a new silhouette for my sleep paralysis demon.

A few passersby give me pitiful looks that only make my plight worse. It's the same look I got inside from the director's assistant. Nothing seemed to convince her to let me audition, not even the recount of my dreadful commute and definitely not my childhood story about my love for ballet. It's the story that got me booked in a winter showcase last year, and I hoped it would work again. Except that showcase was performed at high schools and colleges. It wasn't exactly a grand production.

"Excuse me." A voice pulls me from my thoughts, and I turn to a woman. "I think you dropped this," she says, handing me a single sheet of paper.

I take it from her, only to find my name in familiar bold letters at the top. "This is my résumé. The assistant said I could leave it at the front desk," I explain.

There it is again, that pitiful look. "I found it on the floor by the recycling bin."

Her words strike like a knife to the heart. A half whimper, half groan escapes me, and I plaster on a smile to distract her from how hard I'm clutching my résumé.

"You know," she whispers, cautiously eyeing our surroundings. "The Theatre holds these auditions as a formality. Most ballerinas they've hired this season are ones who have major social media followings."

My mouth parts in shock. They're selecting dancers based on popularity? How is that ethical?

"You seem like a determined dancer, so I wanted to give you a heads-up," she says before rushing inside.

Her heads-up only manages to heighten the doomed feeling in my gut. If it's based on popularity, my ninety-three followers are chump change, and I'll never be considered.

Despair clings to me as I toss my crumpled résumé in the trash and head to the train station, holding back a bucket of tears I'll be sure to release during my shower tonight. It isn't until my phone rings that I shake out of my depressing thoughts.

"I have a last-minute job for you." My uncle's deep voice filters through the speaker.

"Is it that babysitting job for your players' kids? They're cute and all, but one of them bit me, and I still have a scar on my finger."

Postgraduation, I was desperate for a job, but had a rude awakening when I realized even a Yale business degree couldn't get me a job in this market. Yay for Ivy League education!

So my uncle, who works for the NHL, extended a few offers for me to help out his hockey team during the regular season. Including babysitting, dog-sitting, and the one time I cooked for the team last year. They never asked me to cook again, and I can't say I blame them.

"Not this time." He chuckles. "We need a dancer for our fundraiser tonight. We had a last-minute dropout, and I thought you'd like a gig where you can actually do what you love."

My uncle has always been supportive of my ballet career. Sometimes I dreaded looking in the crowd because of the lack of parents cheering me on, but he was always there.

"Thanks, but I'm not feeling very motivated—"

"It's a thousand bucks for an hour-long performance."

My throat dries, and my words catch. That's *three* zeros for sixty minutes of my time? I'm discouraged, not stupid. "I'll be there."

"I'll text you the address."

I locate the nearest Uber because the two-hour bus ride would not cut it tonight. Besides, the money I'll make would be enough to justify this one ride.

Note to self: One bad situation doesn't have to become a bad day.

AMONG THE BACKSTAGE whispers and last-minute run-throughs, I find myself shedding the weight of today's rejection with my clothes. As soon as I slip into my unitard and fit into my pointe shoes, there's a certain tingle that electrifies my body as I wait for my cue.

The first delicate notes of Ravel's "Boléro" hit my ears and I follow the other dancers to the stage, finding my position behind the second row. Polished wood and silhouettes of the audience are visible under the bright lights of the stage, and just like that I'm absorbed into the one thing that never fails to help me escape. My thoughts disappear like mist when I glide in perfect formation with the other dancers, mirroring each step as I learned it only an hour ago.

I have a peculiar talent for replicating dances quickly, and that's probably the reason my uncle was so confident that I could fill in for the last-minute dropout. My focus is on the music, but my eyes still wander the audience for a glimpse of him. It might be the seven-year-old girl in me, but when I see my uncle to the left of the stage, close enough that the bright lights don't block him, a smile stretches my lips.

The group converges into a tableau, and when the end approaches, we dive into grand jetés and lifts, the stage a mix of swirling tutus and poised ballerinas. The applause pulls me back to reality, and somewhere, somehow, I hope Aubrey Zimmerman knows that I won't give up easily.

When the curtains close, encouraging words and high fives fly around the group, giving me the same rush of excitement I'd felt at the age of seven, the first time I desired something.

Up until then, my only focus was making sure the housework was completed and my younger brother, Sean, had everything he needed. I guess that feeling of responsibility comes with being mature for your age. At least, that's what every adult I encountered has had to say to me. Soon enough, you start realizing that's not a compliment. It's a curse.

But the desire? Ballet.

The trip to the bodega by our house was the highlight of my Sundays, but it became the beginning of the rest of my life. The checkout counter was cluttered with magazines of famous faces and gossip wild enough to scandalize my grandmother, but on that particular day, only one stood out to me. Behind the dusty magazine rack and the frayed edges of a plastic cover, I saw a poster. The poster. Misty Copeland graced the cover of the newest production of The Nutcracker, elegant and as beautiful as ever. I knew then that whoever she was and whatever she did, I wanted to be her.

The poster still hangs on my wall.

"Sage!" I turn to find my uncle climbing the steps to head backstage. "You keep dancing like that, and I'm sure they'll hire you full-time."

I shake my head. "I'm not stealing the poor girl's job, Uncle Marc."

"I can pull a few strings," he offers, a glimmer of hope in his eyes, just like every other time he's tried to help me out. All my life, my uncle has felt obligated to care for me and my brother, but I've refused. We aren't his problem, and I never want him to see us as one.

"My auditions are going great. I'll secure that spot at ABT pretty soon," I lie.

His smile doesn't quite reach his eyes. "Never doubted you for a second." His phone vibrates before he silences it. "Get changed, and I'll have a plate ready for you."

I give him a quick squeeze before darting backstage. Slipping into my change of clothes, I head out and find a plate of food waiting for me at my uncle's table, filled with all my favorites. It isn't until I'm scarfing down seconds that I remember I need to call Sean.

He's attending boarding school a few hours away, which has been a difficult adjustment, but I promised to call him every night. Excusing myself from the table, I try to find a quiet corner, but with the auction starting, it's impossible. Outside, the rain brings a breeze to cool my skin in my black silk dress. It's the only nice dress I own, so I was sure to pack it when I headed over here tonight. No one needed to know it was also my prom dress. And my commencement dress.

The phone rings a few times before it's sent to voicemail. I can't help the prick of disappointment that pierces my heart. That's two days without a phone call, and both times it's been because of my crappy schedule. I text him instead.

Am I the worst sister ever? Promise, I'll call earlier tomorrow. I miss you, kid.

It isn't until I'm staring at the rain trying not to pity myself that I notice a couple in the corner. Their proximity suggests they're having an intimate conversation, but the guy backs away, his stance rigid and unwelcoming.

"I'm not interested," he says.

It's assertive, but not assertive enough to get the girl away from him. She is completely oblivious to his closed-off body language. Definitely not a couple.

"You will be," she says, pure determination in her voice.

"Look, Lana, is it?" She must nod, because he continues. "You seem like a nice girl, but I don't know you. Showing up at my hotel and to my work events isn't helping your case."

She laughs. It's a pretty, soft one that most guys would probably love, but he only stands there like a statue. His dark suit suggests he works for the Toronto Thunder, but his height and physique would be wasted if he isn't an athlete.

"I can only play your games for so long," she purrs. This girl cannot take a hint.

"Does that game include showing up naked to ambush me in my hotel room?"

My eyes widen as I stifle a gasp, feeling tense as I eavesdrop on this embarrassing conversation.

However, Lana must not feel it because she scoffs. "You're seriously turning me down?"

Yes! I catch the word before it slips past my lips, barely holding myself back from interfering. But when his head hangs and his shoulders sag, my legs are moving. Confrontation is clearly not his strong suit.

Lucky for him, it's mine.

Without a thought, one I should have had several of before even taking a step, I head straight for them. Suddenly, the double doors screech open, and an employee dressed in black and wearing an earpiece steps outside.

"Eli, you're up in five," he says, waving him inside.

I halt, and Eli breathes a sigh of relief before slipping past the woman. His attention lands on my frozen figure, lingering for a split second, like he's realized I was eavesdropping the entire time, before he disappears inside. Lana watches his retreat with a fire in her eyes, and when her gaze lands on mine, I pivot and slip past the doors too.

The auction has started as I drop back into my seat just as my uncle excuses himself to head to the bathroom. I watch his retreat, only to glance to my right and choke on my saliva.

Aiden Crawford is sitting at my table—or I'm sitting at his. Either way, I'm freaking out. Not for myself, but for Sean because he is going to flip when I tell him about this. I don't pay too much attention to hockey, but from my uncle's praises of Aiden Crawford, and the jersey with his name that Sean wants for his birthday, I know he's a big deal.

"Are you okay?" His deep voice forces me to look at him again, only to see him holding out of a glass of water. I nod a little too vigorously and take the water to hide behind it. "You're Sage, right? Marc told us his niece was performing tonight. I'm Aiden."

I shake his outstretched hand, trying to clear my throat. "My brother's a huge fan."

"Yeah?" He smiles. "I can get—*Shit!*"

My head rears, but when I look at Aiden, his eyes are fixed behind me. Following his gaze, I see Lana, the girl from outside, holding a bidding paddle and looking happier than she did a few minutes ago.

The auctioneer's voice snatches my attention to the stage.

"Next up, folks, we have a date with Toronto Thunder's very own defenseman, Elias Westbrook. Get those bidding paddles ready, and let's see who'll be the lucky winner!"

I'm shocked to see the guy from outside standing on stage, his jaw clenched and posture stiff. Safe to say, he didn't willingly sign up for this.

The auctioneer's voice slices through the hall, loud with excitement. "Let the bidding commence—who's ready for an unforgettable night with Elias?"

"Sage? How do you feel about doing me a favor?" Aiden says.

I pull my gaze from Elias to find Aiden's sheepish smile. What favor could I possibly do for Aiden Crawford? "Depends on what it is," I say warily.

"This is going to sound crazy, but I need you to outbid her." Aiden points at Lana, and my eyes widen. He hands me a paddle and types something into his phone before showing me. It's a sum. A large sum.

"M-me," I stutter, dumbfounded. Although, the request is understandable considering what I witnessed outside. But one look at my bank account, and I'm pretty sure I'd find moths flying around in there.

Determined green eyes lock on mine. "Look, I promised Eli I'd have his back, and that girl cannot win a date. She—"

"Ambushed him in his hotel room?"

His head rears back, and his brows furrow as he studies me.

"I overheard them outside," I explain.

A satisfied look melts his confusion. "Good, so you know her winning wouldn't be good. I'll pay for it, but since I'm a part of the organization, I can't bid. Will you do it?" he asks again.

I fidget with the paddle, just as Lana shouts, "Two thousand!"

Did she say *two*? As in *thousands* of dollars? The amount Aiden typed is more understandable now. However, I'm not confident that my mouth could perform the motor function necessary to say that number out loud.

The older women whisper, paddles in hand like they're preparing for war. "Twenty-two hundred," someone else interjects.

A slight trickle of relief cools my panic as I turn to Aiden. "The other women might outbid her. He seems pretty popular," I point out, desperate for an out.

Aiden nods. "Hopefully, but if not I'll need you to bid."

"Twenty-five," a woman shouts, only for two equally eager women to raise the amount. My jaw drops with each increase, and my palms get sweaty when I realize I'll have to raise my paddle pretty soon.

The auctioneer repeats the number, eyes scanning the room for more.

"Twenty-eight." Lana's smooth voice carries an authority that has the overeager women backing off. *Uh-oh.*

"Wow! Twenty-eight hundred dollars, ladies and gentlemen. Can we top that?"

Elias stands there with an air of confidence, dark hair perfectly styled, and his muscular form cloaked in an expensive suit. It's no mystery why these women are throwing around two grand for one dinner with him. Yet I can't ignore the subtle tightness in his body as tension radiates off him in waves. He manages to stare ahead, doing his best not to engage with a very smug Lana.

"Going once . . ."

Aiden nudges my paddle, and I swallow, scrambling for an excuse. "I don't even know him," I whisper.

"Going twice . . ."

"Please?" Aiden shoots me a killer straight-teeth smile that has me chewing my lip in contemplation. Damn, he's good.

I sigh, knowing Sean would berate me for refusing to help his idol. Without a second thought, my arm shoots up. "Three thousand!"

Elias Westbrook's eyes dart over to me so fast he must have whiplash. I force a wobbly smile as more eyes land on me, but I can't seem to look away from the deep brown ones that anchor me with curiosity and a hint of recognition.

The auctioneer goes around the room three times before he smacks the gavel. "And sold to the beautiful woman in black!"

I won. Holy shit, I *won.*

ABOUT THE AUTHOR

Bal is a Canadian writer and booklover. Before she decided to jump into the romance pool, she spent her time gushing about books on social media. When inspiration strikes, she is found filling her Notes app with ideas for romance novels. She loves reading about love, watching movies about love, and now writing about it herself. There really isn't much else that gets her heart fluttering the way HEAs do. She fell in love with writing and hopes to continue living out her romance author dreams.

VISIT THE AUTHOR ONLINE

AuthorBalKhabra.com
AuthorBalKhabra
AuthorBalKhabra

Ready to find
your next great read?

Let us help.

Visit prh.com/nextread

Penguin
Random
House